The terrace lights backlit a dark figure weaving drunkenly. Xander and Jon materialized out of nowhere at Dinah's side. "It's Claude Ann!" Xander's voice broke and he started running down the beach.

Dinah doffed her shoes and ran after him, her feet sinking in the sand with every step. She felt as if she were running in slow motion. Jon and Steve passed her, but she dug deeper and caught up in time to see Claude Ann, drenched in blood, stagger into Xander's arms and collapse a few yards from the edge of the terrace.

Jon bent down and removed a crumpled piece of paper from her hand. He held it under the green LED light from his wristwatch for Dinah to read. It said GO HOME. In blood.

Previously published Worldwide Mystery title by
JEANNE MATTHEWS

BONES OF CONTENTION

BET YOUR
BONES

JEANNE MATTHEWS

TORONTO • NEW YORK • LONDON
AMSTERDAM • PARIS • SYDNEY • HAMBURG
STOCKHOLM • ATHENS • TOKYO • MILAN
MADRID • WARSAW • BUDAPEST • AUCKLAND

Thanks to my editor, Barbara Peters,
for her help in shaping the story, and for their ideas and encouragement, I thank Joe Winston, Jeanne Kleyn, Gail Boyer Hayes, Sal Gordon, Pat Snider, Dianne Eret, and most especially, Sid.

Recycling programs
for this product may
not exist in your area.

BET YOUR BONES

A Worldwide Mystery/June 2014

First published by Poisoned Pen Press.

ISBN-13: 978-0-373-26898-6

Copyright © 2011 by Jeanne Matthews

Printed in U.S.A.

Acknowledgments

The myths recounted in this book came from the following sources:

Hawaiian Legends of Ghosts and Ghost-Gods, collected and translated from the Hawaiian by W. D. Westervelt, Boston, Ellis Press (1916).

The Legends and Myths of Hawaii, by His Majesty King David Kalakaua, edited with an introduction by Hon. R. M. Daggett and with an introduction to the new edition by Terence Barrow, Ph.D., Charles E. Tuttle Co., Inc. (1972).

Unwritten Literature of Hawaii, The Sacred Songs of the Hula, by Nathaniel B. Emerson, A.M., M.D., Charles E. Tuttle Co., Inc. (1965). Originally published by the Bureau of American Ethnology in 1909.

Materials found in the Bishop Museum, The State Museum of Cultural and Natural History, Honolulu, Hawaii.

On Mauna Loa, the greatest of the Hawaiian mountains, lived Kane-ia-kama, a high chief and an incorrigible gambler. Whenever and wherever the game of konane was played, he bet. Eventually, he gambled away all of his wealth until he had no possessions left. One night while he was sleeping, he dreamed that the voice of a god called out to him from the forest. "Try your luck again, Kane-ia-kama. Challenge the villagers to a game and play the black pebbles."

But Kane-ia-kama cried, "I have nothing left. My treasures are all lost."

And the voice replied, "Bet your bones. Bet your bones and see what will happen."

—Hawaiian Myth

***

Absit omen. (May it not be an omen).

—Anonymous saying

PART I

ONE

On the Philippine island of Mindanao, there are shamans who divine the future by drinking the blood of a freshly slaughtered hog. This supposedly conjures the Spirit of Prophecy, which warns of any trouble looming on the horizon. At an altitude of 30,000 feet over the Pacific Ocean, Dinah Pelerin was forced to rely on the oracle of micro-waved sausage links and Bloody Marys. The Spirit didn't speak to her, but she foresaw only too well the trouble that lay ahead of her: the bride would wear white; the groom would wear black; and she, the reluctant maid of honor, would wear the onus of guilt she'd worn for ten years running. A secret guilt dressed up in—she consulted the letter again—tangerine chiffon, for crying out loud.

Having spent the last two months on Mindanao studying the customs and beliefs of the indigenous tribes, Dinah had picked up the habit of watching for omens. In the Philippines, everything was an omen. Dropping your purse was an omen. It boded poverty. Taking a shower too soon after ironing boded a wrinkly face. Falling asleep with wet hair boded blindness. Dinah wasn't irrational enough to believe these particular superstitions. But playing maid of honor twice for the same bride gave heightened meaning to the word ominous.

She had cordoned off the memory of Claude Ann's first wedding as if it were a crime scene. Whenever she and Claude Ann spoke, neither alluded to that tearful day ten years ago or to the series of misunderstandings and missteps that led to the altar. Dinah never asked and Claude

Ann never reported on the state of her marriage. But it had lasted for a decade and Dinah was beginning to think that, just maybe, Claude Ann had drifted into a life of domestic contentment. Until now. Until out of the blue, Claude Ann had written to say that she was divorced, reengaged, and set to plunge down the aisle again with a man she'd known for barely six weeks. The ceremony was planned to take place on the last day of June on the Big Island of Hawaii. On the lip of a volcano.

Dinah added another splash of vodka to her tomato juice. The volcano sounded like a bad omen.

"Three more hours," said her seatmate. "We'll be in Honolulu by supper time." She was a plump, intense looking Filipina who'd been working Sudoku puzzles ever since they boarded in Manila. Apparently, she'd grown bored with number crunching and wanted to chat. "Are you on your way home?"

"No. I've never been to Hawaii. Do you live there?"

"I wish. I'm visiting my sister. You've got a funny accent. Where do you come from?"

It was the second Bloody Mary, thought Dinah. Alcohol had a way of exposing her Southern roots. "The U.S. Georgia, actually. But I've been away for a long time. I'm an anthropologist." It must be nerves that made such a lie jump out of her mouth. Well, it wasn't a total lie. She was an aspiring anthropologist. Just because she wasn't employed by some university or other didn't mean she wasn't doing anthropology. She'd sweet-talked two professors from Emory into letting her tag along on their Mindanao expedition, hadn't she? She said, "My specialty is myths."

"Then you're gonna love Hawaii. They've got tons of crazy myths."

"Thanks. I'll look into them."

"You ever hear of Pele?"

"I've read some of the legend." Pele had figured in one

of Dinah's college courses, something about the significance of oral literature in the development of preliterate cultures. The early Hawaiians believed that Pele created the volcanoes and they worshipped her with chants they called meles and a risqué dance they called the hula. "She was a fire goddess, right?"

"Was? Don't you believe it. Her spirit still lives inside Kilauea Volcano. My sister, the one I'm visiting, she says Pele's been real angry the last few weeks. Lots of tremors and Kilauea hissing and spitting all the time."

"Which island is Kilauea on?"

"Hawaii, the Big Island. It's growing bigger every day from all the lava spilling out of Kilauea."

Frowning, Dinah skimmed Claude Ann's letter. Had she dropped the name of the volcano beside which she'd be tying the knot? Of course, not. How like Claude Ann to specify the color of the dresses and neglect to mention an erupting volcano.

"A man fell in a steam vent and got cooked just last week down near Ocean View. My sister sent me the news clipping."

Dinah shuddered. "Was he hiking?"

"Nobody knows where he came from or where he was going. No car, no ID. He had a head wound and some broken bones. It's kind of a mystery. The police thought he might have been the victim of a hit-and-run and he stumbled into the vent trying to go for help. Most likely he was drunk or he wouldn't have been crossing the road in the middle of the night." The woman pointed at the empty vodka bottles on Dinah's tray table. "Pele likes booze, too. If you go to Kilauea, you can stay on her good side by leaving her a bottle of gin."

Dinah couldn't decide if she'd been warned or insulted. She didn't reply.

The woman went back to her Sudoku. Dinah polished off

her Bloody Mary and brooded. In spite of the miles that had
come between them and the taboo subject of Claude Ann's
marriage, Dinah and Claude Ann had remained best friends
since they were children. They had grown up together on
the edge of the Okefenokee Swamp in Needmore, Georgia,
a town whose name summed up its cultural opportunities
to a tee. Needmore needed more of everything except scan-
dal, which Dinah's family bestowed upon the community
the way some families bestow monuments and museums.
After her father flipped his pickup and died under a half-
ton of marijuana, the Pelerins became pariahs. If it hadn't
been for Claude Ann's love-me-love-my-dog loyalty, Dinah
would've been the leper of Needmore High. Wussing out
of her wedding, however uncomfortable or close to a spitting volcano, wasn't an option.

"I got to stretch my legs," said her seatmate, folding
her tray table and standing up. "Got to watch out on a long
flight or you'll get blood clots." She straightened her back
and toddled toward the rear of the plane.

Dinah never ran short of things to watch out for. Or people. She reread Claude Ann's description of the groom-to-
be. His name was Xander ("short for Alexander") Garst.
He was a "super brainy scientist with a phenomenal per-
sonality, an absolutely to-die-for house on the Big Island,
and two children from a former marriage." She raved for
half a page about his drop-dead great looks, his sophisticated manners, and his fabulous sense of humor.

That last trait was a welcome twist. Heretofore, Claude
Ann's cup of tea hadn't included a sense of humor. She'd
never shown much of an interest in science either, not that
having similar interests was a prerequisite to marital happi-
ness. Sometimes, opposites really did attract. Anyway, sex
trumped everything, at least in the beginning. Dinah hoped
with all her heart that this new bird was Claude Ann's Mr.

Right. But whether he turned out to be a dreamboat or a disaster, no way could Dinah be blamed. This time, the nuptials would be one hundred percent on Claude Ann's head.

TWO

THE 757 ROARED low over the southeast coast of Oahu and the sapphire-blue waters that had made Honolulu a tourist mecca. Dinah recognized Waikiki Beach from the million pictures she'd seen of it and there was no mistaking Diamond Head crater in the distance. As the plane touched down and taxied toward the gate, she wondered what qualities in addition to looks and humor would appeal to the older and wiser Claude Ann. She was bound to be a lot choosier now. In spite of the letter's giddy tone, the ordeal of divorce would have quelled her youthful tendency to impetuousness and made her more cautious about men.

After the usual delay in hooking up the jetway and unlocking the doors, Dinah wrestled her carry-on out of the overhead bin and melded into the ant column of tourists shambling out of the plane and proceeding toward Customs. Once she'd been cleared for entry, she made a beeline toward ground transportation. As she exited the non-secure area, Claude Ann called out her name and waved excitedly from the back of a crowd of lei-bearing greeters. Dinah forgot about qualms and omens and ran into her friend's outstretched arms.

"Aloha, honey." Claude Ann lassoed her with a garland of fragrant white flowers and gave her a big hug. "You don't look too bagged-out for an aging Pocahontas."

Dinah laughed and gave her a pretend tomahawk chop. She was proud of her Seminole ancestry, maybe even a bit vain, and Claude Ann liked to razz her about it. "Thirty-one's not so old. It didn't keep you from landing a new husband, did it?"

"No, and he's a pip. I can't wait to show him off to you." She hadn't lost any of her sparkle. Her brown eyes shone with their familiar, teasing mischief and her heart-shaped face, framed by a cascade of coppery-blond curls, radiated warmth and vitality.

Dinah stood back and took in her high wattage smile. "You look happy, Claudy. Really and truly happy."

"Honey, I'm over the moon."

A wiry little girl with sulky eyes, sorrel hair, and a face full of freckles shoved in between them. "I'm Marywave."

Claude Ann's smile waned and she looked almost apprehensive. "You remember Marywave, I suppose."

"Of course, I remember." Dinah smiled and held out her hand. "You've grown since I saw you last, Marywave."

She hugged to her chest a small, white leather Bible and ignored Dinah's hand. "I'll be ten in September."

"My, my." Dinah took back her hand. "Time flies."

"Daddy says the reason you don't come to visit us when you're in Needmore is 'cause you can't stand him." Her drawl was even thicker than Claude Ann's.

"Your daddy's mistaken, Marywave. The last time I was in town I had a lot of family business to take care of. I barely had time to meet your mother for lunch in Atlanta before I had to leave again."

Claude Ann gave the child a sour look and turned back to Dinah. "Oh, never mind Marywave. She's goin' through a weird phase. Come on. Let's find the bar and I'll tell you about my new life." She grabbed Dinah's suitcase and started down the concourse, her long tan legs striding out as if she were skating.

Dinah followed a few paces behind, glancing over her shoulder once or twice at Marywave, who poked along clutching her Bible.

Outside the bar, Claude Ann turned around and put a hand on her hip. "Step it up lively, y'all. We haven't got all day."

Marywave scowled. "Daddy says strong drink is an abomination unto the Lord."

"Jiminy, Marywave." Claude Ann made an exasperated face. "Don't be a pain in front of Dinah. Give me a break, okay?"

Dinah still had a buzz from the Bloody Marys. She said, "Maybe we should put off drinks until dinner, Claudy."

"No. I've been lookin' forward to your getting here all week and I won't be pushed around by this pest." She took Marywave by the scruff of the neck, propelled her into the bar, and parked her on a red vinyl bench next to the hostess' station. "You can sit right here and read your book of abominations and thou-shalt-nots and wait for us. Maybe you can latch onto some other poor, thirsty sinner to preach to."

The hostess arrived with menus. "May I seat you ladies?"

"Is there a table where we can keep tabs on my daughter?"

"Of course. This way."

The hostess seated them at a sun-dappled table beside a window under a row of hanging pots with trailing jasmine vines. Claude Ann glared at Marywave. Dinah looked over her shoulder and saw Marywave glaring back.

Claude Ann said, "She's about to moralize me to death. Hank's pumped her full of so much religious rigmarole she can't open her mouth without versifyin', mostly about my sins. Let me tell ya', it's depressin' when your nine-year-old calls you a harlot. And she snubs Xander like he's the Devil incarnate."

"I gather that she's not on board with the new marriage."

Claude Ann rolled her eyes. "She got it in her head that sooner or later, I'd tuck tail and go home to Hank. She doesn't understand how miserable he's made me these last couple of years. I smiled and stuck it out as long as I could.

I didn't want to upset Marywave or scandalize the neighbors. Except for your family, nobody in Needmore gets divorced. But after Hank had that scary car wreck and nearly died, he changed. He was always kind of a fuddy-duddy. But there toward the end, it was like he totally forgot how to have fun."

A waitress came and Claude Ann ordered two "Koko Heads" without asking Dinah what she'd like. "No menus," she said. "We're not gonna eat."

Dinah's stomach grumbled. "But, Claudy, I'm hungry."

"Eat some of these macadamia nuts." She pushed a bowl toward Dinah. When the waitress had gone, she said, "We're gonna have a fancy gourmet dinner with Xander at the hotel." Her eyes darted back to Marywave, as if she weren't sure she'd stay put. "She takes after Hank, doesn't she?"

Dinah answered warily. "A little maybe. She has your nose. And great bone structure."

"Hawaii's gonna be hell on those freckles. The little ninny won't wear sunscreen. Says God'll take care of her. Like He gives a hoot if she's speckled as a guinea hen."

Dinah said, "I don't recall Hank being overly religious in high school."

"He wasn't. He found Jesus after his accident and he's been batty over religion ever since. Not the nice, quiet, do-unto-others kind, but the bullyin', do-what-I-say-or-fry-in-hell kind. I tried to be sweet and understandin'. The poor guy was hurtin' and he couldn't work for months. But one day I woke up to his preachin' and naggin' at me and the frying sounded like a day at the beach. Honestly, I don't know why I stayed with him as long as I did."

Dinah was still puzzling over why she'd married him in the first place, although there was never any question that Hank had worshipped the ground Claude Ann walked on.

"Tell me about Xander. Apart from being brainy and handsome, what's he like?"

"You're gonna just love him to death. He's thoughtful and considerate and he has the most elegant way of talkin', like something out of an old-time book." She wiggled the engagement ring under Dinah's nose.

"Wow. It's stunning."

"He was careful to make sure it's a non-conflict diamond. I swear, he just knows everything."

"What kind of a scientist is he?"

"A volcanologist. He came out here from Maryland to go to the University of Hawaii and stayed on because, I mean, where else would a volcanologist have two active volcanoes blowing their stacks for him every day?"

"No place as heavenly as Hawaii?" ventured Dinah, intoxicated by the perfume of her lei.

"You got that right." Claude Ann broke into a huge, exultant smile. "Can you believe I've come up so far in the world, Di? From a dumb ol' dairy farmer in the Georgia sticks to a brilliant scientist in this incredible place? It's like a dream. Sometimes I get scared I'll wake up and he'll have run off with some egghead who understands what the hell he's talkin' about."

"I'm sure Xander enjoys your sassy, non-eggy take on things," said Dinah.

"Yeah, but I wanted you here so he'd know I have a brainy friend, too. I told him you're the one with a diploma that says magna cum laude. Y'all can talk Latin to each other and I won't know if you're flirtin' or what."

Dinah frowned. She tried to be sensitive to Claude Ann's I-didn't-graduate-from-college-like-you-did complex, but sometimes she felt like smacking her. Everybody had begged her not to drop out of school to get married and Dinah had urged her time and again to go back and finish her education. It wasn't as if the Taliban was preventing her. And that barb about flirting touched a nerve. Did she think…?

"Whatever you're thinking, don't. I'm just kiddin'. You know I want you here 'cause I love you. You're the sister I never had."

Dinah relaxed a fraction. The things unspoken between them had made her touchy.

The waitress arrived with two coconut shells filled with some kind of creamy goop with a yellow hibiscus floating on top.

Claude Ann plunked a straw into the concoction and sucked down a long swig. "This drink is named after an extinct volcano here on Oahu. Seems Pele got chased by a pig god and one of her sisters sent Koko Head crater as a decoy to save her from being raped. Dippy, I know. But folks say dippy stuff all the time around here. Anyhow, this is Pele's favorite drink."

Pele again. She seemed to have a grip on everyone's imagination. Dinah took a tentative sip, expecting gin. It tasted like a coconut milkshake spiked with rum. Where liquor was concerned, it seemed that the goddess had catholic tastes. "A woman I met on the plane told me that Pele's been cutting up rough lately. On the Big Island."

"Aw, just a few little jigglers. Sometimes you don't even feel 'em." Claude Ann added a spoonful of sugar to her Koko Head and stirred it in with her straw. "Earthquakes come in swarms, if you can believe it. Like wasps or hornets. It's a baby volcano that's still underwater off the southeast coast of the Big Island that's causing 'em, but Xander says they're harmless."

"I guess a volcanologist should know," said Dinah, doubtful all the same.

"He's a volcanologist only part-time, really. This past year he's spent most of his time workin' on a major real estate deal. There's not all that much land to build on in

Hawaii and what there is of it is worth a fortune. When it sells, we're gonna be Rockefeller rich." She took a quick slurp and puckered her brow. "Are the Rockefellers still rich? Anyhow, Xan's kept his hand in as a volcanologist because it gives him more credibility with the environmentalists and regulators."

"You're moving awfully fast, Claudy. Shouldn't you live together for a while and see if the infatuation lasts?"

"I knew you'd say that. You've got what they call 'trust issues' on account of finding out at such a young age that your daddy was a drug-runnin' skunk. It's warped your faith in people."

Dinah and Claude Ann had been debating the cause and effects of Hart Pelerin's supposed criminality since they were in the fifth grade. Dinah's slant on her father had mellowed over the last year. Still and all, it was her experience that the capacity of human beings to lie couldn't be overestimated. "How did you meet Xander? And where? At last check, there were no volcanoes in South Georgia."

"I didn't write you, but Hank and I separated last summer. He made a big stink about wanting custody of Marywave and it took a while for the divorce to be final. In the end, the judge liked me best and Hank had to give me a whoppin' big pile of cash. He had to take out a loan on the farm, which really honked him off, but my lawyer said I deserved half the marital assets and I got to keep the money the insurance company paid me after Hank's car wreck for my loss of consortium. Anyhow, when the hoopla was over, I wanted to get as far away from Needmore as I could go where they still speak English. As soon as school was out, I hogtied Marywave and bundled her off to Maui. I met Xan when I went paraglidin' off Haleakala and my feet haven't touched the ground since."

Dinah felt the unromantic prick of skepticism. Just how whopping a pile had Hank coughed up and how recklessly had the gay divorcée been flaunting it? "Are you sure Xander's the real deal, Claudy? He sounds almost too good to be true."

"I'm a thousand percent sure. Hank was plain and borin' as burlap, but Xander's smooth as silk. You know what he says? He says Hank was infra dig. Isn't that a scrumptious word? I love it, even if it is Latin. It means beneath one's dignity and Hank was that, all right."

Hank was about as suave as a herd of Holsteins, but he was honest and hard working and beneath nobody's dignity. He had developed his family's dairy into a top regional brand and, in spite of a sort of innate gloominess, he had tried to make Claude Ann happy—a pied-à-terre in Atlanta where she could shop 'til she dropped and there'd been two or three vacations to Europe. Dinah felt she should put in a good word for him, but there was no percentage in sticking up for an ex. "Is Hank badly crippled from his accident?"

"They had to amputate his left leg, but he's back managin' the farm, bossin' the help around same as always. Sheesh, I can't see why he's so bent out of shape about the divorce. Jiminy Christmas, we haven't had consortium since his wreck."

Dinah didn't need the intimate details. "I guess Mary-wave misses her dad."

"Yeah." Claude Ann looked again to make sure Mary-wave was still there. "I had to give her her own cell phone so she could keep in touch with her friends back home, but she mostly jaws with Hank. After she told him about me and Xander, he started sending me wacko letters warnin' me to repent before it's too late. Wantonness and licentiousness and walkin' after ungodly lusts. Sheesh. To read one of his rants, you'd think I'd taken up streetwalkin'."

Dinah didn't like the drift of Hank's thoughts. Every day of the week some unhinged man gunned down his wife, his children, and any bystanders unlucky enough to be caught in his cross hairs. "Has he threatened you, Claude Ann?"

"Nah. He's gonna leave my punishment to God. I just wish he wouldn't brainwash Marywave." She shook off the mood and put on a big smile. "But I'm not worried. She'll come around once she starts school out here."

"Your letter mentioned that Xander has children. Does Marywave get along with them?"

"She won't have to. They're as old as we are."

Dinah did the math. Xander had to be in his fifties. "How long has Xan been divorced?"

"He's not divorced. His wife died over twenty years ago and he's never remarried."

"How is it that someone that wonderful managed to stay single for so many years?"

Claude Ann added another spoonful of sugar to her Koko Head. "I think he was afraid to let himself fall in love again until now. His wife dived off a cliff into the ocean and killed herself. He must've been super trauma-tized. After all these years, he still gets grouchy if any-body goes near the subject. The only reason I know about it is 'cause Lyssa, that's his daughter, dropped it into the conversation like a live rat. Lyssa's a bitch, but I had to in-clude her in the weddin' for Xan's sake. Thank God she's married and lives way off in Virginia so we won't have to fake the sweetness and light all that often. Her husband is worse than she is. A real snake-in-the-grass. Xan's son Jon lives on the Big Island, but he's kind of a hermit."

"Will he come to the wedding?"

"I hope so. He's the apple of Xan's eye, but there was some kind of a silly rift and they don't talk much." She reached across the table and clasped Dinah's hands. "Gosh, I'm glad you came, Di. I want things between us to be like they used to be. I was mad at you for a long time. Mostly, I think I was mad at myself. Anyhow, I've missed you."

Dinah had a momentary urge to blurt out the truth, but it no longer mattered. In fact, it would be gratuitous cruelty. Claude Ann was in love again and Dinah was beginning to see this breakup with Hank as a culmination of her own guilt. Everything had worked out for the best and she was more than ready to let bygones be bygones. "I've missed you, too, Claudy. More than you know. And it'll be great to see your parents again. Have they arrived yet?"

"They're not coming."

"Why? They're not ill, are they?"

Claude Ann's eyes wandered. "I didn't invite them."

"But, you're their only child. They'll be so hurt."

"They'll be better off waitin' 'til I'm settled." Still, she didn't meet Dinah's eyes. Something was wrong.

"Why aren't they coming, Claude Ann?"

She made an airy gesture of dismissal. "Oh, you know how they are, Needmore through and through. Daddy would want Xander to take him squirrel huntin' and Mama would fire the caterers and serve catfish and hush puppies at the reception."

"You're embarrassed for Xander to meet them."

"I am not! Xan's not the least bit snobby."

"What is it then?"

She clouded up and bit her lip. "Some stupid people have been protestin' Xander's development. Some malarkey about the bones of an ol' Hawaiian king buried on the property. They follow us around wavin' signs and shoutin' all kinds of nutty things. Daddy and Mama wouldn't know what to make of their hoo-ha."

"Can't Xander get an injunction or something?"

"He acts, I don't know, kind of buffaloed. Like he has to tiptoe around 'em. I'll bring the folks out after I'm settled. Speaking of not being settled, you sure jet around. Australia, Panama, the Philippines. Loved your postcards. I want to hear about all your travels and your boyfriends.

Are you still goin' hot 'n heavy with that guy in Seattle? Nick something or other?"

"We split a year ago."

"Oh, honey. I'm sorry. It sounded for a while there like you'd met the love of your life."

"He wasn't the man I thought he was." Dinah concealed a pang of irritation. It wasn't as pleasant to reflect on one's own romantic miscalculations as it was someone else's.

"Well, I hope he didn't aggravate your trust issues. Hold on! I almost forgot." Claude Ann whipped a small, beribboned box out of her handbag. "These are for you."

Dinah untied the ribbon, opened the box, and held up a pair of earrings with clusters of shiny black stones dangling on delicate gold chains. "They're lovely."

"Those doodads shot right out of one of Xander's volcanoes. They're called Pele's tears. I had a jeweler polish them and set them in gold for you. I didn't give you a gift the last time you stood up for me and I wanted to give you something special this time."

Dinah removed her silver hoops and fastened them in her ears. "How do they look?"

"Killer. With that long neck and square jaw of yours, you were meant to wear dangles. And I see you still have great taste in handbags." She held up a black leather hobo purse identical to Dinah's and pulled out her wallet. "We're runnin' late. Dump a handful of those nuts in your purse and let's roll. Xander's meetin' us at the hotel over by Diamond Head. We're gonna spend two nights here on Oahu. We'll do our fittings tomorrow afternoon and Xan's hostin' a party for some of his Honolulu buds in the evening. We'll fly on to the Big Island the morning after that." She dealt a fifty off a deck of new greenbacks, dropped it on the table, and bounced up ready to go.

"Aren't you going to wait for some change?"

"This isn't the Garden of Eat'n in Needmore. People

around here tip big." She hoisted Dinah's suitcase and streaked toward the door like a greyhound after a mechanical rabbit.

Not that big, thought Dinah, shouldering her bag and falling into step behind her.

"Get a move on, Marywave," sang out Claude Ann. "Let's go! Chop-chop!"

Marywave hopped off the bench and scampered along at Dinah's side. As they hustled out of the terminal into the late afternoon sunshine, she said, "If it wasn't for you, I never woulda been born."

Dinah gave her a sharp look. "What do you mean?"

"I heard Mama arguin' with Gran about divorcin' Daddy. Gran called Mama a quitter and Mama said if you hadn't made such a big fat fool of her, she wouldn't have married anybody, especially not Daddy."

Dinah froze. This was an omen. Turn on your heel this instant, she told herself. Turn and take the next flight back to Manila. But Marywave snatched her hand and began running and she felt herself dragged, irresistibly, over the cliff into Claude Ann's life again.

THREE

THE OLOPANA HOTEL was located in a swank residential neighborhood at the end of an alley overarched by massive banyan trees. It was 7:30 by the time Claude Ann turned her rental car into the twilit hotel drive and, at first, Dinah couldn't make out what was happening in front of the entrance. There seemed to be some kind of a disturbance. A shadowy mob brandished torches and waved signs. A police car with its lights flashing sat parked under the portico and two uniformed cops and a valet appeared to be in a dispute with an immense woman who was shaking some kind of a bamboo rattle. As Claude Ann's car pulled closer, Dinah read the crudely lettered signs. UWAHI JOOSE! and GARST STEALS FROM THE KANAKA MAOLI AND SEE PELE'S REVENGE.

"It's those damn people again." Claude Ann parked behind the police car and put a hand to her face. "See what I mean?"

"Roll down your window, Claudy." Dinah craned her neck to see out the driver's side window.

"That ugly ol' battleax has been harassin' us all week and the police can't seem to do a damn thing about it."

The big woman's voice thundered. "Dat buggah Garst tink our land just dirt and rocks to be dug up and planted wid houses. Da land is da body of Pele. No moa houses!"

Claude Ann ticked her fingernails against her teeth, as if poised between fight and flight. "They just won't let up. All those hateful, nutty signs. I thought Hawaiians spoke English." Tears welling, she launched out of the door. "Go away! Go away, you people! Go away and leave me and my fiancé alone."

A burly, brown-skinned cop lowered his arm like a turn-stile in front of Claude Ann. "Go inside the hotel, ma'am. Don't escalate the situation."

Dinah got out of the car, moved around beside Claude Ann, and took her arm. "Let the police handle it, Claudy."

"Well, they're not handlin' it. What's that sign about revenge? Are they threatenin' us, Officer? What do those other signs say?"

"Dey say Pele can't be zoned." The big woman's voice rumbled, low and freighted with foreboding. "Pele can't be platted and subdivided. Tell yo man he bettah leave Uwahi alone." The red light from the police car strobing across her broad, pugnacious face lent an aura of menace.

"It's a free country," said Claude Ann. "People can do whatever they like with their own property."

"Please, ma'am," said the cop, taking Claude Ann by the arm and turning her toward the door. "Do as I ask. Go inside and let the police handle the problem."

Claude Ann threw off his hand. "Whose side are you on?"

"They have a right to hold a peaceful demonstration, ma'am."

The big woman pointed her bamboo rattle at Claude Ann. "If Garst wants a beef, we geev 'im beef. You tell 'im Uwahi bring 'im bachi plenny koke."

"What kind of mumbo jumbo is that?" demanded Claude Ann. "Officer?"

"It's pidgin," said the cop. "She says the Uwahi project is bad karma."

"Sheesh!"

A TV truck rolled up behind Claude Ann's car and a man with a shoulder-mounted camera jumped out and began to film the scene.

A blond reporter got out on the other side of the truck and futzed with her microphone. "Get a tight shot of those signs, Perry. Zoom in on Eleanor and the ringleaders."

"Be careful her ugly mug doesn't break your camera," taunted Claude Ann.

The other cop, a white guy with a horsy face and no neck, slung an irascible look at Claude Ann. "Please go inside the hotel, ma'am. Harsh words will only inflame the situation."

"Then do your job, Officer. The whole bunch of 'em oughta be jailed for trespassing."

"All of Hawaii is our land," came a loud voice from somewhere in the crowd. "Can't trespass on our own land."

The reporter secured her mike around her neck and approached Claude Ann. "Are you a spokesperson for Uwahi Gardens? Has the Land Use Commission okayed the proposed sale?"

"No." Claude Ann backed away. "I mean, I don't know about the Land Use Commission. I'm Xander Garst's fiancée. And these people are nothin' but bullies and hooligans."

"Does Mr. Garst have confidence that the Commission will grant approval?" The reporter held the mike under Claude Ann's nose.

"You'll have to ask…"

The big woman's voice rolled over Claude Ann's. "Dey can approve anyting. Don't mean it's gonna get built. Garst can't cockaroach no more land dat belongs to Pele."

"You're freakin' nuts!" said Claude Ann, and stormed into the lobby.

Marywave, looking curious but uncertain, scrambled out of the back seat and followed her mother inside. Dinah held back, fascinated by the confrontation and the real-life manifestation of the Pele myth in modern Honolulu. Who were these people and what had Xander Garst done to get them so worked up? For all its touristic and commercial trappings, maybe Hawaii wasn't as tame and Christianized as she'd assumed.

"'Aihui!" yelled a bare-chested, angry young man, pointing straight at Dinah. "Pele gonna bust you, too."

Dinah was dumbfounded. What had she done? "Officer, what's that word? What does it mean?"

The white cop rounded on her. "It means go inside. Right now! That's an order."

Well, a-LO-bloody-ha. She about-faced and stalked into the lobby, repeating the strange word to herself so she'd remember it. 'Aihui. 'Aihui. She'd find out what it meant.

At the reception desk, an attractive Asian woman was apologizing profusely to Claude Ann. "The Olopana regrets this unpleasantness, Ms. Kemper. We've asked the police to keep the protesters farther from the entrance, but they haven't been very effective."

"It's not your fault, but this is the third time in a week."

"We appreciate your patience. The manager told Mr. Garst he'd file for an injunction, but Mr. Garst doesn't want to give them any more publicity." She handed Claude Ann an envelope. "He left you a message and he said for me to tell you that every hour he's away from you is torture."

Claude Ann nudged Dinah in the ribs. "Isn't he just the darlingest man in the world?"

Dinah forced a smile. Judging from the hubbub outside, there was some difference of opinion.

While the receptionist checked Dinah in, Claude Ann turned away and read her message.

As with the plane ticket, Dinah's hotel bill was pre-paid, so registration was a simple matter of signing her name and accepting her key card.

Claude Ann finished reading and said, "Xan's runnin' late on account of business. You wanna go to your room and freshen up before dinner?"

"In a few minutes." Dinah surrendered her suitcase to a hovering porter. "I need to walk around a bit and unwind."

"Don't snack and spoil your dinner."

"I won't." She watched as Claude Ann strode across the lobby to the elevators with Marywave scuffing along behind. When they disappeared, she crept back to the door and peeped out at the action.

The fireworks had fizzled and the protesters were already dispersing into the shadows. Dinah felt a sense of relief for Claude Ann, but the anthropologist in her couldn't help feeling disappointed. It wasn't every day one had the chance to interact with pagans. The TV people had turned off the camera and the mike and stood schmoozing with the policemen. Dinah opened the glass door a crack to hear.

"…just rumor and gossip," said the brown-skinned cop. "Nobody alleged foul play."

"He's one powerful kahuna," said the cameraman, who looked Filipino. "That old tita's got a lot of guts to go up against him."

"Isn't she related to…?" The blond reporter caught sight of Dinah in the doorway and pursed her lips, as if evaluating her as a potential news source. The cops looked, too, and Dinah let go of the door and retreated across the marbled lobby. At the far end, there was another glass door through which she could see a terrace with tables and umbrellas. She slammed outside, crossed the terrace, and emerged onto a beautiful crescent of beach.

There was no one on the terrace. The only sound on this side of the hotel was the peaceful whoosh of the surf. She took off her sandals, strolled down the beach, and tried to make sense of the exchange she'd overheard. If Xander was the powerful kahuna, the big woman the reporter had called Eleanor must be the tita taking a stand against him. But foul play? A housing development might be unpopular. It might be controversial or a blight on the landscape. But it could hardly be described as foul play, not by a policeman anyway. Claude Ann had said that the protesters' chief complaint had to do with human bones on the site, but Dinah hadn't seen any signs about that. Did this group of Native Hawaiians really believe that Xander's development would desecrate the body of their goddess?

Oh, for Pete's sake. Her imagination was running away with her. Hawaiians weren't animists who believed that spirits exist in rocks and real estate or blamed their troubles on a disgruntled goddess. However isolated the Hawaiian archipelago, it was part of the U.S. of A. "Pele" was probably just island-speak for the green movement and the protesters invoked the goddess' name to garner media attention for their anti-development cause and exaggerated the small earthquakes as "Pele's Revenge."

In front of her, silhouetted against the reddening sky, Diamond Head rose out of the sea like the fin of some gigantic fish. An article in the Hawaiian Airlines magazine said that the original Hawaiian name for the crater meant "brow of a tuna," but British sailors seeing it from a distance thought that the crystals glistening in the lava rock were diamonds. They turned out to be common calcite, but the misnomer stuck.

After about fifty yards, a jetty of large rocks blocked her way and she turned around and ambled back toward the hotel. It appeared to be a small, boutique affair with Mediterranean style balconies overlooking the ocean. On one side of the hotel, a flock of dolphins cavorted in their private saltwater lagoon. She paused for a few minutes to watch them and pondered Claude Ann's remark that she wouldn't have married Hank if Dinah hadn't made a fool of her. It didn't jibe with her little speech about wanting to be friends again. And it didn't jibe with the truth.

You're being paranoid, she told herself. Claude Ann had been arguing with her mother. Mothers fought dirty.

A woman arguing with her mother might say anything. Daughters, too. And given Marywave's opposition to her mother's remarriage, she might have embellished Claude Ann's words to add to the stress. It was a secondhand remark passed on by an impudent squirt with an ulterior motive. There was no cause to make it into an omen.

One of the dolphins swooshed out of the water and chattered at her as if inviting her to jump in and play. She laughed. He and his pals would make a charming addition to a wedding. Why couldn't Claude Ann and Xander have been content to say their I do's here in Honolulu at the Olopana instead of dragging the party to the Big Island to pose beside a belching volcano? Oh, well. Maybe there weren't as many of Pele's rambunctious disciples on the Big Island.

When she reached the terrace, she brushed the sand off her feet and put on her sandals. Walking back through the lobby, she noticed a corridor of shops and moseyed into a few of them to browse. They carried an array of designer scarves, pricey jade and coral jewelry in a rainbow of colors, Chinese vases, Japanese netsukes, and Louis Vuitton luggage along with a few more prosaic guest needs. She bought a tube of toothpaste, a newspaper and, on impulse, a pack of cigarettes—Sincerely Yours, menthol lights. What were a few paltry carcinogens compared to the deadly gases she'd be inhaling on the rim of that volcano?

In the last shop, she found a book of Hawaiian history, legends, and myths and charged it to her room. That strange fray with the protesters suggested a more complicated Hawaii than the one depicted in the travel brochures. She had a feeling that molten lava wasn't the only fire smoldering under the surface of Paradise.

FOUR

In November of 1880, Mauna Loa burst open and began discharging lava. There was no great concern during the winter, but over the spring the lava oozed closer and closer to Hilo. The forests west of town glowed red and the air was thick and acrid with smoke. By June, the fiery flow had reached the outskirts of town and real estate values plummeted. On June 26th, the flow coursed down from the streambeds above Hilo gobbling as much as five hundred feet of earth each day. Methane explosions sounded like cannon fire and the heat and glare were intense. The Christian inhabitants closed their shops and businesses and thronged the churches to beg the intercession of Jehovah. The Hawaiian inhabitants sent an urgent message to Princess Luka Ke'elikolani, a descendant of King Kamehameha I and an unreconstructed worshipper of Pele.

Princess "Ruth," as she had been re-christened by the Western missionaries, was fifty-five years old and tipped the scales at four-hundred-and-forty pounds. Her nose had been crushed in a pitched battle with her second husband and her voice boomed like thunder. She wasn't one to be overawed by the U.S. government, or the white man's Jehovah, or Madame Pele's flare-ups.

When she came ashore in Hilo in July, Princess Ruth ordered a batch of red silk handkerchiefs, a large quantity of brandy, two roast pigs, and an unrolled taro leaf and commanded her underlings to conduct her royal personage to the edge of the flow. The horse selected to pull her carriage wasn't up to the task and a crew of prisoners from the Hilo jail was drafted to haul her to her destination.

When she was satisfied with her vantage point, she disembarked and directed that a luau be held on the spot. Then, chanting a sacred poem and swaying her imposing hips in a hula, she fed the taro leaf and the handkerchiefs into the flames. When these had been consumed, she smashed a bottle of brandy against the hot lava sending up a hair-singeing gust of fire. The Princess and her party drank the rest of the brandy, ate the pigs, and slept all night in the path of Pele's progress. By morning, the lava had cooled and the goddess had retired to her mountain. Score one for Ruth, whose attitude and description called to mind the formidable woman leading the anti-Garst demonstration outside the hotel.

Dinah closed the book, turned the no-smoking sign to the wall, and lit a Sincerely Yours. Showered and smelling of some citrusy lotion, she lay propped up on her king-sized bed in her luxurious ocean-front room thinking about Eleanor's views on Hawaiian real estate and Xander Garst. Claude Ann had sounded perplexed by Xander's lack of assertiveness with the protesters, even a little fearful. Did she feel she had to stand up to them because he wouldn't, or couldn't? She'd showed her loyalty, but Dinah didn't think her bravado would discourage the woman who resembled Princess Ruth.

She picked up the newspaper and glanced over the front page. The man who'd fallen into a steam vent near Ocean View on the Big Island still had not been identified and no one had come forward to report a missing person. The police were now calling it a homicide. Due to extreme decomposition of the body, fingerprints had not yet been obtained, but with advanced forensic techniques, the police expected the identity question to be resolved within the week.

The telephone rang. Dinah picked it up and listened as

Claude Ann delivered her dinner-time instructions. Dress to the hilt; wear the new earrings; don't tell any Needmore stories no matter how hard you're pressed; and be in the Paliuli restaurant downstairs at 9:00 sharp.

Dinah stubbed out her cigarette, her first in nearly a month. Even the Philippine government had jumped on the health bandwagon to stamp out smoking. Once cigarettes made men look macho and women look sexy. They had bolstered men in times of war and pacified them in times of boredom, and they went so perfectly with martinis and mood music. A cigarette had once been the finale at the end of lovemaking and the final solace of men brought before a firing squad. Now smoking was just one more discredited myth. Like burning witches to prevent sorcery or taking calcium supplements to prevent osteoporosis. While she was thinking about it, she pitched her Calci-tabs, which had apparently been shown to cause heart attacks.

She slipped into her only dress, a sleeveless black sheath with a jewel neckline and a side slit, combed her hair, and assessed her reflection in the mirror. It had been months since she spruced up to go out for a social occasion. She'd almost forgotten what she looked like in a dress. When her fieldwork on Mindanao ended, she would return to the States and rejoin civilization. Maybe she'd return to Emory and complete her graduate degree. In the meantime, this was as close to the hilt as it got. She added a tinge of lipstick, stepped into a pair of sling-back heels, and headed for the elevators.

The Paliuli was two floors down, tucked away on the mezzanine. As she entered, torch ginger and red anthuriums and birds of paradise blazed from every nook and cranny. Xander and Claude Ann were already seated. The maitre d' ushered her past a mural of an Edenic island scene to her host's booth.

Xander stood to greet her. "Dinah, mahalo for coming so far to celebrate with us. I'm delighted to meet you."

He was six-three at least, broad-shouldered, with a wide, rather sensual mouth and penetrating brown eyes. There was a stippling of gray at his temples, but a forelock of still-dark hair fell across his forehead, and he had been blessed with a strong, clean jaw line. He wore a brown turtleneck and a tan cashmere jacket and seemed casually at ease with himself and his place in the world. Whatever his reasons for not wanting to cross swords with the protesters, he didn't look like a man accustomed to tiptoeing.

Claude Ann said, "We're expectin' Xander's daughter, Lyssa, and her husband, Raif, to join us in a little while so scooch in close. Marywave's with the sitter so we can drink and cuss to our hearts' content."

Dinah settled herself next to Claude Ann, who wore an asymmetrical, one-shoulder blue cocktail dress and a radiant smile.

Xander sat back down and held up his hand to summon their server. "Claude Ann refuses to tell me a thing about Needmore, Dinah. I'm counting on you to enlighten me."

Dinah wanted to talk about the protesters, but she tried to contain her curiosity until after the initial pleasantries. "Needmore in the nutshell…"

"It better be an itty-bitty nut," warned Claude Ann.

Dinah held up her hand. "Needmore is best known for its killingly high humidity, its speed trap, and the captivating aroma of its onion processing plant."

Claude Ann laughed. "Don't forget the captivatin' quicksand."

"The quicksand is metaphorical," said Dinah.

Xander grinned a winningly boyish grin. "I'm overjoyed that you two ladies made it out of the quicksand, real or metaphorical."

The waiter breezed by and took their drink order. Claude

Ann wanted a champagne cocktail. Dinah ordered a dirty gin martini.

Xander shot her an amused look and asked for the same. When the waiter had gone, he said, "Claude Ann and I are having our first fight. She thinks of you as a sister, Dinah. Will you please help me persuade her that I can't possibly write my own vows?"

"The first duty of the maid of honor is to support the bride, Xander. Whatever Claude Ann wants, I'm on her side. But why do you feel you can't write your own vows?"

"I'm not a poet. And the examples Claude Ann has shown me of other people's vows are so high-sounding and sappy."

"That just means you'll have to come up with something better," said Claude Ann.

Dinah smiled. A man who could say it was torture being away from his lover for a few extra hours had a finely nuanced concept of sappy.

He raked his hair off his forehead. "Thirty years ago, my wife and I wanted a no-frills civil ceremony, but she was Hawaiian and her family traditional to the nth degree. They insisted on the whole nine yards of Hawaiiana and the show they put on was like something from another century. Somebody blew a conch shell to call forth the gods. There was lots of chanting and hula and some godawful potion that was supposed to be sacred to Pele that we had to drink. My wife and I exchanged maile leis and promised to make the Aloha eternal. It was the ceremony that seemed eternal. It lasted until dawn." He nuzzled Claude Ann's cheek. "You know that I love you, darling, but I want to keep it simple this time. I see no reason to gild the plumerias."

Claude Ann laughed. "The last time I married, all I had was a handful of puny, no-smell roses Mama bought at the Piggly-Wiggly Market. It was a rainy February day and cold as blue flujins. The groom was dressed like an undertaker and he had to bum the weddin' band off of my daddy's finger. This time it's gonna be a sunny June day with a beautiful ring and everybody lookin' like a million bucks. I want to wallow in plumerias and have everything be perfect."

Xander lifted her hand and kissed it. "It will be, Claude Ann. You have my word."

Claude Ann rhapsodized about the absolutely divine Vera Wang gown she'd ordered and the reception she'd arranged at Xander's house on the Big Island—caviar, Dom Pérignon and "the whole cotton-pickin' works." Xander appeared to take a genuine delight in her enthusiasm.

Dinah said, "It sounds lovely, Claude Ann. I'm thrilled for you."

"There's one thing you may not be so thrilled about." She bit her lip and looked sheepish. "I invited Phoebe Marshall. I know she used to say stuff that rubbed you wrong."

Dinah hadn't thought of Phoebe in years. She'd been another of Claude Ann's broken-winged birds, a beneficiary not just of Claude Ann's kindness, but also of her clout. With Claude Ann as her champion, she'd been elected editor of the Needmore Nuggets Newspaper and fancied herself the Boswell of the class. Some of the nuggets she'd printed, especially about Dinah and the goings-on in her family, had been less than complimentary, but it was the maid of honor's duty to back the bride. She said, "It'll be fun to see Phoebe again."

Their drinks arrived.

Claude Ann touched her glass to Dinah's and Xander's. "Here's to happy days."

"Happy days," they said in unison.

Xander held Claude Ann's eyes in a way that made Dinah feel like an intruder. She was about to excuse herself and leave them to their trance when Xander snapped out of it.

"I'm about to retire from the U.S. Geological Survey,

Dinah. I've bought and sold several parcels of land over the years, but nothing as big as the deal I'm working on now. The contract has been signed and it's scheduled to close the day after the wedding. Then Claude Ann and I are off to Bali for our honeymoon. Her friend, Phoebe, has agreed to stay for a few weeks and take care of Mary-wave for us."

Claude Ann said, "I feel kinda bad leavin' Marywave behind, but Phoebe gets along with her real well. She's spent a lot of time handholding the two of us over this last year. Maybe she can talk some sense into the little mule." Her smile was cheery and blithe, but Dinah had a hunch she was more worried about Marywave than she let on.

"Xan, honey, Dinah's prob'ly dyin' to know about that hul-labaloo with the Pele gang. Tell her what you told me."

At last. Dinah sat forward. "I take it they're opposed to your development."

"It's nothing, really. A minor nuisance. As a matter of fact, the Land Commission issued its approval only a few hours ago. That's why I was late." He heaved a longsuffering sigh, like what's a guy to do. "Somebody finds a few bones or an endangered haha plant in a pasture and immediately there's a hue and cry for a moratorium on development. Hawaii is the endangered species capital of the world. There's always some new flora or fauna in danger of extinction."

"Did the protesters find an endangered haha on the land you plan to develop?"

"The environmental studies say not, but the fanatics are never satisfied. I'm all for preserving Nature, but I have all of the requisite county, state, and federal permits. Uwahi Gardens is makai property…"

"Makai means toward the ocean," said Claude Ann. "Uwahi is right on the ocean."

Xander smiled indulgently. "Uwahi is prime ocean-front property, the opportunity of a lifetime. My company has done all of the preliminary studies and we're selling it development-ready to one of the country's premier development corporations. The CEO, Paul Jarvis, took one look at the property and shook hands on the spot. Of course, we had to get the Land Commission's okay and there's a short lag while his attorneys check our bona fides. That's why these protests are a headache. I don't want their rant giving Jarvis or his legal team second thoughts ahead of the closing date."

"What frosts me," said Claude Ann, "is the ignorant way those people talk, dis ting and dat ting. How do they expect you to even understand what they're bellyachin' about?"

"Everybody in Hawaii speaks some pidgin, darling. It's our local language, a mélange of English and Hawaiian with smatterings of every language spoken by the immigrants who came to work the sugar plantations back in the eighteen hundreds—Chinese, Japanese, Korean, Portuguese, Samoan, Filipino. Pidgin is the bridge, the lingua franca." A note of grievance seeped into his voice. "Unfortunately, not everyone wants to bridge differences."

Dinah inferred that reference was to Eleanor. "What does kanaka maoli mean?" she asked, recalling one of the protester's signs.

"The kanaka maoli are native Hawaiians or their descendants. There's always a group of them decrying the exploitation of Hawaiians by white and Asian foreigners and protesting the overthrow of their queen."

"The way that Eleanor struts around," said Claude Ann, "you'd think that she's the queen."

Xander raked his dark forelock out of his face and drained his martini. "I don't mean to be critical, darling, but I wish you hadn't spoken to her. The last thing we need is for that woman to start turning up on the evening news peddling her rubbish. Put her out of your mind. Don't egg her on or let her know that she's rattled you. Three more days and nothing she says or does will matter."

"If you say so. But she better not cross me after Mr. Jarvis has signed on the dotted line."

Dinah sensed a more personal animosity between Xander and Eleanor than any housing development should have caused and a greater fear of her "rubbish" than he was willing to admit. "There was another sign," she said. "Uwahi joose. What does joose mean?"

"It means rigged." His tone turned bitter, as if she'd accused him of a crime. "And there's nothing joose or unfair about Uwahi. I've spent nearly two years and a staggering sum of money acquiring the land and conducting every environmental and archaeological and anthropological study under the sun. Everything to do with Uwahi is completely legitimate and proper."

"I'm sure it is." Dinah offered a mollifying smile. "Oo-wa-hee." She sounded out the syllables slowly. "Uwahi is a melodic name for a housing development."

"It is, isn't it?" His manner became easy and affable again. "It comes from a mele my late wife used to chant. It translates roughly to milk of fire. The land is part of an old volcanic flow."

FIVE

A SLENDER GIRL in her mid-twenties with Polynesian features, pouty lips, and hip-length black hair sashayed through the restaurant and stopped beside their table. "Sorry I'm late." She didn't say it like she meant it.

Xander stood and kissed her on the cheek. "Dinah Pelerin, meet my daughter, Lyssa Reid. Dinah is Claude Ann's maid of honor, Lyssa."

"The same one she had last time, right?" Lyssa smirked and scooted in next to Dinah. She had an arresting notch in her right nostril, which gave her a peculiarly haughty look, and the chip on her shoulder stuck out like a pikestaff.

Xander winced slightly and sat down. "You'll have to forgive Lyssa's flippancy. She's been spending too much time with..."

"My husband?" She tossed her hair.

Dinah affected a smile. "It's a pleasure to meet you, Lyssa. Claude Ann tells me that you'll be one of her bridesmaids."

"That's right."

"What do you do back in Virginia?" asked Dinah.

"I'm a finder. I find unusual things for people, antiques and rare objects for collectors, props for TV shows and movies. Anything, really."

"That sounds fascinating," said Dinah. "How did you get started as a finder?"

"I've always been a natural sleuth, haven't I, Daddy?"

Claude Ann said, "It's a cryin' shame Lyssa and Raif

can't stay all summer, but Raif's a race car driver and he has to get back to the mainland for a big NASCAR race."

"That sounds like an interesting life," said Dinah. "Do you travel with him to the races, Lyssa?"

"Not often." She slued her eyes at her father.

"Raif doesn't think she'd enjoy the society," said Xander. "Not all of the boys behave as they should when they're away from home."

Lyssa unfurled her napkin with a snap. "Has everyone ordered?"

"We were waiting for you and Raif," said Xander. "Where is he?"

"Playing poker in the game room. He'll be along when he finishes the hand."

"I wish he wouldn't flout the law so blatantly. Gambling in a hotel or a public place is illegal in Hawaii. If he's caught…"

"Nobody's going to catch Raif, Daddy."

Xander beckoned the waiter. "Then let's hope the cards are running better for him tonight."

Their server returned to the table and passed out menus. Lyssa ordered Cachi Water.

"It's from Costa Rica," she said to Dinah. "When I do travel, I order a case delivered to each of the places I expect to stay. I'm addicted."

Xander ordered a bottle of white wine for the table and another champagne cocktail for Claude Ann. When the waiter had gone, he smiled at his daughter. "Is it possible to be addicted to a chichi designer water?"

Lyssa cut her eyes at him. "You should be glad that water's my only addiction."

"If only," he muttered, not quite under his breath.

Claude Ann rushed into the breach. "Does anybody know if Jon's gonna show up for the party tomorrow night?"

Xander brightened. "Jonathan is my son, Dinah. He had

to finish analyzing some lava samples and write a report, but he called this afternoon and said he'd be flying over from the Big Island tomorrow afternoon. It took a bit of arm-twisting. He's not exactly a party animal."

"Is he a volcanologist, too?"

"One of the best and brightest in the U.S.G.S. He's going to be a leading light in the field one of these days."

"Who's alight?" A blond dude with blowtorch blue eyes and an arrogant air slid into the seat next to Lyssa.

Xander's mouth tightened. "Hello, Raif."

"Hello, all." He kissed his forefinger and touched it to Lyssa's nose, then introduced himself to Dinah. "I'm Raif Reid. And you must be Claude Ann's friend from Georgia."

Dinah owned as much. "Nice to meet you."

"Ditto. I love Georgia. That Atlanta Motor Speedway's great, especially the night races. The fans tailgate all day. By dark, they're cranked and the drivers are hot to get tearing around the track. The sparks really fly."

Lyssa said, "Raif's won his last six races. He's one of the hottest stars on the circuit."

"On the Southeast regional circuit," amended Xander, his voice edged with contempt. "Raif doesn't drive in the Sprint Cup Series."

"Not yet," said Raif, fingering a gold chain with a Lucky 7 pendant. He draped an arm around Lyssa's shoulders. "Hey, babe, the cards were running hot tonight. I'm up a grand. What do you say? Shall we spend it on a magnum of Cristal?"

"Let's," said Lyssa. "I feel extravagant. Daddy only has two more nights as a free man. We should get him roaring drunk and see what happens."

A muscle in Xander's jaw rippled. "Order what you like. Ask the waiter to put it on a separate check."

Again, Claude Ann tried to defuse the tension. "We were

talking about Jonathan, Raif. He's decided to come to our party tomorrow night."

"Cool," said Raif. "How'd you lure him out of his bunker?"

"It takes a special occasion to bring Jon out," Claude Ann explained to Dinah. "He's kind of a shrinkin' violet."

Xander's eyes betrayed a flash of annoyance. "Jon's not a recluse. He has a lot of work to do is why he isn't with us tonight."

Raif shrugged. "All work and no play. Amounts to the same thing, doesn't it?"

"It amounts," said Xander, "to the fact that he's dedicated to his profession. He knows more about Hawaiian rock and its mineral and geochemical composition than anyone."

The waiter brought the white wine, the champagne cocktail, and the Cachi Water. He poured the wine and asked if they were ready to order. They weren't and Raif seemed to have forgotten all about the Cristal. He ordered a double Jack Daniel's on the rocks and the waiter repaired to the kitchen.

Raif rolled his shoulders and lazed against the upholstered seat back. "Rah for all that dedication, but it can't be much fun cuddling up to a report on rocks at the end of the day."

Xander's eyes narrowed and Dinah forged into the conversational crosscurrents. "Where did you and Lyssa meet, Raif?"

"Right here in the Big Pineapple. My family has been coming to Hawaii every year since I was a kid. After I got kicked out of Georgetown Prep in D.C., my parents talked me into Honolulu's most exclusive educational institution, Punahou Prep. That didn't work out too well either, but I met some of the islands' elite and up-and-coming. They like having a scion of old Virginia aristocracy on their Rolodex, especially one with his feet in two worlds. My NASCAR adventures entertain the hell out of them."

Lyssa beamed him an adoring smile. "Raif doesn't fit anyone's mold. He's one of a kind."

Raif appeared to accept her adulation as no less than his due. "I'm a spark plug. I touch off the combustion and keep the party lively."

"Opakapaka." Claude Ann pored over the menu, or pretended to. "I've had that before. It's the same as pink snapper. What's this a'u, Xan?"

"A'u is Pacific marlin, a'uku is swordfish, hihi-wai is a kind of shellfish, and opah is a moonfish. It's very rich and creamy. Hawaiians call it the good luck fish. And mahi mahi is dolphin fish."

"Not like the dolphins in the lagoon," Claude Ann assured Dinah. "It's a fish, not a mammal."

The waiter returned with Raif's drink and took their dinner order. Dinah, Raif, and Lyssa went in together and ordered a lau-lau—individual packets of pork shoulder, chicken, vegetables, and butterfish wrapped in taro leaves, then tied together in ti-leaves and steamed. Claude Ann ordered the mahi mahi and Xander ordered the good luck fish. After they'd sipped their drinks for a few minutes, the atmosphere grew friendlier.

Xander said, "Jon doesn't have a date for the party, Dinah. Would you allow him the honor of being your escort? I think you'll enjoy his company and I know he'll enjoy yours."

"I'll look forward to meeting him," she said, trapped, "and to learning more about what volcanologists do. Can you predict when a volcano is going to erupt?"

"We have some very sophisticated instruments for measuring any bulge in the mountain or increase in magma, but we still can't predict the exact time or precise impacts of an eruption."

"Like with people," said Raif with a provocative semi-sneer.

Claude Ann plopped a sugar cube into her champagne cocktail, which fizzed angrily. "I'm glad you're retiring, Xan. I'd worry myself sick sittin' home thinking about you tramping around all that hot lava."

Xander gave her hand a squeeze. "Gratifying as it is to be worried about, the majority of volcanologists die like accountants and dentists, in their bed."

"When you write your vows," said Claude Ann, "I want that one in there for sure. And you better promise to be at least a hundred when you croak."

Xander laughed. "How can I possibly object to writing that one?"

"Volcanology." Raif slouched in his seat and stared pensively into his glass. "It's a profession that takes more cojones than I've got. Two hundred miles an hour screaming around a tight track is my idea of a blast, but hiking around the red-hot cauldron of an active volcano? That scares the bejesus out of me."

Lyssa gave her father a black look. "It's hardly a mystery why that should be, is it?"

Xander grimaced, as if he'd been stabbed, and Claude Ann shot him an anxious look.

Raif lifted his glass. "Here's to the happy couple. May you both live to a hundred."

Dinah smiled and seconded the sentiment, but an awkward silence settled over the table. Dinnertime conversation was strained and edgy and the evening ended early.

SIX

Dinah lay sunning on her balcony lanai, drinking her morning cup of Kona coffee and reading the story of Lo-Lale, son of a legendary King of Oahu. Lo-Lale was a bachelor so attractive and so amiable that no woman could be found on the island who was worthy of him. One had to be imported from abroad. The king dispatched canoes to other islands with orders to find Lo-Lale a suitable wife. The questers came up empty on Molokai and Lanai. But eventually, on Maui, they spotted a beauty named Kelea, kidnapped her, and brought her to Oahu. Lo-Lale fell in love at first sight and proposed straightaway. Kelea didn't kill herself, which Lo-Lale took for a yes, and the wedding revelries lasted for a month.

A month! It sounded like hell to Dinah. She dreaded the fittings, dreaded another evening of verbal jabs and innuendo, most especially dreaded her date with the rock expert. When the best a man's own father can say about him is that he isn't a recluse, you know it's going to be a long, grim night. And she'd probably be stuck with him again the following night, as well. On the bright side, a boring disquisition on the geochemical composition of rocks would be restful compared to last night's crossfire.

For such an attractive and amiable fellow, Xander seemed to arouse more than his fair share of hostility. Eleanor had emitted an almost palpable loathing for "dat buggah." His comments about her carried more frustration than heat, but there'd been a twitchy look in his eyes when he asked Claude Ann to keep her head down. The word "hunted" sprang to mind.

And what was up between Xander and Raif? Raif's illicit gambling clearly rankled Xander and Xander made no secret of his view that Raif was not a model husband. That dig about some race car drivers not behaving well when away from home had struck a nerve with Lyssa. There was no doubt that she and her father had argued about Raif before. Maybe Raif mooched off Lyssa and gambled away what he mooched. It was no surprise that Lyssa would go to bat for her husband. Even so, her insinuating malice toward Xander jarred. What had she meant about it not being a mystery why Raif was scared of volcanoes? Had she been thinking of some previous discussion about the unidentified man who'd been cooked alive in a steam vent?

Lyssa seemed to enjoy twitting her father. Claude Ann said that she had brought up the sore subject of her mother's suicide. Maybe she had some sort of emotional hang-up about her death and she was angry at Xander for remarrying. Lyssa couldn't have been much past the toddler stage when her mother died and Xander had probably spoiled her rotten. Dinah wondered if there had been some mental disorder or precipitating event that drove her mother to commit suicide.

Suicide among all indigenous peoples ran high and Hawaii was probably no different. Depression, substance abuse, and poverty topped the list of causes, but there was another theory, something anthropologists called "historical trauma." Historical trauma included conquest and colonialism, forced assimilation, degradation of the environment and, ultimately, the dilemma of being torn between two cultures. Dinah didn't deny that these were depressing things to have to cope with. Her Seminole grandfather and one of her uncles had committed suicide more than a hundred and fifty years after their ancestral lands were stolen and their forebears driven into the Everglades. Be that as it may, it was a reach to think that the overthrow of the Hawaiian queen drove a healthy young woman with two small children over a cliff.

Dinah closed her book and contemplated the pretty white-caps sweeping onto the beach. She could practically feel them sloshing and sudsing around her feet. It was just nine o'clock. She had hours to kill before she was slated to meet Claude Ann and Lyssa at the bridal shop and she decided to take her crummy mood downstairs and pamper herself with a leisurely breakfast on the terrace. Afterwards, she would go for a long walk on the beach, or even huff and puff her way up Diamond Head. The hotel offered a shuttle to the base of the crater. That's what she'd do. Sweating up a hundred and seventy-some steps and down again, followed by a refreshing dip in the ocean would readjust her attitude. She felt better already. She dressed, grabbed her book, and rode the elevator down to the lobby.

A young couple, gazing into each other's eyes like honeymooners, were checking in at the reception desk. Dinah went to the front door and looked out to see if the Pele demonstrators had returned, but there was no one on the lawn or under the banyan trees and the only car parked under the portico was a Royal Hawaiian taxi.

Feeling strangely let down, she donned her Wayfarers and went out onto the terrace. The hostess seated her at a table adjacent to the beach, which was already bustling with walkers, joggers, sun worshippers, shell hunters, kite fliers, sand castle builders, and kids splashing through the waves. A catamaran bobbed in the distance and the air smelled of Coppertone and coconuts. She scanned the menu and, in furtherance of anthropological investigation, decided on something called loco moco. After a few minutes, a friendly woman in a blue sarong took her order, poured her coffee, and traipsed off to the kitchen.

Dinah tried to read more about Lo-Lale, but her thoughts kept circling back to another attractive bachelor named Wesley Spencer and Claude Ann's zinger about Dinah making a fool of her. Before Xander, Wesley had been the love of Claude Ann's life and what happened vis-à-vis Wesley and Dinah had become the fly in the ointment of Dinah's friendship with Claude Ann. Dinah had tried to shield Claude Ann from a truth she thought would be devastating. Like so many good intentions, Dinah's back-fired. She knew now that meddling in another person's love life, however noble one's intentions, was a recipe for regret. But if Claude Ann harbored the notion that, were it not for Dinah's meddling, she would've married her heart's desire instead of Hank, she was deluding herself. Wesley Spencer. That was one bachelor myth that had to be de-bunked or Claude Ann and she would never get their wires uncrossed. The question was how and when to broach the subject. Two days ahead of the wedding, the words "Re-member the handsome guy who ditched you before" prob-ably wouldn't go over too well.

The tropical breeze was like a warm caress. She turned her face up to the sun and was half-dozing when her loco moco came. Meticulous as an archaeologist unearthing a precious shard, she excavated it with her fork. Fried egg on top, a puddle of brown gravy beneath that, then a ham-burger patty resting on a bed of rice. So much for the ex-otic name. Oh, well. She scooped up a forkful of egg, filled her mouth, and nearly choked at the sight of Eleanor, Pele's outsized ambassador, barging barefoot down the beach in a red-flowered muumuu.

This morning Eleanor was alone and carried no sign, but her enormous girth and imperious carriage caused heads to turn. Dinah stared transfixed. Slowly, it dawned on her that this amazing character was looking straight at her. Following Xander's directive, she lowered her eyes, hid her face behind her hand, and waited for the woman to pass.

Useless. In a minute, Dinah heard the unmistakable voice rumbling over her head. "I saw you las' night wid dat woman Garst gonna marry."

Shit. Well, there was nothing Dinah could do now. She swallowed her egg and looked up with a submissive smile. In the light of day, Eleanor appeared even more sinister than she had by torch light. Her bushy eyebrows lowered above her small black eyes and her mouth was as unforgiving as a boning knife. "Boddah you if I sit?" Her tone implied that it had better not.

Dinah glanced around to see if any objection was forthcoming from the management.

"No worry, sistah. All de beaches in Hawai'i, dey public. What's yo name?"

"Dinah Pelerin."

"I'm Eleanor Kalolo." She pulled up a chair. "You a friend of Garst?"

"I'm a friend of his fiancée. A very good friend."

"Den you bettah tell her dat buggah's no good for her."

"Why? Because he's building houses in a place you don't want him to?"

"Dat's one reason." She tipped her head back and squinched her eyes, as if gauging Dinah's niche in the food chain. "You no look like you're all haole."

"What's haole?"

"White. Caucasian. Wat da kine you?"

"My father was white. My mother's Native American, Seminole."

Eleanor's bosom swelled. "I'm full-blooded Hawaiian. Pele is 'aumakua, my ancestor and family god."

That TV reporter had started to say something about someone Eleanor was related to. Could she have been referring to the fire goddess? Dinah said, "I've never met anyone who claimed to be related to a god." Eleanor glowered and she quickly added, "I meant no disrespect."

She gave Dinah that slitty-eyed, speculative look again. "I tink you no like Garst. I tink you plenny akamai."

"What's akamai."

"On da ball. Smart. Like you know wot's wot."

Provoked as she was, Dinah couldn't help but be impressed by the gall of the woman. "Why are you telling me this, Eleanor? I don't hold sway over my friend's choice of a husband, and I certainly don't have any influence over Xander Garst's land deals."

Her glower softened. "We Native Hawaiians have received the same benefits from the haoles as the Native Americans—death from the measles and smallpox, subversion of our customs and our religion, and the appropriation and occupation of our land."

Whoa! So Eleanor could shift registers at will. Dinah's curiosity intensified. Did she use the pidgin dialect to maintain street cred with the locals, or as a guise to make people like Xander think she was ignorant and controllable? "Is your quarrel with Xander Garst about a single housing development or Native Rights in general?"

"It's about making sure Garst gets what he deserves."

"But you can't hold one man accountable for the injustices of history."

"Not all of them." She tilted her head back and fixed her small, shrewd eyes on Dinah. "Have you ever heard of the Great Mehele?"

"No."

"In eighteen-hundred-and-forty-five, King Kamehameha proclaimed that foreigners would be allowed to purchase land that had been set aside for the Hawaiian monarchy. Fifty years later, foreigners owned ninety percent of our islands."

"I can empathize, Eleanor. Aboriginal peoples seem

always to come out on the losing side of history. But you can't dwell on the past. Xander Garst isn't a foreigner. He's an American and so are you."

She snorted. "And we simple savages should be grateful that a hundred years after America ousts our queen and steals our land, Bill Clinton signed an Apology Resolution?"

Dinah bristled. "As you say, it was a hundred years ago and one more housing development in this day and age doesn't warrant the extra effort you're putting into your anti-Garst campaign. This is personal. What did the man ever do to you?"

"You don't need to know."

"Claude Ann said you believe there are bones buried on the property. The bones of an old king. Is that what this is about? Was this king one of your ancestors?"

"You just tell Garst that Uwahi is wahi pana. You tell him this time he's going to pay."

Ordinarily, Dinah tended to side with the natives and the less powerful. But in this case, Eleanor was the one who came off sounding intimidating and prejudiced and Xander who seemed the underdog. It occurred to her that Eleanor might be trying to shake him down for money. "If you expect me to pass along your warning, you'd better tell me what wahi pana is and how much money you want from him."

"Now I tink you not so akamai. You jus' remembah one word. Pash. He'll know. He'll know what he gotta answer for Bumbye."

The growling rancor in her voice sent a chill down Dinah's spine. She tried to imagine what would engender such hatred. Xander said that Uwahi was part of a volcanic flow. Had there been some recent breakthrough of lava? Had someone fallen into a steam vent? "Did this Pash you mention, or Bumbye, get injured on the property? Did someone die?"

She answered with a snort of majestic disdain. "You care 'bout yo friend, you tell her dat kane Garst bring her trouble. Akahele." Her mouth quirked up in a nasty half-smile. "That means she'd better beware what she's getting into, Dinah Pelerin. And so had you." Whereupon, she rose up from the chair like an evil jinn and lumbered off down the beach, her awesome hips undulating hula-like beneath the muumuu.

SEVEN

DINAH HASTENED BACK to the lobby. She felt as if she'd had a visitation from the Spirit of Prophecy and the portent was not good.

Bumbye. Was it a person, one of Eleanor's children, perhaps? Or maybe it was a place or a holy shrine to Pele. After the warm beach, the air-conditioned lobby felt like a refrigerator. She stood fidgeting at the front desk while the receptionist reviewed a bill with a peevish guest. Should she ask the hotel to telephone the police? How specific did a threat have to be to involve the police? Maybe she was overreacting. She took a deep breath. Xander had scolded Claude Ann, albeit mildly, for engaging with the protesters last night and he'd told the hotel receptionist he didn't want any publicity. The prudent thing would be to convey Eleanor's diatribe to Xander and let him handle the situation as he deemed necessary. As for conveying Eleanor's marital advice to Claude Ann, Dinah would sooner be shot.

The receptionist got rid of the complainer at last. "Thanks for waiting, Ms. Pelerin."

Dinah said, "Please ring Xander Garst's room and ask him to come to the lobby right away. It's urgent."

"I'm so sorry. Mr. Garst and Ms. Kemper left in a taxi a half-hour ago."

"Do you have his cell phone number?"

"No, I don't. Is there something wrong?"

"If he calls the hotel, would you please give him my number and ask him to call ASAP?"

"Certainly." She jotted down the number Dinah gave her.

Dinah had another idea. "Is there a computer I can use?"

"Of course." She led her to a room behind the reception area. "Just use your room number to log on."

Dinah thanked her and got to work. If Google didn't come through for her, she'd buy a Hawaiian dictionary. Aumakua, wahi pana, akahele. The ka-hooey word that young protester had flung at her had already slipped her mind. Bumbye didn't sound Hawaiian. She didn't think the Hawaiian alphabet had a letter b. It didn't have an s either and the one word Eleanor had charged her with remembering was Pash.

The online Hawaiian dictionary defined aumakua as Eleanor had—a family or personal god. Aumakua could assume various shapes—a shark or an owl or a rat. Even a rock. Apparently, the aumakua appeared to mortals in dreams to offer guidance or reproach. Akahele meant take care or watch your step, which sounded slightly less threatening than "beware." And wahi pana referred to a sacred place. Bumbye, she learned to her chagrin, was pidgin for by and by. Xander would know what he had to answer for by and by. The only entries brought up by "Pash" were for an indie band whose best known song was "Kill the Rich Boys," the Petroleum Accountants Society of Houston, and Australian slang for tongue kissing.

"Beg pardon. Oh, hello! Are you Dinah?"

She turned and saw a silver-haired man of about sixty with a florid complexion, kinetic blue eyes, and a somewhat manic demeanor. He wore a Hawaiian shirt with coral colored flamingos. The tanned legs poking out below his golfing shorts bowed like the staves of a barrel.

"Yes, I'm Dinah."

"Claude Ann's friend. Excellent, excellent, excellent. Avery Wilhite, at your service. Xander's business partner." He handed her a card. "Heard at the desk you were asking for him. Some kind of trouble. Bride hasn't got cold feet, has she?"

"Not to my knowledge." He was so blithery she had to smile. "It's nothing to do with the wedding."

"Didn't think so. Just joking. The protesters haven't made any more fuss, have they? Pesky lot. Saw a clip of them on TV this morning. Feel bad for Xan and Claude Ann. Her, especially. Dirty pool to hassle a bride at a time like this."

She read the card. SAX Associates. "Are you Xander's partner in the Uwahi project?"

"Partner and primary investor. I'm the A in SAX."

Dinah was eager to unload her worries about Eleanor onto someone else and she could see no reason why Xander would object to her relaying Eleanor's message to his partner and primary investor. She said, "Actually, one of the protesters accosted me while I was having breakfast on the terrace."

"Botheration. Well, no sense burdening Xander. Enough on his plate, poor boy. Let's go to the hotel conference room and you can give me the lowdown. Maybe I can get them off his back."

He shepherded her through the lobby and down a short corridor she hadn't noticed before. He threw open the double doors on the left and blundered into a poker game in progress. "Oh! Wrong room. I do beg pardon."

Raif tongued a swizzle stick from one side of his mouth to the other. "Pull up a chair, Avery. You, too, Dinah. The more the merrier and the richer the pot."

"Raif Reid? Is that you?" Wilhite seemed discomfited out of all proportion.

"None other."

"Raif. Well, well. Raif. Good to see you. Been a while. Lyssa good?"

"She's good," said Raif with what seemed to be his signature semi-sneer. He sat slouched in front of a tall stack of blue chips and a Starbucks' Vente.

"Well, good for Lyssa," said Wilhite. "Excellent."

The two men Raif was playing with were older-middle-aged. One had a heavy five-o'clock shadow, dark circles under his eyes, and a beer gut. One of his hands fondled a short stack of red chips and he didn't appear to appreciate the intrusion. The other player, a fleshy-faced man with a deeply furrowed brow, didn't either.

"Afraid we can't stay and play," said Wilhite, backing out the door. "See you and Lyssa at the shindig tonight?"

"Wouldn't miss it," said Raif.

"Excellent." Wilhite closed the door and tried the one across the hall. "Here we go. This has to be it." He opened the door and gestured Dinah inside.

The last people to meet in this room must have been Eskimos. The air conditioning had been ramped up to near-freezing. Wilhite pulled out a chair for her at the end of a long, teakwood table and sat down next to her. "Astonishing, eh? Never would've imagined it."

"Raif's gambling?"

"No, no. Boy's a pistol. More moxie than's good for him. Drives Xan up the wall, but that's youth for you. No, I meant Xan getting married. I've known him for thirty-five years and, after being a widower and blade about town, it's hard to believe he's making it legal again. Not that Claude Ann isn't the cream. Beautiful girl. Young for him, but then I wouldn't have expected Xander to be dazzled by a woman his own age. Not that older women can't be alluring, you understand. What do they call themselves now? Cougars? But I've never seen Xan with a cougar. Always has a young one on his arm."

Dinah felt as if she'd hit the gossip motherlode. Given the opportunity, her news about Eleanor could wait a few minutes. "Where did you and Xander meet?"

"Oh, at the University. We were on the tennis team. Both of us from back East, both married local girls and decided to stay. We've played a lot of tennis over the years."

"You must have known Xander's first wife. What was she like?"

"Oh, my God. Spectacular woman. Knew it, of course, but that's neither here nor there. Never met a man who didn't fall head over heels for sweet Leilani, myself, included. When Xan married her, his ego shot into the stratosphere and the rest of us island swains moped about like lovesick adolescents." He slapped his knobby knees and chuckled. "Louis Sykes was another one. Besotted. Married, though, like me. Nothing to do but admire from afar. Like her, Louis died young. Tragic. His son Steve's the S in SAX Associates. He's our legal eagle."

Dinah said, "Leilani's suicide must have come as an awful blow to Xander. Had she been ill or depressed?"

"Closed subject. Never talks about it. Too painful. Some of us speculated she might have been despondent because Xander didn't move the family to the mainland. That's what she wanted. Always preferred the company of haoles, didn't want anything to do with her own people. Of course, it was her Hawaiianness that Xan and the rest of us found so exotic and alluring. My wife was never jealous. Not a jealous bone in her body, my Kay. Saw Lani as a marvel of nature, like the o'o bird. Kay, I said, you were damn near clairvoyant when you said that thing about the o'o, being as how the species died out. Hunted to extinction for their yellow feathers to make the kings' capes, the o'o was. No, the brightest and prettiest aren't always the luckiest. Sad, but that's life." He paused for breath. "Now then, tell me what this Pele crowd was on about this morning."

Dinah recapped her conversation with Eleanor. "She seems to have a personal grudge against Xander. I think she wants to rally public opinion against the Uwahi deal to spite him."

"Relatives. What's a man to do?"

"Eleanor's a relative?"

"Leilani's sister."

"She's what?"

"Nothing like her, of course. Night and day. Sisters, wives, daughters, sons-in-law, nephews. Like herding cats. Can't keep 'em in line. Now what was Eleanor squawking about?"

Avery's earful left Dinah feeling slightly punch-drunk. "She thinks Uwahi is a sacred place. She emphasized the word 'Pash' and said Xander would know what it means."

"Pash?" His eyes flicked rapidly back and forth, as if his brain were scrolling through a list of possible meanings and permutations. "No. Can't say. It's gibberish to me. Probably some endangered weed she thinks she's found. A lot of to-dos over nothing here in the islands."

"I thought it was human bones that she'd found."

"Bones? No, no, no. The archaeologist Xander hired gave us a clean bill of health. Not a problem if a stray bone turns up sometime down the line, of course. Minors, as the kids say. Bones everywhere on the island. Up to the Hawaii Burial Council how and where to move them."

Dinah hugged her arms and tried to rub away the chill. Eleanor was Xander's sister-in-law and Claude Ann didn't know. How could he not have told her? "You don't think Eleanor poses a threat to Xander or Claude Ann? Or to your real estate deal?"

"Great Scott, no. Birds, plants, degradation of the Hawaiian language. Eleanor's always fussing about something, always an ax to grind." He took his BlackBerry out of his shirt pocket and checked his schedule. "Don't you worry, Dinah. I'll run the incident by Xander. We're meeting at noon with our buyer's attorneys to finalize the details.

We're in the home stretch now, on cruise control." He stood up to leave. "Can I give you a lift downtown?"

"No, thanks. I'll stick around the hotel until the time I have to meet Claude Ann."

"See you at tonight's party then," he said, and left her shivering in the cold.

EIGHT

DINAH STEPPED INTO the elevator and sagged against the mirrored wall. Was Eleanor merely a crank? A belligerent ex-sister-in-law with a grab bag full of resentments and a yen to see herself on TV? Avery Wilhite hadn't seemed much ruffled by Eleanor's agitating, but Xander was. Of course, she wasn't just badmouthing his opportunity-of-a-lifetime land deal. She was heckling his bride and interfering with his wedding festivities. But why in blazes had he not told Claude Ann about his relationship to Eleanor? It seemed a curiously significant omission in his communications with his wife-to-be. Evidently, it was an open secret. That's what the TV reporter and the cops had been talking about.

To tell or not to tell. Dinah weighed the pros and cons of meddling. Why did she always find herself in the same predicament?

The elevator hadn't moved. Had she punched the button? Absent-mindedly, she punched again.

"Yikes!" A svelte brunette in a fire-engine red Bolero jacket and matching stilettos squeaked inside just as the doors closed. She wore her hair in a kicky, inverted bob and her fire-engine red lips in a pert smile. The air effloresced with peaches and tuberose. Joy, guessed Dinah. Too much Joy.

"Dinah Pelerin. You haven't changed a lick."

"Phoebe Marshall."

"I bet you wouldn't have known me if Claude Ann hadn't told you I was coming." She gave Dinah a big hug.

That was an understatement. Dinah tried to reconcile

this glamorous number with the shy, slope-shouldered girl who caught the bouquet at Claude Ann's last wedding. Hadn't she had a bigger nose back then? And maybe a mole on her cheek? She said, "You've done something different with your hair."

Phoebe cackled. "Anybody would know you're from the South." Her voice was as shrill as a katydid's.

Dinah smiled. Some things weren't yet subject to a makeover. "Did you fly in from Atlanta?"

"No, I've been in L.A. attending a seminar."

The elevator dinged and glided upward. Phoebe wagged her key card and linked her arm in Dinah's. "Let's go to my room and catch up."

When the doors opened on the third floor, Phoebe swished down the hall, pulling Dinah along with her. Her room was only a few doors from Dinah's. She inserted her key card in the lock, waited for the green light, and swept into the room with her arms wide. "This is even more deluxe than I expected."

Dinah sat on the love seat at the foot of the bed. "Have you spoken to Claude Ann yet?"

"I phoned her from the airport, but I won't see her until tonight. I have another seminar here in Honolulu." Phoebe sailed around the room, inspecting the furnishings and the art. She slid open the glass door onto the lanai. "I was planning to be in Honolulu anyway on business, but I'd have stayed in a cheaper hotel. I looked up the Olopana's room rates on the 'Net. Seaside rooms like this go for nine-fifty. Is your room this luxurious?"

"Same view. Very ritzy. Xander seems to have spared no expense."

"You think Xander's paying?"

"Isn't he?"

Phoebe alighted in one of the cushioned rattan chairs across from the love seat and kicked off her stilettos. "I don't know. Claude Ann didn't come right out and say, but I got the impression she was footing the bill for the wedding. It just goes to show, huh?"

Dinah wasn't sure what it showed. "I assumed Xander was filthy rich. He buys and sells real estate, he has a supposedly to-die-for house on Hawaii, and the diamond he gave Claudy must've cost a small fortune." She hesitated. She was no gemologist. She could be all wet, like those British sailors who thought Diamond Head was chockful of diamonds. "Xander is rich, isn't he?"

"I think so. He's just temporarily a little strapped for cash. Would you like a Coke or something?"

"No thanks." It stung that Claude Ann had confided Xander's cash problems to Phoebe and not to her. She didn't like to tap into the money her Uncle Cleon had left her, but she couldn't let Claude Ann pay her airfare and hotel bill. It was too much. "What did Claude Ann tell you about Xander's finances?"

"Promise you won't tell her I said?"

"I promise."

"Because she thinks you'd jump to the conclusion that he's after her for her money or something."

That stung, too, in spite of its being true. She said, "Anyone can have a cash flow problem."

"Exactly. But she thought you might get suspicious what with all the baggage you cart around on account of your father. All I know is, Claude Ann didn't want to skimp on the wedding and she didn't want to put Xander in a bind. She's lent him some money to tide him over until some big deal or other closes."

"How much money?"

"She didn't say, but I wouldn't be surprised if it was six figures. Claude Ann's loaded these days." Phoebe grubbed about in her briefcase for a minute and pulled out a handful of photos. "For laughs, I brought some snapshots I took at Claude Ann's first wedding." She handed one to Dinah. "Claude Ann looked a little flustered, don't you think?"

"Flustered" was a euphemism. She looked like a fever victim in the thrall of some bewildering dream. Dinah handed the picture back. "How much money did she get in the divorce?"

"I don't know the exact amount, but it was substantial. I mean, it's not like Hank's going to the poorhouse. He's still one of the richest dairy farmers in the Southeast. He received a write-up in Kavenger's Wealth Reporter a year ago. Did Claudy send you a copy?"

"No. It seems she's kept me in the dark about a lot of things."

Phoebe's eyes lingered on the photo. "Hank looked so lean and stern and manly. I had the biggest crush on him back then, but of course he adored Claude Ann. Still, you could've knocked me over with a feather when she popped up and married him. I always thought she was gone on Wesley Spencer. Remember the sexy way Wes used to flip his hair out of those big, soulful eyes of his? What do you suppose ever happened to Wes?"

Belatedly, Dinah did remember and the recollection hit her like a stone. Why hadn't she seen the resemblance at once? But for a few gray hairs and laugh lines at the corners of his eyes, Xander was the spitting image of Wesley, right down to the rebellious forelock. "I haven't the foggiest where Wes got to. But tell me about yourself, Phoebe. What kind of seminar brought you to Hawaii?"

"Transformational self-mastery and visioneering. Did Claude Ann tell you that I'm a life coach now? You know what a timid little mouse I was back in high school and college. I worked for the Atlanta Constitution for a while, but all I ever did was file and run errands. Then three years ago, I attended a life training seminar and it turned me completely around. I learned I had to give myself permission to evolve. To envision my butterfly self and begin the journey of emergence to become that butterfly."

Dinah held her breath for the laugh line, but Phoebe looked wide-eyed and sincere as a guppy. "Well, you certainly seem transformed now."

"I outgrew that stutter after I got away from my neurotic mother, but I still had a terrible feeling of inferiority. Remember my impetigo?"

It was never a good idea to remember an unsightly skin rash. Dinah said, "None of us was at our best back then."

"Except for Claude Ann. She was so gorgeous and self-confidant and she was always trying to boost my confidence. I never understood why she went into such a funk. During the bad times with Hank, I kept reminding her she had to give herself permission to be happy and now look how beautifully everything's turned out for her. When she called to tell me about Xan, she sounded positively delirious."

Dinah smiled, but doubts nibbled away at her. She so wanted Claude Ann to be happy, wanted Xander to be a paragon of virtue and a prince of a man. She gave herself full permission to believe in Xander's trustworthiness, but the warning signs kept piling up. Was he truly in love with Claude Ann or was he just a calculating Hawaiian snowman intent on scamming her out of her money?

"Have you met him yet?"

"Yes, at dinner last night."

"And? What did you think? Is he a ten?"

"He seems plausible enough."

"Plausible?" Phoebe pulled a face. "You see? That's why Claude Ann doesn't tell you stuff. You're hopeless. Claude Ann's not afraid to take a chance on love again and you of all people should be ecstatic for her."

"I am ecstatic for her. Cautiously ecstatic."

"There's no such thing. And for your information, I'm

not afraid to take a chance, either." She took a momentous breath. "I've given myself permission to begin a relationship with Hank."

"A romantic relationship?"

"I've been secretly in love with him ever since he took me to the senior prom. It didn't pan out between us then, but we've all evolved and, like they say, first love runs deepest."

It ran contrary to all reason in Dinah's estimation. If she remembered correctly, Hank asked Phoebe to the prom only because Claude Ann promised to dance with him if he did. "Have you and Hank been going out?"

"A few times. I've been his sounding board these last few weeks. He's still boiling mad at Claude Ann and her divorce lawyer. It'll take time for him to simmer down and realize that I'm the right woman for him. But he will. I'm a very spiritual person. I don't come at God the same way Hank does, but I understand his spiritual quest better than Claude Ann did. She should be happy for us both. I don't think she ever really loved Hank, but she's fond of him."

"Have you told her your plan?"

"No. And don't you tell her, Dinah Pelerin. Not yet. I'll tell her, myself, but not 'til after she comes back from the honeymoon."

"Do you know that Hank's been writing Claude Ann crackpot letters and filling Marywave's head with a lot of claptrap about it being a sin for Claude Ann to remarry?"

"He's just venting. He wants what's best for Marywave just like Claude Ann does. He needs to focus on a new life goal is all. Clear life goals and a positive outlook, that's what visioneering's all about."

Dinah's less than positive outlook veered toward the decidedly pissed-off. Why did so many hot potatoes have to land in her lap? Now she had another one to toss or not to toss and this one was sure to turn Claude Ann's honeymoon into a crowd. If there was even a ghost of a chance that Phoebe might invite Hank to Hawaii for some clandestine quality time with Marywave, Claude Ann would have a conniption.

Phoebe's eyebrows rushed together. "I can see it in your face. You're going to tell her, aren't you?"

"No, you are. There are too many secrets swirling around this wedding already. I have to go try on my dress and you have to go to your seminar. But if Claude Ann doesn't know about you and Hank by tomorrow night, I'll blow the whistle."

NINE

THE TINY BRIDAL shop on Kalakaua Avenue was crammed with so many pouffy white gowns and veils that Dinah had the sense of breast-stroking through an avalanche. She could scarcely move without bumping into another snowbank of dresses.

"Hello? Claude Ann? Anybody?"

"We're back here," called Claude Ann from somewhere in the muffled depths. "Behind the mauve curtain."

Dinah pushed on through the racks, through the smothering billows of charmeuse and chiffon and georgette and satin, through the pervasive incense of dried rose petals. "I don't see anything mauve."

"Dinah, where are you?" Abruptly, the whiteness parted in front of her and Lyssa appeared like a bonfire in tangerine chiffon. Whether it was the hot color or the result of a good night's sleep, her disposition had warmed. "Isn't this place fantastic? Follow me. The work room is back here."

She led Dinah through a mauve curtain into a large open space with floor-to-ceiling windows and bright overhead lights. Claude Ann stood in the center of the room on an elevated platform while a bird-like woman with a beaky nose and a row of straight pins clamped between her teeth knelt at her feet, pinning the hem of her billowing white skirt. A dress form clothed in tangerine chiffon stood behind her like a headless vestal virgin. That, thought Dinah, would be my cross to wear.

Claude Ann appeared euphoric. "Dinah, this is Yvonne, the shop owner. She's an absolute genius with a needle and thread. She stitched up Phoebe's dress in nothin' flat just from the measurements Phoebe sent."

Around the pins, Yvonne said, "Have a seat on the sofa. I'll be with you in a few minutes."

"Well?" prompted Claude Ann. "Do I look fabulous or what?"

"Fabulous," said Dinah, preoccupied with Eleanor's threat and Xander's failure to disclose who she was and Phoebe's lech for Hank and Claude Ann's six figure loan to Xander.

"That's pretty lame," said Claude Ann.

"You look sublime. Enchanting. Ravishing. Beyond compare."

"Bullshit. I know you don't approve of my wearin' white. You don't have to say it."

"I don't care what color you wear, Claudy, as long as you're happy. And what does my approval have to do with it? It's your wedding."

"Yeah, but I know what you're thinkin'. You're thinkin', Claude Ann, you're not a virgin anymore. You've calved and you oughta wear somethin' motherly."

"That's not even close to what I'm thinking." She was thinking that she shouldn't have let Eleanor intimidate her. She should have questioned her more closely. What or who was this Pash? What kind of a comeuppance did Xander deserve? And why hadn't Xander fessed up that Eleanor was his sister-in-law? Dinah wished she knew how much money Mr. Smooth-as-Silk had borrowed from Claude Ann, but asking would only reinforce Claude Ann's belief that she was overly suspicious and possibly even get her booted out of the wedding.

Lyssa stepped out of her dress and hung it on a rack.

"Nobody pays attention to that silly rule about white anymore. I wasn't a virgin and I married in white."

"Who can find a virtuous woman? Proverbs thirty-one, ten."

Dinah turned around and saw Marywave sitting on a sewing machine stool with her Bible open in her lap.

"Pay Marywave no mind," said Claude Ann. "Her mission in life is to hammer me over the head with the gospel."

Yvonne stuck the last pin in the Vera Wang, stood up, and rubbed her knees. "The dress is pure romance."

Claude Ann posed this way and that in front of the full-length mirror. "It is perfect, isn't it? Dinah, you remember that drapey, off-the-rack getup I wore at my last weddin' made me look like a trick-or-treater draggin' a sheet. This gown is from Vera Wang's Luxe Collection. It set me back nearly twelve thousand dollars and it's worth every penny."

"It's the most beautiful dress I've ever seen, Claudy. And you're the most beautiful bride."

Lyssa pulled a snug blue tee-shirt over her head, freed her long hair with a sweep of her hand, and shimmied into a pair of tight white shorts. "What made you choose tangerine for the attendants' dresses, Claude Ann? Was it because Dinah and I are both so dark and native looking? Or were you subconsciously repeating the Halloween motif from your first wedding?" Her back was to Claude Ann and her face in the mirror was unreadable as she prinked and applied gloss to her pouty lips.

"It's a happy color," said Claude Ann. "My favorite."

Marywave scowled. "It looks like the flames of hell."

"Another word out of you, Marywave Kemper, and I'll tan your backside 'til it shines like the flames of hell. I hope Marywave's brattiness won't put the rest of y'all off having children. She can be a sweetheart when she wants to be."

Lyssa turned around with a baiting smile. "You mustn't

feel bad, Marywave. My father thinks I'm a brat. We can't always be obedient little angels, can we?"

To her credit, Marywave kept her mouth shut.

"Have you decided what you're wearin' to the party tonight, Lyssa?" Claude Ann's patience was visibly raveling, but she seemed at pains to remain congenial.

"I may wear the dress I wore to the party Daddy threw for Raif and me at the Ko Olina Resort after our wedding. I can't believe you're having such a small reception. We had nearly three hundred guests."

"Your father and I wanted something more intimate."

"I'll bet Daddy doesn't want you to bump into any of his former lady friends."

"That must be it." Claude Ann took off her white satin pumps, hiked her skirt up, and jumped off the platform. "Are you gonna try on that dress, Dinah, or just stand around lookin' feeble-minded?"

"I'm going to do as I'm told. Like an angel." Dinah shed her street clothes, removed the dress from the dress form, and slipped it over her head. She had to agree with Marywave that the color was a shade wicked. But the layers of semi-sheer chiffon against her legs felt like heaven.

Claude Ann fumbled with her intricately buttoned lace sleeves. "Help me out of my dress, Yvonne."

While unbuttoning Claude Ann, Yvonne gave Dinah the once-over. "Too big in the waist. I'll need to make darts." She nodded toward a short, peach-colored dress on a hanger. "Will you try on the flower girl's dress for me, Marywave?"

"I'd rather descend into a fiery furnace like Shadrach and Abednego than be a stupid flower girl. You can donate it to the Salvation Army."

"But it's beautiful. It would make a saint feel just a little vain."

The pages of Marywave's Bible rustled furiously. "Woe

unto them that draw iniquity with cords of vanity. Isaiah, chapter five, verse eighteen."

Claude Ann said, "We'll take Marywave's dress as is."

"But it would be so easy to alter."

"It doesn't matter. If she won't wear it, she can stay at home with the sitter durin' the ceremony and stew over my next iniquity, which will be to cancel her visit back to Georgia come September."

"That's not fair, Mama. You promised Daddy you'd send me home for my birthday."

"Woe unto pissants who don't mind their mamas. I'd rather carry my own flowers anyway."

Marywave leveled sullen eyes on her mother. She was obviously determined to resist her mother's remarriage in every way she could. Dinah wondered whether Phoebe had considered the likelihood that she would also resist any new liaison that Hank might enter into.

"I have to run," said Lyssa. "I'm meeting Raif and one of his friends for lunch."

Claude Ann stepped out of her bouffant skirt and climbed into a pair of pink cropped pants and a striped pink jersey. "Thank you so much for taking the time to come and try on the dress. I hope you'll find another occasion to wear it after the weddin'. Maybe one of those gala NASCAR parties y'all have back in Virginia."

Lyssa looked as if she were about to say something flippant, but checked herself at the last second. "I'll see you both at the party tonight. Ciao."

Claude Ann watched her prance through the mauve curtain. When she heard the front door bang shut, she went off like a Roman candle. "What does she think she's got to advertise in short shorts? She's got a butt like two BBs."

"She seems a mite catty," said Dinah.

"Skanky little heifer. I wish she and that hotdog husband of hers would drive over a cliff and sink to the bottom of the ocean."

"That's pretty extreme."

"Glub, glub, glub. All the way to the bottom."

"She's a pill, but surely she's not worthy of such strong feeling."

"You haven't had the pleasure of her company as long as I have. She's been here for three long weeks and the twerp never misses a chance to devil me or take cheap shots at the man I love, the man who loves her though it's hard to see why. I'll be gracious for Xan's sake. I only have to put up with her for a few more days and she's gone. But she better mind her manners. She's not the only cat who's got claws." She stood back and gave Dinah an appraising look. "Don't they feed you over there on Mindanao? You're scrawny as a slink calf."

Yvonne gathered an inch of fabric on either side of Dinah's dress and marked it for darts. "I can't tell about the length until you put on the pumps, dearie."

Claude Ann handed Dinah a pair of matching tangerine pumps. "I hope your feet haven't spread. I ordered the same size as mine, like always."

Dinah put them on. The right one pinched and the effort of holding back Xander's and Phoebe's secrets put a crimp in the camaraderie. She was on the verge of spilling the beans, but Claude Ann diverted her.

"Do you have something sharp to wear to the party tonight?"

"The same as last night."

"That black thingy is sort of somber, don't you think?"

"I think it's classy. But speaking of what's somber, how dorky is this Jon character Xander fobbed off on me for the evening?"

"Jonathan's ugly as a hatful of pigs' ears, but he's Xander's pride and joy. Just try and act normal and don't say anything mean. I'll owe you one."

"Claude Ann, is something wrong in the Garst family? Or with Xander? I don't do well with hints flying back and forth over my head like shuttlecocks."

"I don't know what you're talkin' about."

"What is Pash?"

"What's whuh?"

"Pash. Eleanor Kalolo said Xander would know what it means. Do you?"

"When did you talk to that ol' biddy?"

"This morning. She confronted me while I was having breakfast on the terrace."

"Too weird. I can't think why she'd know about Pash or give a rip. It's a wedding planner service Lyssa told me about. I was thinkin' about one of those destination weddings, but the closing date for Xan's real estate deal hadn't been confirmed yet. There's a three day window of time when everything happens and we decided to wait until all the t's were crossed and the i's dotted."

"Okay," said Yvonne, standing back for a view of her handiwork. "The hem is marked. I'll have the dresses ready by the end of the day, Ms. Kemper. Shall I send everything to your suite at the hotel?"

"Yes, please." Claude Ann looked at her watch. "I've got an appointment to have my nails done. Will you take Marywave back to the hotel with you, Dinah?"

Dinah stifled a groan. This was above and beyond the call. But she had nothing else to do this afternoon and it was the maid of honor's duty to serve at the bride's pleasure. She would bear her burdens, whether they be ugly as a hatful or bratty as the dickens. "All right, but I don't for an instant believe that Eleanor was talking about a wedding service. I think you should ask Xander to tell you more about this Eleanor woman."

"Like what?"

"I don't know, Claudy. Will you ask him to give me a call? I'd like to tell him what she said to me this morning. He'll want to know if she said something that bears on Uwahi."

"Sheesh!" She reached into her purse and handed Dinah a roll of bills. "Y'all buy yourselves a nice lunch somewhere and when you get Marywave back to the hotel, just drop her off with the sitter. Her name's Tiffany and she's on call for the whole week. She'll probably be in my suite watchin' TV."

"Claude Ann, you shouldn't be throwing your money around like this. Let me at least buy Marywave's lunch. And I'll pay for my hotel room, too."

"Nah. As soon as Xander's deal closes, we'll have tubs of money."

As Claude Ann flitted through the mauve curtain and disappeared, Marywave's Bible spanked shut. Dinah sat down on the sofa, eased her throbbing toes out of the tangerine pumps, and steeled herself for a dose of Jeremiah.

"Can we have lunch at the Dixie Diner? It's not far from here. I know the way."

It was the first time Dinah had seen Marywave smile and, as Phoebe might have said, it was transformative.

TEN

To Dinah's surprise, taking Marywave to lunch wasn't as onerous a chore as she'd feared. They left Yvonne's Dream Weddings, walked past the Honolulu Police substation—surely one of the most attractively situated cop shops in the world—and meandered past the elegantly decorated shop windows of Fendi and Ferragamo and Hermès. The Waikiki Trolley plied up and down the avenue, picking up and disgorging tourists from the numerous hotels and shopping centers.

Marywave seemed to know her way around Waikiki. She led Dinah across the busy street, under the branches of a tremendous monkeypod tree, and down an obscure alley to the Dixie Diner, a homey little eatery that boasted "authentic Southern cooking." Marywave stowed her Bible in her backpack and, after a plate of fried chicken, blackeyed peas, collard greens, and cornbread, she became expansive.

"I have a dog back in Needmore. Her name's Ruby and she's a Hovawart."

"I've never heard of a Hovawart."

"It means guardian in German."

"What does Ruby look like?"

"Sort of like a golden retriever, only not as big. I brush her out every day. She doesn't have a single flea and she sleeps with me in my bed. Daddy takes care of her for me, but he doesn't know what she likes like I do."

"You must miss her."

"She might as well be dead. Xander's allergic to dogs."

Dinah couldn't think of a consoling line. "Do you have room for dessert?"

Marywave smiled again. "Can we please, pretty please, get a shave ice at the snack bar behind the Outrigger? We could walk on the beach."

Dinah's toes still hurt, but she was back in sandals and loath to see Marywave's smile fade. "The Outrigger, it is."

They recrossed Kalakaua, cut between the buildings to the beach, took off their shoes, and started walking. Kicking barefoot along the ribbon of gleaming white sand, with posh hotels on her left and the vista of colorful beach umbrellas and gentle whitecaps on her right, Dinah's forebodings seemed far-fetched. Every face they met sported a sunny smile. Dinah tried to relax and focus on the present.

"Why," asked Marywave, "do people get divorced?"

Too bad the present was so fleeting. "When you're older, you'll understand. People change. Their feelings for one another change and sometimes they don't want to live together anymore."

"I hate change."

"Some changes make people much happier."

"Not me. And not Daddy. You think Mama's feelings about Xander might change?"

"I don't think so, Marywave. She loves him very much."

"Because of sex?"

Dinah sighed. Lunch was one thing. The birds and bees were Claude Ann's responsibility. "Possibly that has something to do with it."

"A wife committeth adultery which taketh strangers instead of her husband. Ezekiel sixteen, thirty-two. Daddy says that God will smite the adulteress with His sword."

"A woman has to be married before she can commit adultery. Your mother's not married to your dad anymore. She's not married to anyone just yet so you needn't worry that she'll be smitten. Smited. Whatever."

"It's not right what she's doin'. She's ruinin' my whole life." She looked up at Dinah with a glum face and Dinah remembered what it felt like when her own mother remarried less than a year after her father died. Dinah hadn't been much older than Marywave and the onslaught of changes had left her confused and resentful. She'd complained to Claude Ann about her own ruined life. Even as a kid, Claude Ann had said the right things. Instinctively, it seemed. She'd reassured Dinah that the world hadn't crumbled, that she was still loved and life would go on. She'd made her see the funny side. It was ironic that, all these years later, she wasn't able to do the same thing for her own child.

"I know it's hard, Marywave, but nobody's life works out exactly the way they want it to, or think they want it to. Life takes unexpected detours. Your mom's and dad's marriage was kind of a detour, not what either one of them expected. Same thing with their divorce. They grew apart and now your mom has found someone new. She's happy and you should be happy for her. It's the Christian thing."

"It was because of Wesley Spencer," said Marywave.

Dinah hadn't heard Wesley's name spoken out loud for ten years and now it rolled trippingly from every tongue. There was no avoiding it. "Just what has your mother told you about Wesley?"

"His folks go to the same church as us. Christmas a year ago, Wesley came to town to visit and they brought him to church with 'em. After the service, Mama asked him about his wife and he said he didn't have one. He never had had one. Mama got kinda bug-eyed and left and when Daddy came home, they had a big fight."

Dinah picked up a sand dab and hurled it into the surf. So Claude Ann knew she'd lied about Wesley being married. In some ways, it was a relief. But why didn't she just come out and ask for an explanation? "What did your mom say to your dad about Wesley?"

"She said it was Wes she loved and she only married Daddy after you told her Wes had run off with another woman and Daddy said yeah, Wes was always full of shit and you must of had somethin' goin' on with him or else why'd you lie."

"What did Claude Ann say then?"

"There it is!" Marywave espied the Outrigger sign and bolted across the beach.

Jerusalem in flames. Dinah trudged through the sand behind her. Did Claude Ann think she'd had a fling with Wesley? Did she think that was the reason he jilted her? She knew Claude Ann blamed her for butting into her affairs. But sex? And what was Wesley thinking to show up in Needmore, tell Claude Ann half the truth, and leave the rest to her imagination? The weasel. Dinah hadn't blabbed his secret.

Well, there was no reason to cover for him any longer. This very night she would give Claude Ann the final, unexpurgated and definitive story on Wesley Spencer. In retrospect, she'd probably say she suspected it all along.

Where was Marywave? She seemed to have evaporated. Dinah went inside the snack bar and looked around, but there was no sign of her. She asked the man behind the counter if he'd served a child in the last minute or so. He had not.

Dinah walked back outside, shaded her eyes with both hands and scoured the beach.

No luck. She turned back and ran into the hotel lobby.

She asked a porter, "Did you see a little girl with a blue backpack romp through here?"

"Sorry, no."

"Have you seen a little girl with reddish-brown hair and

a blue backpack pass this way?" she asked a woman at the reception desk.

"No. Maybe she went to the ladies' room."

Dinah hurried to the ladies' room, called Marywave's name, and checked out the feet under every stall door.

Terrific. Now she'd lost Claude Ann's daughter. She felt the beginnings of panic. She dashed back to the hotel lobby. No Marywave. Had she run away? Had she been kidnapped? Had Eleanor Kalolo snatched her to punish Xander?

She ran out onto the street and looked up and down. Marywave had vanished. Did she have her own money? Could she buy her own shave ice? Make a telephone call? Hire a cab back to the hotel? With all the cash Claude Ann had been throwing around, the little blister could've stolen enough to get to the airport and pay her way back to Georgia. That seemed to be her life goal.

Dinah went back inside and found the main restaurant. She trolled up and down the aisles, looked at every table, questioned the hostess, but Marywave was nowhere to be found. She went out again and made another tour of the snack bar. How many minutes had gone by? How may other places were there to look?

Okay, she told herself. Get a grip. The best plan is to go back to the spot where you last saw her and wait. Let Marywave find you. But how long should she wait before she called Claude Ann or the police?

She jogged back onto the beach and there, happily slurping a purple snow cone, was Marywave.

"You scared me frantic. Where'd you go?"

"The snack bar. Did you want a shave ice, too?"

"Not unless they make one with cyanide." Dinah put her hand over her thudding heart and studied Marywave's cartoonishly wide eyes. It was a fairish attempt, but her lying skills weren't yet so well honed. "You know, Marywave, it's a sin to tell a lie."

"Uh-uh. There's no commandment against regular lyin'. Only bearin' false witness."

"Well, there's a civilian rule against regular lying. Don't try my patience, Marywave. Where did you go? What's up?"

"Why persecutest thou me? Acts five..."

"Oh, can it!" Dinah was tempted to beateth her behind. What was she fibbing about? Had she sneaked off to buy itching powder to exacerbate Xander's allergies or spray paint to trash her mother's dress? Dinah resolved to give Claude Ann a heads-up about possible mischief in the works, but she didn't have the energy or the patience to interrogate the little liar. She herded her back into the Outrigger's lobby and asked the concierge to hail them a taxi back to the Olopana.

ELEVEN

At the front desk, Marywave announced that she had misplaced her key card and the receptionist announced that there was a message for Dinah. Expecting a call from Xander, Dinah was surprised to see that it was from Dr. Sowell, one of the anthropologists she'd been working with on Mindanao. Guerillas from the Moro Islamic Liberation Front had attacked and beheaded a group of journalists and politicians in Cotabata province and the study was suspended indefinitely. Do not return. We will advise you if the study resumes and there is a position for you.

Dinah wadded up the message and stuffed it in her purse. She should feel an outpouring of sympathy and grief for the slain, but all she could think about was her own thwarted career. Another opportunity kaput, as per the usual.

The receptionist presented Marywave with a spare key card and Marywave and Dinah continued on to Claude Ann's suite. To Dinah's considerable irritation, Tiffany wasn't there. She tried calling her room, but she wasn't there either. Marywave guessed she'd be at the swimming pool and would Dinah please, pretty please let her go swimming, too? As if she had a choice. Until she could deliver the pest into the care of the sitter, she was stuck with her.

While she waited for Marywave to change into her bathing suit, she turned on the TV and channel surfed. She wished she'd paid attention to the name on the TV truck last night. If it was a slow news day, the station might rerun the segment and throw in a little background and commentary on Uwahi. But it was too late for the midday news and too early for the evening news. On one station there was a discussion of ho'oponopono. An elderly Hawaiian man was explaining to an audience of people seated on the floor in front of him that in order to heal their errors, which he called hala, and restore harmony within their families and communities, they must confess their hala and apologize. Only through the ancient practice of ho'oponopono could relationships be set right and past quarrels and misunderstandings rectified and forgiven.

Dinah was just getting into it when Marywave capered into the room. She wore a blue and green striped tank suit and a self-satisfied grin. "I'm ready."

"Is there anything you'd like to confess, Marywave?"

"Uh-uh."

"Nothing at all?"

"The Bible says that all the world is guilty before God."

With all her scriptural loopholes and equivocations, Marywave was beginning to sound as if she had something important to hide. Dinah let it go. She had her own hala to reckon with and she was positively yearning for a cigarette. She turned off the TV and the two of them set out to search for Tiffany.

As Marywave had guessed, the sitter was lounging beside the pool in a daring little red bikini, surrounded by a gaggle of libidinous teenage boys. Dinah consigned Marywave into her care and escaped to the sanctuary of her room.

The message light on the phone was blinking red. Maybe it was Xander. She picked up.

Xander's voice said, "Hi, Dinah. I understand you want to speak with me. Give me a call at eight-o-eight, six-two-two, two-four-o-six."

Dinah went into her over-sized bathroom with its dual wardrobe closets and separate vanities and foraged in the mini-bar for vodka and V-8. She mixed herself a Bloody

Mary and sat down on the bed to organize her thoughts. This took almost half of the drink, but she nerved herself and dialed.

Xander answered.

After the preliminaries, she said, "I guess Avery Wilhite and Claude Ann told you that Eleanor Kalolo approached me for a chat this morning."

"Yes, and I am sorry, Dinah. The woman's unstoppable. I don't know why she's rabblerousing here on Oahu. Uwahi's on the Big Island, which is where she lives and agitates normally. But however much of a pain she is, she's harmless."

Like the little jigglers, thought Dinah. "I'm not so sure, Xander. Her anger sounds visceral and very personal. Should you request police protection for yourself and Claude Ann?"

"Eleanor's a blowhard. An empty muumuu." He laughed at his little funny, but it was a tinny laugh. "All she can do is make noise and empty threats."

"Did Avery tell you the word she said I was to pass on to you? Pash?"

"It's meaningless. More of her Hawaiian hocus-pocus to stay in the limelight. Forget her, Dinah. Enjoy your afternoon and…"

"Avery told me that she's your late wife's sister."

The silence on the other end gonged. I've stepped in it now, thought Dinah.

"You're concerned because I haven't told Claude Ann." His voice was flat, resigned. "I should have. When Claude Ann and I met, so many difficult things were going on in my life. She couldn't have been more understanding or accepting or supportive. Frankly, I was afraid I'd lose her if I hit her too soon with the truth about Eleanor. Most of my problems are temporary. But Eleanor is relentless. As I'm sure she made plain to you, she hates me."

"So you are concerned that she can do more than make noise."

"She can slander me. She can slander Uwahi. I don't know if she can torpedo the deal at this point. I don't think so. And the more I know about Claude Ann, the surer I am of her love and her loyalty. You needn't worry, Dinah. I'll tell her about Eleanor tonight." He seemed to have talked himself into a more positive frame of mind. "Things will work out fine. How can they not in the land called Paradise? Look, we'll see you in the ballroom tonight around eight. Jonathan will call for you a few minutes before. He's already checked into the hotel."

Dinah finished her Bloody Mary and mixed another. Between Eleanor's spooky hints and Xander's sunny evasions stretched a no man's land, under which bones might or might not be buried. Dinah didn't buy Xander's line that he didn't know what Pash meant. For all of his seeming candor, he had skipped right over Eleanor's reason for hating him. Did she blame him for her sister's suicide? Could Pash have been Leilani's nickname? Whatever lay behind the feud, there would be no ho'oponopono between Xander and his Hawaiian nemesis anytime soon.

However there could and should be ho'oponopono between Dinah and Claude Ann. Dinah decided that the best way to confess her hala in the matter of Wesley Spencer would be in writing. A letter would give Claude Ann a chance to digest the story in private before they talked. In the rear view mirror, the situation might strike her as funny.

Dinah moved to the desk, took a pen and a piece of Olopana stationery out of the drawer, sat down, and composed her first sentence.

Dear Claude Ann,
It's time we cleared the air once and for all. Whatever
Hank may think, I did not "have something going
on" with Wesley Spencer. I have always been your
friend and I would never come between you and your
boyfriend or do anything to hurt you ever. If that is
what you think, it is absolutely false. And ridiculous.

Did that sound too defensive? In Dinah's mind, defen-
siveness almost always implied guilt. Of course, confess-
ing one's guilt was the purpose of ho'oponopono, but there
were gradations of guilt and she didn't want to give the impression that she was copping to a higher offense than the
one she'd committed.

She lit a Sincerely Yours, nursed her drink, and mulled.
Claude Ann and Wesley had met in college and, after a
whirlwind summer romance, they became engaged. Claude
Ann loved him like the sun. She thought he loved her. Everybody did. And then one day, drunk and barely coherent,
he called her and reneged. No rhyme. No reason. Not even
a decent mea culpa. He quit school, packed his things, and
decamped in the dead of night, leaving no forwarding address. Claude Ann was shattered.

Dinah had watched her cry and pine for days, until she
couldn't stand it any longer. Without telling Claude Ann,
she made a few inquiries around campus and tracked Wesley to his lair in Atlanta. She cornered him and pleaded
on Claude Ann's behalf, reminded him how much Claude
Ann loved him, how brokenhearted she'd be if he didn't
carry through on his promise. She appealed to his sense
of honor, warned him what a mistake he'd be making if he
let a catch like Claude Ann get away, implored him to at
least call her and talk to her. Her arguments collapsed when
Wesley informed her that he had come to the realization
that he was gay. To put the icing on the cake, this realiza-

tion had arrived with the discovery that he was madly in love with Dinah's brother, Lucien.

It was a long drive back to school. A drive during which Dinah despaired of ever really knowing another human being. It wasn't all that great a shock to discover that her artistic, chameleon-like half-brother was gay. It was his duplicity that knocked her for a loop. She had thought they were close. She had thought they entrusted their secrets to one another. But like her father, Lucien had fooled her. It was a second reminder. People lie, even when they don't say anything.

And Wesley? He'd seemed the studliest, red-blooded-est, hetero-male imaginable. Although Claude Ann had never said so, she must have had sex with him. Even in the Bible Belt, most girls lost their virginity by the time they were juniors in college. Especially if they were engaged to be married.

Dinah had agonized over what to do. Neither Wesley nor Lucien had come out of the closet to their parents or her or anyone else so far as she knew. She couldn't blow their cover and she couldn't think of a good way to break the news to Claude Ann that the man of her dreams had switched teams. Claude Ann was loyal to a fault. She would pine her life away waiting for Wes to come back to her. Dinah had to give her a reason for his desertion that didn't shake her self-esteem to the core, but one that would close the door on any hope of a fairy-tale happy ending.

In the end, she told her she had visited Wesley in Atlanta and he'd owned up that he'd been seeing somebody else on the side. She said that he'd fallen in love with this other person and they had eloped and gotten married. She didn't mention the gender of Wesley's new love and the only actual lie was the getting married part. In her naiveté, she assumed that this would bring about closure. Looking back, she should have foreseen that Claude Ann would feel

humiliated that she'd gone begging to Wes on her account
as if she were a charity case. But who could have predicted
she'd freak out and marry Hank Kemper to save face?

Dinah tore up the letter, tossed it in the waste basket,
and began again.

Dear Claude Ann,
I know it mortified you that I took it upon myself to
talk to Wes without your knowledge. It was wrong of
me to meddle, but I was only trying to help. Wes told
me he was gay and living with his male lover. I was
too big a coward to tell you that. But if Hank thinks
I had something going on with Wes, he's wrong. And
if Wes led you to believe that something happened
between us, he's a bigger coward than I am.

Wes had turned up in Needmore a year ago and Claude
Ann walked out on Hank a year ago. There had to be a connection there. How likely was it that Claude Ann had had
further contact with Wes? Maybe they met again in Atlanta
and Wes told her everything. Maybe that was why Claude
Ann said she wasn't mad anymore and wanted to return
her friendship with Dinah to the status quo ante. Lucien
had come out to his family. Maybe Wesley had come out
to his parents and while he was about it, he had made a
clean breast to Claude Ann. If that were the case, there'd
be no reason to revisit the Wesley episode in speech or in
writing. Dinah tore up that letter, too.

Self-justification vied with ho'oponopono. Her reasons
for lying had seemed so selfless and high-minded at the
time. But deep down, had she cared more about protecting her brother's secret than telling her best friend the
truth? Perhaps she'd been afraid that Claude Ann would
hate Lucien and hate her by association. And did she really and truly believe that Claude Ann would have fallen

apart on the news that her boyfriend was gay? Today such an idea seemed melodramatic, an insult to Claude Ann's intelligence and resilience. There must have been extenuating circumstances. Dinah just couldn't remember them at the moment. Good grief, who knew what anyone had been thinking ten years ago? The Past was a galaxy far, far away and the things the natives thought and did there defied present-day comprehension.

She put out her cigarette. She should go out onto the lanai and soak up her thousand dollar view, but the blue sky clashed with her black mood. She flumped onto the bed, and opened the book of myths at random to a chapter titled The Uses of Mana.

The pre-Christianized Hawaiians, like most preliterate peoples, believed in the inherent spiritual power, mana, of all persons and all things. The royals were infused at birth with more mana than commoners, but everyone and everything emanated some degree of spiritual force, either for good or evil. Death did not dispel or diminish the power of mana. The bones of the dead, especially those of the kings, retained such a potent mana that they imparted an almost godlike power to whomever possessed them. Family members kept the bones of their dead and carved them into talismans, which could be used by their owners either to ward off harm from themselves or to inflict harm on someone else. Since the ancestor's mana belonged to every member of the household, the power to hex belonged to everyone. Anyone could send pilikia, the Hawaiian word for trouble, to anyone else for any reason.

The telephone rang. Please God, no more pilikia. And don't let the rock expert be an earlybird. "Hello."

"It's me. Come quick. It's an emergency."

"What kind of…?"

"My suite. Hurry."

"Claudy…?"

The line went dead and Dinah leapt off the bed. Had something happened to Marywave? Had Eleanor Kalolo firebombed Xander's office? She ran out the door and tore down the hall. Claude Ann's suite was at the end of the hall, one floor down. She reached the elevators and jammed all of the down buttons. The doors didn't open and she didn't wait. She ran to the stairs and, in a blind rush, took them two at a time.

The door to Claude Ann's suite stood ajar and she pushed inside, panting. "What?"

Claude halted in mid-stride and spun to face her. "I've been burgled."

"Dear God! Not the Vera Wang."

"My gun."

Dinah stared at her, speechless.

"Somebody took Grandpa Hollis' Beretta out of my train case."

Dinah knew the weapon. She could recite the inscription on the barrel by heart. R Beretta Mo 1934 Brevet. Hollis Albright had confiscated it from an Italian officer during World War II. In his dotage, he showed off his prize to everyone who walked through his door and endlessly repeated the story of how he'd overpowered the Italian to take it.

"Why," asked Dinah, "did you bring a gun with you to Hawaii?"

"I'm not used to gallivantin' around the world by myself like you are, smartypants. I wanted some protection. With that Eleanor skulkin' around, it made me feel safer."

"You obviously thought you needed protection before you met Eleanor. Is it because you're afraid of Hank?"

"The only thing I fear from Hank is a sermon."

"Have you notified hotel management? They should call the police. Is the Beretta registered?"

"Georgia doesn't require people to register their guns."

"The feds do. And I'm guessing that anyone who brings

a firearm into the State of Hawaii is required to register it pretty damn quick."

"Then it's not registered. Sheesh. It's not like I'm carryin' it around in my garters."

Xander walked through the open door. "I just got your message. What's wrong?"

"Somebody stole my gun."

He looked as taken aback as Dinah had been. "You have a gun?"

"I had a gun. Somebody stole it."

"Jesus Christ, Claude Ann."

Dinah said, "The first thing you have to do is report the theft, Claudy. If somebody commits a crime with it, they can trace it back to you."

"No." Xander raked his hair out of his face and kneaded his forehead. "Not right away. Let's sleep on it. Maybe it's just been misplaced and will turn up in the morning." He produced a weak laugh. "There's no need to go off half-cocked."

If this was an example of Xander's fabulous sense of humor, thought Dinah, it was time for an intervention.

TWELVE

THE POLYNESIANS INVENTED kapu, a system intended to suppress objectionable desires by imbuing the desired object with peril. Kapu prohibits what is dangerous, stigmatizes what is unclean, and wields a profound psychological power upon those who believe. The Hawaiian religion designated an oppressive number of things as kapu, forbidden upon pain of death. To cross the king's shadow was kapu. To wear yellow was kapu. To eat turtle or squid was kapu. Women were banned from eating bananas or pork, and it was kapu for women to eat anything at all in the company of men. In the circumstances, Dinah wouldn't have objected if that particular kapu still applied.

She was thoroughly disgusted with Xander. She didn't know if Hawaii or Georgia had a law requiring gun owners to report a stolen gun, but it was certainly the reasonable thing to do. It astounded her that he was so publicity shy he would risk putting his bride crosswise of the law when it would be a simple matter to file a police report. She had a bad feeling about that Beretta. A gun was an inauspicious accessory to pack for a holiday in Paradise. It was downright ominous as part of a bride's trousseau. Claude Ann claimed that she'd transported it to Hawaii legally, in a locked box in her checked luggage. How it got here and why she'd felt the need for it were moot questions. Where it had got to and for what purpose was the mindboggler. It crossed Dinah's mind that Xander might have discovered the gun in Claude Ann's suite and boosted it to keep Claude

Ann from doing anything rash. But why would he pretend he didn't know about it?

She tossed her book aside and picked up today's newspaper. Diplomatic setback in the Mideast, stalemate in the U.S. Senate, bomb blast in Baghdad. Why did they call it news? Her eye fell on an article on page ten.

"The badly burned body discovered in a steam vent on June 22nd has been identified as that of Patrick Varian, 29, an archaeology professor at the University of Hawaii, Manoa. He was on personal leave from the university and believed to be engaged in evaluating a burial site on private property. No one has reported having contact with Mr. Varian while he was on Hawaii and there is no information regarding the location of the property he was evaluating or the individual who hired him."

An archaeologist. Archaeology was one of the four main branches of anthropology. Dinah felt as if one of her own kind had been killed. And in such a gruesome way.

"The women who found the body said they had recently seen a stranger in the forest illegally harvesting 'ohelo berries, which are sacred to Pele. They believe the deceased must be the same man and when he left the forest and walked out onto the lava, the goddess lured him into the steam vent and destroyed him."

The phone rang and Dinah flinched. She tried to muster a cordial greeting, but she was too much on edge. "Yes?"

"Jonathan Garst. I believe you're expecting me."

"Give me ten minutes and come up."

"Fine."

Show time. She squared her shoulders and went to put on her all-purpose little black dress. Could Patrick Varian be Xander's archaeologist, the one who gave Uwahi a clean bill of health? She stuck the clusters of Pele's tears in her ears and frowned. Was Patrick also known as Pash?

The face staring back at her in the mirror looked surly.

If she didn't lighten up, those lines would become permanent. She smoothed them out, added a swipe of lipstick, and tried on a practice smile. Too perky. She toned it down a notch. Too Barbie. Oh, the hell with it.

She was in no hurry to rub eyeballs with Xander or make small talk with a bunch of strangers. It would be best to show up as late as possible and blend unnoticed into the crowd.

Should she risk inviting the hermit in for a drink? How bad could he be? She scraped her brainpan for conversational grist. What did she know about rocks? Sedimentary rocks, igneous rocks, rocks break scissors.

Her date rapped at the door. Shave-and-a-haircut.

Oh, for the love of God. She hadn't heard that cutesy little couplet of a knock since she was a kid. She arranged her face along more or less neutral lines and opened the door.

"Hello, Dinah."

"Hi." It came a beat behind cue. Involuntarily, her eyes gravitated to the right side of his face, which appeared to have melted and hardened like candle wax, pulling his mouth off-center and giving him a look of preemptive self-mockery.

"You'll get used to it in a few minutes. May I come in? I'd like to kill as much time as possible before we have to put in an appearance. That is, if you don't mind."

"No. No, not at all."

He sat down on the love seat. Dinah took the chair across from him and tried not to stare at the scar. He was tall and angular, a shade lighter-skinned than Lyssa, with leery brown eyes and a ponytail of long black hair. He wore khakis, a short-sleeved blue shirt, and Birkenstocks with no socks, whether in defiance of the coat-and-tie requirement or because he hadn't gotten the memo. "So," he said. "What's your opinion of the match?"

Everything about him disconcerted her. Something

Lyssa said to Xander echoed in her mind. Something about it being no mystery why Raif was scared of volcanoes. Xander had reacted as if he'd been stabbed in the heart. Had Lyssa been referring to Jon's scars? She said, "You're very blunt."

"And you're ducking the question. If you were for it, you'd have answered with a big smile and a resounding 'made for each other'."

"Jerusalem, is this your first wedding?"

He threw back his head and laughed, a shocking phenomenon that yanked his mouth back to the center of his face and showed the scar extending down his neck and into his shirt collar. "I wasn't keen on this get-together, but you may surprise me and turn out to be an honest person."

"Jonathan…"

"Jon."

"Jon. Honesty is a heavy liability at weddings. Most people try to be tactful and hedge."

"Not me."

"All right then, what's your opinion of the match?"

"Your friend's getting in over her head."

"In what way?" A half-dozen ways ran through Dinah's head, none flattering to Xander. It might be tradition for the bride or her family to pay for the dress and the wedding reception, but the thought that Claude Ann was paying for the wedding *and* underwriting Xander's business scheme to the tune of six figures offended Dinah's sense of decency. "How is Claude Ann over her head?"

"She seems naïve, like someone who doesn't analyze things very carefully."

"What *things* hasn't she analyzed? Or did you mean your father?"

"Dad's a hard man to know. He doesn't reveal much about himself, even to his family. Six weeks isn't a long time. Your friend might end up wishing she'd waited."

Was this another warning? Like his Aunt Eleanor, did he expect her to pass it on to Claude Ann? According to Claude Ann, there had been a rift between father and son. She put out a feeler. "Your father's certainly waited a long time to remarry. After so many years a bachelor, any idea why he would decide to take the leap on so short an acquaintance?"

"Who knows? Chemistry. The usual mix of oxytocin and dopamine, I guess."

Dinah guessed that cash also figured in the mix, but evidently Jon wasn't disposed to get any more specific with his warning. She couldn't think of a follow-up remark that didn't sound antagonistic or pejorative. The silence built, like sedimentary rock. A minute went by and a cockroach the size of an Airbus buzzed in through the open balcony door. She got up and closed the screen. "Would you care for a drink?"

He smiled a lopsided smile. "Scotch with a touch of water would be good."

She went to the mini-bar and hunted up a bottle of Johnny Walker. She fixed his drink and poured herself a glass of V-8. The Aloha State was raising her alcohol consumption to an unhealthy level and she had a feeling she would need all her wits about her to bandy words with Jon Garst.

When she returned with their drinks, he was leafing through her book of myths. He put it down and smiled. "Sorry if I sounded negative. The best man should be more upbeat and optimistic. Like the bride's maid of honor."

"Optimism," said Dinah, "wasn't what the Romans had in mind when they first came up with the idea of brides' maids. They were afraid that evil spirits might try to molest the bride, so they hid her under a long veil and rounded up a bevy of look-alike brides to confuse any potential evildoers."

"Interesting. Claude Ann said that you're a connoisseur of myths."

"I am. I'm intrigued by the stories people tell themselves to make sense of the universe. A belief only becomes myth when it's proven false or when the next generation comes up with a better explanation."

"I study lava, which in the Hawaiian language is pele. Pele, herself. I guess you could say I'm looking for a better explanation than a petulant goddess. Some days I like the mythological explanation better than the scientific one."

"You must be close to your father to have followed him into the same career."

"Not really. I've lived and played beside the volcanoes since I was a kid. Becoming a volcanologist seemed a natural extension of what I'd always been interested in. It's like being a detective, only the suspects are all rocks. They don't lie."

Dinah held his eyes for a few seconds. Had he put a subtle stress on the word *they* or did she just imagine it? Either way, he made it crystal clear that she was not the only member of the wedding party with trust issues. "I expect you'll miss working with Xander now that he's retiring."

"We've rarely worked together. Different areas of expertise."

"But living on the same island and working for the same organization, you must spend a lot of time together."

"We've shared a place up by Volcano Village for the last three years. He moved in to take care of me after my accident and forgot to move out. After the wedding, he and Claude Ann plan to live in his house on Kapoho Point, south of Hilo. It's ultra-lavish with a panoramic view. He calls it Xanadu."

"Cute."

"Except for the colony of rats that have infested the

garden. The gardener has been trying to exterminate them before the new bride takes up residence."

"Claude Ann's lived in the country most of her life. She won't faint at the sight of a rat." Since he'd brought up the subject of his accident, Dinah assumed it wasn't kapu to inquire. "Was your accident work-related?"

"You could say that." He grazed a finger down the scarred side of his face. "Madame Pele doesn't take kindly to those who invade her privacy."

He didn't elaborate and Dinah took the hint. "Pele crops up in every conversation sooner or later. Hawaii has really embraced the Pele myth."

"And I see you're wearing Pele's tears in your ears."

"A gift from Claude Ann. Xander collected the stones and she had them set for me. What are they, exactly?"

"When particles of molten lava are ejected into the air after an eruption, they cool and solidify, often in the shape of teardrops. You're not superstitious, are you?"

"A little. Why?"

"Hawaiian lore has it that those who steal from Madame Pele's realm are pursued by bad luck."

"Oh." Her hands sprang to her ears.

He laughed his mouth-yanking laugh. "A little superstitious?"

"Okay, more than a little. I was just reading what she did to a man who stole her sacred 'ohelo berries."

"I read that, too. But I believe Pele had human help in the case of Mr. Varian."

"Did you know him? I wondered if he might have been the archaeologist on your father's Uwahi project."

"I'm not in the loop on Uwahi." The word came out charged.

"You disapprove of the project?"

"No comment."

Her curiosity was piqued, but she didn't press. "Over the

last twenty-four hours, I've had two brushes with Pele's disciples. Last night, one of them shouted what sounded like an epithet at me. Ka-ah-ee-hoo…something."

"'Aihui?'"

"Maybe. It sounds like something you wouldn't want to test positive for."

"It means thief. You're in possession of stolen property. No question, you're in deep kim chee with our Lady of the Volcanoes."

"You sound as if you half-believe this goddess actually exists."

"My mother used to sing meles and tell stories about Pele, how she went about digging holes in the ground with her magic stick to make the volcanoes, how she stamps her foot to make the ground shake and the volcanoes spout fire. Pele's as real to me as any other deity from any other religion. More real, I suppose, because I'm hapa…half Hawaiian."

Two pagans in one day, thought Dinah. This was better than Mindanao. "How can I make amends with your goddess? I've heard that she likes gin, but Princess Ruth appeased her with brandy. What do you suggest?"

"Maybe you don't need to do anything. It was my father who took the stones. If Pele played fair, the punishment would fall on him." He swirled his Scotch and downed it in a single gulp. "Then again, I'm living proof that she doesn't play fair."

Dinah couldn't tell if he was wishing calamity on his father or feeling sorry for himself. The remark was certainly fraught with feeling. Like the other pagan's remarks. "Want to hear about my other brush with a Pele disciple?"

"Sure."

"It was your Aunt Eleanor. She warned me that your father was no good for Claude Ann. You and she seem to be on the same page, but neither of you is what I'd call plainspoken."

"It's our Hawaiian mystique. We keep some things huna."

"Under your hats?"

He made a wry mouth and his eyes crinkled at the corners. "I never wear a hat. Let's say hidden."

"Are you hiding the reason you think Claude Ann shouldn't marry your father?"

"No."

She studied his eyes. Rocks might not lie, but rock experts did, and badly. "What about Eleanor? Why is she so down on Xander? She said he'd have to answer for something by and by, Pash. Who or what is that?"

His dark eyes scudded around the room, hither and thither, as if picking up clues from the ceiling and the furniture. "How about...public...access...shoreline Hawaii?"

Damn it. He was hitching words together at random, having her on. She abandoned hope of ever finding out what Pash meant. It might as well stand for Prevaricating, Aggravating, Secretive Hapa Hawaiian. "For someone who doesn't beat about the bush or waste his breath being tactful, you're a very evasive guy."

"The evening's young. Maybe I'll surprise you." He set down his glass and checked his watch. "I expect we should get going."

THIRTEEN

THE PARTY WAS in full swing when Dinah and Jon arrived. A trio of musicians played softly in the background and servers in black livery and white aprons circulated with trays of canapés. Everyone was decked out in their party duds except Jon. Xander gave no sign that he even noticed. He hugged Jon with great warmth and kissed Dinah on the cheek. He appeared relaxed and debonair, although Dinah thought she detected a sort of spring-loaded tension in his body language as he turned to speak to another guest. Dinah hoped it didn't show, but her nerves were taut as a tripwire. The stolen gun preyed on her mind and she couldn't squelch the fear that Eleanor and her troops would crash the party at any moment.

Lyssa's face lit up when she saw Jon. She waved to him from across the room and hurried through the crowd to greet him. She wore a pale yellow, off-the-shoulders dress that set off her latte colored skin and black hair. She reached up and kissed him on the undamaged side of his face. "I told you to dress up, Jonny. Have you no sense of decorum?"

"None." He chucked her under the chin. "Where's Raif?"

"Next to the bar. Why haven't you called us? We've been here for three weeks."

"Just busy. Waiting for the serious partying to begin."

Lyssa's smile dimmed. "Dad says you've met Claude Ann."

"He brought her over to my place soon after they met."

"I see."

Dinah saw. Lyssa was miffed, hurt, or both that Jon hadn't troubled to pay her a call since her arrival.

"I hope you're not embarrassed to be seen with my brother, Dinah. He's pathologically nonconformist."

"Another one-of-a-kind," said Dinah. "Like Raif."

Lyssa flushed and gave her a pettish look.

Xander returned to the group. "Lyssa, would you help me find Claude Ann? I want to introduce her to everyone, but she keeps wandering off. She was last seen at the bar talking to Raif."

"Sure." She smiled, no hint of friction.

"Thanks, sweetheart. Jon, come with me and say hello to Avery. He's been asking about you. You, too, Dinah."

Xander steered them through the crowd, making introductions as they went. Where the room opened onto a tiled lanai and the beach beyond, Avery regaled two giggling young women with a tale about deep-sea fishing.

"Long story short, the boat capsized, the captain drowned, and the biggest marlin in the South Pacific swam away scot-free. It was the bananas." He guffawed until he began to wheeze. "Let that be a lesson to you. No bananas on a boat."

Jon said, "I didn't think you believed in Hawaiian superstitions, Avery."

"Jon! Where've you been hiding this last year? Good to see you, boy. Good to see you." Wilhite's staid blue suit and gray-blue necktie didn't lessen his exuberance. He shook Jon's hand in both of his. "Yes, yes. Dinah and I have met." He shook her hand, too.

Jon seemed glad to see him. "How are you, Ave? And how's Kay?"

"Excellent, excellent. Kay's not here. Off in Wahiawa. Death in her family. Always something. She'll be sorry she missed you."

Xander said, "Jarvis and his wife are here, Avery. They're talking with Steve."

"Excellent. Down to the wire now, eh, Xan? Played golf with Jarvis this morning. He's chomping at the bit. Have you met our buyer, Dinah? Savvy businessman. Texan. Like they are down there. Does a deal on the back of a napkin, but knows his stuff. You must say hello to his wife. Frieda, is it? Yes, Frieda. From somewhere in the South. Mississippi or Mobile."

Xander's eyes searched the crowd. "Have you seen Claude Ann?"

"She was talking to a chappie on the beach a minute ago. All in pink tonight, looking sensational. Careful one of these young buckos doesn't take her away from you, Xan."

"I'd have to kill anyone who tried." He smiled at Dinah, touched Jon and Avery on the shoulder, and headed back into the crowd.

Jon said, "Dinah and I haven't been to the bar, Avery. We'll get something to drink and catch up with you in a few minutes."

"Do that. Love to hear more about your research."

Dinah glimpsed a flash of pink on the lanai. "Jon, I'll join you at the bar in a few minutes." She moved outside and saw Claude Ann idling barefoot down the beach toward the water. Dinah took off her shoes and went after her.

"Claudy, wait up."

Claude Ann turned around and planted her hands on her hips. "You just can't keep your nose out of my personal affairs, can you? Where do you get off raggin' on Xander about what he does or doesn't tell me?"

"I wasn't ragging on him, Claudy. I just thought you ought to know that Eleanor was his former sister-in-law."

"Well, now I know so big whoop. Like there aren't a few polecats in the Pelerin clan? Like you don't have kinfolks you'd rather not display in the family album? Xan's all psyched out now, afraid I'll think he was tryin' to deceive me."

"I'm sorry, Claudy. I'll apologize to him if it will make him feel any better. Or you. I'll leave if you want me to."

"No, I don't want you to leave." She walked back to Dinah and put her arms around her. "I'm the one who should apologize to you, Di. Eleanor ambushed you with her crazy talk and you were worried about me. Everything you've ever done is because you were worried about me. I just want you to know that you don't have to worry so much anymore. Xan's gonna take care of me like I was the greatest treasure in the world."

Dinah felt the urge to knock wood. As none was handy, she crossed her fingers and hugged Claude Ann tight. "Xander's looking for you. What are you doing out here?"

"I'm thinking about how lucky I am. I'm counting my blessings and savorin' this perfect moment." She laughed. "I'm going back to the room for my camera. I want to take pictures so I'll remember all of this when I'm old. Tell Xan to hold his horses. I'll be back in a jiff."

Dinah envied Claude Ann the ability to distill so many volatile ingredients into a perfect moment. She wished she could do the same. It would be nice to leave the worrying to Xander and spend the evening talking with Jon about the gods and goddesses of Hawaii. She felt an odd affinity for Jon—a scientist with a penchant for myth. Lighten up, she told herself. Forget about the gun. And the stupid superstition about Pele's tears. And the menace of Eleanor.

On her way back to the party, she passed Phoebe on the lanai. She was wearing a slinky, floor-length blue dress with a mandarin collar and a contentious expression.

"I'll tell her as soon as I see her. I have no intention of keeping my feelings for Hank a secret from Claude Ann or anyone else."

Hank was the Pluto of the problems orbiting Dinah's

head just now. "Take your time, Phoebe. She's in the middle of a perfect moment. Tomorrow will be soon enough."

"I'll tell her when I'm good and ready and I'm sure she'll deal with it much better than you."

Phoebe flounced off into the crowd and Dinah looked around for Jon. He stood at the end of the bar sipping Scotch. She joined him and ordered a glass of white wine.

He said, "You don't look as though you're having a good time. Something the matter?"

"I keep thinking Eleanor's going to storm the place and all hell will break loose."

"She wouldn't cause a scene at a party for the bride. She's a sentimental old soul."

"And I'm the Queen of Romania."

Raif swaggered up to the bar and slapped Jon on the back. "Look what the cat dragged in. Or is the laid-back attire a sign of mutiny?" He held out his glass to the bartender. "More of the same, Jimbo."

The bartender poured him a generous slug of Jack Daniel's and topped up the glass with Coke.

"Lyssa's worried about you, Jonny. We both are. Good to see you out and about."

"How's it going, Raif?" Jon was stiff and aloof, as if he didn't much care how it was going for Raif. "Still chasing the perfect corner?"

"That's my motto." Raif put out his hands as if gripping the wheel of his car. "Accelerate into the turn, full throttle to the last second, brake hard, and gun it on the straightaway. How about you? Anything hot going on outside of the volcano?"

"Same old, same old." Jon's voice was bland, but there was something akin to revulsion in his eyes.

"You need to rev it up, Jonny. Coasting's for losers." Raif arched an eyebrow and kinked his lip. "You're looking hot tonight, Miss Dinah."

"Thanks." She injected the word with as much sarcasm as a single syllable could hold.

"Say, who's the chick in blue over there? Is she the other bridesmaid?"

"Phoebe Marshall."

"I'd better go introduce myself."

He swaggered off and Dinah said, "I wouldn't want to disillusion Lyssa, but I think Raif is as fast off the track as he is on it."

The observation evoked a sardonic grin from Jon. "It's obvious to everyone but Lyssa. Maybe it's obvious to her and she's too stubborn or too proud to admit it."

A big man with a sandy-blond mane like a Viking's, a full beard, and a gap-toothed grin sauntered up to the bar and gave Jon a shoulder-bumping half-hug. "I wasn't sure if you'd grace us with your presence, buddy."

"Steve." Jon's lopsided smile showed real affection. "You're the one who's hard to find lately. Howzit, brah?"

"I've been working twenty-four-seven on your dad's Uwahi deal. We're counting down the days 'til it's over now."

"Steve, meet Dinah Pelerin, Claude Ann's maid of honor. Dinah, this is Steve Sykes, the S in SAX Associates and the mastermind of all their slick legal gimmicks and angles."

Steve laughed. "Pleasure to meet you, Dinah. Jon and I went to school together like you and Claude Ann. We're best buds—makamakas. I let him dis me, but you should know he's an inveterate liar."

Dinah liked Steve's grin and the twinkle in his Nordic blue eyes. "So you're not a slick finagler?"

"I am a slick finagler. I grease the skids with my seductive charm and legal acumen and make impossible things happen."

"Like Uwahi?" asked Jon.

"No. Uwahi's a piece of cake. Everybody wants it."

"Except Eleanor Kalolo," said Dinah.

"Maybe she'll learn to love it when she sees how many jobs it brings to the island and how much revenue it generates." Steve picked a bottle of beer out of a cooler beside the bar and twisted the cap. "It's prosperity versus preservation."

Dinah quoted the old song. "Pave paradise, put up a parking lot."

"Not all of it," said Steve. "Just a few hundred acres. Anyway, it's a make-or-break sale for Xan. Environmental impact studies don't come cheap. Habitat analysis, marine analysis, ornithological radar, plus you've got your social and cultural impact analyses."

"Isn't the actual developer normally responsible for all that?" Dinah asked.

"This deal's a one-off. A lot of high-level haggling and state politics in play."

Jon tossed off his Scotch and set the empty glass on the bar. "So long as Dad hasn't mortgaged Wahilani, I don't give a rat's."

"I wouldn't bet on it, brah."

Jon's leery eyes turned hard as drill bits. "Are you saying he did borrow against my place?"

"I don't know. He took out a big loan on Xanadu. I'd call that betting the ranch." Steve's attention strayed. "Speaking of betting, isn't that George Knack over by the door?"

"That can't be good," said Jon. "I'd better give him the heave-ho before Dad sees him or there'll be a brawl." He started across the room toward a heavyset man with a black pompadour who seemed to be auditing the room from behind thick, black hornrims.

"Who's George Knack and why would there be a brawl?"

"He's a bookie. He runs an illegal betting parlor in Pahoa on the Big Island. Xander's locked horns with him before over Raif's gambling, but he won't do anything to rock the boat tonight. Not with Paul Jarvis and his wife here."

It was then that they heard the scream. It gathered like a wave, a long crescendo of female terror that climaxed in a crack of anguish.

Dinah's heart lurched. "Someone's being murdered."

The music stopped and the crowd hushed. Everyone looked around wildly.

"It sounds like it's coming from the beach," said Steve.

Dinah's fear surged. Where was Claude Ann? She left her wine and bounded out onto the lanai. The screaming continued, louder and more desperate. She peered up and down the beach. The outside lights were mostly at foot level, designed to spawn romance not clarity, and the moon was no bigger than a toenail shaving.

Steve's voice was right behind her. "Maybe it's just kids raising hell."

"I can't see anything. Where's it coming from?"

Xander's guests began to trickle onto the beach, pointing and murmuring.

"There, coming out of the terrace restaurant," said someone. "What's that?"

The terrace lights backlit a dark figure weaving drunkenly.

Xander and Jon materialized out of nowhere at Dinah's side.

"It's Claude Ann!" Xander's voice broke and he started running down the beach.

Dinah doffed her shoes and ran after him, her feet sinking in the sand with every step. She felt as if she were running in slow motion. Jon and Steve passed her, but she dug deeper and caught up in time to see Claude Ann, drenched in blood, stagger into Xander's arms and collapse a few yards from the edge of the terrace.

Jon bent down and removed a crumpled piece of paper from her hand. He held it under the green LED light from his wristwatch for Dinah to read. It said GO HOME. In blood.

FOURTEEN

DINAH DROPPED TO her knees in the sand. "Is she dead?"

"Call nine-one-one," shouted Xander. "Somebody call an ambulance."

A hundred voices babbled into cell phones.

"Open your eyes, baby." Xander's voice was gravelly, despairing. "Open your eyes."

Claude Ann moaned.

Alive. Dinah drew in a lungful of air. Had she been shot? Stabbed? From the amount of blood, it looked as though she'd been disemboweled.

Two men and a woman, obviously hotel employees, tried to herd the crowd back into the ballroom. "Let's clear a path for the EMTs, people. They'll come through this way. Please move back inside."

Dinah held her ground.

Lyssa touched Xander on the shoulder. "Is she all right, Daddy?"

"I don't know. I don't know." He raked his hair out of his face, leaving a smear of blood across his forehead. "Jon?"

"I'm here, Dad."

"Find out who did this. Follow the trail of blood. She must have run through the lobby to come out the terrace door."

Jon started across the terrace.

"Marywave! Where's Marywave?" Phoebe's flutey voice brought Dinah to her feet.

"Claudy sent her to the movies with the sitter. She might

be back any minute. Please, Phoebe, go make sure she doesn't see or hear any of this."

"Call me the instant you know something?"

"Yes, yes. I promise."

Phoebe hurried away down the beach and the EMTs hurried out of the hotel through the terrace restaurant door along with the same two policemen who'd shooed Dinah away from the demonstration the previous night. The cops pushed everyone away from Claude Ann. As Xander stepped back, Dinah heard Wilhite's voice, high-pitched and querulous.

"Christ on a crutch, man. I thought you said you had it under control."

DINAH RODE IN the ambulance with Claude Ann and Xander to Queens Medical Center and en route, it became clear that, in spite of all the blood, Claude Ann wasn't at death's door. She was dazed and scared, but she was aware of her surroundings and talking.

"I hurt like hell."

Xander held onto her hand as if to a lifeline. "What happened, darling? Who did this to you?"

"Didn't see."

When they reached the hospital, the medics had whisked Claude Ann into Emergency. Xander had paced up and down the waiting room while she was being examined, but when she was moved to Radiology, he was allowed to go with her. Dinah installed herself in an uncomfortable chair across from a hulking boy with a hand-held video game that whirred and sputtered and made explosive little spitting noises. Untold numbers of games and three cups of vending machine coffee later, a sumo-sized cop approached her and identified himself as Sergeant Kama. He held a notepad in one baseball mitt of a hand and a pair of tiny, half-moon eyeglasses in the other. He said, "The blood's not human."

His words couldn't have been more mystifying if he were speaking in Swahili. "Not human?"

"It was animal. Pig, we think. We're having it analyzed."

Dinah was processing this information when a Japanese doctor in a white coat appeared. "Your friend has no puncture wounds of any kind," he said, glancing at his chart. "She has a broken left wrist, a bruised left shoulder, and a lump on her head. The lump's probably not serious, but we'll keep her overnight for observation to be sure there's no intracranial hematoma or bleeding. We've given her a mild tranquilizer and an analgesic for pain. Her fiancé is with her now, but I'm not going to authorize any more visitors tonight."

Sgt. Kama put on his glasses and made a note of the doctor's diagnosis. "The bucket must've clipped her on the head and wrist when it fell off the closet shelf."

"The bucket." Dinah was flabbergasted all over again. "Her closet was booby-trapped with a bucket of blood?"

"Looks that way. The handle of the loaded bucket was tied to the handle of the closet door and when she pulled the door open, the bucket toppled over on her. When will she be awake and able to talk to the police, Doc?"

"Tomorrow morning. Come early. I understand that she and her fiancé are flying to Hilo as soon as she's discharged." The doctor excused himself and moved off to confer with another group awaiting news from the ER.

As Dinah's relief increased, so did her outrage. "But why? Why would anyone douse Claude Ann with a bucket of blood?"

"I was hoping you could tell us. The maids cleaned her suite at one o'clock this afternoon. Who else had access to her suite?"

"I'm not sure. Her daughter Marywave and I were in the room around three-thirty."

"Did you look inside the closet when you were there, Miss?"

"No. Marywave had her own key card. She would've gone back to the room when she left the swimming pool, probably with the sitter, Tiffany. And Dream Weddings was to have delivered our dresses sometime this afternoon. A porter probably took them up to the room." Dinah had been obsessing about the gun since the first scream. Xander's reticence be damned, it had to come out now. "Late this afternoon, Claude Ann noticed that something had been stolen."

"Dinah!" Phoebe and Raif Reid filed into the room.

"You never called. I couldn't stand it. How is she?" Phoebe was breathless.

"A broken wrist and a knock on the head," said Dinah. "They're keeping her overnight to make sure there's no internal bleeding. Otherwise, she's just bunged up and sore. How's Marywave?"

"All she knows is that her suite's been damaged and she can't spend the night there. Housekeeping put a rollaway in my room. She's there now with the sitter."

Raif had lost the cocky sneer. He introduced himself and Phoebe to Sergeant Kama. "The trail of blood leads from the door of Claude Ann's room down the stairs and across the lobby. She must have been terrified."

Kama said, "The receptionist says she tried to stop her, but the lady kept running 'til she got to Mr. Garst. Did either of you go into Ms. Kemper's room at any time during the day?"

"No," said Phoebe, looking frightened.

"Not I," said Raif.

Kama pointed his pen at Dinah. "You were about to tell me about something that was stolen."

"Claude Ann called Xander and me to her room shortly after five. She was very upset. Someone had stolen her gun. A vintage Beretta."

Kama scrawled a note on his pad. "When was the last time she saw the gun?"

"I don't know. You'll have to ask her."

"A gun?" Raif hooted. "What the hell was she doing with a gun? That must've blown old Xan's mind."

It was possible that in other venues, among people who had no connection with his father-in-law, Raif wouldn't stand out as the most obnoxious person in the room. But just now, Dinah couldn't think of anyone who came close. She said, "Claude Ann would've opened her closet when she was dressing for the party. The trap must have been rigged while the party was going on. Her camera must have been in the closet. That's what she went back for."

Phoebe shook her head. "It just breaks my heart. Her perfect wedding sabotaged and all her beautiful clothes ruined. I don't understand how anyone could be so mean."

Mentally, Dinah ticked off the people who might have been so mean. Eleanor Kalolo was certainly high on the list of possible meanies. But her hatred was concentrated on Xander. It didn't make sense that she would target Claude Ann. Marywave was gung ho to go home, but she wouldn't hurt her mother and, anyway, she couldn't have pulled off the stunt without an accomplice. Lyssa didn't like Claude Ann. She probably wouldn't like any woman her own age who came along and usurped her father's love. Maybe she thought Claude Ann was going to usurp her inheritance, as well. But the crudeness of the prank didn't fit Lyssa's passive-aggressive style. Dinah cast a sidelong look at Raif, he of the insolent gibes and the bad-boy swagger. Would he do something this mean? Or Jon who disapproved of the marriage without saying why? Did the same person who rigged the trap steal the gun or did two people visit Claude Ann's closet for different reasons?

Raif contributed his two cents. "It had to be one of those protesters. They've laid siege to the hotel for a week."

Logically, Dinah had to agree. She said, "Eleanor Kalolo sought me out at the hotel this morning, Sergeant. She seems bent on exacting revenge against Xander Garst for something or other. She said he'd have to pay for Pash. Do you know what or whom she could've meant?"

"No, ma'am. We'll interview her and see what she has to say for herself."

Dinah flashed to the sergeant's conversation with the TV crew last night after the protesters had disbanded. "Was Xander ever accused of foul play by Eleanor or anyone in the Native Hawaiian rights movement?"

"Foul play?" Phoebe was aghast. "Xander?"

"Yes, foul play. Yes, Xander. The only people Claude Ann knows in Hawaii are people Xander knows. Whoever did this did it to get at him. Clearly, the man has enemies and people don't acquire enemies by being Mr. Nice Guy."

"It's because your father was a criminal," said Phoebe. "You see foul play and deceitfulness everywhere."

What Dinah saw was red. "You're on notice, Phoebe. Do not drag my family into this or any other conversation. Ever again. Is that clear?"

Kama ahemmed and thumped his pen against his notepad. "Let's stay with tonight's foul play. Can you think of anyone besides Eleanor Kalolo who might want to disrupt the wedding or cause trouble for Ms. Kemper or Mr. Garst?"

"Nobody," said Phoebe. "Raif's right. It has to be one of the protesters."

Xander shouldered through the double doors into the waiting area. His shirt and tux were stained with blood, his hair sweaty, and his face seemed to have aged ten years. "She's resting comfortably. The doctor says it's only a hairline fracture of the radius and he doesn't think there'll be any aftereffects from the blow to her head. It's a miracle. She could've suffered a serious head injury."

"Did she say whether she saw anyone in her room," Kama asked, "or have any idea who the perpetrator might have been?"

"She didn't see anyone. She went back to her room for her camera and…my God. She could've been killed. Did you tell him about the gun, Dinah?"

"Yes, I told him."

Sgt. Kama went on methodically. "What's your best guess as to who might have done it, Mr. Garst?"

Xander rubbed his head. "I can't think. I can't think who'd do something like this."

Kama said, "Any idea who might have taken the gun from Ms. Kemper's room?"

"No. None at all."

"Is there anyone who might have wanted to get back at Ms. Kemper or you, sir?"

"No. No one who'd do such a thing." He darted a beleaguered look around the group. "Officer, I'm exhausted. Would you mind if we talked tomorrow morning?"

"No problem." Kama closed his notepad. "We'll know more by morning and one of the detectives will want to talk to you." He handed each of them a card and headed for the elevators.

Xander put the card in his breast pocket and pushed his hair out of his face. "I'm dead tired. I'm going back to the hotel."

Dinah could scarcely believe her ears. How could he bail out on the woman he claimed to love after she'd had such a horrible experience? It seemed wormy in the extreme. She said, "I'll wait around the hospital for a while in case Claude Ann gets scared and wants somebody to hold her hand."

Xander's eyes showed that he'd felt the cut, but his mouth smiled. "Thanks, Dinah. I appreciate that. If there's any change, or if she asks for me, please call."

Phoebe said, "I need to get back and look in on Marywave."

"Raif, will you give Phoebe a ride?" asked Xander.

"Sure. I'll drive you both back."

"No," said Xander. "No, I'll take a taxi. I have to drop off a document at my lawyer's office."

Phoebe also declined Raif's offer. "I need to make a stop on the way back to the hotel, too. A friend from my self-mastery seminar is staying downtown and I need to collect some materials from her before we leave for the Big Island. I'll see you all in the morning."

Raif gave Phoebe a derisive look, as if to say "your loss." "I'll stay with Dinah and give her a ride back when she's ready."

"No need." Dinah didn't dislike Raif in a small way. She had taken a huge scunner to his sneering arrogance and the sooner he moved on, the better she'd feel. "I may be here for hours. Please, go back and get some rest."

"I never go to bed before three or four. I'll keep you company as long as you like."

Xander and Phoebe left and Dinah sank into one of the chairs lined up against the wall. Raif sat down next to her and rested his head against the wall. Dinah ignored him. She tried to put herself in Claude Ann's place. What horrors must have reeled through her mind when that bloody deluge hit her? Even if there were no physical aftereffects, there would be emotional ones.

Raif loosened his tie and fingered his Lucky 7 pendant. "You think Claude Ann will give Xan his ring back now and buzz off back to Georgia?"

"I doubt it."

"Probably not. He must be a prize catch for a girl like her."

Dinah bit her tongue.

"How did you and poor old Jon hit it off? You'd think he wouldn't dress like such a slob. It makes him even more of an eyesore."

"I think he's rather dashing. And remarkably stoical about his scars."

"Lyssa worries that he's turning into one of those anti-social loners, maybe not the kind that amasses an arsenal and goes on a killing spree. But a headcase just the same. She keeps bugging him to have reconstructive surgery. It wouldn't get rid of all the scars, but it might help him to feel less of an oddity. He used to be a good-looking dude."

Dinah had no trouble visualizing the intact Jon, or imagining how tough an adjustment it must have been for an attractive man to have his curb appeal so thoroughly demolished. She said, "He obviously doesn't like to talk about the accident. How did it happen?"

"He was collecting lava samples, not wearing his protective gear. I guess the heat burned through his boots. He jumped wrong and lost his balance. At least, that's all I've ever heard him say about it. You know what Xander said? He said he wished it had been him who got burned instead of Jon." Raif uttered a bark of scoffing laughter. "Everybody lies about something right?"

Dinah didn't doubt that, present company in no way excepted. Raif seemed to delight in disparaging Xander. Whatever issues Lyssa had with her father, Raif stoked the fire. Lyssa would naturally be torn between her father and her husband, and maybe between her brother and her husband. It must make her life a tricky balancing act.

She said, "Jon told me that after the accident his father moved in with him to take care of him."

"That must have been a drag. The way those two circle around each other like a pair of boxers on guard for the next punch, it makes everybody jumpy."

"They don't get along?"

"They don't go at each other. It's more like the air between them is combustible."

And how, Dinah wondered, is that different from the air between you and Xander? "You seem to despise Xander. Why?"

"I don't like the way he leans on Lyssa and tries to tell her how to spend her money. It's hers. Her grandfather left it to her and Xander's got no right."

"He probably resents the way you gamble with your wife's money."

"Takes one to know one." He curled his lip. "At least I'm not a hypocrite. Like they say down South, if you can't race it, play with it, or take it to bed, who needs it?"

FIFTEEN

CLAUDE ANN DIDN'T call Dinah to come and hold her hand and Raif's snide backbiting taxed Dinah's endurance to the limit. At midnight, she decided that Claude Ann must be sleeping soundly through the night and there was no point in hanging around any longer. She stood up and stretched. A dull pain drummed against her temples and it occurred to her that she hadn't eaten in hours.

"Had enough?" asked Raif.

"Yes. Would you mind stopping off for a burger on the way back to the Olopana?"

"Sounds like a plan. I'm hungry, too."

They left and Raif drove to a drive-in with a blazing neon sign—The Shark Bite. He parked under a carport strung with red and blue Christmas lights. A well-endowed young woman in a tight tee and short shorts roller-skated up to the car window and smiled.

Dinah ordered a burger and fries and a large coffee. She already knew she wouldn't be able to sleep, so she might as well be fueled to think straight.

"Give me a cheeseburger and a cola," Raif said. "Any kind. It doesn't matter."

While they waited, he lolled against the driver's door and seemed to consider. "You really care about her, don't you? Claude Ann, I mean."

"I really do." The question surprised her and not only because it came from Raif. It had been a while since she had reflected on the reasons she loved Claude Ann, but she certainly did. She loved her for her loyalty and her high spirits, for her spontaneous and arbitrary acts of kindness, for her lack of pretense and her easy laugh. Claude Ann was the only person outside of Dinah's family who knew her when. When she was young and trusting. Before Needmore and her father's betrayal made her cynical. She and Claude Ann were the repository of each other's earliest history and now Dinah was bearing witness to another crisis in Claude Ann's life. At the moment, it seemed as if this one, too, was trending toward heartbreak.

She had been dubious about Xander from the start, but with this bizarre attack on Claude Ann, her doubts metastasized. Claude Ann had trusted Xander with her heart, trusted him with God only knew how much of her money. He seemed to be genuinely in love with her, but seeming and being were two entirely different things and so far, he hadn't shown the kind of commitment that would redeem him in Dinah's eyes.

The food arrived. Raif pulled a fifth of Jack Daniel's out of the glove compartment and added a splash of high octane to his cola. "Want a shot?"

"No thanks."

"Suit yourself."

They ate in silence and Dinah began to feel a little better. Less empty, anyway. Tomorrow she'd have a heart-to-heart with Claude Ann and, without divulging her misgivings about Xander or putting Claude Ann on the defensive, she would convince her to wait a few weeks before plighting her troth.

Dinah finished her burger and wiped the mustard off her fingers with a paper napkin. "Thanks for dinner."

Raif topped up his cola with more whiskey and slid a hand down her thigh. "You want to go to a motel?"

She recoiled and stared at him. "Are you flat-out crazy or just a conceited cheat?"

"Like Mick Jagger says, marrying money's a full time

job. I take a night off now and then. We could say we spent all night keeping vigil at the hospital. It's the perfect cover."

"Go to hell."

"What's the matter? Aren't I as dashing as Jon?"

"You're repulsive."

He grabbed her arms and pulled her into him, crushing his mouth against hers, forcing his tongue into her mouth. She squirmed out of his grasp, jerked open the door, and jumped out.

He smirked. "Lyssa won't believe you, so you needn't bother tattling."

She slammed the car door, turned on her heels, and fumed inside the drive-in. Some days it was hard not to give up in disgust on the whole catalog of humanity.

HER HABIT OF carrying a hundred dollar bill pinned in the hem of her dress had paid off. The taxi dropped her off under the portico of the Olopana and she handed the driver the bill.

"I can't make change for a century."

"Keep it. I don't have a pocket anyway."

The Olopana looked deserted. The lobby was lit, but the receptionist must have stepped away for a break. Too angry and restless to sleep, Dinah drifted out to the beach, took off her shoes, and started walking. She couldn't stomach walking where the horror had taken place. Eleanor had said there were no restricted beaches in Hawaii, so Dinah availed herself of the beach belonging to the hotel next door.

The sand felt cool under her feet and the soughing sound of the surf calmed her. Out here, there were no trust issues. Everything was controlled by the gravitational pull of the moon. She waded up to her ankles through the lapping waves and halfway thought about stripping off her blood-stained dress and skinny dipping, but the floodlights around the hotel threw off too much light and the possibility that her blood might attract a shark stopped her cold.

She hadn't noticed it before, but a hundred yards along there was a lifeguard tower. As she drew closer, she saw Jon, elbows leaning across the rail, staring out at the water.

"Ahoy."

"Come aboard. I scavenged a bottle of Scotch from the caterers if you're interested."

"I could use a bracer."

He offered her a hand and she climbed up the ladder.

"Dad called and said Claude Ann wasn't seriously hurt."

"Not physically."

They sat in canvas chairs and he drizzled a couple of inches of Dewars into a plastic cup and placed it in her hand. "Soda?"

"Yes, please." The strong, peaty smell of the Scotch had an astringent effect and, in close quarters, he transmitted a distracting sexual vibe along with the scent of Scotch and sandalwood soap. "Romantic setting, mood-enhancing libation. You're the perfect date."

He gave a mordant little laugh. "When the moon's behind a cloud." But the moon wasn't behind a cloud and there was a floodlight at the base of the tower. He replenished his Scotch and brought out a bottle of soda. As he poured, she fixated on his scars. Dashing they were not. And it was curious that he'd made no attempt to get himself surgically reconstructed.

"Hell of a day," he said.

She thought about Claude Ann's toast—was it only last night?—to happy days. "It's a day with nasty repercussions, and not just for the bride and groom. Your Aunt Eleanor is the prime suspect."

"From what I know of her, Eleanor doesn't do anything anonymously. She's pretty much in-your-face."

That much, Dinah could believe. "Maybe she got tired

of Xander being a no-show at her demonstrations. Maybe she decided to do something outrageous to dynamite him out of his foxhole." She thought about Avery's sketchy description of Leilani, an exotic beauty who died young—the night-and-day antithesis of Eleanor. But sister love could be strong. Was Leilani's suicide the impetus for Eleanor's resentment of Xander? "Tell me about your mother's death, Jon. If it isn't huna."

"I was six years old, Lyssa four. Dad was away in California. I remember her being on the telephone, crying really hard. When she hung up, she said she was sick and had to go to the doctor. She took Lyssa and me to Eleanor's house in the country. It was the first time we kids had ever met Eleanor. She and my mother had a big fight, mostly in Hawaiian. It sounded like they were calling each other names. Lyssa cried. My mother kissed us, then got in the car and drove away. Eleanor took us to town and bought us a colossal dish of Roselani ice cream—Menehune mint. We never saw my mother again."

"Did you ever find out who she was talking to on the telephone or what had upset her?"

"No."

"You're sure her nickname wasn't Pash?"

He flicked a sideways glance at her. "Everyone called her Lani." His gaze returned to the ocean. "I know that from your perspective and probably Claude Ann's, Eleanor is the logical culprit. But I don't believe it. She wouldn't do something this cowardly and mean-spirited to a woman who's done nothing wrong except to fall in love with the man she has a beef with."

Dinah was prone to agree. Maybe in the fervor of her hatred, Eleanor had made up the word Pash as a sort of curse or incantation. But why did Jon seem so ambivalent about Xander? She didn't give much credence to Raif's slurs, but there did seem to be something huna in the way everyone spoke about Jon's accident. "You were blunt with me, Jon. May I ask you a blunt question?"

"Turnabout's fair play."

"How did your accident happen?"

"Like Kamapua'a, I encroached on Pele's domain."

It required an effort not to snap at him. Nobody loved a myth more than Dinah, but the idea of Pele as the agency behind every occurrence in the State of Hawaii was becoming tiresome and Jon's evasions in particular irked her. She said, "I ran across that name in my book of myths. Wasn't he Pele's lover?"

"One of them. The goddess favored him for a while, but when he grew too bold, she chased him into the sea with streams of fire."

"And you identify with this myth because you became too bold to wear your protective clothing?"

"Who told you that?"

"Does it matter?"

He shrugged. "Maybe I identify because Kamapua'a was half man and half monster."

"That's a terrible way to see yourself."

"It's not a matter of how I see myself. It's how others see me."

"I thought you had too much, I don't know...intelligence to indulge in self-pity."

"No, you didn't. You were just relieved when I pretended not to notice your pity. I've come to terms with the man in the mirror and I wouldn't trade skins with anyone. But I'm not oblivious to the effect my scars have on people."

She didn't know what to say without making it sound like a condolence. "Like you said, once a person gets used to you, you're not so bad."

He laughed that mordant laugh. "The early Hawaiians mutilated themselves with all kinds of gashes and burns to prove their devotion to a lover. Their scars were called alina and they were all the rage. I'd have been quite a knockout back in the day."

Dinah was too squeamish even to get a discreet little tattoo. She didn't think she would've gone for gashes or burns, however artistic or faddish. But with the moon beginning to slide behind a cloud and the Scotch seeping into her bloodstream, Jon's alina were growing on her in a disturbingly paganish way. She eighty-sixed herself. "What were you doing next to red-hot lava without your protective gear?"

"I was testing a lobe of pahoehoe lava. Pahoehoe is beautiful. It flows in a smooth, rolling motion and as it cools and hardens, it looks like coils of twisted rope. It doesn't radiate as much heat as a'a lava. If you've got sturdy boots and gloves and work quickly, you don't need the full suit."

"Were you angry at your father before the accident or did you fall out afterward?"

His body stiffened. "Who said I was angry?"

"Everything you've said to me about him contains a not-so-veiled distrust of the man. Claude Ann mentioned a rift and Raif said that you and Xander were wary of each other."

"Wary's a good word. Raif is surprisingly perceptive up to a point. My father and I have had our differences, some of them fierce. But he raised Lyssa and me single-handed, he took care of me when I was burned and sick, and I believe that he loves us. Some problems in life are insoluble. Dad and I try to steer clear of those. I'm happy he's finally found somebody he loves and wants to spend the rest of his life with. It should happen to us all." He belted the last of his Scotch and stood up.

"Give me your hand." He pulled her to her feet and she was seized by an untoward urge, almost like a tic, to kiss him. Big mistake, she thought. Sexual curiosity mingled with compassion, ticklish in the extreme. But sex won out. She stood on her toes, closed her eyes, and kissed him on the mouth.

His response was more than she'd bargained on. When she came up for air, her knees were rubbery and her dopamine level dangerously high. So this was what it felt like to kiss a heathen descendant of a fire goddess.

He said, "That didn't taste like consolation."

She was casting about for words when something bumped the back of the tower. She looked around the side of the structure and saw a lanky figure in a billed cap limping hurriedly down the beach.

"How long do you suppose he's been listening?" asked Jon.

"I…don't…know." She watched the man until he hobbled out of sight behind the hotel.

Sorrowing Jesus. Well, that solved the bucket of blood mystery and probably the missing gun, as well. So it wasn't Eleanor or any of the local meanies after all. How could she have thought even for one second that Hank would stay at home and miss Claude Ann's next wedding?

SIXTEEN

"I WANT HIS miserable teetotalin' liver on a stick. I'd like to rip his sanctimonious tongue right out of his head. I'd like to lop off his cracker balls and feed 'em to the fish. I'd like to…"

"Claudy, I take your point." Dinah speared a chunk of the pineapple garnish off her plate and stuffed it into her mouth. Room service had delivered her breakfast eggs and bacon at six a.m. They sat congealing on the serving trolley and she hadn't managed to eat more than two bites.

"Of all the lowdown, contemptible, dirty tricks. I wish he were dead, dead, dead, dead, dead, dead, dead!"

Dinah held the receiver away from her ear until the tirade subsided. "I reported Hank's appearance to the police and Marywave gave them the name of his hotel. By the time you're released from the hospital, the police will have nabbed him."

"What does Marywave have to say for herself? Did the little traitor cook it up with her daddy to put me in the hospital?"

Dinah looked at Marywave, her eyes rimmed red from crying and her lips quivering. "No, Claude Ann. Hank didn't think you were reading his letters so he told Marywave he was going to leave you a message you couldn't ignore. She didn't know about the blood. She's scared sick and worried about you and her father, too. We're all worried about Hank. He's obviously gone off the deep end and now he has a gun."

Marywave sniffled. "Tell Mama it wasn't my fault."

"Marywave says to tell you it wasn't her fault."

"Ask her when he got here? How long's he been spyin' on me?"

"Do you want to talk to Marywave, yourself?"

"I can't talk to her. I'm too keyed up. Tell her she's a sneaky little pissant and a complete pain in the ass. And I love her."

"Your mother loves you, Marywave." Dinah ate another piece of pineapple. "The police think he got the blood from a luau or a hotel kitchen. They recommend that you apply to the court for an injunction in case he makes bail."

"Sheesh! I don't know how I can make it up to Xan. He's walkin' on eggshells because his deal's gotta close right on time or else. His buyer was at the party last night thinkin' we're all nice as pie and along comes my crazy-ass, infra dig ex-husband and causes a bloody horror show. Xan'll be here any minute and I don't know how I can explain."

It irritated Dinah that Claude Ann felt she owed Xander an apology. "You couldn't possibly have foreseen that Hank would show up and assault you. And how can what happened to you make any difference to the Uwahi deal? Anyway, it's not just Xander's deal. It's your deal, too. Phoebe says you've lent him a good deal of money."

"Yes, I put up some money." She sounded as if she might be about to cry. "And now I've balled things up. Everything would be perfect if I hadn't brought my holy mess of an ex-husband from Needmore on my coattails."

If the buyer was the eager beaver Steve said he was, Dinah didn't see the problem. Hank, on the other hand, had shown himself capable of wreaking serious havoc. "I think you should postpone the wedding until after Hank is behind bars for good or has left the state. If he stays out of jail, injunctions are no guarantee that he'll leave you alone. Hold off for a month."

"I won't, I won't, I won't! I won't be bullied, Dinah

Pelerin. Not by you or that ugly witch Eleanor or Hank freakin' Kemper."

"Come on, Claudy. Use your head for something besides a hairdo. Think about your safety. Think about Marywave's safety and Xander's. It can't hurt to put off the wedding for a few weeks. I'll stay. I received a message this morning from one of the professors I've been working for on Mindinao. Some journalists and politicians were beheaded a few days ago and the anthropology team has decided to call it quits and go home. I can stay on for a while and be your bodyguard."

"You can stay as long as you want, but somebody's gonna have to behead me before I call it quits. Yvonne was late sending our dresses to the hotel so they weren't damaged. I'm gettin' married bright 'n' early on the day after tomorrow no matter if God turns the whole bleepin' ocean to blood."

It was no use. Dinah had been down this road with Claude Ann before. Once she made up her mind, she was like a stuck accelerator pedal—flat-out, headlong, full speed ahead. "How much time before we leave for Hilo?"

"Xander's packed my things for me and as soon as the doc gives me my walkin' papers, we're outa here. We'll meet the rest of y'all at the airport at ten-thirty sharp. We're gonna fly on Avery Wilhite's private plane. Jon'll drive you and Phoebe and Marywave."

"Tis not mine to reason why."

"What?"

"Nevermind. I'll see you at ten-thirty." Dinah hung up the phone.

"Does she hate me?" whined Marywave.

"Of course, she doesn't hate you. But what your dad did to her is hateful. I don't know if he intended to hurt her, but if he didn't, he showed a total lack of foresight."

"I still don't believe Hank did it," said Phoebe, coming

out of the bathroom. She'd been alternately throwing up and
bursting into tears ever since Dinah had rousted her out of
bed in the wee hours with the news that Hank was prowl-
ing around outside the hotel. When Marywave confessed
to giving him a key card to Claude Ann's suite and Dinah
telephoned the police, Phoebe's stomach had rebelled. Physically and emotionally depleted now, she drooped onto the
loveseat next to Marywave. "Just because he went into
Claude Ann's suite, and grant you he shouldn't have done
that, it doesn't mean he dumped the blood or took her gun.
You said yourself this Eleanor woman is dangerous and a
local person would know better than Hank where to get a
gallon of pig's blood." Her shrill voice grated on Dinah's
caffeinated nerves.

"Get real, Phoebe. He's been writing Claude Ann threatening letters, he sneaked into Hawaii without telling her, he
had the key to her room. And as for the pig's blood, Hank
puts the husband in animal husbandry and always has."

"You've never liked him." Phoebe hooked her arm pro-
tectively around Marywave's shoulders. "But you shouldn't
talk about him like that in front of Marywave."

Big tears rolled down Marywave's cheeks and Dinah
eased up. "Your daddy's been going through hard times
since his car accident, Marywave. He may have sustained
a head injury the doctors didn't find. Maybe he needs to
get checked out by a neurologist or a psychiatrist. Maybe
if he pays restitution for the damage he did and agrees to
get professional help, he won't have to go to jail. At least,
not for long."

"You're not much of a comforter, are you?" Phoebe stood
up and took Marywave's hand. "Let's go back to my room
and pack your things, sweetpea."

"Wait." Dinah held out her hand. "Give me your phone,
Marywave. I assume Hank has your number, too, Phoebe."

Phoebe was indignant. "I'm not giving you my phone."

Dinah stared her down. "He's wanted for questioning by the police, Phoebe. Aid and abet at your own risk."

Marywave handed over her little pink Kajeet. Dinah opened the door and watched them walk down the hall and go inside Phoebe's room, then closed her door and flopped onto the bed face-first. She tried to envision her butterfly self, any self at all with wings to fly her out of here in the opposite direction from Hilo. She thought about the next forty-eight hours and moaned out loud. "As God is my witness, I will never attend another wedding as long as I live."

SEVENTEEN

THE COFFEE HAD left a bitter taste in Dinah's mouth and she went to the bathroom to brush her teeth. Her face in the mirror looked like death on a cracker. A seedy, brittle cracker. She should go back to bed and try to sleep until Jon arrived to chauffeur her to the airport. But she was too wound up to sleep. Maybe when the caffeine and the adrenaline wore off, she could sleep this afternoon. She'd like to sleep all the way through until the wedding. Another party had been scheduled for tonight, but with Claude Ann in a cast and all of her clothes but the wedding dress splotched with blood, Xander would be wise to scratch the affair and barricade himself and his bride behind closed doors. Double-bolted steel doors.

Dinah finished brushing her teeth, spat into the sink, and chased the bad taste down the drain with a froth of tap water. The aboriginal kings of Hawaii preserved their saliva in a vessel studded with the teeth of their ancestors and kept the spittoon under heavy guard. They believed the essence of their spirit resided in their spit. If an enemy got hold of even a single drop, he could cast a spell and zap the king through sorcery. For Dinah, it was too late for precautions. She'd swapped spit with Raif Reid and Jonathan Garst and the way her head felt, she'd been zapped already.

She rinsed and spat again. She needed a hard run to clear the cobwebs. One of the "things to do" magazines on her bedside table recommended a sort of cave or blowhole. She thumbed through the magazine and found it—Spitting Cave. Terrific. It was less than three miles from the hotel.

She could do a mile in a little over eight minutes. She could do six in an hour easily and be home and hosed by the time Jon showed up. She memorized the directions, threw on her running shorts and a tee, and set out.

The route took her along mostly residential streets. There were some lovely homes and magnificent trees, but she wasn't interested in scenery. Her thoughts revolved around Leilani's suicide and the mysterious phone call that preceded it; Eleanor's crusade for revenge and her baffling allusion to Pash; Jon's insoluble problem with Xander and his careless fall on the pahoehoe; the appearance of an unwelcome bookie at the party; Raif's gambling and his allegation that Xander gambled, too; Claude Ann's maddening disregard for her money and her safety; and a dead archaeologist that nobody claimed to know in a land where people took their ancestral bones very seriously. The fact that a jealous ex-husband was running around loose with a handgun was almost refreshing in its simplicity.

There were too many mysteries revolving around Xander Garst. Something was hinky. Could Phoebe be right and someone other than Hank was trying to derail the wedding train? Dinah wished she didn't have such a suspicious mind. An old boyfriend who did brain research once diagnosed her problem with trust as the result of a chemical deficiency—some peptide or other that, produced in adequate amounts, induces faith in one's fellow man. If Dinah's brain was lacking in the stuff, Claude Ann's brain must manufacture it by the gallon.

At the intersection with Lumahai Road, Dinah stopped to fish a stone out of her shoe and reconsidered. Why should she distrust Xander and swallow whole what Eleanor and Raif and even Jon had to say about him? They could be full of selfish motives. Raif was a proven sleazoid, Jon's insoluble problem with Xander could be a disagreement over the U.S. invasion of Iraq for all she knew, and

Eleanor's cryptic admonitions didn't inspire trust. Furthermore, it was patronizing to assume that Claude Ann wasn't capable of vetting a husband. She and Xander had spent the last six weeks together and, apparently, he had exhibited no signs of treachery or corruption or deal-breaking kinkiness. It was Claude Ann's heart and Claude Ann's money and Claude Ann's choice to make. To each her own. Everyone had flaws and if there was something flawed or fishy about Xander, it wasn't Dinah's place to point it out.

She turned down Lumahai Road and ran until it deadended. There was a sign to Spitting Cave with an arrow pointing down a steep dirt trail. Hair whipping in the breeze, she followed the arrow toward the sound of crashing waves. Where the trail ended, she was standing atop a bowl-shaped cliff of craggy, layered rocks that looked like brownie batter. Far below, where the waves pounded against the rock, a torrent of white water spat out of a cave and gushed into the turbulent blue water.

"The locals used to dive from here."

Dinah jumped back and whirled around. A few feet to her right, Lyssa Garst perched on a rock like the Little Mermaid.

"Lyssa." She blew out a breath. "You startled me."

"I thought you'd seen me." She adjusted her big, square sunglasses and turned her face toward the water. "It must have been exhilarating. Sixty feet into that maelstrom. They viewed it as a rite of passage."

"It must have been the last passage for some," blurted Dinah and kicked herself. Was this the cliff Leilani leapt from? Couldn't be. The family lived on the Big Island at the time.

Lyssa said, "It's a good place for thinking."

It seemed creepily morbid for a woman whose mother died in a suicide leap to spend her afternoon perched on a precipice musing about the thrill of it all. It seemed like a good idea to draw her away from the brink. She was wearing a blue track suit and running shoes.

"Did you jog here? We could jog back together."

Lyssa gathered her long hair on one side of her face and clambered to her feet. "I drove. May I give you a lift back to the hotel?"

"Sure."

"Raif said you didn't want to leave the hospital last night. I was asleep when he finally came in."

Dinah was immediately on her guard. "Xander went back to the hotel and I didn't want to leave Claude Ann alone in a strange place. I didn't mean to inconvenience Raif."

"I'm sure you didn't. He's a night owl."

They climbed back up the trail together. Two cars were parked in the cul-de-sac. Dinah hadn't noticed them on her way down. Lyssa pulled her key out of her jacket pocket, pushed the electronic door lock, and the taillights of a red Ferrari 458 winked on.

Dinah slid into the passenger seat with a tweak of envy. "I like your wheels."

"Raif bought it for me last year. He's a Ferrari devotee. I don't know why I haven't had it shipped back to the mainland before now. It's silly not being able to drive it except when I come to Honolulu. I wish Jon could enjoy it, but he almost never comes to the city." She opened the console and pulled out two bottles of Cachi Water. "Thirsty? I always carry extra."

"Thanks." Dinah luxuriated in the soft leather seat and rehydrated.

Lyssa started the engine and pulled into the street. The vroom of all those powerful Italian horses under the hood sent a tingle up Dinah's spine. It must be sweet to be able to afford a toy like this, and strange that the pleasure of driving it should be limited to periodic visits to the island. She recalled Xander's little gibe that Raif was only a regional driver. What kind of money did a regional NASCAR driver earn? She said, "Raif must be doing very well for himself. Who sponsors his racing team?"

"Durante's Auto Parts."

Dinah had never heard of it. "I guess he does product endorsements, too."

"Not yet."

Coy. Studied. Defensive. Lyssa must have had to defend Raif's reputation and accomplishments to Xander many times, and probably to Jon, as well. Perhaps she felt the need to defend her own judgment for marrying him. Maybe Raif was one of those Internet poker whizzes in his spare time and he really could afford to buy her a Ferrari, but Dinah shared Xander's suspicion that Lyssa subsidized her husband's high-rolling lifestyle with the money her grandfather left her and her finder's commissions on Hollywood props.

"Raif thinks Claude Ann is marrying Daddy for his money."

"Really?" Dinah kept her tone nonchalant. "And what do you think, Lyssa?"

"I think he's right. I wouldn't say she's a total gold digger, but Daddy's stinking rich. Has he told you about the brewery his German great grandfather founded in Munich?"

"Xander is one of the Garsts of Garst Brewery?"

"That's right. When my grandfather died, he divided his fortune between me and a female cousin. He was old-fashioned and believed that men should make their own way in the world, but girls should be cocooned in banknotes and securities. Of course, Daddy owns tons of stock in the company. Claude Ann is probably salivating to get herself named as a beneficiary in his will."

Dinah wasn't about to disclose Claude Ann's contribu-

tions to Xander to this cough drop, but there was a limit
to how much snarkiness she could stomach. "After what
happened to Claude Ann last night, it makes a person wonder if someone already named as a beneficiary is trying
to scare her off."

"That's absurd."

"So is the idea of Claude Ann as a gold digger."

"Money's always part of the equation." She turned her
head and her strangely notched nose twitched. "By the way,
I don't appreciate the way that you and your friend, Phoebe,
were hitting on Raif last night. Consider this a warning.
Lay off."

A string of scathing put-downs ran through Dinah's
mind, but the glaze of tears in Lyssa's eyes brought her up
short. Hard as it was to believe, she loved the rotter and
nothing Dinah could say would disabuse her. "I'll keep my
distance, Lyssa. You can rest assured."

Lyssa stopped at a crosswalk and waited for a mob of
pedestrians to straggle across. "Did Claude Ann tell you
that Daddy was once accused of rape?"

Dinah's jaw dropped. "By whom? When?"

"Oh, a few years ago. There were no charges. It may
have been a misunderstanding. The girl was kind of a flake.
She didn't go to the police."

"How do you know about this? Who's the woman? What
happened?"

"I'm sure Daddy's told Claude Ann. I mean, he'd have
to, wouldn't he? To inoculate her against hearing it from
somebody else."

The last straggler made it to the other side of the street.
Lyssa stepped on the gas and turned up the stereo full blast.
The pulsating beat of the Talking Heads' "Psycho Killer"
precluded any further inquiry. *Run, run, run, run, run, run,
run away.* Dinah leaned her head back and closed her eyes.

Oh, oh, oh, ay, ay, ay, woo. How, she asked herself, can otherwise intelligent women be so confoundingly, perversely, off-the-charts wrong about men?

EIGHTEEN

"Crazy what happened last night, eh? There's no telling anymore. Crazy world out there. Crazy, crazy. Who'd have believed her ex would blow in and go berserk? Watch your step." Wilhite welcomed Jon and his charges aboard his corporate plane, a twin engine Gulfstream turboprop, and guided them into the club-like cabin. This morning, he was clad in an eye-popping shirt that featured lime green and cobalt blue fish swimming against a magenta background.. Dinah wondered if he wore the loud shirts to draw people's eyes away from his ungainly, bowlegged spraddle.

The aircraft's plush leather seats were arranged for conversation like those in a train compartment with two facing forward and two aft. Xander and Claude Ann were already ensconced in the first two forward-facing seats drinking coffee from china cups. Claude Ann's left arm was in a sling. She wore a cast on her wrist and a skittish smile. Xander looked haggard, as if he hadn't slept in days.

Claude Ann held out her free arm to Marywave. "We're all gonna be okay, baby."

Marywave wrapped her arms around Claude Ann's neck and hugged her. "I prayed for you, Mama. I didn't mean for you to get hurt."

"I know you didn't. You just did what your daddy told you to do."

"I'm gonna wear the dress and carry your flowers, too. A froward heart shall depart from me. Psalms one-o-one, verse four."

"That bucks me up more than anything. I knew I could count on my girl."

Raif and Lyssa sat across from Xander and Claude Ann facing aft. Raif slouched behind his tray table shuffling a deck of cards. Lyssa browsed through a magazine.

Xander touched Jon's arm. "Jon, I need a few minutes. Raif and Lyssa, would you change seats and let Jon and Phoebe sit here? Jon and I need to talk and Claude Ann wants to brief Phoebe on how we're going to arrange for Marywave's care in light of Hank's attack."

"No problem." Raif closed his tray table, stood up and moved into the seat behind Xander so that they were sitting back to back.

Lyssa shot her father a resentful look before moving around to the seat next to Raif. She leaned close to Raif, but he didn't respond. He had already pulled down the tray table and resumed his trick shuffles.

"My pilot's ready as soon as we're all settled," said Wilhite, fiddling with his mobile. "Vaughn? Vaughn, can you hear me? Come back and clear these coffee cups, will you?"

A disembodied voice came over the PA system. "No problem."

Claude Ann let go of Marywave's hand. "Avery, will you show Marywave to her seat?"

"No problem."

If one more person said "no problem," Dinah was sure she would lose it.

Wilhite motioned Marywave into the seat across from Raif and Lyssa and made sure she was buckled in. Marywave nestled in and opened her Bible. The last two seats were situated in the very tail of the airplane. Dinah felt as if she'd been relegated to the back of the bus.

"Go ahead, Dinah," said Wilhite, gesticulating. "Sit, sit. I'll join you as soon as I've made sure we have all the bags and gear aboard. You gals don't travel light. Not a problem, of course. Lots of space."

Dinah sat down and glanced out the window. Was Hank out there somewhere watching them, plotting some fresh mayhem? Her brain was sluggish from information overload and sleep deprivation. When she and Jon were talking on the beach, had Jon mentioned that they'd be flying to Hilo on Wilhite's plane? Hank had probably heard everything they said. Was he crazy enough to plant a bomb? No. Not with Marywave on board. Anyway, surely the police had posted guards at the airport.

Hank was no longer a faraway problem, but if the police did their jobs, he was a jailable problem. The problem of Xander was more complicated and Dinah's determination not to meddle wavered with each new disclosure about him. An allegation of rape was pretty damned serious and, reported by his own daughter, it warranted a bit of Q and A. She wished she could have had a few words alone with Claude Ann. Hopefully, Xander wouldn't monopolize her all afternoon.

A crisply uniformed man with "Vaughn" stamped on his name tag took away the cups and saucers. Wilhite pulled out a walkie-talkie and informed somebody named J.J. that they were ready for take-off and, as the plane was backing away from the gate, he trotted to the rear of the plane and sat down next to Dinah. He had a file folder in his hand and flipped through a bunch of papers, moistening his thumb repeatedly.

The turboprop rolled out onto the tarmac and lined up behind a large commercial jet awaiting take-off. Dinah fastened her seatbelt and tried not to think about a bomb. She thought about Pash. Maybe the flaky girl who cried rape but didn't go to the police was named Pash.

In a few minutes, the Gulfstream accelerated down the runway and hurtled into the sky at a cookie-pitching angle.

Dinah's stomach tingled. She counted to ninety. Nothing exploded and she relaxed a hair.

Wilhite closed the folder and elbowed her in the ribs. "Nice view of Punchbowl crater."

She looked down at the sprawling city whose name in Hawaiian meant place of shelter. Where Claude Ann was concerned, it hadn't lived up to its name. "Mr. Wilhite, what does the name…?"

"Avery, please."

"Avery. What does the name Hilo mean?"

"Means to hang by a thread."

She tensed again. "Because it's in the path of a volcano?"

He erupted into convulsive laughter. The fish on his shirt jittered and shook. "A joke, Dinah! A joke! Hilo means thread in Spanish." His laughter tapered into a series of asthmatic wheezes. "Let's see. Hilo was an ancient Hawaiian navigator who sailed by the stars and the moon. Some call the first night of the new moon hilo, some say it's the first day of the month. Some of the old kam'ainas say it means twisted. You'll have to ask Jon what it means. He's a walking encyclopedia of Hawaiiana."

Thus far, Avery had been a walking encyclopedia of Hawaiian gossip. She had a feeling his brief explosion of temper last night was because he thought Eleanor had attacked Claude Ann and mucked up the party and he didn't want Mr. Jarvis, the prospective buyer of Uwahi, to see it. He had probably blamed Xander for not keeping his troublesome relative at bay. Xander had obviously put him wise this morning and Avery was animated and chipper. Jarvis would have no reason to associate an unfortunate domestic fracas with the Uwahi deal.

"Did you socialize much with Xander after Leilani died, Mr.…Avery?"

"Oh, sure. Not as much. Kay was all tied up with the children. Soccer and drama class, this and that. Of course,

whenever we barbecued or what have you, we included
Xander and his kids. Jon and Lyssa are the same age as
our two kids. They all grew up together."

"After Leilani, did Xander date anyone for very long?"

"No. None lasted longer than a year or so. All of them
dazzlers, but no point trying to remember their names.
Sally, Sara. They came and went. I think he was up-front
about not wanting to marry again 'til his kids were grown
up."

Dinah gave up on the girlfriends line of inquiry. Even if
Xander had dated a woman named Pash, she hadn't lasted
long enough for Avery to remember her name. However,
he seemed to know a lot about Jon and Lyssa.

She asked, "Has Jon changed much since his accident?"
Avery frowned and she realized her gaffe. "Psychologically, I mean."

The frown deepened and his eyes became solemn. He
glanced toward the front of the plane where Jon was sitting
and lowered his voice. "I've always felt guilty about what
happened. At the time, my daughter Tess was engaged to
marry Jon, but when she saw his burns, she couldn't go
through with it. Made me ashamed of her. Felt guilty for
bringing her up to be so wishy-washy. Don't be superficial,
I told her. It's what's under the skin that counts and Jon's
solid as they come, back of the net. Brains, integrity, all the
right stuff. But his scars grossed her out. Her word. Child-
ish. Put me off. Tells you something about the seriousness
of girls these days, eh? Of course, Tess was always high-
strung. In therapy ever since she left school."

Dinah caught her breath. Was being high-strung the
same as being a flake? "Were, or are, Tess and Lyssa good
friends?"

"The best, until Tess treated Jon so shabbily. Can't blame
Lyssa. Blood's thicker and all that." He skimmed a look
down the aisle toward Lyssa. "My personal take? Lyssa's

changed more than Jon since his accident. If you didn't know better, you'd swear…"

"What?" asked Dinah, anticipating the answer.

"Great Scott. I hadn't thought of it this way before, but… Well, it's almost as if she holds Xander responsible. Young girls. Strange as weather. Don't get 'em, myself."

NINETEEN

CLAUDE ANN HAD booked a hair appointment in Hilo for herself and Marywave and she was raring to be on her way. Dinah had no chance to speak with her alone. Xander had arranged a car for her and glued himself to her side as they walked through a mizzling rain to the Hertz lot.

Dinah poked her head under the umbrella Xander held over Claude Ann's head. "You can't drive with your arm in a sling, Claudy. I'll drive you."

"The sling's just 'cause my shoulder's sore. See?" She slipped her arm free and moved her arm up and down. "This little cast won't keep me from steerin' straight. You go on with Jon."

Xander said to Dinah, "I've assigned Jon the job of transporting the luggage and wedding paraphernalia and, of course, yourself to his place in Volcano. We'll camp with Jon tonight because Volcano's closer to the wedding site. You'll have your own cabin and nothing to do but relax until the party tonight."

"Fine." Dinah thought it something of a solecism to lump the maid of honor in with the wedding paraphernalia, but that was the least of his sins. "Claude Ann, my only dress was totaled in the blood bath last night. Let me go with you into town to buy another one."

"Not all of my clothes were ruined and I've got a couple of dresses that'll fit you just fine. Don't worry about anything except how you're gonna safety-pin me into my weddin' dress. This cast will never fit into the sleeve. Do you think we could slit open the seam and Velcro the thing closed around this cast? Oh, never mind. It's no biggie. We'll make it work."

Xander stopped next to a blue Buick and opened the driver's door for Claude Ann. He kissed her, helped her into the car, and stood back. "Be careful, darling."

"I will. Come on, Marywave. Hop in, baby. This'll be fun."

Marywave smiled and climbed in on the passenger side. Mother and daughter seemed to have forgiven one another their hala and put things to rights, their ho'oponopono brought about by Hank's insane act of spite.

Xander folded the umbrella and chucked it into the back seat. "You don't mind, do you, Dinah? Claude Ann and Marywave will need it to protect their coiffeurs." He gave Claude Ann's uncasted hand a last squeeze, as if he almost couldn't bear to see her go. "I love you."

"I know you do."

He waved good-bye, stuffed his hands in his pockets and, shoulders hunched against the heavy mist, walked back toward the terminal.

Claude Ann said, "He's got his own car parked here somewhere. He and Avery are going into town to talk business with Steve Sykes. He doesn't blame me at all for last night, Di. He was so sweet. He said nothin' in the world mattered to him but that I'm safe." She fastened her seat belt, started the car, and looked at her watch. "Omigosh! Gotta go. Bye!"

Dinah watched her drive off, then walked to a covered walkway across from the terminal and sat down on a bench to wait for Jon. She was glad, at least, of a chance to talk with him in private. She would ask him, obliquely, about Tess and see if she could coax some information out of him. If his fiancée was the girl Xander raped, that would definitely qualify as an insoluble problem.

Lyssa had rented a nondescript beige compact, quite a

comedown from the Ferrari on Oahu, and in a surprising turn of friendliness, she offered to take Phoebe to her favorite spa in Pahoa for a lomilomi massage. Phoebe jumped at the offer, probably in no small part because she didn't want to take any more flak from Dinah about Hank.

Raif rented a red Corvette. As he drove past Dinah, he cocked a finger pistol at her. "If anyone asks, I'm off to a private poker game in Pahoa." He spotted Avery, who was walking toward the parking lot with Vaughn, and cocked another finger pistol at him. Avery waved back distractedly, as if he had a million things on his mind, and glanced at his watch.

A half hour went by while Dinah sat looking out at the rain and brooding. She had read that Hilo was one of the wettest towns in the world, but the gray skies and drizzle seemed like a personal affront—a thumb in the eye from the local deities. Rain was part of the ceaseless war between Pele and her lover, Kamapua'a. Pele sent the fires that gave birth to the land, then Kamapua'a sent the rains that extinguished her fires. Wild boars dug up the lava and softened it so that seeds could take root and plants and trees eventually covered the island. Then Pele came along and destroyed it all again. Today, Kamapua'a clearly had the upper hand. Dinah was thinking about Jon's identification with Kamapua'a when a beat-up Suzuki Sidekick pulled up in front of her bench and beeped. Shave-and-a-haircut.

Jon leaned across the passenger seat and threw open the door for her. "This has worked out better than I thought it would. I'm glad it'll be just the two of us on the drive to Volcano."

She crawled in and buckled up without looking at him. That ill-considered kiss was going to come back and bite her. She just knew it. "How far?"

"To Volcano, thirty miles. To my place, another three." He seemed to sense the chill and curbed his enthusiasm.

The wipers scrubbed across the windshield and thunked at the end of their arc in a particularly irritating way without doing anything to improve visibility. She pulled a tourist map out of her purse and rubbed away the condensation on the inside of the windshield so she could see where they were going.

Highway 11, otherwise known as the Belt Road, was a two-lane thoroughfare that cut through the green interior of the island toward Volcanoes National Park. Modest houses lined the road on either side. As they got farther from Hilo, the houses became more widely spaced and the countryside more rural.

The Suzuki hit a pothole and jounced annoyingly. She said, "You need new shock absorbers."

Jon's burned side was toward her. He didn't turn, but his eyelid fluttered slightly, like a shrug. She found that even more annoying. "Tell me about Tess." So much for obliqueness.

He kept his eyes fixed on the road. "I see Avery's been bending your ear."

"He seems to think more of you than he does of his own daughter."

"I wouldn't put too much stock in his analysis of people or events. He's not someone people confide their secrets to."

"Did Tess not tell him that your father raped her? Or tried to rape her?"

He clenched his jaw. Shit. And she'd lectured him about tact. She massaged her temples. "I'm sorry, Jon. Truly, I am. I hope you'll chalk it up to a sleepless night and an overabundance of troubling indicators. Maybe I put something your sister said together with something Avery said and came up with a total blooper."

He made no comeback.

"Did I? Because I will grovel. I will abase myself. I will…"

"Tess was looking for an excuse to break it off with me. When she wasn't being cool and distant, she complained that she was bored. I thought she might be seeing someone else. I asked her if she wanted out of the engagement. She said no, she was just feeling nervous. Then one day she came to me crying hysterically with a story that Dad had raped her. I was stupefied. It seemed incredible. I didn't know whether to believe her or not. She could be fairly intense, but I couldn't believe she'd hallucinate being raped. I got drunk and fought with Dad. He denied it, said she must be crazy. The next day when I went to work, I was still angry, still not sure, probably still half-drunk. What happened was my own stupid fault, but Dad blames himself. When I ended up in the burn ward, Tess dropped by for a quick visit, recanted her story, and gave me back my ring."

"And she never told her father this story?"

"Obviously not. If Avery knew, he wouldn't still be chummy with Dad. He sure wouldn't have bought into his Uwahi deal."

"She told Lyssa."

"Somebody told her. Lyssa means well, but I don't need her pity and the last thing I want is for her to keep needling Dad. It's water over the dam. She's chosen to believe that Tess' recantation was the lie. I choose to believe the original accusation was the lie. And Dad just wants to make believe none of it ever happened. It's ripped us all apart."

Dinah felt an ache of sadness for them all. What a tangled web. If Xander had been falsely accused and it cost him the love and trust of his two children, how sad for him. How disheartening and lonely. It entered her mind that Xander might be another of Claude Ann's broken-winged birds, that her willingness to trust him so completely and her unshakable loyalty would be a balm to his spirit. But if Lyssa was right—

Jon said, "When Tess took back her story and kicked me in the teeth, Dad's version of events became a lot easier to believe." Dinah could commiserate. Too much of her own life had been spent choosing whose version of events to believe. "How long was it before she recanted?"

"Six days. That's how long before she visited me in the hospital."

"Does she still live in Hawaii?"

"She works for a travel agency in Hilo." He smiled that lopsided, self-mocking smile. "Makes for a sticky situation when we cross paths now and then. But she travels a lot and, anyhow, I don't get out as much as I used to."

"Stop! Pull over." Dinah rolled down her rain-streaked window.

The enormous banner was strung between two coconut palms in front of a yellow clapboard house with a corrugated metal roof. Jon drove onto the shoulder and she read the manifesto emblazoned in big red letters.

GOD IS NOT HAPPY! 50 YEARS OF LIES! SHAME ON YOU WHO CELEBRATE FRAUDULENT STATEHOOD AND HONOR THE THIEVES! THIEVES WHO LOCKED UP OUR QUEEN! THIEVES LIKE GARST WHO STEAL OUR LANDS! THIEVES WHO BEAT OUR ANCESTORS FOR SPEAKING THEIR LANGUAGE!

"Does one of Eleanor's disciples live here?"

"Eleanor, herself. It's an easy commute to the University of Hawaii campus in Hilo where she teaches."

"She's a professor?"

"That's right. Ethnobotany's her field. She knows everything there is to know about Hawaii's indigenous plants and how they've been used and misused over the years. She writes a weekly column for *The Tribune Herald*. Locals call her the poison lady." Dinah ran her eyes over the metallic lilac Cadillac taking up most of the length of the driveway. It looked like a relic from the Fifties with its elongated tail fins and protuberant red taillights. Even in the rain, they glittered like the orbs of Satan. "Is it also an easy commute from here to the wedding site?"

"It's not far."

Dinah took a deep breath. Why did everything have to be so complicated? She couldn't keep yo-yoing back and forth. She had to make up her mind whose version of events to believe, whether to support and defend the bride and forever hold her peace or gang up with the groom's many detractors. Somehow, Eleanor's over-the-top banner decided her. "Claude Ann's had enough bad luck, Jon. Will you ask Eleanor not to interfere with the wedding? You're her nephew. She'll listen to you."

"Nothing I could say would have any effect. Eleanor has her own agenda."

Dinah's temper boiled over. "Well, for crying out loud, what is it? Does she intend to kill Xander?"

He did the shrugging eyelid thing again, merged into traffic, and stepped on the gas.

Jerk. Dinah stared out at the wet road and listened to the annoying goddamned windshield wipers as they scrubbed and thunked like a jug band. At mile 29, a sign indicated the turnoff to Volcanoes National Park. Jon turned in the opposite direction onto Old Volcano Road, which seemed to have been hewed out of a rain forest.

Dinah rubbed her bare arms. "How can it be so cold in Hawaii in late June?"

"We're at four thousand feet. You may want a fire in your room tonight."

He turned down a one-lane road choked by tree ferns and honeysuckle and jounced along for about a mile before turning again onto a still narrower track. He drove for another mile and turned in through an open gate. There was a vine-covered, multi-car carport with a hanging wooden sign that said Wahilani, the place Xander had better not have mortgaged. Jon parked next to the only other car, a red Jeep Wrangler.

"Whose car is that?"

"Dad's. He keeps it around for the occasional guest. I'm supposed to crank it up every now and then, but I haven't done it in a long time. The battery's probably dead." He got out and opened Dinah's door for her. "I'll show you to your cottage and come back for the luggage." He led her along a misty footpath bordered by tree ferns and travelers trees and wild red anthuriums. "There are five cottages on the place. You'll be staying in mine. I've moved into the one next door for the weekend."

"That seems like a lot of unnecessary trouble."

"Less trouble than being dragged out of bed in the middle of the night to rescue you from the mongoose that lives under the cottage next door. I call him Hairy Potter." He spelled it.

"Ha-ha."

"Hairy sometimes slithers inside when the weather's nippy. When Phoebe gets here, she'll be in the third cottage, then Raif and Lyssa in the fourth. Dad's place is the one at the end of the property if you want to visit Claude Ann this afternoon before the party. It's the largest and has a spare bedroom for Marywave."

After about twenty yards, they arrived at a small cottage enveloped in a jungle of ferns and vines. He stepped up onto the lanai, took off his shoes, unlocked the door, and waited. Dinah noted the MAHALO, NO SHOES sign, slipped off her sandals, and set them on the rack. There was nothing else on the lanai except a single rocking chair, a barrel for rain catchment connected to the corrugated metal roof, and a weathered teak table upon which sat a fly swatter, a flashlight, a pair of binoculars, and a clean ashtray.

He held the door open for her. "A family of Kalij pheasants lives on the property and the birdwatching's good, especially early in the morning. You're welcome to stay on after the wedding." He said that last without looking at her.

They went inside and Jon's style was immediately apparent—spare and practical, yet refined. The walls, the planked floor and the high, beamed ceiling were gold cedar and none of the large windows had coverings or needed any. The view on all sides was forest. A sweet, woodsy smell permeated the room, which appeared to serve as both kitchen and den. There was a round table under one window with a bowl of anthuriums, a basket of fruit, a bottle of red wine, and a corkscrew. A pair of well-worn beige club chairs sat in front of a large black heater. The rest of the furnishings consisted of a tiny, two-burner stove, a large cupboard with a mini refrigerator on the bottom shelf, and a microwave oven on the top. A small stainless steel basin had been wedged into the corner.

"You'll find glasses in the cupboard and there are some fresh papayas and cheese in the fridge if you're hungry. The bedroom's in here." He opened French doors into an airy room with cedar book shelves on the back wall and, on the facing walls, the same wide, uncovered windows looking out on the jungle. There was one leather armchair, a card table with an open laptop and a stack of books and papers, and a platform bed under a rattan ceiling fan. "The bath and shower are through there. If you want to check your e-mail, feel free to use the computer."

"You have Wi-Fi here in the jungle?"

"All the conveniences of civilization." He turned back into the kitchen. "Come and I'll show you how to turn on the gas heater if you need it."

Dinah watched as he pointed out the switches and

buttons. "How long have you occupied this little corner of Paradise?"

"About five years. Dad wanted to build a resort hotel on the property, but I persuaded him to leave it green and let me build what I want. It's handy to the volcanoes and the U.S.G.S. Observatory where I do most of my work."

"It's beautiful. This close to the national park, it must be worth millions."

"Dad's promised it to me in his will."

"Aren't you afraid he'll change his mind after he and Claude Ann are married?"

"No." The voice of Johnny Cash blared from his jacket pocket. "I fell into a burnin' ring of fire..." He pulled out his cell phone, glanced at the caller's name, and shut it off. "I'll go and bring in the bags."

There was a loud clap, like thunder, and the floor jolted. Dinah grabbed onto him.

"Quake," he said as the bowl of anthuriums jumped off the table and smashed to smithereens at her feet. The dishes in the cupboard trembled and clinked for a few seconds and then the shaking stopped, as suddenly as it began.

"That was a good one. I'd better unload the luggage and head over to the Observatory to check the seismometers."

"Flaming Jerusalem! You're not going to leave me here alone, are you?"

He laughed. "You're not scared of a little earthquake, are you?"

She glared at him.

"I'll shut off the gas before I go. If there are aftershocks, keep away from the windows and crouch down in an interior corner. And if you want to visit any of the others when they get back from town, follow the path to your right where it forks."

TWENTY

DINAH PICKED UP the pieces of the broken bowl, threw them in the trash, and mopped up the water. She tossed the heart-shaped anthuriums loose into the sink and turned on the faucet to a slow drip. She didn't feel like looking for another vase or flower arranging. She fetched her pack of Sincerely Yours and her book of myths, put on a sweater, and went out on the lanai. As the crow flies, she couldn't be more than a couple of miles from the entrance to Volcanoes National Park and scores of people, but she'd never felt more isolated in her life. She wished she'd gone to the spa with Lyssa and Phoebe.

She lit a cigarette, inhaled like there was no tomorrow, and opened her book to the story of how the world was created. All was Chaos. She blew out a cloud of smoke. Based on her Hawaiian experience, not much had changed.

She read on. There was no form or meaning until the god Kane lobbed a giant gourd into the air and created the sky. (There was no explanation as to how the gourd came into existence, but Dinah wasn't a stickler.) The seeds of the gourd scattered across the darkness and became the sun and moon and wheeling constellations. Kane used the rest of the gourd to fashion the earth. A few helper gods pitched in and formed the sea and land and living creatures and when Kane was satisfied with the end product, he set about to design an ali'i nui or ruling chief who would have dominion over this new Earth. After tinkering around for a while with stone and bark, he took a hunk of red clay, shaped it in his own image, breathed life into it, and dubbed this first man Kumu-honua. After Kane made his Adam, he tackled the job of making a first woman. And just as in the Hebrew book of Genesis, he made her out of the sleeping man's rib. Her name was Ke-ola-ku-honua and, right off the bat, she let a lizard con her into eating a kapu breadfruit, which got the couple evicted from their pleasant garden.

According to this version of the myth, there were so many parallels between the Hebrew and the Hawaiian creation stories that some religious anthropologists theorize that there must have been a cross-cultural link between the early Polynesians and the Jews. One historian even surmised that the Menehune, a race of dwarfs from whom the Hawaiians were thought to have descended, might be one of the lost tribes of Israel.

Dwarfs. She squashed her cigarette in the ashtray. Why had no one ever told her that Hawaii was this weird?

There was an aftershock. The shoes danced on the rack and a windchime made of mangled spoons and forks jingled madly. Just a little jiggler, she told herself. She went to the kitchen and raided the fridge. There were some individually wrapped wedges of cheese and sliced papayas. She sat down at the table and ate. This was the perfect opportunity to nap, but she was too nervous and antsy. She looked out the large picture windows at the rain forest. What if Hank had slipped through the police net? He could be lurking out there with Claude Ann's Beretta, waiting for her to return. Maybe he had tried to communicate with Marywave again. Dinah pulled Marywave's cell phone out of her purse, flipped it open, and tried to check the voice mail. The battery was dead.

An hour had passed since Jon left. Where did he keep the keys to that Wrangler? Maybe that battery wasn't dead. Maybe she could take it out for a short drive, get a better sense of where she was, and lose the heebie-jeebies. She ransacked the place, but had no luck. She was stranded with nothing to do but wait, her least favorite thing.

She went back to the lanai, picked up the book of myths, and read about Lono. Lono was one of the founding movers and shakers of the cosmos—god of the sun and of wisdom, god of fertility and agriculture, and CEO of the weather, including hurricanes and earthquakes. He was a happy god, happy in his work and happy in his marriage. His wife was the comely Kaikilani, a goddess in her own right. While Lono went about presiding over the rain and wind and ambient temperature, Kaikilani disported herself from island to island as a sort of ambassadress to the little people. The kanaka maoli. One day, in her democratic zeal, she had an extramarital roll in the ferns with a no-class kanaka from Molokai, a perfidy Lono could not tolerate. He slew the faithless goddess, packed his canoe, and vacated the islands, leaving the weather to regulate itself. His Second Coming had been prophesied for generations. The long, humdrum stretch of time, during which there was nothing to do but wait for his return, was called kulo'ihi.

There was no second coming of Jon or anyone else. The only thing that came was another aftershock. I'm trapped in kulo'ihi, thought Dinah. Another hour crawled by and then two. She smoked another cigarette, but she couldn't read anymore. Lono reminded her of Hank and Hank reminded her of the Beretta. It was only a half-hour drive from Hilo to Volcano. How long could they dilly-dally with their hair and their lomilomis? Why hadn't she written down Claude Ann's cell phone number?

She searched the cottage until she found the Hilo Yellow Pages tucked away in the cupboard and called every beauty salon and spa in the list, but none had heard of Ms. Claude Ann Kemper. She found the Volcano Village directory, looked up the number of the U.S.G.S. Observatory, and asked for Jon. The man she spoke with said that Jon had taken a few days off for his father's wedding and would she like to leave a message. She considered asking whether Jon made a habit of going walkabout in the wake of Pele's tantrums, but self-censored and rang off in frustration. Where had he gone and why had he lied?

Well, there was nothing for it but to chill out and entertain herself as best she could until the laggards returned. She looked through the shoebox of CDs she'd seen in Jon's bedroom. He seemed to favor an artist named Israel "Iz" Kamakawiwo'ole. As shown on the cover of one CD, Bruddah Iz was a mountain of a man, 700 pounds at least, with dark shades on his eyes, a straw boater on his head, and a small, round mouth overarched by a thin mustache. She was unfamiliar with Hawaiian music, but assumed it would be soothing. She pulled out a few disks, inserted them in Jon's Bose, and lay down on the bed to listen.

Bruddah Iz's voice was surprisingly light for such a large man. It seemed to float on a strong current of melancholy. He strummed a ukulele and sang alternately in Hawaiian and English. When he crooned the words "cry for the land that was taken away," Dinah felt a tug at her heart. His voice expressed with a soft poignance what Eleanor and her partisans expressed with threats and angry signs. The music lulled her into a Hawaiian state of mind where time ceased to matter. She was on island time. By the time Bruddah Iz segued into a bouncy rendition of "Over the Rainbow," she was feeling as soothed as if she'd spent the afternoon being coddled at the spa.

At four o'clock, the drizzle stopped and an anemic sun filtered through the trees. She went onto the lanai, laced up her Nikes, and went for a jog. At four-forty-five, she returned to the cottage. Still no one had returned. So much the better. She took a leisurely shower, picked out a not-too-wrinkled shirt and slacks for tonight's party, and dressed. She went back to the kitchen area and noticed the forgotten red anthuriums in the sink. She supposed she ought to be a good guest and find another container for them.

She went to the cupboard and rummaged around behind the mugs and plates. A cereal bowl was too shallow and a tea glass too tall. She pushed aside a platter on the top shelf and saw a framed 5 x 7 photograph of the smiling young Xander standing on a beach next to a smiling, dark-haired beauty who had to be Leilani. In the foreground, two laughing little children, a boy and a girl, chased after a beach ball. Dinah took the picture to the table and sat down to study the happy family. How could anyone look at this idyllic scene and imagine that the woman's pretty smile hid thoughts of suicide?

An edge of paper peeked out from the back of the frame. Dinah removed the back and unfolded a yellowed photocopy of a news article datelined San Francisco, November 4, 1989. "Earth Sciences Conference Marred by Death."

Someone tapped smartly on the door. She looked up and two policemen in uniform were peering in at her through the glass panel. One of them signalled for her to come. A queasy sensation came over her, a premonition that what they had to say would not be good. She forced herself up, forced herself to walk across the room, forced herself to open the door.

"Is Lyssa here?" asked a baby-faced cop with a blond soul patch and a grave manner.

She shook her head.

"How about her brother, Jon?"

"No."

"Do you know how to reach either of them?"

"No. What's wrong?"

The other cop had sad, pouchy eyes that telegraphed bad news. "Are you a relative?"

In the sense that all mankind descended from the same Mitochondrial Eve, she was a relative. "Yes. Has something happened to their father? To Xander Garst?"

"It's Mr. Raiford Reid. He's been murdered. His body was discovered next to a fresh lava flow a little over an hour ago."

PART II

TWENTY-ONE

DINAH SAT DOWN on the lanai and smoked another cigarette. She was in a state of suspended animation, unable to process this whammy and unwilling to think about what might follow. The younger policeman had apparently gone to school with Lyssa and he'd asked permission from his supervisor to deliver the news to her in person. The two men made a few desultory comments while they waited, mostly about the earthquake. It had cracked a couple of side streets in Hilo and they'd heard a report of a landslide makai of Pahala. They recalled the quake of 2006, which had cause considerable damage to the northwest corner of the island. This time it was the south's turn. But as Dinah struggled to assimilate the stark reality of Raif's murder, the earthquake's terrors receded in her mind.

At six o'clock, the sound of slamming car doors brought her to her feet and galvanized the cops. They hurried down the path toward the carport. Dinah slid into her sandals and tagged after them. The widow had arrived. Lyssa wore an inquiring half-smile as she got out of the car. "Mark, hello. Did somebody vandalize Jon's mailbox again?"

The younger policeman, Mark, took her arm. "It's about Raif, Lyssa."

"Come on, Mark, did you have to arrest him? You've been known to play a friendly game of cards, yourself."

"It's not that. He's been murdered, Lyssa. Shot to death in a lava field west of the Pahoa Highway near Kalapana."

She looked blank. "Murdered?"

Mark held onto her arm. "A couple of park rangers on horseback found him."

Phoebe came around the side of the car and covered her mouth with her hands. "Dear God! Raif's dead?"

Mark said, "Homicide detectives and the medical examiner are on the scene now. They'll be here to talk with you in a little while."

Lyssa broke into a welter of sobs. Dinah vacillated, waiting for Mark or Phoebe to do something or say something. When they didn't, Dinah put her arms around Lyssa and murmured something inane. "There, there" was about all she could come up with. She wished she could offer the girl some interpretation of this horror that she could understand and take comfort from, but she couldn't. She could think of no silver lining, no light at the end of the tunnel, no mitigating factors of any kind whatever. She felt, as she always did, useless in the face of grief. Raif's death was a bolt out of the blue and Dinah had no inkling how to construe it, let alone how to help Lyssa bear up to it.

"Phoebe? You're a comforter. You're a life coach. Help me out here."

But Phoebe stood frozen with her hands still covering her mouth.

"There, there, Lyssa. There, there." Where the hell was Xander? Where was Jon?

At last, Mark took the initiative. "Let's walk up to Jon's cottage, Lyssa. Come on. Ms. Pelerin can make you some tea or something while we wait for Jon to get home." He took her arm and nudged her ahead of him up the path. "Travis, will you give her dad's number another try? And her brother's?"

"What was he doing in Kalapana?" Lyssa asked in a broken voice. "Mark, are you sure?"

"That's what the detectives are trying to find out. He

left his rental car on the side of the road. That's how they know it's Raif."

Dinah frowned. His wallet must have been stolen or they'd know who it was from his driver's license. He must have been robbed by one of the people he'd played poker with. Raif was a smart-alecky playboy who relished acting like an outlaw, probably because he thought it made him look cool. But not all of the people who violated the state's anti-gambling law would be harmless rascals. Raif must have tangled with a player who didn't care for his attitude or his winning ways.

Another car pulled into the drive. Dinah turned and saw Jon get out of the Sidekick.

"Officer Travis, what's up?"

Travis walked over and said a few words to him. Jon flung an uncertain look up the path and started after Lyssa.

"I guess there won't be a wedding after all," he said to Dinah and kept walking.

For the first time, Dinah thought about Claude Ann and the hideous undoing of her perfect wedding. She would need a lot of there-thereing, herself. Jon could give Lyssa her tea. Or Phoebe, who had rallied enough to follow the others toward the cottage. The maid of honor would wait here by the carport for the bride and give her a shoulder to cry on. Claude Ann would probably feel guilty for her facetious wish that Raif and Lyssa would drive off a cliff into the ocean.

Xander pulled his gold Lexus under the carport and got out. "Is something wrong, Officer?" He huddled with Travis for a few minutes and reacted as if he'd been physically struck.

Travis reached out and steadied him. "Do you need help walking to the cottage, sir?"

"No. No, I'm all right. Is my daughter, is Lyssa here? Has she been told?"

"Yes, sir. Her brother's with her."

As Xander slogged up the path, he looked like a man on the way to his own hanging. He seemed not to see Dinah as he passed by. He was probably grappling with how to express his sympathy and regret for the death of a man whom he detested.

Travis followed Xander, as if he didn't believe he could make it by himself.

Dinah said, "I'm waiting for Xander Garst's fiancée and her daughter. They should be here any minute."

"So should the detectives. Tell them where we are, will you?"

"Yes, of course."

Dinah tried to swallow the knot in her throat. This would be the second time she'd had to tell Claude Ann that her dream wedding had turned into a nightmare. Thank God, she didn't have to tell her that Xander was dead. Their wedding could never be entirely dissociated from the terrible thing that had happened today, but they were alive and in love and not all happy marriages were formed in the month of June.

A car squealed around a corner close by and Dinah found herself wringing her hands.

The blue Buick swerved into the driveway, slinging gravel, and screeched to a stop behind the patrol car. Claude Ann swung out of the car with a big smile. "I shopped too long and the time got away from me. We're gonna be late to the party. Come on with me and I'll show you a darling dress I think you should wear."

"There won't be a party, Claude Ann."

Her smile wilted as she took in the police car. "Have those protesters been here?"

"No, Claudy."

Marywave got out of the car and came around to her mother's side.

"Did they bring my daddy? Is he here?"

Claude Ann pulled Marywave in front of her and rested her hands on the girl's shoulders. "They wouldn't do that, would they?"

"No."

"Then what's the fuzzmobile doin' here?" She tightened her grip on Marywave's shoulders. "You look like hell. Did something bad happen to Hank?"

"It's Raif, Claudy. He's dead. Murdered."

TWENTY-TWO

THE SAVAGE, UNABLE to grasp the mysteries of nature or control its upheavals, ascribes his ups and downs to the will of some all-powerful, all-knowing deity—a deity who can send rain or drought, feast or famine, victory or defeat. But the deity's criteria for meting out these rewards and punishments aren't always clear. It's the shaman's job to interpret the deity's judgments and policies in terms the savage mind can understand and accept. In ancient Hawaii, this job fell to the kahuna pule, or priest. The detectives' dry account of Raif's demise fell short of imparting understanding.

One of the detectives, a youngish Japanese man with spiky, bleach-blond hair who identified himself as Lt. Kimo Fujita, described the circumstances of the murder. "Mr. Reid's body was discovered at approximately three-fifty this afternoon by park service personnel near Kalapana. He had been shot in the forehead at point-blank range and either fell or was dragged very close to a bed of liquid lava." He opened his notebook and read. "Due to the extreme heat, it will be difficult to establish an exact time of death."

Jon was the first to register acceptance of the murder as a fact. "He must have been at least partially cremated."

"You'll want a closed casket," said Lt. Vince Langford, the senior detective. He had beady, suspicious eyes and an underslung, bulldog jaw.

Dinah shuddered. No wonder the police had to confirm his identity through the rental car agency.

Lyssa buried her face against Jon's chest and sobbed. He held her, but his expression was strangely cold and absent.

Claude Ann and Phoebe, who sat across from each other at the kitchen table, traded horrified stares.

"Yuck," said Marywave, clinging to the back of her mother's chair.

Xander went to the cupboard, pulled out a bottle of Scotch and five glasses, and poured. He offered one to Lyssa, but she wouldn't take it. Claude Ann and Jon each took one. Phoebe pressed a tissue against her nose and shook her head, no. Dinah, her back braced against the wall, accepted her glass with alacrity but her hands shook so that she had trouble getting it to her lips without spilling. Xander returned to stand beside the cupboard, but his eyes stayed on Lyssa.

Lt. Langford stood in front of the door with his hands behind his back and surveyed the room. "We'll need to know how and when Mr. Garst and the rest of you arrived on the island?"

Jon helped Lyssa into a chair and chugged his Scotch. "Our flight from Honolulu landed in Hilo at eleven-thirty. It was a corporate plane owned by my father's business partner, Avery Wilhite."

"Eleven-thirty," repeated Langford. "Didn't take long for Mr. Reid to get himself killed."

"The earthquake must have opened up a skylight," said Jon.

"What's a skylight?" asked Dinah.

"Magma is what lava is called before it breaches the earth's crust. Magma flows underground through long tubes. When the roof of one of those tubes collapses, the magma is exposed. Volcanologists call those openings sky-lights. The earthquake or the aftershock must have frac-tured the crust down near Kalapana, or maybe the weight of Raif's body caused it to break through."

Lyssa raised her swollen eyes to Jon. "Raif was afraid

of volcanoes and lava. Why would he be walking around in a lava field?"

Langford's eyes roved the room scrutinizing everyone and everything. He stopped in front of Jon and gave him a hard look. "In the span of two weeks, Hawaii County's had two homicides. One man beaten and shoved into a steam vent, now another shot in the head and shoved into a sky-light. I'm seeing what I guess you could call a geothermal pattern. Would you agree, Mr. Garst?"

"So it would seem." Jon came across as guarded and defensive, a cat with his back up.

"Ever meet an archaeologist named Patrick Varian?" goaded Langford.

"No."

"Hmm." It was the hmm of a prosecutor. Langford rambled around the room with his hands behind his back. "Did Mr. Reid own a gun?"

Lyssa roused herself. "He hated guns."

"Maybe Raif had changed his mind," said Xander. "He had a gambling problem or, I should say, a money problem. He owed quite a lot. I don't know how much, but he was worried. He had asked me for money several times."

"Liar." Lyssa's mouth contorted with rage. "You've always despised him and now you're glad that he's dead. I hate you."

"You're wrong, Lyssa. I'm…I won't lie to you. I didn't respect Raif. Maybe I did despise him, but good God, I never wished him dead." Xander drank his Scotch and poured himself another. "I love you. I'm appalled by Raif's murder, if that's what it was."

Claude Ann left the table and went to stand beside Xander. "Xan's right. How come you're so sure it was a homicide, Lieutenant? Maybe it was suicide. Maybe he shot himself."

Lyssa lashed out at her. "How can you suggest such a

horrible thing? Raif wasn't like my mother. He loved his life. He loved me." She dissolved into tears again.

Phoebe walked over and tried to take her hand to comfort her. "You were blessed to have Raif for a little while, Lyssa. Be thankful for the time you had."

"Shut up or I'll kill myself," Lyssa snarled.

Langford paced around the room for a minute. After a couple of circuits, he came to a halt directly in front of Lyssa. "Did Mr. Reid carry a cell phone?"

"Of course, he did. An iPhone. He called the spa where Phoebe and I were and left a message. He wanted to meet us and go for a drink when we were finished with our treatments."

"What time was that?" asked Langford.

"I'm not sure. A little after four, I think."

Langford and Fujita exchanged a look.

Dinah got it at once. If Raif's body was discovered at three-fifty, he couldn't have made that call. "Did you not find the phone with the body?"

"We did not," said Langford.

Jon walked over to the cupboard and refilled his glass with Scotch. "A murderer would've tossed the gun and the phone into the lava. They would've melted and been untraceable."

"The only smart murderers are in murder mysteries," said Langford. "And tossed phones don't call and leave messages. But it's funny you should mention tossing the gun into the lava. Mr. Reid's murderer tried that, but either he throws like a girl or his aim was off. The gun missed the fire and I guess the surrounding ground was too hot for him to retrieve it and try again." His suspicious eyes panned the room. "Any of the rest of you own a gun?"

"No," said Claude Ann.

Dinah lanced her a warning look.

"Not at this time," she said without batting an eye.

"My ex-husband kept guns." She held up her casted wrist. "Thanks to him, I spent last night in the Honolulu hospital. I'd like to know if he's been arrested yet."

"Name?" growled Langford.

"Henry J. Kemper. Hank. The police on Oahu were still looking for him when we left this morning."

"We'll look into it. Can you think of any reason why Mr. Kemper would want to harm Mr. Reid?"

"No." Claude Ann appeared nonplussed. "No. Hank and Raif never met."

"My daddy wouldn't break the Commandment against killing," said Marywave. "He's a born-again Christian."

Xander wrapped an arm around Claude Ann's shoulders. "Why are you asking us about guns, Lieutenant Langford? No one in this family had any reason to harm Raif. You should be questioning the gamblers he kept company with, the people he owed."

Dinah remembered Raif's finger-pistol farewell. "When Raif drove away from the airport this morning, I think it was about eleven forty-five, he told me he was on his way to a private poker game in Pahoa."

"Probably run by George Knack," said Xander. "I can't believe the police haven't been able to shut Knack down. Everybody knows what he does."

"Everybody suspects what he does." Langford's voice was matter-of-fact. "If Knack runs an illegal game, he hides it well. The FBI has been sniffing around him for two years and they can't nail him. He has a sixth sense about undercover heat."

"You might ask him why he was in Honolulu last night," said Jon. "He horned in on the family's private party. I was showing him the door when we heard Claude Ann call for help."

Fujita stood next to the front door in his sock feet. Dinah

had never encountered such a polite cop. He jotted a lengthy note on his notepad, which had alphabetical tabs.

Langford waited for him to stop writing. "Other than Knack or the people Reid played poker with, is there anyone else who.might have a grudge against him? Anyone who felt strongly enough to murder him?"

Lyssa blew her nose. "Raif played poker, Officer. It was recreational. There are illegal games going on all over Hawaii—illegal card games, illegal video slots, illegal bookmaking, and cock-fighting, too. My God, even Bingo's illegal here. People want to gamble. This state's stupid law was made to be broken. As for the money, Raif was a professional race car driver and I have money of my own. He would have told me if he had gambling debts. We could have paid them. Whatever the reason he was murdered, it had nothing to do with his gambling."

"There's some logic to that," said Langford. "Wouldn't make much sense to kill a man before he's paid his debt. But these private games, you never know. Somebody could've gotten his ego bruised or owed your husband and didn't want to pay. Did Mr. Reid tell you about any big wins he'd had lately?"

"No."

"We'll dig around and see if we can find out who else might have been playing poker in Pahoa today. Meanwhile, we'll need statements from all of you regarding your whereabouts between eleven-thirty and four and the names of any witnesses who can corroborate it. We'll want to obtain fingerprints, but that can wait until tomorrow."

"From us?" Lyssa's eyes riveted on her father. "Why do we have to be fingerprinted?"

"A formality," said Fujita. He shifted from one socked foot to another, as if he'd found some glass shards Dinah's cleanup had missed. "To rule out those who didn't handle the weapon."

"Let's begin with you, Mrs. Reid." Langford rubbed his palms together in a manner that Dinah saw as almost sadistic. "Where did you go when you left the airplane?"

"Phoebe and I went to a day spa. Peacequest, in Pahoa."

"Peacequest." The name seemed to surprise Langford. "Were you in the same room?"

"No. We opted for different treatments."

"I had the seaweed facial and the salt glow," said Phoebe.

"Thank you." Langford didn't ask Lyssa about her treatment. He turned to Jon. "And you, Mr. Garst? Where were you?"

"I drove here from the airport with Ms. Pelerin. We got here about twelve-thirty and I showed her around. When the quake struck a little after one, I left. I intended to go to the Observatory, but I changed my mind and drove down the Chain of Craters Road to Holei."

"And why was that, sir?"

"To look for damage. I sat on the cliffs for a while, thinking."

"Thinking." Langford's eyes glinted.

"That's right."

"Alone?"

"Yes. Alone."

Dinah massaged her temples. What was it about these Garsts that moved them to do so much of their thinking alone on clifftops?

Marywave allowed as how she and her mother had gone to the beauty parlor to have their hair done for the wedding. "I got a princess updo. Mama got a Grecian goddess."

Dinah hadn't even noticed their hair. Marywave's looked sleek and carefully arranged. She couldn't tell any difference between Claude Ann's regular style and the Grecian goddess.

Claude Ann provided the name of the salon, Nani's Cliptomania on Kalanianaole Street. "When Nani finished with me, I left Marywave there and went shopping in the Prince Kuhio Plaza."

"Which shops did you visit?"

"Macy's and maybe another boutique or two. I don't recall the names."

"Make any purchases?"

"No. When I was through shopping, I went back to Nani's and picked up Marywave."

Langford swiveled around to face Dinah. "What about you?"

"I was here. I tried to find the keys to Xander's Wrangler to go for a drive, but I couldn't. Anyhow, Jon told me the battery was probably dead."

"Hmm. And Mr. Xander Garst, where did you spend the afternoon?"

"I drove to my house in Kapoho. Ms. Kemper and I are to be married—were to be married—tomorrow morning. I was making sure everything was ready for us to move in."

"Kapoho. That's what, eight, ten miles from Pahoa? Maybe ten or twelve to Kalapana?"

"Thereabouts." Xander fixed him with a stony look.

Fujita turned to the W tab in his notepad. "You said that you flew to Hilo with Mr. Avery Wilhite. Where can we reach him?"

"Christ!" Xander raked his forelock out of his eyes. "He's probably at the Kilauea Lodge right now. We were supposed to meet there for dinner and a pre-wedding party. We should be there now. I'll call the lodge and explain."

"You're free to go if you'd rather explain in person," said Langford. "We're finished here for now."

Fujita passed out cards with his and Langford's contact numbers. "We'll be back in the morning with our forensics people to collect everyone's fingerprints."

As the detectives prepared to leave, so did everyone else.

Lyssa clutched Jon's hand. "Will you come with me while I phone Raif's parents?"

"You know I will."

"You, too, Phoebe. I'm sorry I snapped at you. I'd like you to stay with me for a while."

Lyssa was the first out the door, followed by her two comforters, Jon and Phoebe.

Xander whispered something in Claude Ann's ear. She whispered in Marywave's ear and the three of them left without so much as a backward glance at Dinah.

Langford stood on the lanai and watched everyone troop off into the gathering gloom while the exceptionally polite Fujita sat down and put on his shoes.

Nothing ventured, nothing gained, thought Dinah. "Lieutenant, if it's not classified information, what kind of gun was used in the shooting?"

His jaw jutted as he appeared to take her measure. "I don't see that it matters. It was an old Beretta. Until it landed near that skylight, somebody had taken real good care of it."

Dinah made a superhuman effort to return Langford's stare without shrieking. She thanked him, said good-bye, and went back inside. Shell-shocked, she sat down at the kitchen table to think. The framed photograph of Xander and Leilani was still there, but the article about the death that marred the conference in California was gone.

TWENTY-THREE

DID CLAUDE ANN think the Hawaii police wouldn't communicate with the Honolulu police and find out about the missing gun? Jon was back at the door before Dinah had conjured up anything close to a rational reason for her lie. "Dad and Claude Ann have gone to the lodge for dinner. Will you come?"

"What about Lyssa?"

"After she talked to Raif's mother, she took a sleeping pill. She'd rather be unconscious."

"What about Phoebe and Marywave?"

"Phoebe volunteered to stay with Marywave. They've ordered in a pizza. I haven't eaten all day and I'm starved. How about you?"

Dinah wasn't hungry, but she didn't want to be alone and she was in a swivet to speak to Claude Ann about the gun. She grabbed her purse and followed him to the car.

"What do you think Raif was doing out on that lava field, Jon?"

"He may have gone to meet someone on the sly."

"A woman, you mean?"

"Lyssa would never believe it but, as you've guessed, Raif played around."

"But he would've met a lover at the No-Tell Motel, not in the middle of a lava field."

"Maybe she wasn't a tourist. Hawaii, or at least this corner of it, is like a small town. Everybody knows everybody. Maybe they planned to make love in the back seat of the car."

"The 'Vette he rented didn't have a back seat."

"I don't know, Dinah. It was probably connected to his gambling. Like Langford said, maybe somebody owed him and chose not to pay."

Dinah wished. But how likely was it that another somebody in this corner of the island had a grandfather who willed him an Italian gun? "Who died in California back in eighty-nine?"

"I don't know what you're talking about."

"There was an article about a death at an earth sciences conference behind a picture of your mom and dad."

"I'd forgotten I had it. It was Steve's dad."

"Louis Sykes?"

"That's right. He got tanked and drowned in the hotel swimming pool."

"Why would someone take it?"

"Why would you take the picture apart to snoop?" He let out a prodigious sigh. "Sorry, but I've got more pressing things to think about than a death that happened over twenty years ago."

"Right."

He drove to the front door of a rustic lodge lit up like Christmas. The parking lot overflowed with traffic and the raucous sound of Bavarian polka music spilled out into the night. Dinah flashed him a quizzical look. "This is where you come after a death in the family?"

"The Kilauea's a busy place, but the back room's reserved for us. Go on in and I'll try to find a place to park."

She had a yeasty feeling in the pit of her stomach, a feeling that several members of the wedding were lying their heads off. Claude Ann's lie about the gun was the most bothersome. She had no conceivable motive to murder Raif, but the world was too full of nuts for cops to be finicky about motive. If Claude Ann's Beretta was the murder weapon, if her fingerprints were found on it, if Hank didn't come forward and confess to having stolen it—well, the fallout didn't bear thinking on. Xander's reaction to the murder had seemed labored and unnatural, and to say that Lyssa had looked at him askance was putting it mildly. Jon's alibi, not to mention his scientific detachment and his defensive attitude, hadn't gone over with Detective Langford. It pained Dinah to acknowledge any similarity between herself and a sourpuss like Langford, but his barefaced disbelief mirrored her own exactly.

She climbed the steps and entered the noisy dining room. On one side of the room was a cheerful fire blazing in a big stone fireplace. A roisterous group milled around the sofa and coffee table in front of the fire, toasting each other with ornate beer steins. Some wore green paper Bavarian hats with feather flourishes. Others wore pointy alpine hats with colorful braid bands. The men wore lederhosen and suspenders. The women wore dirndls. An accordion player in full Tyrolian garb strolled among the tables. The rest of the band—a trombone, a tuba, a trumpet, and a zither—occupied a makeshift stage in the far corner and played as if to raise the roof. A couple polkaed somewhat drunkenly in front of the stage.

Dinah cupped her hands to her mouth and shouted at a harried looking waitress carrying a tray full of drinks. "Where is the Xander Garst party?"

"You'll have to ask the hostess. It's Volksfest night." She balanced her heavily loaded tray against her mid-section and plunged off into the hurly-burly.

Dinah stood at the vacant hostess station and scoped out the crowd. At the rear of the room, she spotted Avery Wilhite in a neon-blue shirt with electric yellow lines squiggling across it like sea snakes. At least, he wore long pants. He waved to her and she threaded her way between the tables until she reached him.

"Hell of a thing," he said, taking her hand and patting

it as if she were the bereaved. "Shocking. Unbelievable. Guns everywhere. Jon with you?"

"He'll be in as soon as he finds a parking space."

"Most of the guests have been sent home, but Steve and I stayed. What are friends for? Go on in. Go, go." He pointed at a door with a Private sign. "Jon and I will round up a waiter."

She opened the door and went inside. The first thing she noticed when she closed the door was the tomb-like quiet. The second thing was the odor of stale grease and cigar smoke. The room was windowless and mirrorless and the walls had been padded with a quilted, maroon fabric that muffled sound and collected odors. The murky lighting brought to mind stories of the yellow fogs of Victorian London. On the side of the room opposite the door, Claude Ann and Xander sat on a maroon velveteen banquette gabbing with a very large man who made sweeping gestures with a fat cigar.

In the center of the room was a rectangular table. At the far end, Steve Sykes sat with three men she'd never seen before. Steve looked up and showed her a smile and she realized how long it had been since she'd seen one. It was magnetic. She had to hold herself back from running toward him.

He stood up. "We keep meeting in the scariest circumstances. How's Lyssa?"

"I don't know what she must feel. I hope I never do."

He introduced her to the other men at the table. They were all Xander's co-workers from the U.S.G.S. They asked her to pass on their condolences to Lyssa, but they seemed ill at ease. Obviously, murder wasn't the attraction that had brought them to the lodge this evening and it had put the quietus on their revelry. They must have felt obliged to stay on a decent length of time to show solidarity with their colleague.

Steve walked her away from the table. "Those are the oldtimers who've worked with Xander for years. They were at Lyssa's wedding, although I doubt they knew Raif except in connection with her. They're friends of Avery's, too, going back to the time he worked for the Survey."

"Avery's a volcanologist, too?"

"He was some variety of geologist before he began dabbling in real estate and started his own acquisition business. He knows the older U.S.G.S. crowd anyhow."

"Who's that talking with Xander and Claude Ann?"

"Paul Jarvis. Uwahi closes day after tomorrow and Paul was invited to the party and the wedding. Xander and Avery called off the party and notified most of the guests not to show, but they wanted Paul here to reassure him that what happened to Raif was unrelated to business and all systems are still go with Uwahi."

The door opened and Avery and Jon walked in to the rollicking strains of Beer Barrel Polka. When the door closed, it was quiet again.

"The bar's back in the main dining room," said Steve. "Would you like something before dinner?"

"I had a hit of Jon's Scotch earlier. I'll coast." The word reminded her of Raif, who said that coasting was for losers. "Maybe a glass of red wine. You choose."

Steve left and she sat down with the oldtimers and listened as they talked shop. One of them talked about doing a flyover of Mauna Loa with thermal imaging cameras. Another expounded on a paper he'd submitted for publication, something about convection and vertical pipes of molten material venting where the earth's crust was thinnest. He nattered on, seemingly forgetful of the fact that Raif had fallen through said thin crust mere hours ago.

Jon and Avery pulled up a couple of chairs and joined the group. There was another round of condolences.

Avery tut-tutted about the proliferation of illegal gambling in the state and the fast and loose tendencies of young people these days. "All want instant gratification, caution to the wind, no appreciation of the consequences. Poor boy probably done in by a sore loser. Too few sensible ones like Steve and Jon. And Dinah, of course. Not enough self-discipline."

Jarvis' cigar smoke was gassing the room and causing Dinah's eyes to burn. Xander and Claude Ann appeared unfazed by the smoke or by grief. Raif was a rotter and Lyssa might be the only one who would truly mourn his passing, but surely the murder of one's daughter's husband, however unlovable, should be cause for more consternation.

She had to separate Claude Ann from Xander and pin her down for a serious powwow. Excusing herself from the table, she forged across the room to the banquette. Xander was in the middle of a spiel about property taxes. He and Jarvis stood and Xander introduced her to Jarvis.

"Pleasure," said Jarvis, pumping her hand.

"Likewise. Sorry to interrupt, but I need to speak with you, Claude Ann. In private."

Claude Ann smiled at Jarvis. "I'll be back in a jiffy, y'all. Dinah, throw your purse down there next to mine. I think we can trust Paul and Xan to guard our valuables." She took Dinah's arm and walked her toward a pair of tub chairs in the far corner of the room. "What's up?"

"The gun that killed Raif was a Beretta. An old one."

"Mine?"

"It would be a remarkable coincidence if it weren't."

"But that means that Hank is here, on this island, and he really did kill Raif."

"Not necessarily. You noticed the gun was missing in the late afternoon. You must have gone into your closet after that to dress for the party. It had to have been taken sometime before Hank rigged his bucket of blood. Where did you keep it and when did you last see it?"

"Sheesh, I don't know. I kept it under the cosmetic tray in my train case. Yesterday I just got fed up with Eleanor harassin' us. I thought if she came back, I'd show her the gun and scare her off, only it was gone."

A tall, thirtyish woman with a good figure came into the room carrying a drink. The piercing sounds of the zither accompanied her and died when the door flew shut.

"That's Frieda Jarvis," said Claude Ann. "I have to go and be gracious. I'll talk to you later." She rushed off, leaving Dinah none the wiser.

Dinah sat down in one of the tub chairs to wait for Steve. As she did, Avery left the table of oldtimers and joined her.

"Kay, I said, what's the world coming to? First an assault and battery and now Raif dead. Terrible. Jon says the police haven't caught Kemper yet. Let's hope they get Raif's killer fast."

Dinah said, "The police think there may be a connection between Raif's murder and the murder of that archaeologist, Patrick Varian, who was found murdered in a steam vent. I wonder if Eleanor Kalolo could have hired him to authenticate her claim that the bones of one of her ancestors are buried on the Uwahi property."

"Eleanor? Great Scott, hadn't thought of it." His eyes blinked rapidly, like the shutter of a camera shooting multiple frames per second. But whether it was her question that perturbed him or he was having one of his normal hyperkinetic fidgets, she couldn't tell. "Expensive proposition, hiring an archaeologist. Can't see it would do her much good. Most of 'em talk gibberish. Layers and mounds and articulations."

Steve came through the door along with a blast of frenzied accordion music and a drunken chorus singing, "Someone stole the keeshka, someone call the cop." An older man in a business suit followed him in.

"Great Scott, it's Norris Frye. Running for Senate. Must

introduce him to Jarvis." Avery practically vaulted out of his seat and rushed off to greet the newcomer.

Steve returned and handed her half a glass of wine on a soggy pink napkin. "Sorry it took so long. It's wild out there."

"So I see."

He sat down and quaffed the foam off his beer. "They're almost out of Garst on draft."

"I understand that Xander owns stock in the brewery."

"I don't know now. He's sold off a lot of his investments to finance Uwahi."

"He's comfortably well-off, rich by most standards. Why has he staked everything he owns on this one deal?"

"He owns some choice real estate, but land values went south just as he was approaching retirement. His Garst stock was in the toilet and I'm sure his U.S.G.S. pension wouldn't begin to keep him in the style he's grown used to. He probably felt vulnerable and then this golden opportunity came along. He didn't plan on staking everything, but putting all the pieces together turned out to be more costly than he'd anticipated and the deeper he got in, the harder it became to cut his losses and get out."

With his fortune and Claude Ann's on the line, Dinah could see how Uwahi was all-important to Xander. But why did Steve sound so serene? Did he have nothing at stake? "I know that you and Jon are longtime friends, but how did you and Xander become business partners?"

"My father, Louis, was a U.S.G.S. scientist. He and Avery and Xan were at the U together back in the seventies and our families were all close. After I finished law school in California, I came back to Hawaii to take care of my mom. At the time, Xander was trying to arrange a land swap so he could acquire Uwahi and he hired me to do the legal stuff. I was brilliant, of course, so when Avery came into the deal, Xan recommended me as legal counsel. Avery one-upped him and made me a partner in the company."

"Did you have to put up money for Uwahi?"

"No. Avery and Xander have been very generous to me. I'll get a token share of the sale price when the deal closes, but mostly I bill by the hour. I have other clients. My office is down in Pahoa and I live upstairs. Pahoa is a great little town. It's in kind of a time warp, lots of hippies and New Agers and eccentrics and the air redolent of pakalolo."

"Pot?"

"The best. If you get down that way, drop by and I'll roll you a joint to round out your experience of the island."

"I wouldn't think an upstanding attorney like yourself would risk getting caught smoking dope."

"I don't smoke with just anyone." There was an invitation to something more than pakalolo in his twinkling blue eyes.

Dinah smiled and placed a rendezvous in Pahoa in the Rain Check section of her brain. "Jon told me that your father drowned at a conference in California."

"That's right, on the same day Jon and Lyssa lost their mom. Afterward, Xan included me whenever he took his kids fishing or camping or sailing. He took us all to Yosemite one summer. Lyssa used to contrive all kinds of schemes to get Xander and my mother together, but it didn't work out."

Dinah thought about the phone call that triggered Leilani's suicide. "It was an amazing coincidence, the two of them dying, drowning actually, on the same day."

"No kidding. Over the last twenty years, Jon and Lyssa and I have wasted many hours chewing over the coincidence of their deaths. We never made a connection. Sometimes, a coincidence is just a coincidence."

"Steve, I don't mean to delve into painful memories, but

why would Jon keep a newspaper article about your father's death behind a photo of Xander?"

"Does he need a reason? I don't know. People put things where they put them and half the time they forget where or why. I probably have an article somewhere about Jon's mom's suicide."

"Did you ever think your father's death might not have been accidental?"

He seemed to deliberate. "A long time ago the thought entered my overheated young mind. But facts are facts. He had a few too many, he fell and hit his head against the edge of the pool, and he died. There was a woman on a float who paddled across the pool and tried to save him, but he went under and she couldn't swim." He took a slow sip of beer. "Scuttlebutt has it that the lady who couldn't swim was my father's roommate."

"Ah."

"I've never told my mother. I don't know how she'd feel about it, but there's no sense dredging up his infidelities at this late date."

Dinah pondered the arbitrary nature of the cosmos. Coincidences happened. Doppelgangers, synchronicities, flukes of all kinds. But they didn't happen in swarms, like earthquakes. "It's another amazing coincidence that only a few days ago an archaeologist was murdered in the same way as Raif?"

"They weren't killed in the same way. Raif was shot."

"Don't quibble. They were both pushed into fiery holes in the ground. Hellholes."

"From what I understand, hell opened up coincidentally under Raif's body."

"All right, all right. Maybe that was a coincidence. Patrick Varian wasn't by any chance the archaeologist you hired to evaluate Uwahi, was he?"

"No. Our archaeologist is very much alive and still sending us bills."

Jon left the table of U.S.G.S. oldtimers and drifted over to chat with Avery and Xander. Xander shoved purses and wraps aside for him and he sat down next to Paul Jarvis. Maybe Xander thought Jarvis should hear from a leading light in volcanology that Uwahi was safe from volcanic flows. She wondered if anyone from SAX Associates had apprised Jarvis that ancient Hawaiian bones might lie under his proposed development. Wouldn't they have an ethical obligation to disclose the information?

"Steve, what do you know about Eleanor Kalolo's claim against Uwahi?"

"So far, she hasn't filed a claim, although she's hired an attorney. He called me a few weeks back alleging that there were bones in a lava cave on the property."

"Not just any bones," said Dinah. "The bones of a king."

"The alleged bones of an alleged king."

"Did her attorney say she'd hired her own archaeologist?"

"No, but it was under consideration. Xan and Avery and I discussed the matter and we're standing by our guy's findings. No human remains. Not so much as a fragment. His Highness' bones are a figment of Eleanor's imagination, or a ploy to extort money from SAX."

"Shouldn't you inform Mr. Jarvis of the risk of bones?"

"Not if no claim has been filed. It's up to his lawyers to exercise due diligence and lay out the potential risks for him."

"Do you suppose his lawyers hired Varian?"

"If they did, I'm sure they would've informed the police. Jarvis has big plans for development here in Hawaii. He wouldn't do anything to jeopardize his squeaky clean image."

Jarvis sat forward, head down, apparently all ears while Jon talked.

Dinah wished she could read lips. "If Eleanor's right and bones are found, what would that mean to your sale?"

"There are always obstacles to buying and selling land in Hawaii. Ownership rights aren't as unambiguous here as they are in the rest of the country. The law grants Native Hawaiians usage rights for certain protected practices, but there's no definitive list of those practices. It could be anything. Somebody like Eleanor with a Hawaiian pedigree and a bee in her bonnet can claim that a piece of property has some cultural or religious history and a buyer and his lenders can find themselves screwed at the last minute and unable to get title insurance. It's buyer beware."

"Akahele," said Dinah. "Watch your step."

Across the room, Johnny Cash burst into "I fell into a burning ring of fire." Jon pulled his phone out of his pocket and walked away from the group, looking uneasy. In a minute, he returned and said something in Xander's ear. In the murky, yellow light, Xander's face morphed into a mask of misery. He stood up, kissed Claude Ann on the cheek, shook Jarvis' hand, and conferred briefly with Avery.

Jon walked across the room to Steve and Dinah. "Something's come up. Will you give Dinah a ride back to the cottage after dinner, Steve?"

"Of course. Not more bad news, I hope."

"No. No problem."

Dinah sank the last of her wine. She hated that expression.

TWENTY-FOUR

DINAH SAT DOWN and took off her shoes on Jon's lanai. She breathed in deep drafts of the cool night air, looked up at the infinitude of stars, and decompressed. Her clothes reeked of cigar smoke, but she wanted a cigarette anyway. She dug inside her purse and found the Sincerely Yours. Tomorrow was to have been Claude Ann's big day and Dinah had scheduled her return flight to Manila for the day following. Claude Ann had informed everyone at dinner that she and Xan planned to marry in a civil ceremony in a week or two, after the Uwahi closing and Raif's funeral. Now that Dinah's Mindinao study had been abandoned, she had no plans. She was, as her detective ex-boyfriend Nick was wont to say, in the wind.

Once these awful murders had been solved, Hawaii wouldn't be a bad place for a budding anthropologist to settle down and study. Her acquaintance with the soon-to-be Senator Norris Frye would stand her in good stead. At dinner he had talked her ear off about his friends in academia and Xander and Avery and Jon were all alums of the University. They might help her get her toe in the door. She didn't have a Ph.D., but she had tons of practical experience and being part Native American never hurt. Maybe she could parlay her research on the customs of the T'Boli and the B'laan of Mindanao into some sort of internship. She conceded that at least part of her interest in staying on could have something to do with sex. She remained inexplicably attracted to Jon and, more explicably, to Steve.

She put out her cigarette, took a last look at the stars, and pulled out her key. But she turned the knob and the door opened. In her haste, she'd forgotten to lock it. She went in and locked it behind her, then headed for the shower. She walked into the bedroom and a hand sprang out of the darkness and clapped over her mouth like a vise.

"Don't yell, Dinah. I'm warnin' you."

Wailing Jerusalem. It was Hank. The accent was unmistakable and the smell of his sour perspiration was even stronger than the smell of her smoked clothes.

"I'm gonna let you loose now, but don't yell, you hear?" She made a compliant mmm-hmm sound and tried to nod. Slowly his fingers relaxed and he moved his hand. "You can turn on the light if you want. Can't anybody see in through all those trees."

Her heart was flapping like a wild bird in a net. She clicked on the bedside lamp and turned to look at him. He was gaunt and unshaven and the loose-fitting shirt he wore made him look like a scarecrow.

"What are you doing here?"

"I'm tryin' to atone. I know what I did was wrong. I don't know what I was thinkin'. I was so damn mad. Claudy takin' me to the cleaners and then givin' my money away to some bozo with a slick line of bullshit. But I never meant to hurt her. I waited at the hospital 'til you left and followed you to that drive-in. I would've given you a ride back to the hotel, but I was afraid you'd holler and start a riot. Anyways, I eavesdropped on you and the deformed bub to find out if Claudy was all right." Dinah's heart rate slowed and her thoughts caught up with the situation. "You need to turn yourself in to the police, Hank, and get this mess straightened out. Don't get yourself in worse trouble than you're in already."

"You mean that boy that was killed? Phoebe told me about it. I didn't have anything to do with that."

"You talked with Phoebe? When?"

"Tonight while everybody was gone. I tried to talk to Marywave, but she wouldn't come out of her room. She called me a fallen man and she's right." His knees buckled and he dropped into Jon's chair and hung his head. "I should never have come out here, only Marywave was homesick and beggin' me all th' time to bring her home. She misses me and I miss her. How can I share custody with Claude Ann movin' her way off to the middle of the ocean? Took me a whole day and half the night to get from Needmore to Atlanta to L.A. to Honolulu."

"Claude Ann's not unreasonable, Hank. If you hadn't tried to turn Marywave against her and written those letters, she'd be more accommodating."

"It's my right and duty as a father to see what kind of a man she's taken up with and I can tell you, he ain't what she thinks. Claudy tells you stuff she doesn't tell anybody else, stuff she doesn't tell Phoebe. What does she say about how this Garst bozo gets along with Marywave?"

"She thinks Marywave will come around to like him if you stop putting him down. And she told Phoebe one thing she didn't tell me."

"What's that?"

"That Claude Ann had lent him money. Phoebe's been keeping you well informed, hasn't she?"

"Yeah, well, the money stuck in my craw. I'd have thought Claudy had more common sense." His voice hoarsened. "But there's other stuff Claudy tells you and I've gotta ask. I know she had a thing for Wes Spencer, but when we married, she said that was over and done. She said she wanted a dependable man who'd cherish her and take care of her. She acted like I was the one. Have I been her chump for all these years?"

Despite his bloody-mindedness, Dinah felt a twinge of sympathy for Hank. It couldn't have been easy appeasing his homegrown Aphrodite over the years, living with the ghost of Wesley Spencer and the awareness of smalltown opinion that Claude Ann could have done a lot better for herself. She said, "You weren't a chump if you loved her. You got the girl you wanted."

"I'd have chosen her over God if she'd have stayed. That's my sin and I'm damned for it. Damned and beat out by the likes of Xander Garst. He's phony as a rubber wiggler. I can't believe she went for him hook, line, and sinker."

"Why do you say he's phony?"

"Consortin' with other women for one thing. I followed him into town today and saw him pick up a blonde. And him supposed to marry Claudy tomorrow mornin'. What kind of a life is he gonna lead her?"

Dinah sat down on the bed and tried to collect her wits. "You stalked Xander from the airport today?"

"Call it what you will. I saw what I saw."

"Which was what, exactly?"

"He drove into Hilo and went into a travel agency."

"He was probably picking up their airline tickets for their honeymoon trip to Bali."

"You think I'm such a hick I don't know how to pick up airline tickets? I know you don't have to go sit in your car for a half hour with a big-breasted blonde negotiatin' the price."

This tidbit tore through Dinah's brain like a bullet. Tess Wilhite worked at a travel agency in Hilo. Was this yet another coincidence? "Did Xander and the blonde go to a big, fancy house somewhere down by Kapoho Point?"

"Nah, she went back inside the agency and he left by hisself. I'd seen enough. I drove on up here to Volcano and found a motel. I need to talk to Marywave and Claudy. I have to find a way to tell 'em I'm sorry. Claude Ann won't believe anything I tell her about Garst. Will you try and talk some sense into her, Dinah? We can't let her throw her life away on a user like Garst."

Dinah got up and started into the kitchen. "I'm going to brew us a pot of strong coffee. Why don't you take a shower and I'll find you one of Jon's shirts to wear. Both of us need to take a few minutes to think about this."

The floor juddered.

"Jerusalem!"

Hank dropped to his knees. "It's the End."

"No, Hank. It's only an earthquake." She crouched in the corner farthest from the window and rode the waves. Since when had "it's only an earthquake" become a comforting thought?

Hank stayed on his knees and prayed. "Yea, though I walk through the valley of the shadow of death, I will fear no evil."

The shaking stopped. Dinah felt a spasm of regret. When the earth is shaking like a wet dog, survival is the only concern. Everything else is on hold. There was a lot to be said for crouching in a corner. She sensed she was going to miss it. Reluctantly, she got up and dusted off her hands. "Hawaii's an adventure, isn't it, Hank? Always something going on."

"Earthquakes and hellfire bubblin' up out of th' earth. It's God's wrath comin' down. Have you seen the signs? Pele's Revenge, Hawaiians for Obama. This place is full of false gods and idolaters. Beware them that forget the Lord. Beware and take heed lest ye also fall."

TWENTY-FIVE

DILEMMA, TRI-LEMMA. Dinah put her head down on the kitchen table and banged it several times, but no happy solution fell out. Her instinct told her that Hank didn't kill Raif, but Hank was an odd duck with an obsession about stopping the wedding and no alibi for the time of the murder. The question of when the Beretta had been taken was problematic. Langford could clear that hurdle without breaking a sweat. Hank had been in Honolulu for several days before Claude Ann noticed it was missing. The cops would assume he had gained admittance to her suite on more than one occasion. They would assume he'd mistaken Raif for Xander, or even that he had intended to pick off the members of the Garst party one at a time.

She also knew in her heart that Claude Ann didn't kill Raif, but the murder weapon belonged to her and she had no alibi, either. And Xander, who admittedly despised Raif, had lied about his whereabouts at the time of the murder. At least he had omitted one of the stops he made. Why would he do that? Tess Wilhite could have given him an alibi for at least part of the afternoon. And what were those two saying to each other that couldn't have been said in her office?

Tchak, tchak, tchak. Something was barking. She raised her head. Attached to the window across from her, a little green gecko with lavender feet and round, blue-shadowed eyes observed her with brazen curiosity. Tchak, tchak, tchak.

"Okay, buddy. What's your bright idea? Should I go

to the police and lay all these worries and suspicions and hearsay on them?"

Tchak, tchak, tchak. He skittered down the window and disappeared into the woodwork, which is what she wished she could do. After a stimulating read from the Book of Isaiah, something along the lines of *The earth shall reel to and fro like a drunkard and shall fall and not rise again*, that's what Hank had done. He'd waltzed out the door and disappeared into the darkness and she hadn't uttered a word of argument. Cowardice or concern? Definitely procrastination. Maybe she would wake up tomorrow morning and learn that Langford had solved the crime, or the crimes, and she needn't have to think another thought about it. Them.

God, she was tired. She showered and climbed into bed, not expecting to sleep a wink. Mercifully, she was wrong. She woke up six hours later wondering if she'd dreamed that strange interlude with Hank. But when she went into the kitchen, she saw two cups of half-drunk coffee on the table and reality returned in spades.

Light streamed in through the windows as cheery as marmalade and the birds chirruped and tweeted to beat the band. Not a care in the world, the little slackers. Sometime today, Fujita and Langford and their forensic team would show up to fingerprint the human inhabitants, but they hadn't given a specific time. Did that mean there was leeway to do other things? She felt claustrophobic here in the forest. She needed to venture out and see where she was on the map, have a look at what was on the other side of these enclosing trees and forty-foot ferns.

She dressed and brewed a fresh pot of coffee. She wondered if Jon was up yet and whether he'd lend her his Sidekick for an hour or two. She wondered what fresh misfortune had summoned him and Xander out of the lodge last night. It must have been something to do with Lyssa. But having heard no sirens and received no middle-of-the-night call, Dinah was content to leave that worry on the back burner for the time being. Sufficient unto the day is the pilikia thereof.

Still curious about the missing newspaper article, she went back to the bedroom, turned on Jon's computer, and Googled "earth sciences conference marred by death, San Francisco, 1989." The results were not helpful. Scientific treatises of Ptolemy marred by errors, anti-Islamification conference marred by protesters, Mineralogical Society meeting marred by non-appearance of guest speaker. She modified her search, adding Louis Sykes' name and U.S.G.S. and Hawaii. Nothing came up. After several failed attempts, she gave up. Apparently, the story hadn't merited a lot of media attention or it had never been scanned into Google's database. Anyhow, Jon was right. There were far more pressing matters.

She needed to talk to Phoebe and find out if she knew where Hank was hiding out. Not that Dinah wanted to sic the cops on him, but it would be prudent to know where he was in case his prints turned up on the murder weapon and proved her instinct wrong. And she wanted a tête-à-tête with Tess Wilhite to find out if the blonde Hank had seen "negotiating" with Xander was, in fact, Tess. With this agenda in mind, she finished her coffee, put on her running shoes, and started down the path.

The morning air was laden with the smell of jasmine. She stopped beside a tree with multiple, vine-covered trunks and sniffed a pretty white flower with a red center. It smelled like a rotting carcass—an unpleasant reminder of just how wrong her instinct could be.

When she reached the carport where the path forked to the other cottages, she saw the unmarked car the detectives had arrived in yesterday afternoon. Fujita was nowhere to be seen, but Lt. Langford was sitting behind the wheel of the Wrangler. It was humming like a sewing machine. He smiled a gotcha smile, shut off the engine, and opened the door.

"Battery's fine," he said. "For future reference, Mr. Garst keeps the key on a chain next to the front door. Pretty obvious place if you think about it."

Terrific. So now she had no verifiable alibi for the time of Raif's death. "Thank you," she said, holding out her hand for the key. "I was planning on going out for a while this morning. Would you like to take my fingerprints first?"

"Forensics won't be around for another day or so. I'm just here to iron out a few inconsistencies and update everyone on the progress of the investigation. Seems the Honolulu police let Hank Kemper get away from them. He made it to Hilo on a charter flight about noon yesterday. He might try and contact his ex-wife or his daughter. Haven't seen him snooping around, have you?"

"If he's evading the police, I'm sure he'll keep well out of sight. And Claude Ann's and Xander's cottage is much farther down the path."

He showed her his underbite. "I hope evading the police doesn't turn into an epidemic."

She nodded and hiked back to Jon's cottage to get her driver's license. She would talk with Phoebe later. An hour from now everything could be changed. Hank might turn himself in or Phoebe might turn him in, or Langford might lose his patience and unleash a pack of bloodhounds. Langford gave her the hives. That knowing glint in his eyes reminded her of a loaded mousetrap poised to whomp down on some hapless neck.

Since Jon had already given her permission to drive the Wrangler and Langford had given her the keys, she saw no reason to disturb anyone with her good-bye. She stuffed her license, her Visa card, and a few dollars in her pocket and went back to the carport. Langford's car was still there, but neither he nor Fujita were anywhere in sight. Feeling vaguely like a fugitive, she started up the Wrangler, backed quietly down the driveway, and headed toward Hilo.

ACCORDING TO HANK, Xander had visited the Casino Royale Travel Agency, which was listed in the Hilo Yellow Pages on Lanikaula Street. Dinah wended her way through town until she found it in what looked like a private residence set back from the street in the shadow of a Marriott. She maneuvered the Wrangler into a tight parking spot on a side street and walked back to the agency. Only as she marched through the Casino Royale's frosted glass door did she think about what she would say to Tess. "Were you or were you not raped by Xander Garst and, if yes, why in the name of God are you still seeing him?" seemed unlikely to lead to a fruitful exchange.

The walls of the large front room were plastered with posters of fabulous casinos and gambling destinations—Bellagio Las Vegas, The Venetian Macau, Fairmont Monte Carlo, Conrad Cairo, Casino Baden-Baden. Royal Caribbean Cruises and Norwegian Cruise Lines apparently also catered to high rollers with onboard casinos. One poster featured a background seascape and in the foreground, a Sean Connery look-alike hoisting a martini at a roulette table. Another showed two women simpering at one another in front of a row of slot machines.

A dapper Chinese man with an unctuous smile stood up from his desk and bowed his head. "May I help you?"

"Is Tess Wilhite in?"

"That's Tess on the phone over there. You can have a seat at her desk and she'll be with you in a few minutes."

Dinah thanked him and sat down. Given Jon's love of Nature, she had expected that Tess would be an outdoorsy looking girl with at least a passing resemblance to Avery. This woman surprised on both counts. Her skin was very fair and creamy and her eyes amazingly large and violet.

Like a baby's eyes. At first, Dinah thought she might be wearing those circle contact lenses popularized by Lady Gaga, but she changed her mind when Tess settled a pair of purple glasses on her nose to read a price list to the person on the other end of her phone call. She had fine, white-blond hair, bee-stung lips painted the perfect shade of raspberry, and a sultry voice even when explaining the surcharge for checked baggage and the cost of a single room supplement. She and Jon must have made a striking couple. Dinah thought she perceived a gloss of artificiality about Tess, but attributed the judgment to petty jealousy. How artless and sincere could a person be, after all, when selling an expensive junket to Vegas?

Tess finished booking her client at the Mirage, shook her tinkling gold charm bracelet down her willowy, white arm, and smiled at Dinah. "How may I help you?"

"My visit is personal, Tess. My name is Dinah Pelerin. I'm a friend of Jonathan Garst's. I'd like to ask you a few questions if you can spare the time."

Her big, violet eyes skewed toward the clock on the wall. After a second or two, they skewed back to Dinah's face. "Of course. There's a little place on the bay that I like. I'm parked in front. I'll drive." She informed her Chinese co-worker that she'd be gone for an hour, donned a pair of Chanel sunglasses, and led Dinah out the door to a red Miata convertible.

The day was gloriously sunny. Dinah didn't see how the woman could keep her skin so milk-white and drive a convertible, but with Hilo's rainy weather she probably kept the top up most of the time. And Jon had said she traveled a lot. She probably spent much of her time scouting out casinos where Hawaiians could indulge their craving to gamble.

The Miata sliced through the city streets like a Jedi light-saber, coasting through stop signs and romping it through yellow lights. At the first red light, Dinah said, "I've never run across a travel agency that specializes only in gambling destinations."

"That's because gambling is illegal in Hawaii. No games for money, on shore or in Hawaiian waters. No cruise ship that has a casino on board can start or end its cruise here. If you want to gamble, you have to go elsewhere."

When they reached the waterfront, Tess careened down a narrow alley and jerked to a stop in front of a hole-in-the-wall called Kava-Kava. "Have you ever drunk kava?"

"No."

"It alleviates stress, but doesn't impair thinking."

Dinah was all for alleviating stress. She followed Tess into the grungy little coffeehouse. It had only three tables, none of them occupied, but there were three large, morose looking employees behind the counter. Tess ordered two kavas and two glasses of guava juice and sat down at the table farthest from the door.

"What is kava?" asked Dinah, dusting crumbs out of the chair before sitting.

"It's a South Pacific shrub. It's been used for thousands of years to help people relax. Fijians say it makes people talkative. Some people say it lets them see into the future."

"Sounds like the magic potion I've been searching for all my life."

Tess smiled. "In Hawaii, it's mostly drunk during naming ceremonies, when boys are consecrated or when girls are initiated into the traditional hula."

A fat-faced man arrived with a tray and offloaded two wooden bowls of what appeared to be liquid mud with a skim of yellowish slime on top and two glasses of juice. "Anything else?"

Tess said no. The man grunted and went back behind the counter.

The kava smelled like a mixture of Pine-Sol and rotting leaves. Dinah tried not to gag. "What's the yellow goop on top?"

"Mashed hibiscus. Gives the kava more of a kick. Drink it down fast. Like this." She took the bowl in both hands, turned it up to her mouth, and drank. She set the empty bowl on the table and smiled. "Try it."

Dinah lifted her bowl to her lips and tasted. "Ugh!"

"Where's your spirit of adventure?"

Dinah choked down a few more swallows, forced herself not to urp, and reached for the guava chaser. "If that's what seeing into the future tastes like, I'd rather be surprised."

"It's an acquired taste. Your lips and tongue will start to feel a little numb. It takes a while, but you'll find it reduces your inhibitions."

With her huge, violet eyes and voluptuous mouth, Tess didn't look like the inhibited type. Avery had described his daughter as high-strung, Jon had described her as intense and, when professing his innocence to Jon, Xander had called her crazy. But looks and descriptions to the contrary, Tess seemed at the moment almost preternaturally cool and composed.

Dinah didn't know if it was the kava already at work reducing her inhibitions, but she got straight to the point. "What did you and Xander Garst talk about yesterday afternoon?"

Tess' raspberry lips parted and formed a round O, like a Lifesaver. "What makes you think I talked with him?"

"You were seen together in Xander's car shortly after noon."

"By whom?"

"By the ex-husband of Xander's fiancée."

"He was spying on Xander? How creepy." She shook her charm bracelet down her arm, rested her elbows on the table, and steepled her fingers under her chin. "What is it you want from me, Ms. Pelerin?"

"Your father told me that you were close to the Garst family at one time, engaged to marry Jon."

"That ended a long time ago. Are you interested in Jon? Is that what this is about?"

"It's more about Xander, actually. You told Jon that he raped you and then you retracted the accusation. Which statement was true?"

"That's hardly any of your concern."

"Whether it was true or not, the way matters were left between you and Xander wouldn't exactly foster warm relations. Why are you still seeing him?" Dinah had a brainstorm. "Did you threaten to tell your father that he raped you? Or his fiancée? Are you blackmailing Xander?"

"That's preposterous. I'm not 'seeing' him. Our conversation yesterday was about business. He booked a trip through the agency."

"A trip to where?"

"My clients' travels are confidential. And anyway, why should I tell you?"

"It might be less disagreeable telling me what went on between you and Xander than it would be telling the police?"

Her unnerving eyes flattened Dinah against the wall. "Are you trying to blackmail me? Why would the police become involved?"

"Because your meeting with Xander provides him with a partial alibi for the time of his son-in-law's murder."

Dinah hadn't thought that skin that white could go any whiter.

"Murder? Who was murdered?"

"Don't you read the newspapers or listen to the news? Raif Reid was murdered yesterday afternoon."

"No!" Her fists crashed onto the table and her face congested with fury, or was it fear? She was in the throes of some overwhelming emotion.

The employees behind the counter looked up sharply.

Dinah cringed. All of a sudden "high-strung" and "crazy" seemed like accurate descriptions. "Did you know Raif?"

She clawed at her face leaving bright red marks and Dinah reached across the table and took hold of her hands. "Tess, take it easy. What's wrong? Do you need a glass of water?"

She fought Dinah's grip and shook her arms so that her charm bracelet tinkled wildly. One of her gold charms caught Dinah's eye. She pulled Tess' forearm closer.

"Let go of me."

Dinah let go of her left arm, but held onto the right. With her free hand, she singled out the Lucky 7 charm and turned it over to read the engraving on the leg of the 7— Your Playmate RR. She dropped Tess' arm. "I don't know if kava is any good at divining the future, but it's dynamite for seeing into the past. Were you and Raif playmates when you made the accusation that Xander raped you? Were the two of you working some variation of the badger game on Xander, threatening to tell your father that he'd raped you? Did you cook up the rape allegation by yourself or did Raif put you up to it?"

Tess jerked her arm away. She was breathing hard, but she'd stopped clawing at herself. "Why would Raif do such a thing?"

"Apart from bleeding Xander for money, you mean? How about to undermine Xander's influence over Lyssa and make her easier to manipulate? How about to stick it to his sexual rival, Jon? Is blackmail how Raif bankrolled his gambling habit?"

"I don't know what you're talking about. But if any of what you're saying were true, Xander must have been wanting Raif dead for a long time. And me, too." She stood up, tottering slightly. "I'm going to the police."

"You're in no condition to drive, Tess. Sit down and talk for a few minutes."

And then miraculously, whether from the anesthetizing effects of the kava or some mental trick, her eyes iced over and the air of preternatural aplomb returned. "You'll have to find yourself another ride."

As she left, her heels clacking against the wooden floor sounded like gunshots. Dinah sat for a minute absorbing the implications. Xander had been a victim of Tess' false witness and Raif's blackmail and now, thanks to her meddling, he was being promoted to Prime Suspect in Raif's murder.

The server who'd brought the kava interrupted her thinking. "You ready to pay?"

"Yeth." Her lips and tongue felt as if they'd been injected with Novacaine. Maybe the effects of kava came on in stages. First the loss of inhibition, then numbness, and soon Stage Three—clairvoyance. She would need a sibyl's clairvoyance to see through the maze of mysteries surrounding Xander Garst. She looked at the tab, fished the money out of her purse, and handed it over. As she was leaving, a customer in a dark hoodie sprawled face down on the table in what Dinah hoped did not augur Stage Four.

TWENTY-SIX

ONCE AGAIN, DINAH was stranded. Fortunately, the Hilo Hawaiian Hotel was only a short walk from Kava-Kava and she had no trouble finding a waiting taxi. She returned to Lanikaula Street and looked for Tess' convertible, but either Tess had parked somewhere else or she hadn't gone back to work.

Dinah walked back to the Wrangler and reviewed her Big Island map. It looked to be about thirty miles from Hilo to Kalapana, where Raif had been murdered. Had Xander driven from his meeting with Tess to a pre-arranged meeting with Raif and killed him? Getting rid of a blackmailer was certainly a compelling motive for murder, one of the classics. He'd had access to Claude Ann's gun, giving him the means. And he had plenty of time to get to Kalapana, shoot Raif, and get back to Volcano in time for the party. It was bad luck that the gun wasn't devoured by the fire, but it was the chance he took. It made the case against him seem open-and-shut.

Unless. Everyone deserved at least one unless. Could Tess have killed Raif? Her response to the news of his death had been dramatic, but had she overplayed it a bit? If she could put on an act about being raped, she could put on an act about not knowing that Raif was dead. Hadn't Avery mentioned that she attended drama classes as a kid? Maybe Tess decided she didn't want to split the booty with her playmate anymore. Maybe she'd decided she didn't like playing second fiddle to Lyssa anymore. Or maybe Raif had gone on a Casino Royale junket with some of Tess' money and either swindled her out of her share of the winnings or saddled her with the loss. Ginning up a motive for the woman was easy and she could have whacked Raif on her lunch hour without breaking a sweat. Putting Claude Ann's gun in her hand was the rub. Of course, if Raif had stolen the Beretta, it wasn't unthinkable that Tess could have gotten it away from him somehow.

On the spur of the moment, Dinah decided to drive to Kalapana. On the way, she might stop off in Pahoa where Raif had said he was going to a private poker game, where George Knack ran an illegal betting parlor, and where Lyssa and Phoebe had spent yesterday afternoon at the spa. Pahoa was a scant ten miles from Kalapana. Come to think of it, Lyssa wasn't immune from suspicion. Jon had said that everyone knew Raif was a bounder but Lyssa, but she knew he was on the make. And she was insecure enough and jealous enough to warn Dinah to stay away from him. If she had found out about Tess, she would have gone ballistic. It wasn't unreasonable to think that she could have been inside Claude Ann's suite alone at some time during the last week and, given her belief that Claude Ann was a gold digger, it wasn't unreasonable to think that the self-proclaimed "natural sleuth" would have rifled Claude Ann's room looking for some compromising evidence. She could have glommed onto the gun with the intention of killing Raif and framing Claude Ann for his murder. Two birds with one stone. She could have arranged a secret meeting with Raif somewhere near the spa and opted for a treatment that didn't necessitate that a therapist be in the room with her the whole time. She could have slipped out from her hot stones or whatever, sneaked away and shot Raif, and returned without anyone having noticed she'd been gone.

George Knack would have been a dandy suspect except that he couldn't have gotten hold of the Beretta. Unless. The unlesses were rolling now. What if Raif had pilfered the gun? If he owed Knack money and Knack was pressuring him, he might have felt the need of a weapon. He could've trumped up an excuse for going into Claude Ann's suite. The Olopana staff would have no reason to suspect Xander's son-in-law. Maybe Knack called Raif to Pahoa and demanded his money, Raif pulled the Berretta, the two struggled, and pow! And since it wasn't his gun, Knack would have no reason to take it away with him.

Filled with purpose and awaiting the onset of clairvoyance, Dinah drove out of Hilo and turned south onto Highway 130. Highway 130 was wide and straight, with businesses and subdivisions branching off on either side. It could have been Anywhere, U.S.A., except that somewhere near the place where it dead-ended into the Pacific Ocean, molten lava had ruptured the earth's skin. The farther south she got, the more farming she saw—papayas, mangoes, anthuriums, orchids. And sooner than she'd expected, she was entering the quaint little town of Pahoa.

Main Street looked like the set of an old spaghetti Western—raised wooden sidewalks and false-front buildings painted in a who-gives-a-rip patchwork of red and aqua and chartreuse. The hodgepodge of New Agey shops, funky taverns, ethnic restaurants, and Internet cafés conveyed a sort of outlaw ambience wherein smoking pakalolo wouldn't stir much controversy. She shivered as she passed a sign pointing to the Steam Vent Inn and Health Retreat, but she saw nothing that looked like a betting parlor. She assumed that illegal betting received more scrutiny than illegal smoking and George Knack didn't advertise.

Steve's law office was somewhere in town, but she was too engrossed with thoughts of murder to think about romance. She looped around the town and returned to the main drag. A yellow Victorian house with blue gingerbread trim and flower boxes full of tropical blooms caught her eye. It was set well back from the street with a curved paving stone walkway lined with multi-colored flowers. A sign in the front yard read PEACEQUEST and painted on the side of the house was a mural of a sheltered cove under the words Wellness, Rejuvenation, Vibrational Healing, Holistic Therapies, and Ancient Wisdom through Modern Modalities. Peacequest was the spa that Lyssa and Phoebe had visited. A young man with headphone cords sprouting from his ears and a baseball cap worn backwards ambled out the front door and paused to light a cigarette.

Dinah pulled to the curb and parked. While she was in the neighborhood, she might as well have a looksee and pin down the exact time of the call the murderer made to Lyssa on Raif's phone. It would be a bonus if she could speak with the person who took the call.

She waited until the young man had loafed down the block. When he was out of sight, she marched up the walkway to the front door and walked inside. Bells on the front door jingled and the heady smells of eucalyptus and lavender engulfed her. The Victorian façade gave way to a thoroughly modern interior with muted colors and Chinese massage music in the background. In the lobby, several ladies in plush terry robes sat reading magazines.

A wholesome, twenty-something blonde in green scrubs greeted Dinah with a smile. "Hello. Do you have an appointment?"

"No. I'm, I'm a friend of Lyssa Reid."

"Oh, poor Lyssa. How is she? All of us here at Peacequest were blown away to hear about Raif. Nothing like that's ever happened here. It's horrible."

"You know Raif, too?"

"He and Lyssa are both regulars. He's so…I mean he was so good-looking and so good-natured. He always had something nice to say."

Dinah didn't know what parts of the body vibrational healing involved, but she couldn't picture Raif swaggering into a place like this to imbibe the ancient wisdom. And unless the kid with the earbuds and the cigarette was elderly when he first entered, he didn't look as if he were in need of rejuvenating. Lyssa wouldn't have brought Phoebe to some kind of a swingers' retreat, would she? Dinah studied the blonde's face. Her smile was as wholesome as a glass of milk. "Were you the person who took Raif's call?"

"That was Emily. She's new and she didn't recognize the voice. And Lyssa was in the water shiatsu treatment and didn't speak with him. Was it Raif? The police acted like maybe it wasn't."

"I don't think they know. Is Emily here today?"

"Yes, but she's giving a Zoku Shin Do."

"What's that?"

"Foot reflexology massage."

"Do you suppose Emily could squeeze me in for a short Zoku?"

"I'll have to check her availability this afternoon." She opened the appointment book, but a phone call interrupted her. "Peacequest. Oh, yes, Mrs. Culler. No, Rory's doing the Kupua this week."

An ox-eyed woman with a towel around her head put down her magazine and spoke to Dinah. "If you're new, I can't say enough about the Kupua Earth and Fire treatment. I signed up for a full year of once-a-week treatments and it's changed my life. My fibromyalgia is completely cured and I sleep like a baby."

"Sounds wonderful. Is it expensive?"

"Not if health is your priority. Individually, the Kupua costs five hundred dollars, but if you buy fifty-two, it's only four hundred per. It's quite a savings and tipping's not allowed. Ask George about it. Tell him Sylvia recommended it. Of course, you'll probably want to try several treatments before you decide on a single therapy."

Dinah was impressed. If there were many patrons like Sylvia, this establishment must be a cash cow.

The blonde finished her phone call. "You're in luck. Emily can take you at one o'clock. I'll show you back to the dressing room and, if you like, you can enjoy our Jacuzzi while you wait."

"I didn't bring a bathing suit."

"Most of our clientele bathe in the nude, but if you're shy we have cover-ups." She stamped Dinah's credit card and led her down a narrow hallway with closed doors on either side which Dinah assumed to be massage rooms. At the end of the hall was a door to the outside and a breezeway connecting to another, much larger house. Dinah followed her through another lobby where both men and women waited in robes and showed her into a large dressing room replete with all of the spa essentials. She handed Dinah a numbered key. "Leave your clothes and valuables in the locker and help yourself to a robe and towels. You can go into the Jacuzzi or wait in the lobby and Emily will come and find you."

When she had gone, Dinah took a bottle of water from a large oval ice bucket on a stand. The label informed her that it had taken two thousand years for MaHaLo Hawaii Deep Sea Water to flow from the glaciers in Greenland to the Water Rejuvenation Zone off the Kona Coast, that it was pumped from three thousand feet below the ocean's surface, that the salt had been filtered by a patented process while maintaining the ancient minerals, and that there was no purer water on the face of the earth. Dinah removed the plastic cap, drank with all due reverence, and reconsidered why she was wasting her afternoon here. Her initial thought had been that Emily could describe the voice of the caller purporting to be Raif, but voices were impossible to describe and anyway, he would have disguised it.

In spite of the semblance of purity, something felt wrong

about this place. She could see Raif hanging around a place where sex was dispensed, but not holistic therapies. On the other hand, if Lyssa also hung out here, it wasn't likely that anything nefarious was going on. Maybe Raif just liked to unwind here after playing poker all night.

Dinah undressed, stowed her things in her assigned locker, slipped on a robe, and went out into the lobby. It was empty now, everyone presumably having moved on to their respective treatment rooms. With time to kill before her Zoku, Dinah went exploring. She walked outside and checked out the large Jacuzzi under an elaborate yellow and blue gazebo. The grounds were meticulously tended in the style of a Japanese garden with lanterns and basins, sand and pebbles, dramatically shaped rocks, mini-waterfalls, and more paving stone walkways. There were several hot tubs behind privacy screens and a few small out-buildings—saunas, probably. She followed the walkway around to a tiny, prefab shed between two huge stone urns containing Poinciana trees. It looked like a child's playhouse. There wasn't a Keep Out sign on the door and she went inside.

It was someone's office. The wraparound windows under the roof let in plenty of light, but guaranteed privacy. There was a desk, a custom job inlaid with various exotic woods and not a single scrap of paper to hide the sheen, and one sumptuous leather chair on castors. Behind the desk was a credenza with the same beautiful inlay. She was running her fingers along the top when the door opened. Embarrassed, she turned around and stared straight into the reptilian eyes of George Knack.

TWENTY-SEVEN

"I'M SORRY. I didn't realize this was someone's office." She started to leave.

"No need to rush off. I like to meet the new clients. Take a load off." The deep-set black eyes behind the thick lenses of the hornrims practically pushed her down into the leather chair. "What'll you have? Green tea? Carrot juice? Resveratrol concentrate?" He opened the credenza, part of which seemed to be a mini-refrigerator.

"Nothing, thanks." She held up the bottle of MaHaLo water she still carried.

He took out a bottle of carrot juice, twisted off the cap, gave her an assessing look, and leaned his back against the door. "I saw you at Xander Garst's party in Honolulu. What's your name?"

"Dinah Pelerin. I'm a friend of his fiancée." Her thoughts were racing. Even holding a bottle of carrot juice, Knack looked like a mafioso. She cinched her robe tighter. Was Peacequest a front for his illicit betting operation? She recalled the surprised look on Langford's face when Lyssa named the spa where she'd spent the afternoon. Maybe the spa was a lawful enterprise and the employees didn't know about his sideline. He could be funneling his gambling profits through the spa. It would be a perfect way to launder his dirty money.

"And what brings you to Peacequest?"

"Lyssa told me it was a great spa. I'm going to have a Zoku something."

"Zoku Shin Do." He took a sip of carrot juice while his

impassive eyes seemed to pat her down. "Ever had your feet worked over before?" He made it sound like the treatment would include burning cigarettes.

"No."

"Emily's good. She knows all the right pressure points. Jessica at the front desk said you were interested in the phone call Raif Reid made to the spa before he died. Are you doing some kind of independent investigation?"

"No."

"Don't trifle with me, Dinah. Did Xander send you?"

"No."

"Because I don't want any trouble out of this Reid business. I don't like the police coming around and roiling the waters. I don't like anybody roiling the waters. Peacequest is a nice, quiet operation. I aim to keep it that way."

She found what should have sounded threatening strangely liberating. If Knack didn't want his waters roiled, he wasn't going to work her over or do anything that would call attention to what went on in the back room of Peacequest. "Did Raif owe you a lot of money?"

"Raif liked the Tahitian black pearl scrub and the Hot Jade Stone Massage. They're on the high end of what we offer. He always paid, although he hadn't been as prompt the last few weeks."

"I'm not the vice squad. You don't have to speak in riddles."

"I don't have to speak to you at all."

Dinah decided that the only way to extract any information from him was to roil. "Everyone knows that Raif gambled. I think he got in over his head and maybe you leaned on him when he was slow to pay. He's been blackmailing Xander for a long time, but Xander was in debt, himself. If Xander turned off the spigot, or if Lyssa did, and if the cards were running cold for Raif, he wouldn't be able to repay you before he went home to Virginia. Viewed in that light, the police could get the idea that you took drastic action."

Knack's black eyes bored into her. "I run a holistic health center. I pay my taxes and keep my nose clean. But say for the sake of argument that a client owes me money. It wouldn't behoove me to kill him. I'd never get my money back. And if I killed him in my own backyard, the police would start poking around and business would suffer. So you see, killing a non-paying client is a lose-lose situation. Theoretically."

"If you weren't turning the screws on Raif, why did you show up uninvited at Xander's party?"

"As a rule, I don't get involved in my clients' problems, but every so often there's an exception. I went to the party to see another of my clients."

"Xander owes you money, too?"

"I went to see Lyssa. She promised to retire Raif's debts if I helped her take care of another matter. It seems Raif had been seeing one of my employees on the side and Lyssa asked me to put a stop to it." He finished his carrot juice and tossed the bottle into a metal waste can next to the door.

The sound jangled Dinah's nerves. Surely, Raif was too fond of Lyssa's money to play around with somebody at the spa where she routinely came for lomilomis. "Is Tess Wilhite one of your employees?"

"That's right. I asked her to cut Raif loose or see him someplace other than here on my turf." His phone rang and he pulled it out of his pocket and answered. "A lost client? I'll have a look around. If I find her, I'll send her to Emily." He slipped the phone back in his pocket.

Dinah stood up and stepped around the desk. "Will Lyssa pay you now that Raif's dead?"

He frowned. "What's your angle?"

"The only thing I care about is making sure that my

friend and her fiancé aren't framed for murder. Do you know who played poker with Raif yesterday?"

"If he had a game, I don't know anything about it. Like I told the police, I've heard that a lawyer here in town hosts a game from time to time. They might play for money or for matchsticks. I wouldn't know."

Dinah so wished he hadn't said that. She told herself that Pahoa must be teeming with lawyers. "Will you tell me how much money Raif owed you?"

Knack walked around her to the credenza, pulled out a slim little notebook computer, and sat down at the desk. He opened it, hit a few keystrokes, and took a pen and paper out of the desk drawer. He scribbled a note, folded the paper, ripped off the bottom half, and handed it across to her. It said $80g/w/vig.

"Raif owes you eighty thousand with the vigorish. That's the interest, right?"

"You can decipher it however you like. I'd probably say it meant an eighty dollar grapefruit sugar scrub followed by a vigorous herbal oil treatment."

"How is it that so many people know that you're a book-maker and the authorities don't do anything about it?"

"Gambling's illegal in Hawaii. If you're interested in what we do here, I'd recommend the Laa hot stone-cold marble treatment. It's relaxing as a coma and I'd consider giving you a discount."

TWENTY-EIGHT

DINAH DECIDED TO pass on the Zoku Shin Do treatment and
the interview with Emily. She dressed in a hurry and returned to the car convinced that George Knack, for all of
his malevolent posturing, didn't kill Raif. He had too much
to lose. He might not take a welsher's bet again if he didn't
pay, but he would eat a loss if he had to in order to remain
under the police radar.

She spotted a food mart on Main Street and stopped off
for a sandwich. At the cash register, she asked a bald man
with spectacular full-sleeve tattoos on both arms about Kalapana. She had no idea what the scene of the crime might
tell her, but for some reason, she wanted to see it.

"Can't get there. You want chips?"

"Yes, please."

He threw a bag of Hawaiian taro chips into her lunch
sack. "That'll be four-eighty."

"Why can't I get to Kalapana?"

"Lava's severed the road. The new flow took out two
houses, one of them new. Kalapana Gardens subdivision's
still there, but people are evacuating. This flow isn't as bad
as the one back in ninety. A hundred houses destroyed then
and Kaimu buried under fifty feet of lava. But what you
gonna do? Pele's raising hell again."

"Can I get to the place where the man was murdered
yesterday?"

"If that's the kind of thing you're into." He showed her
a ghoulish grin. "It happened this side of the flow. But if I
was you, I'd be careful."

She took her ham and cheese sandwich to the car and ate it, but her appetite had flagged along with her courage. Did she really want to go jaunting about in an area where hot lava could sever the road at any minute? But she didn't intend to linger at the scene of the crime. All she wanted was to nip by for a quick look and anyway, lava must move like molasses. Princess Ruth had time to sail from Oahu to Hilo before the stuff reached Hilo.

Putting Pahoa in the rear view mirror, Dinah rejoined Highway 130 and drove south. She noted the time and mileage leaving Pahoa. The road was undistinguished except for one area along the shoulder where the trees and shrubs had been blackened by fire. She drove ten miles until she reached a large RESTRICTED ACCESS, AUTHORIZED PERSONNEL ONLY sign across the road. There was a parking lot off to the side and she nosed the Wrangler into an angled space and cut the engine. A towering column of steam rose in the distance where the hot lava was entering the water and building a brand new beach.

She got out of the car and walked between a gauntlet of cautionary signs.

VISITORS ARE REMINDED TO STAY AWAY FROM THE STEAM WHICH CONTAINS HYDROCHLORIC ACID, GLASS PARTICLES, AND EXPLOSION EJECTA.

REMAIN WITHIN PERMITTED AREAS ONLY. LAVA BEYOND THE ROPE BARRICADES IS EXTREMELY UNSTABLE AND CAN COLLAPSE AT ANY TIME.

BEWARE HOT ROCK FALLS.

Hawaii was a hotbed of bewares. Akahele. Watch your step ye who travel here.

She stepped lightly across the pavement, imagining subterranean rivers of lava coursing beneath her feet. The air smelled like a struck match, but nothing felt hot underfoot and she continued walking. Where the pavement ended, a well-beaten path led through a copse of scorched trees. Another sign warned VIEWING AREA CLOSED. GROUND UNSTABLE.

And then she saw the bright yellow crime scene tape strung between two charred trees. Why would Raif have come here? This was no place for a tryst. Had someone held the gun on him and forced him to walk back here or had he been murdered in Pahoa and his body driven here and dumped?

She stood staring at the trail on the other side of the tape. It wasn't lava. It was dirt. Trees had grown out of it. How dangerous could it be? She laughed. That had to be the question that winners of the Darwin award asked themselves just before they did some ludicrous thing that permanently removed their idiot genes from the gene pool. But the park rangers who'd discovered Raif's body had walked here and they'd had horses. And the police had walked here, too.

She ducked under the tape and, very gingerly, inched forward one baby step at a time along a trail fringed by scorched trees. Five feet, ten feet. Her cat-killing curiosity impelled her forward. After maybe twenty feet, the trees ended abruptly and a barren tract of lava stretched out in front of her. According to the map, this was part of the East Rift Zone and the Keauohana Forest Reserve. A few steps to her right, a lurid red glow emanated from a depression about the size of a coffin. That must be the skylight where Raif died. The person who shot him might have stood where she was standing now.

What kind of a man, or woman, could have dispatched a fellow human being into that inferno? It would make Dinah feel more favorably disposed toward the human race if she could lay off the cruelty on the caprice of a mythical goddess. But however cruelly the fire had seared Raif's body, Pele hadn't pulled the trigger.

Something tickled Dinah's neck and she gasped. Mosquitoes. And whether it was her imagination or surging magma, the soles of her feet began to feel warm. Swatting madly at the hungry horde that buzzed around her face and eyes, she hotfooted it back to the car and drove north toward Kapoho and the stately pleasure dome called Xanadu, the house where Xander and Claude Ann planned to live after they were married. She didn't have the address, but she would find it. She had no idea what the house could tell her about Xander, but hadn't Jon mentioned a gardener? Maybe he could tell her something useful. Maybe he'd been hunting rats when Xander arrived yesterday and could substantiate his alibi for part of the afternoon. As Fujita had said, the medical examiner could only guestimate the time of Raif's death. It couldn't hurt to establish the fact that between the hours of X and Y, Xander couldn't have shot him.

She phoned Claude Ann for directions to Xanadu. Claude Ann was in a tizzy. Hank had been calling her repeatedly. She hadn't answered, but had alerted Lt. Langford. She didn't know where Xander was, but he and Jon must have taken Lyssa with them because she was gone, too. Xander was in torment for fear that Lyssa would commit suicide. Phoebe was acting strange and Raif's father had gotten grumpy when Claude Ann informed him that the memorial service he'd arranged for Raif had to wait until after the Uwahi closing tomorrow morning. Dinah said something bromidic and encouraging and Claude Ann said she would phone the security guard at Kapoho Beach and authorize him to let her in.

Kapoho Beach Estates was a gated community on the easternmost tip of the island. By the time Dinah tooled through the gate, it was three o'clock. None of the multistory homes were what she would have described as palatial, but they all had picture postcard views of the ocean. Many had their own private lagoons and tidepools, some had exquisitely manicured Japanese gardens, and all of them were set amidst palm trees and verdant tropical foliage.

Like a great white egret poised for flight, Xanadu stood alone on a promontory overlooking the water. The style was South Seas colonial, with a green winged roof and a wraparound porch on each of its three, rather narrow stories. On either side of the white pebbled drive, six-foot tiki totems with fierce faces stood guard and at the end of the drive, directly in front of the green garage doors, sat Xander's gold Lexus.

Oh, brother. This was an interview Dinah would rather kick down the road or at least wait until Claude Ann was present. She had neither the standing nor the chutzpah to ask him what went on between him and Tess and her instinct about Xander was hazy in the extreme. Maybe he'd brought Lyssa with him, which would make any reference to Tess radioactive.

Deciding to play it by ear, Dinah left the car and walked through a side garden toward a tiered wooden deck overlooking a natural, kidney-shaped tidepool at least eighty feet long. Xander slumped in a green-striped deck chair staring out at the white combers skirring toward the black sand beach below.

She said, "It's an inspiring sight."

He looked up from his reverie. "The view from here has always lifted my spirits. Not so much today."

"Claude Ann told me that you're worried about Lyssa."

"She's distraught. She feels cursed."

"Where is she?"

"With Jon. She'd rather he look after her." He stood up and eked out a thin smile. "I'll show you around if you like."

"Later. I'll sit with you for a while if you don't mind."

"Please do." He sat and gestured her into a chair. "I'd welcome any comfort or counsel you have to offer."

Dinah gnawed her lip and watched a long comber curl sideways across the water and crash onto the beach. The only counsel she could offer was to get out ahead of the tide of bad news. Maybe she should prod him. If she prodded him now, he'd be better prepared to answer questions from the police. And from Claude Ann. "Xander, why didn't you tell the police that you'd met with Tess Wilhite yesterday afternoon?"

He kept his eyes resolutely on the next wave. "How did you know?"

"Someone saw you together. I talked with Tess a few hours ago. She didn't know that Raif had been murdered."

"How did she take it?"

"I'm not sure. She seemed overwrought at first, and then she turned to ice and said she was going to the police. She thinks that you killed Raif. That you might kill her."

"I've thought about killing Raif. He was a heartless bastard. He had Lyssa hypnotized. I couldn't believe she didn't see how promiscuous he was. Now, it seems he was destined to break her heart one way or another." Xander got up and walked to the edge of the deck. With his back to her, he said, "I didn't kill him."

Ordinarily, Dinah didn't like talking to a person's back, but in this case maybe it was easier on both parties. "I made a few inferences while talking with Tess. She and Raif were lovers, weren't they?"

"Oh, yes. She wasn't his only dalliance, but Raif and Tess were uniquely suited to each other. Neither was capable of love." Dinah made no inferences about love. "Was there ever anything sexual between you and Tess?"

He turned around and met her eyes. "No."

"Did I guess wrong then? Were they not blackmailing you?"

"Oh, yes. Raif gambled that I wouldn't tell Lyssa about his relationship with Tess, or if I did, he could convince her that I was only trying to malign him and destroy his marriage. He held it over my head that Tess' false charge could be renewed. He had already poisoned Lyssa's mind with so-called rumors of a girl I raped, rumors he said he picked up from his Punahou chums. He didn't tell her it was Tess making the claim. Lyssa hated Tess for the shameful way she'd treated Jon."

"But, Xander, if it was all a lie, why did you pay?"

"Because she's insane. And frighteningly believable. I couldn't have her go back to Jon with more of her lies. I couldn't risk being estranged from my son. Jon says he believes my denial, but he loved her. In his heart, I think he's still unsure. She could twist him around her little finger again. So I paid to keep her quiet until last week."

"Let me guess. Last week Raif presented you with a demand for eighty grand."

"How did you know that?"

"Never mind. Did you give him the money?"

"I couldn't. I told him I was tapped out. He'd have to wait until after Uwahi closed. He said he couldn't wait. He showed me some pictures he'd doctored with Photoshop and said he'd show them to Claude Ann and Jon if I didn't give him the money as soon as we got to Hilo."

"What did you do?"

"I had no choice. I told Claude Ann everything and I told Jon."

"You told Jon that Tess and Raif were lovers?"

By his frown, she supposed he realized he'd just given Jon a motive for murder. "No. No, what I told Jon...I told Jon that Raif was blackmailing me, but I didn't tell him that Raif and Tess were lovers."

Dinah's truth meter was far from infallible, but that was a particularly bumbling lie. She wondered if the call

Jon received just before he left her alone on the day of the murder was a call from Xander. Jon could have called him back on the way to the Observatory and Xander's revelation sent him roaring off in search of Raif.

Weeping Jerusalem. With such a surplus of suspects, why did the only two men she'd found attractive in the last six months have to land on the list? "What about Avery? Weren't you afraid Tess would tell him if you stopped paying and he would back out of the Uwahi deal?"

"Avery has been a good friend over the years. I would hate to have him think that I raped anyone, certainly not his daughter. But at this point, he needs Uwahi to succeed as much as I do. Tess has always been a strange girl, reckless and devil-may-care. If Avery knew for a fact that I raped her, he'd rationalize and say she'd asked for it. He'd show up at the closing tomorrow and sign the papers with a smile."

"How can Avery be that callous? Or that desperate? He's your primary investor. I thought he had gobs of money."

"He thought so, too. Unfortunately, he invested most of it in Bernard Madoff's hedge fund. As I'm sure you've read, that fund turned out to be a massive Ponzi scheme, Avery's hemorrhaging money and it'll be years before he recovers anything from the Madoff bankruptcy trustee, Uwahi is triage."

TWENTY-NINE

DINAH NEEDED TO be alone. She needed quiet and anonymity. She probably needed to share the information she'd gleaned today with Langford and Fujita, but the sum of what she'd gleaned only added up to confusion. Passing the turnoff to Jon's Wahilani, she turned into the entrance to Volcanoes National Park.

As the brochure handed out at the entrance gate explained, Kilauea is merely a four thousand foot bump on the southeast flank of Mauna Loa, which rises some thirty thousand feet from the ocean floor. Mauna Loa, or Long Mountain in the Hawaiian language, is a "shield" volcano, one of five that make up the Big Island of Hawaii. Shield volcanoes have gentler slopes than cone-shaped stratovolcanoes and their eruptions tend to be less explosive. In fact, Mauna Loa doesn't look all that tall in comparison to the surrounding terrain, but at sixty miles long and thirty miles wide, it is the largest volcano on earth by volume and area and it comprises fully half the area of the island.

Kilauea, though it's only a bump, is considered a separate volcano. It has its own plumbing system through which magma percolates up from deep inside the earth and it has a coterie of seismologists and volcanologists and geophysicists who study its every hiccup from their state-of-the-art Observatory on the rim of the caldera. Because Volcano Village sits at roughly the same elevation as the summit, there's little or no ascending.

Dinah parked at the Visitor's Center and walked to the caldera overlook. A cloud of gray volcanic gases, which the brochure called vog, rose from the hellish depths of Halemaumau crater and boiled across the landscape toward the other side of the island. It looked as if a dirty eraser had rubbed across the blue sky. This was Pele's stomping ground. To the Hawaiians, she encompassed all things volcanic—steam, lava, noxious vog, eruptions—and the caldera below afforded an amazing view of the first three.

Was this where the wedding was to have taken place? She hugged herself to keep from shaking. It was impossible not to visualize Raif's flesh roasting beside a stream of liquid fire. The police hadn't said, but she assumed that even a few minutes at two thousand degrees Fahrenheit would make it impossible for the coroner to determine whether he'd been shot before or after he fell into the lava. She prayed that the bullet came first, then remembered that she was praying at the altar of the goddess who'd immolated him. She thought, too, about the archaeologist, Patrick Varian. Steve's idea that the two deaths were a coincidence was beginning to bear out. If Raif was killed because he gambled with the wrong guy or blackmailed the wrong guy or screwed the wrong woman, there could be no link to Varian.

She had to think about something else for a while or she'd go bats. It was only a little after five. The sun was still bright and hot. Maybe she could walk off this turmoil, or at least avoid worsening it for a while. She reviewed the park map. Crater Rim Trail was closed due to dangerous amounts of sulfur dioxide gas, but the Kilauea Iki Trail was deemed safe enough for the casual tourist in sneakers provided that one "take care at cliff edges and cracks." That was one warning she definitely would heed. She bought a bottle of water at the Visitor Center, drove to the trailhead, and began walking.

Kilauea Iki, like Halemaumau, was a smaller, circular crater inside the much larger caldera. The descent to the hardened lava floor of the crater followed a series of switchbacks through a lush rain forest. Except for the birds, she had the trail all to herself. The view of the crater floor below was obscured by trees and overhanging foliage. Strange plants and ferns abounded. Where the sun knifed through the thick canopy, puffs of vapor wisped off the leaves. The moist, earthy smells conveyed an almost primordial sense. She felt as if she were breathing the same molecules that the first Hawaiians had breathed. The same molecules that Captain Cook had breathed when he dropped anchor off the Kona Coast in 1779. The molecules he breathed before the natives deduced that he wasn't the reincarnation of Lono after all and killed him.

For all its beauty, Hawaii did not lack for violence. And Pele seemed to go especially hard on lovers. Dinah recalled a myth about Pele falling in love with a handsome chief named Lohi'au on the island of Kaui. But being a goddess carried responsibilities and she was obliged to return to Hawaii to churn out more lava and make more land. She promised Lohi'au that she'd send for him as soon as possible. True to her word, she asked her most trusted sibling, Hi'iaka, to go and ferry him back to Hawaii. Hi'iaka agreed, asking only that while she was away, Pele protect a grove of pandanus trees that she treasured. Pele promised and Hi'iaka set out for Kaui. But by the time she arrived, poor lovelorn Lohi'au had hanged himself.

Hi'iaka revived him and enticed his errant soul back into his body, but when he woke up and saw her sweet face, he did an emotional one-eighty and declared his love for her instead of Pele. Hi'iaka rebuffed him and dragged him back toward Hawaii. But as they drew near, Hi'iaka spotted a wildfire devouring the trees Pele had promised to protect. Enraged, Hi'iaka pasted a long, retaliatory kiss on Lohi'au's fickle lips in full view of her pyromaniac sister. But hell hath no fury like Pele when she's scorned. She flooded the mountain with fire and incinerated her faithless lover.

Apparently, it was no accident that the Hawaiian word for "love" also meant "good-bye" and "alas." Aloha had its dark side and Dinah couldn't seem to say aloha to thoughts of murder.

The forest ended abruptly and the bleak, black expanse of the crater floor opened out in front of her like Hell's foyer. There were several groups of hikers. Some gathered around numbered cairns, which marked the trail, to peruse the correspondingly numbered descriptions in their guide brochure. Some snapped pictures. Some explored the off-trail sights—cinder cones and steam vents and weird rocky depressions.

Dinah had no desire to explore this charred and eerie landscape, the aftermath of a flood of Pele's fire. She was about to turn around and start back up the hill when she clocked Eleanor Kalolo in a red-striped muumuu like a carnival tent. Eleanor stood under a flowery parasol minutely examining the single flame-red blossom on a lone, incongruous tree. As Dinah and any number of tourists watched, she pulled a pair of shears out of her pocket and, indifferent both to federal law and Pele's wrath, snipped off the blossom.

Dinah walked about a hundred yards across the lava to speak to her. "Hello, Eleanor."

She looked up with a testy expression. But when she saw who it was, her expression changed to one of benevolence, more or less. "You come wid me. Time we talk story." She took Dinah's arm and leaned heavily against her. "You help me back up the mountain. I haven't walked this far in a long time. When Leilani and I were little, our father brought us down here and we cooked a chicken in the hot lava. It was against the law, of course. Haole law."

Dinah supported Eleanor's unsteady bulk as best she could. "Did you hear about Raif Reid's murder yesterday?"

"Of course, I heard. He was my niece's husband." She

handed Dinah the red blossom she'd picked. "It's called an ohia. It's one of the first to grow in lava. It was named for a handsome warrior Pele wanted to marry, only he fell in love with another woman, Lehua. Pele punished Ohia by..."

"Incineration," supplied Dinah. "That seems to be Pele's modus operandi." She couldn't keep the sarcasm out of her voice. She was losing her taste for Pele myths.

Eleanor glowered as if to say, pearls-before-swine. "Pele punished him by turning him into a tree. But the other gods felt sorry for Lehua. They turned her into the red flower that grows on the tree so that the two lovers could always be together."

Talking story was apparently not the same as talking turkey or, if it was, Eleanor must enjoy having the story gouged out of her. "What do you know about Raif's sins, Eleanor?"

"He cheated."

"I know he cheated on Lyssa. Did he cheat at cards, too?"

"Cheat at one thing, cheat at everything. He was kolohe when he played cards and moekolohe when he slept with other women. He was scum."

Dinah was surprised by her vehemence. She wouldn't have thought that Eleanor cared one way or the other about Raif's transgressions. "Did Jon tell you about Raif's kolohe ways or was it Lyssa?"

"I talk to my nephew sometimes. Lyssa hasn't talked to me since she married that bum. She's my niece, my own blood, and I love her. But she's vain and willful like her mother. She didn't care that her husband was a parasite. All she saw was his handsome face and his hiluhilu friends."

"What do you mean Raif was a parasite?"

"It's just a word. It's what Jon called him."

"Do you have any idea who killed him? Besides Pele, I mean."

Eleanor stumped along in silence for a minute. The only

sounds were her whistling breath and the scuffing of her ankle-high brogans across the lava. When she deigned to answer, her words were dipped in acid. "Xander Garst kill 'im. 'Apaka, kolohe, ho'opunipuni. It's his hala dat brings po'ino to both his children. What goes around comes around."

Dinah's temper flared. "Stop it. Stop toggling in and out of pidgin and Hawaiian and stop your mysterious hints about Xander's crimes and misdemeanors and hala huna whatever. Either spit out your criticism in the language I speak and tell me what this Pash thing is about or put a sock in it."

"Kaii. Boddah you I talk stink 'bout Garst, eh? Boddah you I talk pidgin and Hawaiian? If there were any justice in this world, Garst would be dead instead of my sister and you'd be deferring to me, speaking my language in my homeland."

They had reached the trail leading up through the forest and back to the road. Eleanor let go of Dinah's arm and sat down heavily on a boulder. She closed her parasol and blotted the sweat off her forehead. "I feel junk."

With a mixture of concern and contrition, Dinah offered her her water bottle.

She took it and drank. When she was finished, she screwed the top back on the bottle and handed it back. "Mo bettah. Mahalo." With the thank you, her voice softened, as if she were feeling a little contrite, herself, and she reverted to standard English. "I don't wish Garst dead. I want him to lose his money on Uwahi, I want him to lose his good name, and I want your friend to see that he is a liar and a fraud and save herself. He killed my sister."

"How could he have killed your sister? He was in California when she died. Did something happen there that made her want to kill herself?"

"Yes."

"What?"

"Garst was unfaithful to her."

"How do you know that? How did she know that?"

"Somebody called her from the convention, somebody who'd seen him carrying on with a woman. Leilani was furious. She cried all the time she tried to talk to me."

That phone call again, and yet more infidelity. Louis Sykes had been fooling around with another woman, too, or so went the gossip among the U.S.G.S. "oldtimers." The earth sciences people must be a lusty bunch and a gossipy bunch. The blabbermouth who'd tipped off Leilani to her husband's fling must have been shocked by her reaction. Shocked and guilt-ridden.

"It must have been one of Xander's colleagues who called her. You never found out who it was?"

"No. She didn't say."

"What did you and Leilani argue about when she brought the children to your house the day she killed herself? Jon remembers you yelling and calling each other names."

"We argued about what we always argued about. I told her she should stick to her own people, stop being embarrassed by her ancestors. I said raise your children like Hawaiians. They were born in Hawaii to a Hawaiian woman descended from royalty. There's no blood quantum that makes Jon and Lyssa less Hawaiian. But she wanted them to be haole. She said the old ways are pau, finished, and that I wanted something that doesn't exist anymore. She called me old, antique, kahiko. I was about your age." She made a guttural noise in the back of her throat.

It took Dinah a few seconds to recognize the noise as a laugh. She felt obliged to say something consoling. "Leilani sang meles to the children. Jon seems proud of his Hawaiian ancestry. He seems in love with the land and the culture."

Eleanor didn't reply.

"Did you see Leilani again after you argued?"

"No. We had no reconciliation. No kala 'ana." She squinted up at Dinah, shielding her eyes from the sun with one hand. "Kala 'ana is kala 'ana. It means what it means. Hawaiian isn't a code for something else. But I will tell you what it comes closest to meaning in English. To give kala 'ana is to lift the burden of anger. It is forgiveness. I can never have my sister's kala 'ana now. I can never tell her that I loved her. Love her still. That's what Garst took from me."

"And you're getting back at him by obstructing the sale of Uwahi?"

"Uwahi was salt in the wound. My family owned the land back when Garst married Leilani. It wasn't a lease-hold on trust lands. We owned it in fee simple. My father revered the land and wanted to protect it. He signed a conservation easement, a legal agreement that restricts future uses of the property regardless of who owns it. When he died, my mother was forced to sell the land, but we knew the land would be preserved because the restrictions still applied. They ran with the title. No building. But Garst had always coveted the place. He brokered a land swap between the owner of a much larger tract and the land trust charged with enforcing the easement. He and his lawyers gamed the system. The trust consented to lift the easement and Garst bought it. That's when I turned to lawyers, myself."

"What did you mean by Pash? What is it?"

"It's a law. Public Access Shoreline Hawaii. The law grants us Hawaiians access to land that has cultural and religious uses. The bones of King Keawenui are buried under the lava at Uwahi. I pray there. I won't let Garst defile it."

"But the closing is tomorrow morning, Eleanor. You won't be fighting Xander anymore. You'll be fighting a Texan named Jarvis."

"Kaiii! I know who he is."

"Then why haven't you gone directly to him with your claim?"

"Jon told me about the sale, but he didn't tell me who the buyer was until you told me just now." Using her parasol as a cane, she pushed herself off the boulder. "I thought the land would be used for building houses, more seaside mansions for haole millionaires. I didn't know that Paul Jarvis was conniving to buy Uwahi. He and his boosters have been lobbying the legislature for over a year to legalize gambling in Hawaii. He wants to build a chain of casinos and, if the state so chooses, it can dole out some of the profits to Native Hawaiians. He says that gambling will make us all rich."

THIRTY

CLAUDE ANN SAT alone at Jon's kitchen table in front of a glass of red wine, drumming her fingers and looking daggers. "It's about time you dawdled in. I have something to say to you."

"Hold the thought." Dinah proceeded into the bedroom, threw off her clothes, stepped into the shower, and turned the water on full force. She was tired. Tired from towing Eleanor up a hill no woman her size should have walked down in the first place. Tired of mixing with people who minced the truth into misleading little bites, people who acted as though they'd sooner chop off an arm than cough up the whole truth. In the space of a single day, she'd been privy to Tess' bizarre emotional outburst, George Knack's coded threat, Xander's questionable disclaimer, and Eleanor's insistence that Xander's far-off hanky-panky had killed her sister as surely as if he'd pushed her over that cliff. Eleanor is oversaturated with Hawaiian myth and so am I, thought Dinah. A long-distance phone call couldn't kill a person the way Pele's spate of fire killed Ohia.

Dinah walked out of the shower feeling prickly, in no mood to take any shit from Claude Ann. Instead of slamming Raif and wishing he was dead, Claude Ann should have taken Dinah into her confidence and told her he was blackmailing Xander. Either they were friends or they weren't. She swaddled herself in Jon's oversized robe, combed her wet hair, and marched back to the kitchen. She took a wine glass out of the cupboard, clunked it on the table, and sat down. "I suppose Xander's told you that

I pried into his personal affairs this afternoon. You can lay into me about it if you want, Claudy, but we're past the time for fabricating excuses or editing out the uncomfortable parts of the story. We've got a murder on our hands and you and Xander could both end up as suspects. So no more lies, no more holding back, no more waffling."

Claude Ann poured Dinah a glass of wine and pushed it across the table. "The thing that ticks me off is the way you stirred up Tess Wilhite. Didn't growin' up in Needmore teach you anything? Jiminy Christmas, you don't have to wake up a snake to kill it."

"That's a peculiar thing to say, especially as Tess seems to think that Xander killed Raif and that he wants to kill her."

"You know what I meant. You shouldn't have clued her in about Raif's murder. She could have read about it in the papers and never connected Xander or any of us to the crime. Now Xander says she's all riled up and threatening to go to the police. She'll dish up another crock about Xander and make everything that much worse."

"Maybe. But if she goes to the police, she'll have to cop to blackmail. She'll have quite a lot of explaining to do about her relationship with Raif. And her employer, or one of them, has good reason to rein her in."

Claude Ann finished her wine and emptied the rest of the bottle into her glass. "I'm fated. Every time I start to get married, my life falls to pieces."

Dinah forbore to remark that, considering Raif's fate, Claude Ann's wasn't half so bad. But more than a few things had gone awry and Claude Ann was entitled to feel rotten. Dinah certainly did. She said, "Maybe I'm the jinx. If you ever decide to marry again, don't invite me. Just e-mail me your new name and address."

"This will be my last weddin'. I just hope it doesn't take place in the prison chapel."

It was pitch dark outside now and the rain had returned. It pelted against the metal roof and dribbled down the window panes—the pathetic fallacy. Dinah couldn't tell whether Claude Ann believed that Xander had, in fact, killed Raif or whether she merely feared that he would be blamed. Either way, she sounded determined to marry him and Dinah could only wonder what that kind of unconditional love must feel like.

The room felt cold. Dinah went to light the gas heater, but Jon hadn't turned the gas back on since the earthquake. She pulled his robe tighter around her. It smelled of Scotch and sandalwood soap and she felt a stab of almost Pele-esque jealousy. Had Tess worn this robe after passionate nights of lovemaking with the pre-scarred Jon? Had she really twisted him around her little finger? Had Jon blown his stack when he found out that she'd been doing Raif at the same time she was doing him? Had Jon swiped Claude Ann's gun in Honolulu, tracked Raif down in Pahoa, and given him a taste of what hot lava felt like against the skin before shooting him?

"Open another bottle of wine," said Claude Ann, emptying Dinah's undrunk glass into her own.

Dinah hunted in the cupboard and found a bottle with a label that read "Deadly Zin." How apropos. She opened it, and went back to the table. "I don't know who killed Raif, Claudy, but the more the police know, the better the odds of catching him. Or her. We have to tell them everything and trust them to nail the right person."

"Since when are you gonna trust anybody, let alone the police? You made it sound like that detective you lived with in Seattle disappointed the crap out of you. And this Hawaiian outfit, Langford and Fujita, they don't act like they're wowed by our Southern charm and high moral tone. Langford keeps pesterin' me about the gun, like he thinks

I'm gonna break down and admit that I shot that black-mailin' varmint."

"And all you did was wish that he was dead." Dinah filled her glass with Deadly Zin. "Who else besides you knew that you had a gun?"

"Nobody except Hank and maybe Marywave. I didn't take it out and spin it or play quick-draw at parties."

"Okay, then who was in your suite? Think. Xander, of course, and Hank. Who else?"

"Gosh, Xan and I had been on the Big Island for a couple of weeks and when we moved over to Oahu, I had a party in my suite the first night we checked into the Olopana. Raif and Lyssa were there."

"Jon?"

"No, he wasn't there."

Dinah took heart. "So unless he broke in on the day of Xan's big party, he couldn't have filched the gun."

"I guess that's right."

"Was anyone else at the party in your suite?"

"Avery Wilhite and his wife, Kay, were there. And Steve and his girlfriend, Jessica."

"Steve has a girlfriend?"

"Well, I don't know if they're a regular item. She was a real pretty blonde and he was all over her. I had just bought into Uwahi as a sort of silent partner and Steve added my name to the official documents, whatever you call 'em, and we drank champagne."

Dinah downed several sips of Deadly Zin. Wasn't Jessica the name of the girl at the front desk at Peacequest, the one who looked like a glass of warm milk? What did Steve see in her? Dinah banished the thought. Sometimes a coincidence was just a coincidence.

"How much money did you put into Uwahi, Claude Ann?"

"Seven-fifty."

"Seven hundred and fifty thousand? Holy shit. How much money did you walk away with after the divorce?"

"Seven-fifty. Not counting my alimony and Marywave's child support."

"You gambled your whole nest egg on this land deal?"

"It's not a gamble. It's a sure thing."

Dinah put her head in her hands. "If you're worried the wedding might have to take place in prison, isn't it time to rethink the groom and his assurances?"

"Stop actin' so superior, Dinah Pelerin. You always act like you have some, I don't know, some deep insight into the men I love. Like you know what makes 'em tick and I don't know squat. That's how it was with Wesley and Hank and now you're doin' it again with Xander."

"Okay, Claudy. Let's deal with those first two. I have to get something off my conscience once and for all. My big insight about Hank is that you never loved him. You took advantage of the fact that he loved you and you married him to save face. You couldn't stand anyone thinking you'd been jilted, but you were. And here's my big insight about Wesley. The reason he punked out and didn't marry you is that he's gay."

"Gay?" She seemed stunned. "You mean, homo gay?"

"Yes, and that derogatory spin you put on the word 'homo' is the reason he didn't tell you and stayed in the closet. He ran off to Atlanta to live with my brother."

Claude Ann let this sink in and, after a minute, threw back her head and laughed so hard she cried. "I should've guessed. After the first couple of times we did it, he didn't seem all that interested in sex. Lucky for me that Hank was hot to trot."

It was Dinah's turn to be stunned. "What?"

"God's garters, Dinah. How'd you get through school if you can't even count to nine? I was pregnant when I married Hank in late February. Marywave's birthday is September third. She's Wesley's child."

"And all that business about me making a fool of you and you had to get married to keep from being a laughing stock, that was all a lie?"

"No, it wasn't. How would you feel if I galloped off to Seattle to find that Nick guy you were so crazy about and told him how he'd broken your poor heart and you were pinin' away for him and would he please, please come back to you or you'd wither up and die?"

"I'd wring your neck."

"Well, so there. I told you the truth, only I left some stuff out of the story."

"And threw some stuff in," shot Dinah, cursing herself for her blind stupidity. "She favors Hank, doesn't she? Yeah, right."

"I'm sorry if I made you feel guilty, Di, but I kept my secret for the same reason Wes kept his. It was Needmore. I'd have had the baby out of wedlock if it was anyplace else. But you know how folks treated you after your daddy ran afoul of the town's morals. If I hadn't gotten myself a husband fast, Mama and Daddy couldn't have held their heads up. They'd have had to sell the farm and move and Marywave would've been as much of a social reject as you were."

"Does Hank know about Marywave?"

"Are you kidding? No, Marywave was a real tiny baby and Hank's no better at math than you are, thank goodness. He loves her like she was his and after all he's been through, I could never tell him. Someday when Marywave's all grown-up, I may tell her. But it would be the last straw for poor Hank." She laughed again. "Wesley gay. Jiminy Christmas. No wonder he looked so funny when I told him he was a papa."

THIRTY-ONE

DINAH'S BED BUCKED. Once, twice. She opened her eyes. Another little jiggler, not half as violent as the knocking that had been going on inside her head for the last hour. She threw off the quilt embroidered with scarlet lehua blossoms and looked out the window. The rain had ceased and the sun poured through the jungle like pancake syrup. The birds had set up an energetic racket and paradise was revved up and doing its thing. The intense green made her slightly nauseous. She swallowed three aspirins and plodded into the kitchen. The Deadly Zin had lived up to its name. She felt like the walking dead.

Nine o'clock. She wondered if Claude Ann had a hangover, too. She'd intended to attend the Uwahi closing with Xander. It must already be well underway by now. If everything went through as planned, SAX Associates would be rolling in dough and the bones of King Whatshisname would be Paul Jarvis' lookout. Even if the burden of ferreting out the risks was on Jarvis and his lawyers, it still seemed unethical to Dinah. But Jarvis was no babe in the woods. He looked like a man who was working angles of his own behind the smoke screen of his big cigar. Anyway, when the check was cut, Claude Ann or Xander would be able to afford first-rate legal representation should either of them be charged with fraud or, God forbid, murder.

While Dinah was schlepping up the hill with Eleanor yesterday afternoon, Langford and Fujita and the forensic squad had shown up to fingerprint everyone. Maybe she should go to the police station, apologize for being truant, and volunteer to be fingerprinted. If she shared what she'd learned from George Knack, maybe Langford would reciprocate and share any additional information that he'd learned. He'd told her about the Beretta. But after a cup of strong coffee, she decided that Langford was unlikely to share anything else with her.

Knocking again. This time not under her feet or inside her head. She went to the door and saw Jon. In the harsh light of day, her jealousy of Tess seemed like a figment brought on by too much Deadly Zin.

He said, "I thought you'd want to know. The police picked up Hank Kemper last night."

"That's a relief," she said before remembering that Hank would tell Langford about Xander's meeting with Tess.

"They're calling him a 'person of interest.' But I think we're all persons of interest."

"There does seem to be a plenitude." Dinah's head wasn't clear enough to discuss the subject. "There was another earthquake this morning."

"I've just come back from the Observatory. The seismographs picked up a harmonic tremor under the East Rift Zone." He made it sound dire.

"Isn't it a good thing to be harmonic?"

"A harmonic tremor means that magma is moving through underground chambers. It might signal an eruption, or it might not."

"Uncertainty seems to be the watchword in Hawaii. Would you care for a cup of coffee?"

"No. I was wondering…would you like to go for a drive? I know a pagan temple where you can get rid of those bad luck earrings of yours."

How could the opinion of a leading light in the field of volcanology that Pele's tears were bad luck not magnify Dinah's own retrograde superstitions? The bride converts a handful of volcanic pebbles into a pair of earrings and the groom's son-in-law is murdered. Who could say for sure that it wasn't Pele's revenge? It didn't pay to ignore local legends.

"How long will it take? The memorial service for Raif is this afternoon."

"It's in Hilo. Wear what you were going to wear to the service and we'll go together. Bring along some walking shoes, too. The temple's not far off the road, but the footing's rough."

Dinah dressed in the blue linen suit Claude Ann had left for her and put the offending earrings in her pocket. She wore her sandals, but grabbed her Nikes off the rack as they left the cottage.

As Jon pulled out of the driveway, she asked after Lyssa. "Can she be left alone? Xander says that she's distraught."

"Having a mother who committed suicide...it's not a good role model when you're depressed. But she's with Raif's parents this morning. Dad thinks we should get her some kind of grief counseling, but I...I don't think she'll go for it."

Dinah considered telling him about her meeting with Tess, but thought better of it. Maybe he'd heard already from Xander. Maybe that's why he seemed so halting and self-conscious this morning.

He reached behind him and pulled out a pint of gin and handed it to her. "I brought this along for Madame Pele. Something to sweeten your offering."

Dinah dandled the bottle on her knees, feeling more than a little ridiculous. Maybe Jon was, too. "You don't seriously believe that Pele is causing the bad luck, do you?"

"I wanted some time alone with you. If getting right with Pele is what persuaded you to come, she's good luck."

"So this is just a pretext."

"A plan can have a dual purpose."

And so can a man, she thought. There was a hesitancy

about Jon in the back of her mind now, an apprehension that she didn't understand the first thing about him. The Jon she thought he was didn't mesh with the Tess Dinah thought she was and it was hard to recalibrate first impressions in the middle of a murder investigation.

As the Sidekick spiraled south along the Chain of Craters Road, he amped up the volume on the CD player. Bruddah Iz was singing "You Don't Know Me."

It was a lyric Dinah could relate to. She didn't feel as if she knew anyone. She had misread Claude Ann as badly as she had misread her brother all those years ago. She was forever being blindsided by secrets, the back story tucked away behind the smiling faces. Knowing that Wes was gay had blinded her to the possibility that he might be Marywave's father. Knowing that Raif was a hustler and that he gambled with punters and pros made her less willing to believe that someone more sympathetic had killed him—Jon, for instance. People seemed a certain way, but the more she learned about them, the more she realized that the seeming was all in her head. For all she knew, she was on her way to the temple of a mythical goddess with a murderer as her guide. And Eleanor's duality made Dinah's head spin. She said, "You were right about what PASH means. Pacific Access Shoreline Hawaii."

"It gets mentioned in a lot of natural resources reports."

"Where is Uwahi?"

"The property's on the Puna Coast, southeast of Mauna Loa."

"It's all over but the shouting now. After the closing, Xander and your buddy Steve will be rich."

"I guess."

"What do you know about the burial cave that's on the property?"

"I don't know that there is one."

"Your Aunt Eleanor says there is. I've read that a king's

bones contain some pretty potent mana. A king's bones could put the kibosh on the closing if Mr. Jarvis knew about them. It doesn't seem cricket to withhold the information from the buyer."

"I don't know."

"Eleanor says you told her about the pending sale. You've been in cahoots with her against Xander from the get-go. Why did you lie?"

"Maybe I just wanted to even the playing field."

"But you didn't tell her that Jarvis was the buyer. Why?"

"Dual loyalties, I suppose. A lot of big-money interests have been working in the shadows to push through the deal. Hawaii's broke and legalized gambling in a glitzy new casino could be a boon to everyone. Not just Dad and Claude Ann and Avery and Steve."

"With all the earthquakes and harmonic tremors, do you think Uwahi is safe to build on?"

"It's lava land. It's been overrun before. It could be overrun again. Lava is what Hawaii is made of. Lava is Pele."

The road dropped away in a breathtaking zigzag to the sea. A tall plume of smoke coiled above the horizon. Volcanic gas. Dinah looked around at the black and barren lava as far as the eye could see. The continuous eruptions from Kilauea had added hundreds of acres of lava land just like this and, in the process, houses and roads and entire communities had been annihilated. On Hawaii, everything was in a state of perpetual flux.

Jon pulled off the road and parked. "The temple is about a half mile from here. All that's left of it is a stone slab. The ancients used to place gifts there to be sanctified, then they'd take the sanctified object into a game or a battle to test its potency. If it brought them luck, that meant the god liked it."

She changed her shoes and stuffed the gin into her hobo bag, but that sense of hesitancy mounted. It occurred to her that no one else in the world knew where she was or who she was with. It occurred to her that Raif had walked onto a lava field much like this one and it turned into a one-way trip. "Jon, I have an awful hangover and I forgot my sunglasses. Will you take the earrings and the gin and leave them for me?"

He didn't say anything. He just looked at her.

Shit. She flogged herself for her cowardice, for not trusting anyone, not even her own intuition. She didn't believe that Jon killed Raif and, even if he had, he had no reason to kill her. A George Santayana line popped into her mind, something about daring to trust the soul's invincible surmise. "Oh, all right. You lead the way."

There was no trail and the lava was so jagged and uneven that she had to keep her eyes on the ground in front of her, glancing up from time to time to see which way he was heading. There was a tang of sulfur in the wind and the sun reflecting off the rocks hurt her eyes. After about ten minutes, she saw a small clump of ohia trees and bushes like an island rising out of a choppy black ocean.

Jon was standing beside a rough, bed-shaped stone, maybe four feet high, in the center of the island. "It's called the Heiau He'a. Temple of Blood Sacrifice."

She felt a rabbit run over her grave. "Did the Polynesians offer human sacrifices here?"

"Not to Pele. But when the Tahitians emigrated to the islands, they brought along a war god named Ku who demanded human sacrifice. Luakini. This was one of Ku's luakini temples."

"Lu-a-ki-ni. The Hawaiian language makes even human sacrifice sound melodious."

"At least, the Hawaiians only sacrificed enemies they captured in battle. They didn't kill people just because they disagreed on matters of doctrine."

She pictured the victims splayed upon the altar waiting to be disemboweled. "It gives me goose bumps."

"It gives the locals goose bumps, too. They call this a chicken-skin place."

"Won't Pele resent that I'm returning her belongings at Ku's altar?"

"You're standing on a kipuka, an area of land surrounded by lava. Pele's diverted lava flows around this heiau for probably hundreds of years, so she must regard it as hers now. Give me the earrings and the gin." He laid the offerings on the altar and rattled off some Hawaiian words.

"What did you say?"

"I asked for kala 'ana."

"Eleanor told me that means forgiveness."

"Dinah…I want you to…" He seemed at a loss for English words. "I haven't felt the desire to explain myself to anyone in a long time, but I…I want you to understand that the rift between me and my father isn't about Tess."

"Xander told you that I met her?"

"Yes. I already knew that she and Raif were lovers. I've known that since I saw them kiss outside my hospital window the day she came to tell me the rape story was a fantasy and we were finished. I've shunned Raif as much as possible. Unfortunately, that's meant seeing less of Lyssa, which she's never understood. I hoped she'd come to her senses and realize what a lowlife Raif was, but she wouldn't hear a word against him from me or from Dad. Raif banked on that. Anyway, I've been over Tess since the day I walked out of the hospital. If I had ever been tempted to kill Raif, it would've happened a long time ago."

Dinah set aside for the moment George Knack's assertion that Lyssa knew all about Raif's philandering and may have been tempted to kill Raif, herself. She said, "If Xander had known that you were aware of Tess' amour with Raif, it would have saved him a lot in blackmail."

"I didn't know about the blackmail."

"So if it wasn't Tess' rape accusation, what did cause the rift between you and Xander?"

"That's what I want to try to explain to you. I want to show you something. Will you come with me?"

This would be the dual purpose of the outing. Her reservations about him hadn't entirely lifted with this speech, but they had abated and she was anxious to get away from this evil altar. "As long as we get back to Hilo in time for the memorial service. I promised Claude Ann I'd be there."

They returned to the car and Jon drove on toward the ocean. The road swept downward in wide curves and near the point on the horizon where the water touched the sky, the road bent sharply to the left. Ahead she could see where a thick tentacle of lava had snaked across the road and blocked it.

He parked facing the water. "That's Holei Sea Arch. Come, I'll show you."

He helped her out of the car and they walked past another cautionary sign. HAZARDOUS COASTLINE, FREQUENT HIGH WINDS AND WAVES, STEEP CLIFFS. Where the land ended, she held her thrashing hair out of her eyes with both hands and looked down. They stood some ninety feet above the sea while below her, wild waves churned and crashed against the soaring cliffs, eating into the base of the rock face and sending up a stupendous white spray.

Dinah looked across at the dizzying bridge of the arch. She wasn't usually acrophobic, but the slashing wind confused her sense of balance and she felt the need to cling to the low rock barrier in front of her. "Is this the place you came to think on the day of Raif's murder?"

"Yes. There are sea arches all around the island, but this is one of the few that's easy to get to. I've been coming here off and on for years, doing the Camus thing, wrestling with the only truly philosophical problem—suicide."

Dinah's stomach tensed. "Is this the cliff where your mother jumped?"

"Yes. Did you know that the children of a parent who commits suicide are statistically more likely to die by suicide?"

"It doesn't surprise me. Is that why you and Xander are so worried about Lyssa?"

"She was younger when our mother died and, I guess you could say, more psychologically vulnerable. I must have been a hardhearted little devil because I didn't start thinking about my mother and why she found life not worth living until I was in my teens. You know, there's a theory that suicide is really just murder by proxy. The suicide has someone in mind that he wishes to kill, but the kapu against murder is too strong and so he kills himself. It's a powerful statement of hatred."

"You think your mother wanted to kill someone else?"

"She was angry. She climbed out onto that arch, God only knows how she did it, and stood upright. A tourist standing just about where we are now took her photograph. It appeared on the front page of the next day's newspaper. Her expression was spiteful and defiant and she was blowing a kiss."

"To Xander?"

"It's a question I keep asking myself."

THIRTY-TWO

"DEAR FRIENDS, WE have come together today to give thanks for the life of Raiford Reid," intoned the minister in a buttery voice. He was a round-faced, cherubic man in his middle years. He wore Episcopal robes and a rueful smile. The funeral program identified him as Father Phoenix. "We commend his soul to the Almighty and ask God's heavenly mercy on the loved ones he left behind."

Jon, Lyssa, and Raif's parents occupied the right front pew and a large number of strangers—Lyssa's local friends and Raif's alums from Punahou Prep who'd flown in from Oahu—crowded into the pews behind. George Knack and two of the girls Dinah recognized from Peacequest were also in attendance. Claude Ann and Xander snuggled close together on the left front pew and next to them sat Avery and Kay Wilhite.

Dinah, in the pew behind, studied the back of Kay Wilhite's head. Her straight, gray-blond hair was crowned with a flapper-era black cloche adorned with a large, black satin flower. It fit Dinah's stereotype. Even if her daughter weren't psycho, Kay would have to be somewhat kooky to be married to Avery.

"What's with the shoes?" whispered Steve in Dinah's right ear. She and Jon had run late getting to Hilo from Holei Arch and she'd hurried into the chapel in her Nikes.

"Shh."

Steve had brought his mother, who leaned around him to see who he was talking to. She was a frail looking woman with deep lines between her eyes and hard parenthetical lines around her mouth. The adjective that came to Dinah's mind was careworn. It would be interesting to see if, after the service, Steve cozied up to Jessica, the glass-of-milk blonde from Peacequest.

"Not a religious man, but a spiritual one," droned Father Phoenix. "A vital young man with a tremendous zest for life, Raiford was admired and respected by his peers and beloved by his friends, his family, and his young wife, Lyssa. Raif would be surprised to hear us speak today of the many ways he has touched the lives of those who knew him. But Raif has left a very special mark on the hearts of each of us gathered here today."

If eyebrows made a noise when they flew up, the sound would have been deafening, thought Dinah. She looked at Raif's smiling picture on the program cover—so handsome, so clean-cut, so deceptively winsome. She looked across the aisle at George Knack, his eyes inscrutable behind his thick glasses. Had he come to demonstrate that his relationship with Raif had been innocuous, or had he come to lean on Lyssa for Raif's unpaid debts? She wondered who among the congregation might have played cards with Raif and how many IOUs had been canceled by his death.

"While we rejoice that one we love has ascended to sit at the feet of our Lord, our joy is leavened with our human grief. The brutal manner of Raif's passing has sickened us all. And yet as I walked along Leleiwiwi Beach this morning, I saw the spirit of rebirth and renewal in so many small but hopeful ways."

Dinah's eyes wandered around the chapel, from the wreath of black anthuriums that stood as the focal point of the chancel décor, to Jon's inappropriate plaid shirt, to Xander's frowning profile, to Avery's bobbling head. The man couldn't hold still. Of course, it could have been a reaction to Marywave, who sat on Dinah's left side thumping her feet metronomically against the pew under Avery's behind. "Stop it," she hissed, and pinched Marywave's arm.

"Ouch!"

Claude Ann twisted around and gave them both a sharp look. Phoebe, who sat on the other side of Marywave, was sniveling audibly. Claude Ann put her finger to her lips and turned back around. Dinah didn't think Phoebe's tears were for Raif. She must have heard about Hank's arrest.

Dinah looked behind her. Would Tess have the audacity to show up at her playmate's memorial service? If she did, it would certainly liven things up. But, apparently, she'd decided to pass. Lts. Langford and Fujita, alert as Dobermans, were on hand for the proceedings. They had positioned themselves at about the midway point. Langford gave her a considering look and she turned back around, wondering if Tess had carried through with her threat to reveal Raif's blackmail scheme and Xander's motive. It was possible, but it wouldn't necessarily be in her best interests or the best interests of George Knack.

"Why are you so hyper?" whispered Steve.

"No reason. How'd the closing go?"

"We're golden. Tell you all about it after the service."

There was a lot more about Raif's racing career, his ambition to go into politics someday, and his all-around youthful promise. Dinah hadn't heard about Raif's interest in politics, but in hindsight, his blackmailing skills would have stood him in good stead in either the Democratic or Republican hierarchy.

"Let us bow our heads," said Father Phoenix. "Grant us, Lord, the wisdom and the grace to use aright the time that is left to us on earth. Lead us to repent our sins, the evil we have done and the good we have not done. Help us through our tears and pain…" he faltered.

There was a commotion at the back of the chapel. "Move. Move out da way, bruddah."

Heads jerked around and Dinah groaned as she saw a whole row of people being displaced to the far end of a pew to make room for Eleanor. Kingdom come. What was she doing here? Had she come to denounce Uwahi and Xander? To crow over the death of her niece's no-good husband? There was a sharp intake of breath in the front row and a general stiffening of backs. Lyssa sat bolt upright and glared behind her.

Looking bemused, Father Phoenix shut his eyes again and went on with his prayer. "Help us, dear Lord, to glimpse your loving hand at work and bring blessing out of our grief. Reach out to Lyssa and to Raif's mother and father. Enfold them in the circle of your love and may the afterglow of Raif's life light their way to a happier tomorrow." Father Phoenix raised his arms over his head. "Now receive, O' Lord, your servant, Raiford Reid, for he returns into your hands." He nodded at the organist and she launched into a recessional hymn.

Over the music, Dinah heard Xander say, "Don't, Claude Ann. Please don't."

But Claude Ann stepped into the aisle and started toward the rear of the church. Eleanor rose and started toward the front. Dinah flashed to that old math problem, two trains leave the station at the same time, traveling in opposite directions. Dinah squeezed past Steve and tripped over his mother's cane. Lyssa and Jon and Raif's parents, Xander and Avery and Kay—everyone poured out of their pews and clogged the aisle.

Xander tried to jockey around the Reids, but Raif's father grabbed his arm. "I'd like you to think about going in with me to set up a memorial fund in Raif's honor."

There seemed little hope of averting a head-on collision between Claude Ann and Eleanor. Dinah and Xander looked on helplessly as Claude Ann and Eleanor met mid-way up the aisle. The organ drowned out their words.

"Dinah, this is my wife, Kay. Kay, young woman here's from Georgia by way of Manila. What d'you say?"

"Pleased," said Kay. "Dreadful place, Manila. Dreadful climate, wall-to-wall people. All those peasants in from the hinterlands."

Dinah shook her hand. "I wish we were meeting in happier circumstances, Kay. It must have been a sad week for you. Avery said there'd been a death in your family, too."

"My brother's son."

"Stepson," corrected Avery.

"Frightful tragedy." Kay lobbed a pitying look over Avery's head toward Lyssa and shook her head. "Terrible. Can't believe it. Just like Raif."

"Young," said Avery. "Same age, same school, and dead in the same month and year."

Kay dropped her voice. "Not to speak ill of Raif, but Rick was a hard worker. A lot of promise. Conscientious. Taught at Manoa."

"Adjunct," said Avery. "Sharp as a tack, but Ph.D. not worth a sack of sand these days."

"Avery, I said, that boy will make something of himself one of these days, but there you have it."

"Wasn't to be," finished Avery. "Wasn't to be."

Dinah didn't know whether Avery had adopted his wife's speech patterns or she'd adopted his, but if this was the kind of ricochet dialogue Tess grew up with, no wonder she was schizo. Dinah tried to see where Claude Ann and Eleanor had gotten to, but they'd disappeared. "What did your nephew teach?"

"Hear, now. Enough about our kin, eh, Kay? No need to pile tragedy on tragedy. We're here for Raif today."

"Avery." Xander wrapped an arm around Avery's shoulder. "I've invited everyone down to Xanadu after the service for a post-funeral reception. Lyssa and Raif's parents will be there along with a few of Raif's local friends."

"Good idea. Keep things moving. Maybe we can take Lyssa's mind off her troubles for a little while. Can't speak for Kay, but I'll be there. How about you, Steve?" Avery snagged him as he stepped into the aisle.

Steve's mother kept on walking and Dinah jostled through the crowd and followed her. As the older woman cleared the door, she stumbled over a raised floorboard and Dinah plowed into her back. Dinah regained her balance and caught Mrs. Sykes before she tumbled off the stoop and down the stairs.

"Sorry, dear. I'm rickety."

"Let me give you a hand down the stairs."

"Thank you. I don't know where my son got to."

Dinah helped her to ground level. On the side lawn, she noticed a glider swing under an arbor of white flowers. "Would you like to sit over there and wait for Steve?"

"Yes, I'll do that."

She looked as if the slightest zephyr would blow her over, so Dinah walked her across the lawn to the bench and sat her down. "So many terrible things happening all at once on our little sliver of Paradise. All this violence. I still can't believe that poor little Lyssa's husband was murdered. Steve and Jon and Lyssa were inseparable when they were kids. I haven't seen much of her since she married and moved away, but I think of her almost as family."

On the sidewalk in front of the chapel, Dinah caught sight of Eleanor and Claude Ann standing toe-to-toe, or as close as Eleanor's size permitted. Eleanor cocked her head and squinted into the sun. Claude Ann appeared to be the one doing most of the talking. Neither was shouting or waving her fist. Dinah couldn't imagine what they were saying to each other.

Mrs. Sykes said, "Xan has done so much for Steve. Hitting balls and shooting baskets when Steve was young, taking him to sports events, being a sort of substitute father.

And now that Steve's an attorney, he's giving him a leg up in his career."

"You and Xander must have depended on one another for moral support, losing your mates so close to the same time."

"I wasn't much support for Xander. I've felt guilty about my standoffishness toward him. It must have hurt his feelings. Once or twice I thought about explaining, but time got away from us. To say anything now would only trouble the waters."

"Why were you standoffish, Mrs. Sykes?"

"Call me Sara, dear." Her bony fingers worried the folds of her skirt. "It's strange how Raif's murder has brought back sad memories for me. I wasn't much older than Lyssa when I was widowed."

Dinah took her veiny hand in hers. "Steve and Jon have told me about the accident. It must have come as a great shock and a loss."

"A shock, yes. But I had lost Louis long before he died. I had become quite invisible to him. He was in love with another woman, you see. At his funeral, the minister heaped kudos on his fine character and devotion to his wife and family. No one laughed or contradicted the pretty picture. I didn't. You can't tell a six-year-old that his father was a shit."

Her sudden acerbity struck Dinah dumb. Steve had been protecting his mother from rumors that his father had a lover and she'd been living with the knowledge since the day Louis died. "Sometimes, it's better to talk these things out. Protecting people from the truth is a kind of robbery. Steve's a big boy. You wouldn't want to deprive him of the chance to decide for himself how to think about his father."

"I disagree. Some secrets are best kept. They can only bring pain and unhappiness to the people who least deserve it." She patted Dinah's hand. "And yet here I've gone and told you my secret. Why is it so much easier to talk to a stranger than a friend or a relative?"

"Maybe because it's easier to control the story. A stranger can't argue with your characterizations." Dinah turned around and Claude Ann and Eleanor had disappeared. Mystified, she sat down beside Sara Sykes.

She laughed. "You're a very astute young woman. My characterization of my husband would certainly differ from others who knew him and worked with him."

"Did you know the other woman? His lover?" Just then, Steve walked out of the chapel with Avery and Kay and Dinah had an epiphany. What was the word Avery used? Besotted. Like himself, Louis had been besotted by Leilani Garst. "Was it Xander's wife?"

"Why, yes. How on earth did you guess?"

"Did Xander know or suspect that Louis and Leilani were having an affair?"

"I doubt it. Even if he did, he was completely mad about the woman. If she'd taken a hundred lovers, he'd have forgiven her. And he loved Louis. Xan was lecturing at Stanford the day Louis died. When he got back to the hotel that night and learned that Louis was dead, he called me in tears. I was the one who told him about Leilani. That she'd killed herself."

Dinah thought about Jon's theory that suicide was murder by proxy. She pictured Leilani perched atop Holei Arch blowing a kiss. Was that kiss a message of hatred? Had she killed herself to spite someone else? "Sara, who was it who told Leilani about Louis' death?"

"I don't know. The police probably, or one of the U.S.G.S. people at the conference. Avery is the one who called me."

THIRTY-THREE

THE GATHERING AT Xanadu following the memorial service, like the gathering at Kilauea Lodge following the discovery of Raif's murder, was rife with emotion. But not all of the emotion was grief. There was an irrepressible light of triumph in the eyes of the SAX Associates. The deal they had wanted so badly had finally closed and their relief was conspicuous.

A table of wine and cold cuts had been set up on the deck. The centerpiece was a blown-up photograph of Raif posing beside his hot yellow race car with a bright red 7 painted on the door and roof and Durante's Auto Parts in white on black on the rear fender. Several guys about Raif's age reminisced about seeing Raif do a backflip once after winning a race.

Xander stood beside the lagoon talking with Raif's parents. His father, an older, beefier Raif, seemed to have cottoned on to the fact that Claude Ann might be implicated in his son's death. "We're staying on at our condo in Honolulu until the police can give us some answers. It seems the gun that killed our boy belonged to your girlfriend or her ex. The police tell me they've got the man behind bars. If they can't get to the bottom of this, I'll hire private cops."

"I hope they get to the bottom of it, too, Robert." Xander's reply was mild and amicable. He seemed to be going out of his way to paper over his dislike for Raif, presumably for Lyssa's benefit. "My daughter needs to put this tragedy behind her and move on with her life."

His daughter languished in a chaise longue at the edge of the deck. Raif's mother sat at the foot of the chair, dabbing at her eyes. Dinah wished that she didn't know about Lyssa's arrangement with George Knack. Every time she looked at Lyssa now, she thought of Pele and the jealous rage that moved her to incinerate her two-timing lover.

Dinah was dying to talk to Claude Ann and find out what she and Eleanor had been yakking about, but every time she got within earshot of Claude Ann, she dashed off to answer the phone or tend to something in the kitchen.

Jon and Steve had walked down to the beach where they seemed to be having a weighty discussion. Steve had dropped off his mother before coming to the party, but Dinah felt that she had solved the mystery of Leilani's and Louis' near-simultaneous deaths. Avery Wilhite had worked for the U.S.G.S. way back when and attended that earth sciences conference in California. He sussed out that Leilani and Louis had an extramarital thing going on and it must have infuriated him. Not only did Xander have a sexual relationship with this enchantress, but so did Louis. When Avery saw Louis fooling around with another woman, the jealous old gossip decided to rat Louis out by telling Leilani. He didn't count on her jumping off a cliff to spite Louis. Or had she done it to spite Avery?

Dinah took a Sincerely Yours out of her purse and went to smoke and look out at the ocean. She leaned over the rail and exhaled a mare's-tail of smoke and suspicion. Was Avery the source of the scuttlebutt about the woman on the float? What if Louis hadn't cheated on Leilani? What if Avery conked Louis on the head, pushed him into the pool, and made up a story to cover it up, or even paid a woman to say she'd witnessed the drowning?

"Beautiful sight, eh, Dinah? Never palls. Ever think about moving to the islands? Everything you'd ever want.

Year-round swimming, snorkeling, sailing, fishing. You can even ski on Mauna Kea if that's your thing. And your friend Claude Ann lives here now."

Dinah looked at Avery in a new light. Was she hatching a boogyman out of a few snippets of information and her over-fertile imagination? "I don't know, Avery. I tend to get claustrophobic on islands. I'd be afraid I'd get rock fever."

"Like Raif, poor boy. Couldn't hack it for long periods, but liked to visit. Liked pushing the envelope here in our little corner of the world. Poker parties, sports betting. Drove Xan crazy. But pretty soon, we'll have legalized gambling. Kay, I said, hang on to your hat. We're catching up to the rest of the country. Glad you got to meet my Kay. She liked you. Girl's got the aloha spirit, she said. She was sorry she couldn't come to the do here this afternoon. Baby shower, book club. Can't keep up. Always something."

"Officers!" Xander's voice was too loud, too hearty. "To what do we owe this visit?"

Lt. Langford and Lt. Fujita strode up onto the deck.

Langford smiled, friendly as a gallows. "We have some new information. Since you all were going to be together in one place this afternoon, we thought we'd drop by and bring you up to speed."

"About time," said Raif's father. He motioned to his wife and Lyssa. "This is more like it."

Claude Ann appeared in the door and slung Dinah a look, like this is your fault.

If Xander expected bad news, he concealed it. "Shall we go inside?"

Avery cupped his hands around his mouth and called over the rail to Jon and Steve. "The police are here."

Jon looked up and frowned. He said something to Steve and the two walked back toward the house.

"Hold on to your hat, eh, Dinah?" Avery put his hand on the small of her back and nudged her toward the door.

She tried, but couldn't quite repress a shudder. She flashed him a nervous smile, stubbed out her cigarette, and joined the migration into the living room.

"Y'all sit down wherever." Claude Ann waved an arm around the room in a gesture of all-encompassing disgust and curled up on the end of a black leather sofa.

Raif's mother took the opposite end of the sofa and Lyssa rested one hip on the arm next to her mother-in-law. Mary-wave sat cross-legged on the floor with her back against the middle of the sofa playing with her pink phone. Phoebe and Dinah sat down in facing club chairs. Phoebe looked as if her visions of a happy future had gone poof. Xander brought out several folding chairs, but Robert Reid refused to sit. Xander settled on the arm of the sofa next to Claude Ann. Jon and Steve each took a chair and parked themselves on either side of Dinah. Avery stepped around Marywave and sat down next to Mrs. Reid. The detectives remained standing.

"As you know," said Langford, "Mr. Hank Kemper was taken into custody late yesterday and was questioned regarding the murder of Mr. Reid."

Lyssa skewered Claude Ann with a red-eyed stare. "If Dad hadn't hooked up with Claude Ann, Raif would be alive today. She's the reason that lunatic came here. If it weren't for her, Raif would be alive."

"Mr. Kemper remains a person of interest," said Langford. "But as of this time, he has only been charged with vandalism."

"Why not burglary?" asked Xander.

"His daughter gave him a key to the room, which is as good as an invitation, and there's no proof that he's the one who removed the gun."

"My Daddy wouldn't kill anybody," said Marywave.

"It's against the Commandments. Want me to get my Bible and read it to you?"

"That's okay," said Fujita. "We, um, we know that commandment."

Langford said, "Mr. Kemper posted bail this morning and was released."

"You let him loose?" cried Claude Ann.

"What the hell?" demanded Raif's father.

Langford held up a hand for silence. "Read us what Mr. Kemper said in his statement, Fujita."

Fujita riffled through his notepad until he found what he was looking for. "He said that on the day of the murder he observed Mr. Xander Garst meeting with a blond woman from the Casino Royale Travel Agency. We've identified the woman as Theresa J. Wilhite."

"Tess?" Avery looked befuddled.

Langford smiled. "You didn't mention that when we spoke earlier, Mr. Garst. Could you just clarify why it was you omitted to tell us about your meeting with that lady?" He was all purring menace.

Xander kept his cool. "With the shock of bad news, it escaped my mind. I didn't think it was important."

"That's for us to decide," said Langford. "As a matter of fact, we followed up with her this morning. She recalled that you were angry with Mr. Reid. What were her exact words, Fujita?"

"Ms. Wilhite stated, 'Xander Garst always hated Raif, but Raif told me that it came to a head last week and Xander threatened to kill him.'"

Robert Reid's face reddened. "What the hell? Is Garst a suspect in my son's murder?"

"She's lying," said Lyssa. "My husband would never talk to that woman, not after the way she treated Jon."

"Raif was all heart," said Jon.

"What the hell?" Raif's father was like a parrot with one phrase.

Langford seemed to be enjoying the discord. "We've reviewed the phone records and it turns out that Mr. Raiford Reid spoke frequently with Ms. Wilhite, both at her office and at her home."

Raif's mother spoke up. "You said that Raif's phone wasn't recovered at the scene."

"That's correct," said Langford. "The murderer used his phone to make a phone call to a spa where his wife says she was having a water shiatsu."

"Says?" Lyssa's voice rose. "Are you insinuating that I wasn't there?"

"What the hell! They're all in it together." Raif's father seemed to be skidding toward apoplexy.

"Raif called me on my phone once," said Marywave.

Langford's eyes scrunched. "And when was that, young lady?"

"Lyssa and Mama and me went to see 'Avatar' in Honolulu and both of them had their phones turned off inside of the theater and Raif had to talk to Lyssa right away and Xander gave him my number. My phone remembers everything. I got it right here." She pushed a button and somewhere close by, a phone rang.

Langford and Fujita scanned the room.

"What the hell!"

"Great Scott!"

"It's coming from the deck," said Raif's mother.

Fijita walked outside and came back holding a black leather hobo bag by the straps like a dead cat. He handed it to Langford.

Langford smiled. "Now which of you ladies would this bag belong to?"

"It's mine," said Dinah. Her purse was identical to

Claude Ann's, but she recognized a white scratch on the outside pocket.

Langford stretched a latex glove over his hand, flexed his fingers, opened the purse, and reached inside. The phone continued to ring. Stares shifted from him to Dinah and back again. Dinah looked at Claude Ann. Someone—it had to be Raif's murderer—was trying to incriminate Claude Ann. Or was Dinah the intended scapegoat?

Langford pulled Raif's phone out as if he were a surgeon removing a tumor and held it up for all to see. "Well, well, well. This adds a new wrinkle to the investigation, wouldn't you agree, Ms. Pelerin?"

PART III

THIRTY-FOUR

THE EARLY HAWAIIANS didn't count past forty thousand. They couldn't comprehend anything bigger, more numerous, or longer. They called it kini, the ultimate number. The clock on the wall said 10:10, but it might as well have said forty thousand. Kini. Forever. That's how long Dinah had been sitting in the police interrogation room in Hilo bashing her brains and trying to figure how Raif's phone had ended up in her purse.

Langford tapped a Bic against a yellow legal pad. "Help us to understand. If you didn't put it in your purse and you didn't see anybody else put it in your purse, how do you suppose it got there?"

"As I've told you a hundred times, I don't know." Dinah's thoughts seethed with stories of people unjustly convicted—people who spent years in prison for crimes they didn't commit. She was sitting in a hard plastic chair in a stark, windowless room that was as uncomfortable as they could make it without placing it in a dungeon and across the table from her was the implacable face of a man who sent people to the clinker for a living. The trapped air ponged of fear and suspicion and the B.O. of the last customer interrogated in this room.

"What say we buy you another cup of coffee and see if that stirs a memory."

Fujita yawned and arched his back. "I'll go make a fresh pot." He left and Langford sorted through the items in her purse as if he were doing an inventory.

"Aren't you supposed to have a warrant before you search someone's personal property?"

"When a dead man's phone rings inside a lady's purse, that's what we professional law enforcement people call probable cause. In which case, we don't need a warrant." He pulled her book of myths out of the purse. "This sure looks interesting. Myths and Legends." He opened the book and read, or pretended to read, while Dinah worst-cased the course of her life from here on out. A grueling trial during which she could produce no alibi and no explanation for Raif's phone; the sentencing—she'd probably get the death penalty due to the heinous nature of the murder; and years and years in jail while she waited for a date with the electric chair. Were prisoners on death row allowed to work in the prison laundry? As she contemplated her future, the prison laundry seemed like a bright spot.

Fujita returned with the coffee in one of those cone cups in a brown plastic holder. He set it down in front of her.

"We should have copies of this book lying around the station, Fujita." Langford stabbed his finger at a passage in the book. "There's a whole chapter on crime. You read about the pu'uhonuas, Ms. Pelerin?"

"Not yet."

"They were places of refuge. In old Hawaii, anybody who broke the law, no matter how minor, would be put to death. The chiefs had no patience with lawbreakers. There was no such thing as an accident. The law was the law. But if the lawbreaker could get to a pu'uhonua, he'd be safe, absolved of his crimes. All he had to do was confess. We're kind of like a pu'uhonua here, isn't that right, Fujita?"

"Absolutely. And the way Mr. Reid's family was looking at you, Ms. Pelerin, you'd be smart to trust us. Talk to us. A lot has changed since the old days. We believe in accidents. We know how situations can spin out of control when you least expect them to. Tell us how it broke between you and Raif. We can help you."

Co-habiting with Detective Nick Isparta had taught Dinah many things she'd rather forget, but it had left her with a fair knowledge of how the police operate. They did not hand out absolution. They did not make idle chitchat with people they invited into the interrogation room or, as Nick called it, "the box." And they most definitely could not be trusted. These cops hadn't read her her rights or informed her that she was under arrest, but she was under no illusions. Everything she said could and would be used against her in a court of law.

Fujita sat down next to Langford and picked up her passport. "You must care a lot about your friend to fly all the way from Manila to be in her wedding. Were you out there for business or pleasure?"

"I was assisting an anthropological expedition. There was no salary, but my food and lodging were paid." She tried to recall Nick's checklist of "tells." If the perp's eyes move right, he's remembering. If they move left, he's concocting a story. Or was it the other way round? She focused on Fujita's hands as they turned the pages of her passport and concentrated on not licking her lips.

"You do a lot of traveling. That must get pretty spendy."

It wasn't a question. Dinah didn't comment. She took a sip of the coffee, which was lukewarm and evil tasting, and tried to project where Fujita was going with this.

"I'll bet a lot of these countries you visit have a problem with illegal gambling. Weren't you reading about some big uproar in the Philippines, Lieutenant Langford?"

Langford closed the book of myths and inclined his bulldog face across the table. "A big gambling syndicate paid bribes to some of the president's cronies to cover up an illegal numbers game they call Jueteng. You know what Jueteng is, Ms. Pelerin?"

"No."

"Long odds, no limits on minimum or maximum bets. Poor people love it. And so do the syndicates. They rake in millions every year."

"Of course, they have to hire the right kind of intermediaries to pass the bribes to the politicians. The kind of people who can come and go without raising questions. People with American passports," said Fujita. "When did you first meet Mr. George Knack?"

"Yesterday. Actually, I saw him in Honolulu, but we didn't meet. What are you getting at? If you think I have anything whatsoever to do with any gambling syndicate, you're a zillion miles off base." She sounded spluttery and she realized that she was nervously winding a lock of her hair around and around her finger. Excessive grooming was another sign of guilt on Nick's checklist. She clasped her hands together tightly in her lap and sat up straighter. "Is George Knack involved with a Philippine gambling syndicate? Is Tess Wilhite?"

Fujita opened his notepad and leafed through the tabs. "Mrs. Reid says that you and her husband spent the night together in Honolulu after the attack on Ms. Kemper."

"That's not true. We sat together in the hospital waiting room for a couple of hours and then went our separate ways."

Langford leered. "You have to admit Raif was an attractive young man. And from what we're hearing, he spread his charms over a wide swath. Did you and he have a little something extra-curricular going on?"

"No. Definitely not."

"Come on, Dinah," purred Langford. "We're not here to pass judgment. Love's a many-splendored thing, right, Kimosabe?"

Fujita flashed his partner an offended look. Dinah remembered that his first name was Kimo and assumed he didn't care for the sobriquet. But instead of shooting back at Langford, he transferred his displeasure to Dinah. "Maybe you decided you didn't want to share the gentleman's attentions with his wife and his other women friends. Maybe you borrowed Ms. Kemper's gun and put a stop to his bed-hopping."

"I could not care less about Raif's sex life."

"How about Ms. Kemper? Did she care? Was she one of his close friends?"

"What?"

"A lot of sex can break out before a wedding." Langford's face was ill-suited to a leer, but he kept on trying. "The thought of all that monogamy ahead. Some brides will jump at a last chance to be bad. Did that happen with your friend? Did she give Raif a tumble and then get worried that he'd snitch on her? She wouldn't want to risk losing a rich husband like Xander Garst. Maybe you helped her dispose of her problem."

"That's ridiculous."

Langford twiddled with his Bic. "Claude Ann was probably the shooter. Hers are the only prints on the gun. Then maybe you helped her drag Reid's body toward the skylight to confuse the time of death, and one of you had the bright idea to take his phone away with you and call Lyssa Reid to further confuse the time of death."

"None of it's true. I don't know how that phone got in my purse. I've never seen it before."

"There's no use denying it," said Langford. "Look, Ms. Pelerin, we're just trying to work out the why and how. If you tell us that Claude Ann did the murder and just asked you to hang onto the phone for her, then you need to give us a statement and set matters to rights."

"Obstruction of justice isn't much of a crime," offered Fujita. "You were only trying to help a friend. Heck, maybe she didn't even tell you it was the dead man's phone. Why don't you write it all down for us and clear things up?"

They were all over the map. Throwing ideas against the wall to see what stuck or what got a rise out of her. All they had to go on was a gun that could have been swiped by any number of people and Raif's BlackBerry, which the murderer had planted in her handbag. Which he, or she, would have purged of any incriminating evidence. The police hadn't had time to find out what secrets the phone held. They weren't ready to make an arrest. She said, "If Claude Ann had shot Raif, she wouldn't have left the gun for you to find with her prints on it and if I were trying to hide his phone, I wouldn't be toting it around, fully charged and turned on, inside my purse." She looked directly at what was probably the one-way mirror where somebody was ogling her for signs of guilt. "And unless I'm under arrest, I'd like to leave now."

Langford made a mouth of peeved impatience. "We'll get back to you with an answer in a few minutes. Bring that phone, Kimosabe." He pushed his chair back, tossed his Bic on the table, and bulled out of the room.

Fujita's lips moved silently in what Dinah assumed was an unflattering retort. He ran a hand through his bleach-blond hair, picked up the bagged BlackBerry, and followed Langford.

The skin on the back of Dinah's neck prickled. Maybe they were going to arrest her after all. She looked around at the blank walls and felt like a monkey in a cage. She twirled the same lock of hair around her finger, caught herself, and put her hands down on the table.

Fujita's notepad lay right there in front of her. He wouldn't have left it there on purpose, would he? Were they watching? She picked it up and thumbed through the alphabetical tabs. What did the police know that she didn't? She glanced at the door, which would be bursting open any second and turned to the R. In a neat, almost calli-graphic hand under the name Raiford Reid was a précis of the known facts.

Last seen alive 6/29 at 11:45 by D. Pelerin. Vic stated he was off to play poker in Pahoa. Est. time of death 12:30–3:30 near Kalapana. VA resident, no priors. Witness state-ments—see tabs. Connection to Varian killing? See V.

Hurriedly, Dinah flipped to V.

Patrick Varian—Punahou '94–'98—Raiford Reid.

Rented by wk., Bayside Apts., Hilo. Clothing, books, papers, PC. Computer forensics report pending.

The door bumped open and Dinah dropped the notepad.

Langford was talking over his shoulder as he shoved inside. "Take your gripe to Larson and see where it gets you, Kimosabe." He gathered up the items he'd taken out of Dinah's purse and piled them back in. "You're free to go for now. We'll be in touch." He glanced down at Fujita's notepad and his beady eyes went beadier. He snatched it off the table and pitched it to Fujita. "Looks like you forgot something, Kimosabe."

Fujita caught it and glared.

Dinah said, "It's nearly midnight. Will someone please give me a ride back to Volcano?"

"There's a pay phone downstairs," growled Langford. "Call one of your friends to pick you up."

"This way," said Fujita. "I'll show you."

She followed him to the phone, thanked him tersely and, when he'd gone, she dialed Jon's cottage.

"Leave me a message," said his voice on the answering machine. "I la maika'i nou. Have a nice day."

THIRTY-FIVE

CLAUDE ANN THREW her arms around Dinah and hugged her tight. "I thought you'd never call."

"I wasn't sure you'd come."

"Then your brain's sprung a leak. You should've known we wouldn't cut and run. We had a lawyer and a bail bondsman lined up and ready to go into action, didn't we, Xan? Oh, honey, you look beat. You must be ready to keel over."

Coming from the fetid smell and chill of the indoors into the warm, fragrant night air had a tonic effect on Dinah. "I'm okay. Just take me away from this place."

Xander hooked arms with both women. "The car's across the street. This way."

Claude Ann pushed Dinah into the back seat and crawled in next to her. "It's closer to drive down to the big house. You need a hard drink and a soft bed fast. I'm gonna stay with you tonight. Xander's goin' back to Volcano with the others."

"Where's Marywave?"

"With Phoebe. Phoebe's a godsend. She's always gotten on with Marywave, but lately she's just knockin' herself out bein' sweet."

Xander took his place alone in the front seat and played chauffeur.

Dinah looked out the window as they cruised along the deserted streets. The blackness of the bay and the ocean beyond drove home to her the blackness of her situation. Of Claude Ann's situation. Of their situation. She had a sense of impending doom, or impending incarceration which seemed tantamount to doom, and she hadn't the faintest glimmer what to do next. The prospect of Hank and Phoebe raising Marywave while Claude Ann wasted away in prison accentuated the blackness. "Your prints are on the gun, Claudy, and the killer planted Raif's phone in my purse. He may have thought he was planting it in yours, but either way, he's trying to make one of us the patsy."

"But who? I can think of people who might've wished Raif dead, or at least out of their hair, and I'm one of 'em. Xan is, too, and maybe even Jon. Xan and I have talked about it. We know how bad things look. But who would want to frame you or me?"

Xander stopped at a traffic light and Dinah felt rather than saw him looking at her in the rear view mirror. She leaned her head back against the seat and feigned sleep. She wished that she could eliminate Xander from the list of people who might want to frame Claude Ann. Legally, they were only business partners at this point. Did he stand to benefit if she weren't free to claim her share of the profits from the Uwahi deal? There was no way to ask with him listening, probably no way even without him listening. Claude Ann would brook no doubts about the man she loved.

The miles slid past. Dinah didn't open her eyes and Claude Ann and Xander didn't speak to each other until they reached Kapoho Beach and the guard had to lift the gate for them. Xander drove on to the house. Claude Ann jumped out of the car, gave Xander a quick kiss, and went ahead to unlock the house. Dinah yawned and opened the door.

"Dinah?"

She looked back.

Under the grainy overhead car light, Xander frowned in a way that reminded her of one of those morally conflicted, shady characters in film noir. "I said it before, I'll say it again. I didn't kill him. But you need to know that if Claude Ann or you or either of my children should be charged, I'll confess to the crime. Do you believe me?"

"I want to, Xander. I'm trying." She started to get out, but turned. "Did Jon attend Punahou school?"

"No. He had the grades, but he didn't want to leave the Big Island. Do the police think someone from Punahou had something to do with Raif's death?"

"It's not clear. It's a link to the other murder. The archaeologist."

"Ask Steve. He graduated from Punahou."

That morsel was hard to swallow. Steve and Varian and Raif were all in their early thirties. If they all went to Punahou Prep, wouldn't they have been aware of each other? Why had Steve not mentioned this coincidence when he was riffing on the subject of coincidences? Still harder to swallow was Xander's promise to confess to Raif's murder if the police came after his nearest and dearest. Was he an innocent man prepared to forfeit his freedom and possibly his life to save the people he loved, or was he a guilty man beguiling them with a promise he didn't intend to keep? She didn't take overmuch comfort from hearing her name on the list of those he'd go to prison to protect. Taking the fall for one's beloved might be romantic. Taking the fall for the beloved's maid of honor was crackbrained. As he drove away, she imagined him congratulating himself with something noble like, it is a far, far better thing I do than I have ever done.

She trailed Claude Ann down the driveway, across the deck, and into the house, ablaze with lights. Claude Ann was already pottering among the bottles and glasses at the bar.

"Make mine light," said Dinah. "I woke up about forty thousand years ago with a hangover and nothing's gone right since." Claude Ann thrust a tumbler of amber liquid into her hand.

"When do you think that phone was sneaked into your bag?"

"I've been going over and over that question. The only time I remember it being out of my sight was at the Kilauea Lodge when we both left our bags on that banquette next to Paul Jarvis and Xander."

"There were a lot of people millin' around that night, Dinah." Her defensive tone made it clear that Xander was off-limits as a suspect.

And then there was Marywave, presumably also off-limits. Dinah called to mind the triumphant look on the kid's face as she dialed Raif's number. Could her father have given her Raif's phone and inveigled her to smuggle it into the purse? She wouldn't conspire with him against her mother, would she? No. And even if Hank had killed Raif, he would have no reason to take his phone and no reason to call Lyssa at the spa. He wouldn't even know she was there.

Dinah took a sip of her drink. "Jerusalem, Claudy. What's in this?"

"Mostly bourbon." She turned back to the bar, strained the juice from a jar of maraschino cherries into her drink, and plopped down in one of the club chairs.

Dinah set her glass on the coffee table and lay down on the black leather sofa. "Had Paul Jarvis ever met Raif? Could there be any reason on earth for him to want Raif out of the way?"

"They met socially once or twice. Lord knows what rude thing Raif might've said to him, but it wouldn't have been enough to stir Paul to murder."

"Was Jarvis ever in your hotel suite in Honolulu?"

"No. If the phone was put into your bag at Kilauea Lodge that night, turned on so it would ring, how long would it hold a charge?"

"I don't know. Maybe it had one of those automatic power save features."

"One thing bugs me," said Claude Ann. "The murderer takes the phone to confuse the time of death or give himself a better alibi, whatever. But why keep it? Why didn't he toss it after he made that call to the spa? Was his plan all along to land us in the soup?"

"Maybe he wanted to make sure Raif hadn't stored any incriminating data on the phone. And when he saw that he hadn't, he decided he could send the police off in the wrong direction by planting it on one of us."

"Yeah, but wouldn't he need Raif's password to find out what was on the phone?"

"Maybe he knew the password." Dinah sat up. "I just remembered one other time when my purse was out of my sight. I left it in one of those locker baskets at Lyssa's spa, which by the way is a front for illegal gambling."

"Places like that always have extra keys," said Claude Ann. "Do you think that George Knack guy is the murderer?"

Dinah was still trying to connect Varian's murder to Raif's murder and, apparently, so were Langford and Fujita. Varian and Raif had gone to the same school, along with Steve. Did all three of the former schoolmates like to gamble? Did that connect them? Knack had teased her with the information that a lawyer in Pahoa organized poker games. Suppose it were Steve. Suppose Varian had joined in one of Steve's games after he arrived on the Big Island. Suppose he'd won more than he should off Steve and Steve killed him. Maybe Raif put two and two together and threatened to go to the police. Maybe he'd been blackmailing Steve, too. Steve would have needed to assure himself that Raif hadn't recorded anything incriminating on his BlackBerry. He'd taken it away from the scene, checked it over, and later that night at the Kilauea Lodge, he could easily have dropped it in Dinah's purse. She said, "I'm going to go to Pahoa in the morning and pay Mr. Knack another visit. If he confirms my suspicion, then I may have figured out who done it."

Claude Ann's eyes welled. "I'm afraid I know who done it."

Dinah's eyes widened. "Who?"

"Lyssa. She acted all lovey-dovey, but she knew Raif was cheatin' on her. He made a big fat fool of her and she killed him and if she's caught, her father's gonna take the blame. Did he tell you?"

"Xander said he'd confess if you or either of his children were in danger of being charged."

"I won't let him do it, Dinah. He shouldn't have to spend the rest his life stampin' out license plates to make up for the sad fact that Lyssa lost her mama. When you go to that spa tomorrow, you find out if she was where she said she was, doin' what she said she was doin'. Phoebe can't vouch for her. If nobody else on the staff can, I'm gonna make her confess. I don't know how, but I will if I have to beat it out of her."

Dinah took a last sip of bourbon, closed her eyes, and laid back down. Claude Ann's guess was as good as hers, maybe better. If Lyssa could buy Knack's help to take care of the Tess problem, she could buy his help to provide her with an alibi. And here was the kicker: Lyssa could have picked her husband's pocket and boosted his BlackBerry before he got off the plane in Hilo. In a place like Pahoa, how many cell towers were there? Could the cops pinpoint whether that call to the spa came from inside the city limits or ten miles south? Lyssa could have timed the phone call to give herself an alibi.

So many possibilities. So many secrets. Kini went by an eon ago. She felt a puff of air as Claude Ann spread a blanket over her. Her last thought was of Langford. She hoped the son-of-a-bitch didn't sleep a wink.

THIRTY-SIX

THE SUN DIDN'T loiter about playing peek-a-boo through the trees. Here at Kapoho Beach, it came up like a fireball and flashed through the windows with the intensity of an incendiary rocket. Dinah sat up blinking. Propped on the coffee table was a note from Claude Ann.

Gone to breakfast with Xander. Coffee, donuts and paper on kitchen counter. Extra toothbrush in bathroom cabinet, extra clothes in my bedroom. Help yourself. Back by ten. If you need anything before then, there's a mini-mart two miles from the entrance gate. Keys to my car on the dresser in bedroom. CA

Dinah went to the kitchen and poured herself a cup of coffee. In all of the excitement last night, she'd forgotten to ask Claude Ann about her head-on with Eleanor. It couldn't have been too scary or Claude Ann would have filled her in. Maybe Eleanor had only wanted to offer a show of sympathy to her niece.

The headline of the *Hilo Tribune-Herald* caught Dinah's eye.

BILLION DOLLAR BUDGET DEFICITS MAY BRING SLOTS TO HAWAII.

HONOLULU, Las Vegas has long been known as Hawaii's ninth island, but soon Hawaiian residents may not have to fly six hours to place a wager. Lawmakers

looking for ways to increase revenues and jump-start
the state's troubled, tourism-dependent economy will
consider allowing gambling in Waikiki and on Native Hawaiian lands. A casino on Waikiki would need
only state approval. A casino on Hawaiian crown
lands would need federal approval. The Akaka Bill,
currently pending in Congress, would confer sover-
eign control of Hawaiian lands to Native Hawaiians,
many of whom support legalization of gambling. At
present, the bill does not contain an explicit ban.

The early Hawaiians resented the missionary's ban
on gambling and the general populace today loves to
gamble. Hundreds of thousands of Hawaiians flock
to Las Vegas each year to gamble and illegal gambling thrives on the islands, primarily in the form of
sports books, cock fighting, and card houses. Pro-
ponents of legalization cite the prospect of job gains
and increased tourist dollars from high-rolling Asian
gamblers who won't have to travel so far to get to the
roulette tables. Opponents fear that our cultivated ambience of family-friendly tourism and natural beauty
would be tarnished with the advent of gambling. They
fear an increase in drugs, prostitution, and gambling
addiction.

Notwithstanding Eleanor's objections, gambling seemed
inevitable. Uwahi wasn't Hawaiian crown land and if there
were enough Native Hawaiians who supported the plan to
build a casino on the Big Island, a few awkwardly located
bones wouldn't stop the gambling juggernaut. Paul Jarvis might have no problem at all. But if gambling became
legal, George Knack's operation would shrivel and die. He
was smart enough to read the writing on the wall. Dinah
wouldn't be surprised if he had opened a back channel to

the squeaky clean Mr. Jarvis and proposed an accommodation of some kind.

She eyed the selection of doughnuts, most of which were coated with sprinkles. All that sugar made her teeth ache. She found eggs in the refrigerator, put a pot of water on to boil, and went to shower and dress. It was convenient that she and Claude Ann could still wear the same clothes. She chose a black peasant skirt and gauzy white blouse. If she was going to Pahoa, it seemed fitting to dress like a hippie.

The water was boiling when she returned to the kitchen. She boiled a couple of eggs, scraped the sprinkles off a doughnut, and sat down to eat. Claude Ann was due back in less than a half-hour. Was it a bad idea for Claude Ann to accompany her on this foray into Pahoa? She'd sounded a hair too fired-up when she talked about Lyssa last night. But the more Dinah thought about Xander's vow to confess if one of his children was charged with Raif's murder, the less sense it made for Claude Ann to impugn Lyssa's alibi. After Claude Ann talked with Xander this morning, the two of them would probably team up and ask Dinah not to stick her nose in and make waves. The best plan, Dinah decided, was to scoot into Pahoa and put her questions to Knack before Claude Ann got back.

IT WAS GOLDEN Soul Day at Peacequest and tents representing each of the energy fields—earth, water, wind, and fire—had been set up on the front lawn. The air was spiced with incense and potential customers clustered around the individual tables, reading the literature and considering whether to invest in a $25 Vibrational Assessment. A silver-voiced man in priestly raiment held a group of German tourists mesmerized as he described the varying types of live and intelligent frequencies that comprised the energy field surrounding the body and the drastic deterioration in health and well-being that resulted when these frequencies became blocked or damaged.

The Germans talked amongst each other. "Gesundheitsproblem?"

"Aber ja! Gesundheitsgefahr."

Jessica oversaw the wind energy table. Dinah waited in line until she could speak with her. "I'd like to see Mr. Knack. Is he in?"

"After the way you wasted Emily's time, I don't think Mr. Knack will want to see you." She delivered this rebuke with a perfectly pleasant smile.

"I'm sorry about that, but I'm quite sure he'll want to see me. I have some extremely troubling vibrations he'll want to assess."

Looking uncertain, as who didn't these last few days, Jessica summoned a stand-in and led Dinah down the walkway to the front door. Once again, bells clamored and the smells of eucalyptus and lavender assailed her nose. The ladies in their terry robes glanced up from their magazines.

Jessica stopped at the front desk and rang Knack's extension. "The lady who was here before, Ms…?"

"Dinah Pelerin."

"Ms. Pelerin is here to see you. She says it's…"

"A matter of life and death."

Jessica frowned. "Important." The girl turned her back on Dinah and listened. After a few seconds, she turned back, still frowning. "Mr. Knack says to go on back."

Dinah walked back to his office, thinking belatedly that she should have left Claude Ann a note about where she was going. She should have left word to call the cops if Dinah hadn't phoned in by noon. She rapped twice on the door and pushed it open. Knack lounged in his leather chair with his feet up on the beautiful desk. The pompadour, the pose, the apathetic black eyes—he was the perfect stereotype of a mafia don.

He said, "I didn't expect to see you again. And now it's life and death."

"The police grilled me last night about Raif's death. Their investigation is unsettling my life and the life of my friend."

"As I told you before, I don't know anything about Raif's death."

"Whoever killed him stole his BlackBerry. I wouldn't be surprised if he kept sensitive information on it. Raif had a taste for blackmail."

"What's that got to do with me?" He swung his legs off the desk and stood up. He was taller than Dinah had remembered and more heavily muscled.

"Your line of work makes you susceptible to blackmail."

"You're off in la-la land. Anyway, I've got an ironclad alibi. I was here at the spa all day. My staff will testify to that if they have to."

"How about Lyssa? Will they testify that she was here when she says she was or are you and your staff covering for her? If you are, you're an accessory to Raif's murder. It'll look all the worse if Lyssa's paying you for your silence. And if you know where and with whom Raif was playing poker on the day he was murdered and you haven't disclosed that information, then you're guilty of obstructing justice."

"Listen to you. You sound like a TV cop. I've given my statement to the police and they've gone over it with a fine-tooth comb. Far as I know, they've verified Lyssa's story with my employees. Whatever it is you're fishing for, you can go fish someplace else."

"Did I mention that somebody planted Raif's Black-Berry in my purse? My purse that I left unattended in a locker here the day before yesterday?"

"Well, talk of things looking bad, that's got to look bad for you, doesn't it?"

"You don't have to help me, Mr. Knack. The only leverage I have is the leverage of noise. I can make a lot of noise and the more stressed I get, the more noise I make. You have a lot of balls in the air—setting odds, taking bets, collecting debts—all of that while administering Tahitian black pearl scrubs and vibrational assessments and keeping the police off your back. And now there's this murder of a non-paying client on your doorstep."

"Ten miles south isn't my doorstep."

"Ten minutes there, ten minutes back. Too close for a really ironclad alibi. And depending on how you and your syndicate see proposed changes in the law, you're either working quietly behind the scenes to prevent gambling from being legalized or you're quietly lobbying state VIPs to make sure that it is. Noise is the last thing you want."

He removed his hornrims and polished the lenses with his sleeve. "I don't know how Raif's phone got into your purse. I didn't put it there and none of my people did. There are two numbered keys to the lockers. Jessica gives one to the customer and she keeps the other. A lot of rich folks get naked in here and stash their cash in the lockers. Jess is a Mormon. Honesty's their thirteenth article of faith."

The gratuitous bit of religious trivia rendered Dinah momentarily speechless. She almost asked him if he could name the other twelve. "What about Lyssa? Are you sure she was in her shiatsu water treatment on the afternoon of the murder?"

"She was here. She could've hired somebody to pop her husband, but she didn't do it herself."

"Do you know where Raif went to play poker?"

"I don't know."

"Guess."

"Steve Sykes has a group of poker pals. Strictly private, not open to outsiders. I don't know when they meet or how often."

"Is Steve one of your clients? The Hot Jade Stone treatment, perhaps?"

His eyes frisked her as if he were looking for a wire under her blouse.

She felt her face grow hot. "Well?"

"Once in a while, some of them lay off bets with me. Car races and ball games. Steve will put down a few Benjamins on the Bruins occasionally. Does that allay your stress?" He replaced his hornrims and went back to his desk.

"What about Patrick Varian? Was he one of your clients?"

"What the fuck?" He pivoted on one heel and lunged forward.

Heart hammering, she stepped back. "Was he?"

"Hell, no."

Dinah watched his internal fight for control play out on his face. After a long, excruciating minute, he walked over to the credenza and brought out a carrot juice. She let out a sigh of relief. "Did you know Varian?"

"All I know is what I read in the papers and if you're looking to tie that can to my tail, you'll find yourself stressed like catgut."

THIRTY-SEVEN

STEVE WASN'T HARD to find. He was listed in the Pahoa telephone directory. Dinah decided not to phone ahead to say she was coming, but after her scare with Knack, she did call Claude Ann.

Claude Ann hadn't gone back to Kapoho as planned. Marywave had complained of a bad stomach ache and Claude Ann and Xander had rushed off to Volcano to check on her. "She's runnin' a fever and complainin' about a tummy ache. It's probably just some twenty-four hour bug, but I'm getting ready to take her to the doctor in Hilo."

"How's Lyssa?"

"Refusing to eat, rantin' and ravin' about her dead mother and her dead husband. She's probably feelin' guilty."

"I don't believe she killed Raif, Claudy. Xan won't have to confess on her account."

"I don't know how I feel about that. I should feel glad for Xan that it's not his daughter, but I'm scared. Who could have done this thing, Dinah? And don't you dare suggest that it was Xan."

"Okay, I won't suggest it. Where is he?"

"He and Jon are with Lyssa, tryin' to calm her down."

"When she's calm and you have a chance to talk with her, ask her about Raif's Punahou friends, Claudy. Ask her if Raif partied or played cards with a guy named Patrick Varian."

"That archaeologist who was murdered?"

"Yes. The police think the murders are connected and so do I. If the same person killed both men, Lyssa couldn't have done it and neither could you or I. It would have taken a strong man to break another man's bones and push him into a steam vent. That's probably why Langford didn't arrest me last night."

"Jiminy. Not a woman and not Hank, because he wasn't on the island when Varian was murdered. And not Xan because I'll never believe it in a million years, so don't even go there. Have you thought any more about who could've snuck Raif's phone in your bag?"

"I think of almost nothing else. It had to have been the murderer, Claudy. Somebody we know. Somebody who's been that close to us. I think I've eliminated George Knack as a possibility. My next stop is Steve Sykes' office. If I don't turn up by dinnertime, start the search for my body there."

"Don't talk like that, Dinah. Quick. Cross yourself."

"We're not Catholic, Claudy."

"Do it anyway. And say a prayer."

"I'll cross my fingers, for us and for Marywave, too. Hope she hasn't caught the flu."

They said good-bye and Dinah followed the town map to Steve's office, a solitary white house off the main road between what appeared to be a vegetable garden on one side and a large cemetery on the other. She tried not to think of the cemetery as an omen. A group of people were working in the garden, raking and hoeing and filling their baskets with tomatoes and lettuces and herbs. Dinah parked on the street and surveilled the house. He had said that his office was downstairs and his living space upstairs, but there was no sign. Were attorneys in Pahoa in such demand that they didn't need to hang out a shingle? She wondered what kind of clients Steve serviced in addition to Xander and Avery. Gamblers? Pakalolo smokers? DUIs?

She sat in the car thinking. The pivotal fact, or so it seemed, was the planted BlackBerry and that night at the

Kilauea Lodge, Steve could've slipped it into her purse without her noticing. Of course, so could Xander or Jon or Avery or even Paul Jarvis. But Steve had sat quite close. He could have palmed the phone in a cocktail napkin so as not to leave his prints on it. Luckily, she hadn't touched it, although fingerprints on a phone wouldn't prove anything. People were constantly passing their electronic gadgets back and forth and anyone might have handled Raif's BlackBerry for completely innocent reasons.

The gardeners hefted their baskets and began to leave and she had a rush of the heebie-jeebies. Peacequest was a busy place with lots of people coming and going. There wasn't much risk confronting Knack in so public a place. This was different. When the gardeners were gone, there'd be no one to hear her if she screamed. Her cries would carry unheard across the graveyard. Perhaps she should call Langford and lay her theory on him. But even if Langford were open-minded and sympathetic, which he was not, he knew everything that she knew except that she was innocent. There was no reason why Steve would want to frame her, but what if he had drawn up the Uwahi documents in such a way that he and Avery would reap more of the profits if Claude Ann or Xander were out of the picture? He was good at devising slick legal gimmicks. He could have planted a subversive clause like a land mine in the fine print before planting the phone in what he assumed was Claude Ann's purse.

Dinah's nerves were jittery as a tambourine. Maybe she should call Jon. But he wouldn't believe that his makamaka was a cold-blooded murderer and anyway, Jon was preoccupied trying to keep his sister from committing suicide. Dinah thought about the twinkle in Steve's eyes and the grin she'd found so appealing. Was he really a murderer or was she doing to him what Langford and Fujita had done to her? Innocent until proven guilty, she reminded herself.

She got out of the car, walked across the rather unkempt grass, and climbed the steps to the concrete porch for a minute. On a whim, she knocked Jon's silly shave-and-a-haircut knock.

The door opened almost immediately. "Hey, I thought you were Jon. Come in."

Said the spider to the fly, thought Dinah. But she'd come this far. She marshaled her thoughts and walked inside.

"I was cleaning out my files." He was shirtless and barefoot and the twinkle and grin were on full display. His office, however, was a pit. Heaps of paper littered the place—old newspapers, legal briefs, cardboard boxes filled with books. She couldn't imagine holding a poker game in here, let alone a client meeting. He moved a pile of papers off a grungy brown chair and motioned her to sit down. "Glad to see the police cut you loose. Sit down. Would you like a beer or lemonade or something?"

"I can't stay. I need to ask you some questions."

"What's with the long face? They didn't charge you, did they? I gave Claude Ann and Xander the name of the best criminal attorney on the island, but I didn't think you'd need him."

"No, I didn't need him." She stayed close to the door and watched as he crammed reams of loose papers willy-nilly into a box and stacked the box against the wall. "Are you packing up to move or gearing up for the lawsuit Jarvis will bring against you for fraud and failure to disclose Eleanor's claim?"

"There was no fraud, Dinah. If Eleanor had come forward before the deal closed with any tangible evidence that called our archaeologist's report into question, or if her attorney had filed a claim, then we would have been obligated to disclose it. But that didn't happen. We saw nothing that contradicted our information and the contract clearly stated that the seller would guarantee the property to be free of encumbrances only up until the time of closing. Hell, Jarvis saw her and her groupies railing against the project on the nightly news. If that didn't put him on notice, it's because he and his legal team chose to assume the risk."

"It still sounds unethical. And letting Eleanor and everyone else think that Uwahi was intended to be sold for a housing development when you knew all along that Jarvis wanted to build a gambling casino, that was unethical, too."

"They may call Hawaii heaven, Dinah, but it's still Earth. Nobody sports wings and a halo. You want my opinion, I think Eleanor's just blowing smoke. There are no bones. But if there were, if she were to trot out King Kawhosits entire skeleton this very afternoon with a certificate of authenticity signed by the Lord God Kane, Himself, it would be the buyer's headache and there's nothing illegal or unethical about it." He picked up an official looking paper with a court stamp on it, folded it into an airplane, and sailed it into the box. "Did you figure out how Raif's phone wound up in your purse?"

"Raif's murderer put it there." She cleared her throat and bluffed a bravery she didn't feel. "I've been racking my brain trying to understand why during our lengthy conversation about Patrick Varian and his unfortunate death, you neglected to mention that you'd gone to school with him."

The twinkle and the grin vanished. "I'd never heard of Patrick Varian before his name appeared in the newspaper."

"You went to Punahou with him, Steve. You and Varian and Raif must be close to the same age. You must all have been classmates."

"Raif was a year behind me. Varian may have been in his class, but I didn't know him. The name didn't ring a bell."

"His photo was in the paper. Didn't you recognize him?"

"No, Dinah, I did not. High school was a while ago and there were nearly five hundred in my graduating class."

"You also neglected to mention that you played poker with Raif. Did you play poker with him the day he was murdered?"

"He was supposed to play. He warned me that he would come carrying a bundle and betting big, but he never showed. I gave the police that information."

"You told them you hosted an illegal game?"

"Social games in a private home aren't illegal. If it were, the state wouldn't have enough prisons to house all of the offenders."

"Who else was with you? More of your Punahou posse?"

"A couple. They hadn't talked with Raif, but they corroborated the rest of my statement, that it was a friendly game. All of us equal, no house rake, no minors present."

"Were these Punahou guys the same ones who attended the memorial service and went to Xander's house afterward?"

"That's right." He reprised the grin, like everything was back to hunky-dory. "I'm going upstairs for a beer. It's a lot more comfortable up there. Come on. We can look through my Punahou yearbooks for Patrick Varian." He pointed to a narrow staircase directly across from the front door.

Dinah's fingers began to cramp and she uncrossed them. Who all had been mingling on Xander's deck after the memorial service? She remembered setting her purse on a bench with a lot of other purses and jackets. She'd taken out a cigarette and gone to look at the ocean. Xander and Raif's father had been standing beside the lagoon and the guys who reminisced about Raif's backflip had been standing beside the drinks and cold cuts. The Punahou posse. One of them could have dropped the BlackBerry into her purse while her back was turned. After Langford and Fujita arrived, everyone had gone into the house, but in what order? The cops behind Claude Ann. Lyssa and Raif's parents and Xander next. Dinah and Avery behind them and then the others. Steve and Jon had walked up from the beach. They were the last to arrive. Which one came in last?

Midway up the stairs, Steve looked back over his shoulder. "Aren't you coming?"

She really wanted to see that yearbook. "Bring the book down here. Please."

"What's wrong with you?" He started back down the stairs.

She backed against the door, found the handle with one hand, tried to remember the self-defense moves Nick had taught her—palm heel strike, knee thrust, side kick, upward elbow jab.

"Don't come any closer, Steve. Just bring me the book."

"You don't think that I…? Hey, wait one goddamned minute. You came here thinking that I killed Raif?"

"I came here to ask you to explain your relationship with Patrick Varian and Raif."

"All right, Dinah. I'll bring you the book. And I'll retire to the far corner of the room and let you read it in safety. But I can tell you right now that you are one twisted wahini if you think I had any part in Raif's death." He tromped back up the stairs and she reminded herself again, innocent until proven guilty. Maybe he hadn't known Varian.

He returned with two yearbooks. "This one is for my class. The names and pictures are alphabetical." He handed it to her open to the Vs.

She ran her finger down the page. There was no student named Varian.

He handed her the second book. "This one is for the class that graduated after me. The reason I have a copy is because my mother taught at Punahou for a few years to help pay the cost of my education."

Dinah turned to the Vs. "Here he is. Patrick 'Rick' Varian." He had soft, delicate features and a bashful smile. She read the sentiment next to his picture. "Thanks Pete and Liz. Go Buffanblu! Go Punahoopsters!"

"What's Buffanblu?"

"The school colors. Buff and blue."

She looked for Raif's photo, but there wasn't one. What was it he'd said? His time at Punahou hadn't worked out well. Probably he'd flunked out or been expelled before the yearbook was published.

Steve said, "Let me see Varian's picture?"

She showed him.

He studied it for a minute. "That's funny. I did know this kid, only his name wasn't Varian. It was Shirley."

"What?"

"Patrick Shirley. He got teased a lot because of his name. Patty Shirley, he's so girlie." Steve sat down in the grungy brown chair and studied the photo. "I remember going to a party at his house once. We hardly knew each other, but a lot of us kids who'd come to Oahu from the Big Island to go to school were invited. Me, Tommy Ong, Tess Wilhite. When I got to the party, Kay Wilhite was there with cookies and care packages for all of us. Turns out Pat's dad was Kay's brother. She was his house guest."

"Varian was Kay's maiden name?"

"I guess so. I didn't give it a thought at the time. All I knew was that her brother had married Pat's mom. Varian must have adopted Pat. I'm sure Pat welcomed the name change."

Dinah's thoughts reeled. Patrick Varian was Avery Wilhite's nephew. He was the Rick whose funeral Kay had attended. He was the sharp-as-a-tack archaeology professor who'd come to the Big Island for some mysterious client and been murdered.

And Avery hadn't acknowledged knowing him. How odd was that? She harked back to her first conversation with Avery after she'd been accosted by Eleanor. Avery had blithered about not being able to keep sisters-in-law or nephews in line. It was like herding cats. Had Avery hired his nephew to validate the opinion of Xander's archaeologist? Adjunct professors were poorly paid. Avery could have gotten Rick's services cheap and Rick might have jumped at the opportunity to earn some extra money. Kay had said he was conscientious. Had he been too conscientious for Avery's liking?

Steve said, "I'd never have associated Pat with archaeology. As I recall him, he was always acting the clown, probably trying to deflect the teasing that came his way."

She'd almost forgotten about Steve. Her thoughts were in ferment. "At Xander's party in Honolulu, I remember Avery saying his wife couldn't be there because there had been a death in the family. It must have been Rick Varian. Why didn't he say so? And then at Raif's memorial service, Kay spoke about the death of her brother's son and Avery cut her off."

"Avery cuts people off all the time. Have you noticed that he likes the sound of his own voice?"

"But Kay seemed genuinely to care about the boy. Why did Avery keep the fact that Varian was his nephew a secret?"

"Who knows? Absentmindedness. Maybe he didn't want to inflict his family's troubles on others."

"No. Avery loves to gossip too much. He had to have a reason for dodging the subject."

"I'm not following you. Why should he volunteer to you or to anyone else that the unfortunate man who was bludgeoned and stuffed into a steam vent was his nephew by marriage?"

"Because it's titillating. Because he had special knowledge of Varian that nobody else had. It would have been such a natural thing for him to volunteer and totally in character. As for not telling me, I'm inconsequential. I'm a nobody. If he's hiding it from me, he's hiding it from everybody and that's suspicious in the extreme."

"You're letting one fact send you off on a tangent. Maybe he told the police. And even if he didn't, failing to confess that a corpse was your nephew isn't a felony in any jurisdiction that I know of."

"Maybe so, but something's hinky. I don't know how you can blow off the fact that Varian was an archaeologist. According to the newspaper report, he had come to the Big Island to evaluate a burial site on private property. A Native Hawaiian woman claims that Uwahi is a burial site. Hello?"

"But why would Avery have hired another archaeologist when we already had a clean report?"

"All right, all right. Are you absolutely sure that Jarvis or his lawyers didn't hire Varian? Or Eleanor and her lawyers?"

"No, I can't be sure. They wouldn't be obligated to disclose their experts to me if they didn't want to." He picked up another armful of papers and piled them on his desk. "Avery came to me a couple of weeks ago and asked about the legal ramifications if some bones or artifacts were discovered on the property after the closing. I told him the problem would belong to Jarvis. The contract was clear that any warranties we made would terminate at the time of closing. The thing about Uwahi was, it had to close yesterday or else. Politics were involved. The timing was crucial. If anybody balked, it could have been months or a year before we had another viable offer."

"So if Varian discovered something, it would be in Avery's interest to keep him quiet until after the closing."

"What of it? It was in everyone's interest for the deal to close—Xander's, Claude Ann's, and mine."

"Be that as it may. Avery said that archaeologists spoke gibberish. 'Articulation.' That was the example he gave.

Did your archaeologist, the one Xander hired to evaluate Uwahi, say anything about articulation?"

"I don't think so. Does it mean something besides clear speaking?"

"In archaeological jargon, it refers to a find of two or more bones in their original configuration. Rick may have found the king's bones."

"Where are you going with this? Are you thinking Avery killed his nephew because he found something Avery didn't want him to find? Because, I mean, Avery? That's surreal. I've known him for years. He's a pussycat."

"People aren't always the way they seem."

"Avery is. He can sometimes get worked up if things don't go his way. But overall, he's the dullest, most domesticated man I've ever met."

"You said that the closing date was crucial. If Varian had found bones and he wanted to announce his find right away, before the closing took place, that would have gotten Avery worked up."

Steve kicked another box of documents against the wall. "None of us would have felt happy about that."

"But who," she mused, "would have felt the most unhappy? Xander, perhaps. But Xander says that Avery lost his shirt in Bernie Madoff's bogus hedge fund. He needed the deal to close as badly as Xander did."

"Avery's broke? Judas Priest, he was never short of cash when I went to him with some new expense. He must've borrowed big-time."

"Just like Xander," she said. "He bet the ranch. He was all in."

"Avery Wilhite, killer and archvillain." Steve went behind his desk, opened a drawer, and pulled out a half-smoked joint. "I can't see it. You walked in that door convinced that I killed Varian. In twenty minutes time, you've talked yourself into believing that it was Avery. But if Varian was murdered because of something he found at Uwahi, you're back to square one on Raif's murder. Raif had zero to do with Uwahi."

Stymied, Dinah was considering whether to throw in the towel and get stoned when a loud knock sounded at the door. Shave-and-a-haircut.

THIRTY-EIGHT

"CONSULTING WITH your attorney?" Jon's tone was accusatory.

"Thanks so much for asking, but I haven't engaged one yet. The police released me without pressing charges, as I'm sure you must have heard through the grapevine."

"I thought you'd call me."

"I did call you. Your answering machine bid me to have a nice day."

"You should have called my cell. I've been on non-stop suicide watch."

Dinah noticed his bloodshot eyes and dropped the sarcasm. "I thought you were spending today with Lyssa."

"I had to get away. Her emoting began to sound less like grief and more like…"

"Guilt?" suggested Steve.

"A performance."

Steve laughed. "Mind what you say, brah. Dinah's on a prosecutorial tear. In five minutes, she'll have you doubting your own innocence." He motioned Jon toward the stairs. "Let's all go upstairs and kick back for a while. Come on, Dinah. There's safety in numbers."

Caution to the wind, she followed the smell of pakalolo up the stairs.

Steve's living quarters weren't spick-and-span, but the floor was passable and the chairs free of clutter. She and Jon declined to smoke and Steve brought out a cold six-pack of Big Bang Pale Ale and three clean pilsners. They sat down at the kitchen table like old friends.

After the first few sips of beer, Jon said, "Thinking about death and murder all the time eats you up inside. Lyssa see-saws between anger and agony. It's hard to watch."

Dinah recalled the bitter look on Lyssa's face when she saw Langford pull Raif's phone out of her purse. "Lyssa probably thinks that I killed Raif."

"We're all looking at each other sideways," said Jon. "Lyssa doesn't trust Dad or Claude Ann. Dad's on tenter-hooks because he thinks either Lyssa shot him or I shot him. We're a mutual circle of suspects."

"Cheer up, brah. We don't know who killed Raif, but Dinah thinks she knows who killed that archaeologist, Pat-rick Varian. Go ahead, Dinah. Fill him in."

"First, I should fill you both in on why Jon's mother killed herself."

"Say what?" Steve jerked his chin back.

The eyebrow on Jon's good side spiked up. "Have you held a séance without inviting me?"

"Leilani was in love with Louis Sykes. Your mother has known it from the beginning, Steve. They were having an affair. After your father's drowning accident, someone tele-phoned Leilani and told her that Louis had been cheating on her with another woman. I think the person who made that call was the same person who called Sara to tell her that Louis was dead."

"Avery," said Steve. "I've always known that. But why did my mother not tell me about the affair?"

"She didn't want you to think less of your father. She didn't want to blame a dead woman. She didn't want to hurt Xander. Unfortunately, Eleanor fixed her blame on the wrong man and her hatred of Xander has festered for all these years."

"Jesus, when I think how much mental energy we've

squandered on the suicide question." Jon rubbed his eyes with the heels of his hands. "And all because of a love triangle."

"Actually," said Dinah, "it was more of a quadrangle. Avery was in love with Leilani and jealous of both Xander and Louis. When he called Leilani, he probably described Louis' carryings-on to Leilani in a way that inflicted maximum pain and humiliation. Maybe he suggested that she should have an affair with him now that Louis was dead. Maybe Leilani believed that he had murdered Louis. She was furious and, of course, grief-stricken at the same time. I don't suppose you'll ever know whether her suicide was because she couldn't bear living without Louis, or whether in her mind she was punishing Louis or Avery or both."

Steve finished his Big Bang and opened another. "How could Xander not have known that his wife was having it on with one of his best friends?"

"I don't know," said Dinah. "There's a peptide that instills trust. Maybe he has a lot of it."

Jon smiled his lopsided smile. "Oxytocin."

Steve shook his head. "Like I said before, when I was young I wondered if my father's death was an accident and then I heard the story about the woman who tried to save him. Now I'm wondering all over again."

Dinah said, "At first, I thought Xander had tumbled to what was going on between Leilani and Louis and murdered his rival. But Xander was lecturing at Stanford when Louis died. He called Sara when he got back to San Francisco. It was she who told him about Leilani's suicide."

Steve extinguished his joint. "Avery could have killed my father and paid the woman to lie, or it could have been an accident and he called Leilani to rub it in. And to gloat."

"Unless he confesses," said Jon, "we'll never know."

"Maybe he'll go down for another murder. Dinah, tell

Jon what you found out about good old Ave's relationship to Pat Shirley, a/k/a Rick Varian."

Dinah summarized the family connection. "All along I've been thinking that Raif's murder stemmed from his gambling habit or his womanizing. But what if he had managed to interject himself somehow in the Uwahi deal?"

"But how?" asked Steve. "He couldn't have known anything that wasn't said in general conversation. And we were fairly economical with what we said."

"Raif and Varian were schoolmates. Varian could have called him when he came to the Big Island and, over a friendly game of cards, mentioned that he'd found bones on property his Uncle Avery had asked him to evaluate." Dinah was thinking out loud. "Maybe Avery ordered his nephew to deep-six his find and when Varian's scruples got in the way, Avery killed him. Raif was desperate. Lyssa was beginning to suspect that he was only interested in her money. If she tightened the purse strings and if Tess couldn't or wouldn't pony up the cash to cover his debts, Raif had no place else to go. Xander was tapped out. When the body in the steam vent was identified as Varian, Raif saw his chance. He threatened to go to the police or to Paul Jarvis unless Avery bought him off."

"That's a lot of could-haves and maybes," said Jon. "And Avery as a killer? Come on."

"My thought exactly," said Steve. "But it makes a certain amount of sense. Even if there was no evidence to link Avery to Varian's murder, the investigation would have delayed the closing and Jarvis was adamant that he would walk if the sale didn't close on time."

Dinah had another timing question. "Jon, when did you tell Eleanor that Xander was getting ready to sell Uwahi?"

"A few weeks ago. I knew that Uwahi was special to her, that it had been in the family for generations. I thought she deserved a chance to go and commune with her ancestors before the spirit of the place was destroyed. I'm sure Dad considers my talking to her a betrayal."

Steve frowned. "Damn right it was a betrayal. Of me, too. Eleanor could have thrown a monkey wrench into the deal and left me without a nickel for all the work I've put in."

"It wasn't my intention for her to mobilize an army of protesters. At least, I didn't tell her that Jarvis was the buyer. If she'd suspected that a gambling casino was being contemplated for Uwahi, she'd have stormed the governor's office."

"Your display of friendship is duly noted, brah."

"I owed her, Steve."

"For what? Hounding your father for failing to keep your mother alive?"

Dinah intervened "Stop it. We were talking about murder. About the possibility that Avery committed both murders. He acted as if Eleanor's protests were a trivial problem, more of an intrafamily spat than a threat to Uwahi. But she had rattled him. Soon after her first protest, he must have called his nephew over from Oahu to do some additional bone hunting on the QT."

"That's the part that makes no sense." Steve took away Dinah's undrunk beer and poured it down the sink. "Buying a second opinion would just be asking for trouble, shooting himself in the foot if the new man turned up something the first archaeologist had missed. Sorry, but it won't wash. You weave a good story, Dinah, but there's not a shred of evidence linking Avery to either murder."

"Can he be absolutely sure of that?" She took a deep breath and placed her hands on the table palms down as if preparing herself to summon the spirits of the dead. "Maybe we should hold a séance. Spirits sometimes come back to haunt the ones who hurt them. If Avery is the murderer, I have an idea that might smoke him out. Will the two of you help me?"

Jon's leery eyes narrowed. "How?"

She smiled. "Steve bragged that his seductive charms could make impossible things happen. Let's put him to the test."

THIRTY-NINE

In Hilo, Jon turned off the Bayfront Highway onto Banyan Drive, a shaded avenue lined with huge banyans, each of which had been planted by a famous person whose name appeared on a plaque at the base of the tree. Presidents, movie stars, athletes, adventurers.

"These old trees have survived some major disasters," said Jon. "A twenty-five foot wave obliterated the waterfront back in forty-six and Hilo was hit again in sixty by a thirty-five footer. With all the big quakes that've been happening around the Pacific lately, we've had a number of tsunami warnings."

Dinah gazed out at the peaceful shoreline and the blue waters of Hilo Bay sparkling under the noonday sun. The one thing she'd learned about Hawaii was that safety is an illusion. The very ground you walk on is provisional and the gods can drop the trapdoor in the blink of an eye.

Jon drove past the Hilo Hawaiian Hotel, turned right and parked in the Coconut Island lot facing the water. Coconut Island was an emerald-green, palm-studded islet no larger than a football field and connected to the Big Island by a picturesque stone footbridge.

"The island's name is Moku Ola in Hawaiian," Jon informed her. "In olden times, it was a pu'uhonua, a place of refuge. Anyone who violated kapu could come here, make an offering to the gods, and swim away free and forgiven."

Dinah had heard all about pu'uhonua from Lt. Vince Langford, but the refuge he had offered was behind prison walls topped by concertina wire. Setting that aside, forgiveness was very much on her mind. She hoped that Steve was making more headway than she had made in trying to convince his mother to break her silence and open up about Louis and Leilani. "Are you sure Eleanor will come?"

"She'll come, but how receptive she'll be is anyone's guess." Jon gave her a jaundiced look. "This idea of yours, this bluff the murderer game. It's stupid. A cliché out of an old whodunit and dangerous as hell."

"We'll let Langford in on the plot if and when everyone agrees to participate. For heaven's sakes, I know that it's iffy. I know that it's amateur hour. If you have a better idea, then for heaven's sakes, shoot it to me this instant."

"Let the police finish their investigation. You don't have enough facts to make a valid judgment."

"Policemen are not renowned for their patience, Jon. They don't have enough to book anyone yet, but Raif's father will keep turning up the heat. Eventually, they will get tired of the aggravation and decide that Claude Ann's prints on the gun or Raif's phone in my purse or the fact that Raif was blackmailing Xander is enough evidence to convict and life as we know it will end. My idea is a long, long shot, but I can't just sit around waiting and hoping."

He got out and went around to open the car door for her. "This is going to be one strange meeting."

"Whatever happens, at least we can set the record straight about Xander's role in your mother's suicide and maybe generate some ho'oponopono."

The Hilo Hawaiian Hotel was an older hotel with a spectacular view of Coconut Island and, in the distance, Mauna Kea. Jon and Dinah followed the walkways along the shore and entered the hotel from the waterside. They found the restaurant and sat down. A waiter brought water and menus. Jon toyed with his watch while Dinah mentally enumerated all of the ways in which her bluff could go wrong. She could have constructed a case against an innocent man and enlisted the real murderer to help her trap him. Avery could be guilty, but too cagey to take the bait. The bait could be too flimsy to persuade him. He could take the bait, but change his mind and skip town. Or he could take the bait, realize that he'd been tricked, and blow away everyone in sight with yet another gun. She hadn't run out of worst case scenarios when Jon stood up.

"Hello, Eleanor. Glad you could make it."

Eleanor's eyes transmitted a comprehensive skepticism. "This must be ke panepo'o." Her tone implied that Jon didn't ask her to lunch often. Dinah translated the Hawaiian as "earth-shaking."

Jon pulled out a chair and Eleanor sat, but he had trouble pushing her toward the table and she didn't budge. He gave up and sat down. "Sorry I haven't been in touch."

"I saw you at the memorial service. You didn't look glad I could make that."

"We didn't know what to expect."

"I went to talk to Lyssa." She eyed Dinah as if she were a stink bug. "Your friend Claude Ann stopped me."

Interesting as that encounter must have been, Dinah cut to the purpose of this encounter. "Eleanor, I've learned something about Leilani. Something that will change the way you think about things."

"I taught my last class of the day. I'll have a Mai Tai." The subtext was clearly, I will let you know when it's time to call this meeting to order.

Jon hailed the waiter and ordered Eleanor a Mai Tai and a beer for himself. Dinah didn't want anything to drink. She was too nervous. She was already thinking that Jon was right and her bright idea was supremely stupid. A huge mistake. She looked around. What if Sara Sykes didn't come or didn't want to air the truth? What if Eleanor was so invested in her prejudice against Xander that she refused to believe her? What if she accepted Sara's story and still declined to cooperate?

Eleanor stared across the table, mute as a statue, and Jon did a conversational tap-dance to fill the void. He stuck to non-controversial topics—the rash of harmonic tremors over the past week, the upcoming 4th of July fireworks show, and did Eleanor read about the one hundred and fifty pound Kahala fish caught off the Kona Coast. She didn't say whether she had or had not. When their drinks were served, she removed the pineapple wedge, the sugar cane stirrer, and the paper umbrella from her Mai Tai and tasted. Seemingly satisfied, she broke the ice. "How is Lyssa?"

Jon didn't sugarcoat the situation. He described Lyssa's mercurial emotions and said, "I worry that she's going to imitate our mother."

"She won't. I went to a kaula." She gave Dinah a condescending look. "A kaula is a prophet. A seer. She told me that something very bad would happen soon, but not to Lyssa. Not to you, either, Jon."

Dinah's skin shrank. She tried to resist the inclination to superstition, but it would have been nice to hear her name included in the list of those to whom something very bad would not happen. Claude Ann's, too. "What kind of a very bad thing?" she asked.

"The kaula saw a box of papers, a fountain of fire, a mound of broken stones, a child sick with fever, and a woman carrying a stick."

The woman carrying a stick arrived as if on cue.

Jon stood up. "Sara. Thank you for coming."

Dinah's angst escalated. Was Marywave the sick child? Claude Ann had been about to take her to a doctor the last time they spoke.

Jon took Sara's cane and hung it on the back of an extra chair. He pulled out a chair for her next to Eleanor. Eleanor and Sara apparently needed no introduction. To Dinah's surprise, Eleanor reached a hand out and covered Sara's. "The Mai Tai is good, Sara."

"I guess I'd better have one." Sara looked more careworn than ever. "If my attorney deems it advisable."

Steve smiled. "It's advisable. I'd say we can all use some fortification."

He showed no ill effects from the pakalolo, but Dinah was mulling the significance of a box of papers and second-guessing herself. She was less sure than she'd been two hours ago when she'd hatched this plan. But whatever the result of her ploy to entrap Avery, surely it was in everyone's best interest to put to rights the misunderstanding that had concentrated Eleanor's hatred on the wrong man.

Steve ordered his mother a Mai Tai and a beer for himself. "Are you up to this, Mom?"

"Yes. I'm ready."

Jon said, "Eleanor, Sara has something to tell you about Leilani. It changed the way I think about her death and I think it will change the way you feel about my father."

Eleanor leveled a hard stare on Dinah. She seemed to intuit that, whatever was about to issue from Sara Sykes' mouth, Dinah had been the catalyst. She turned back to Sara and nodded, as if granting her permission to speak.

Sara spoke in a soft, clear voice and she aimed her words directly at Eleanor. "Do you remember my husband, Louis? I met and married him when we were at the U together. Louis, Xander, Avery, Leilani and I had our own clique. The boys all competed for Leilani's attention, but I was a friend. Leilani's friend, too. Soon after the boys went to work for the U.S.G.S., Xander married your sister. Louis and I were at the wedding."

"I remember," said Eleanor.

"Some time after that, Louis asked me to marry him. I thought he'd outgrown his infatuation with Leilani, but he still carried a secret torch. I don't know what caused Leilani to lose interest in Xander, but it wasn't long after Lyssa was born. She and Louis began an affair and Louis was so enamored with her, so thrilled by her change of heart, that he scarcely bothered to hide it from me. He spent more and more time with her. She had been my friend and so I humbled myself and went to ask her to break it off. But she had no remorse, Eleanor. None at all. She told me she was in love with Louis, that she should have married him instead of Xander. She said Louis was applying for jobs on the mainland and as soon as he received an offer, she would divorce Xander and Louis would divorce me and take her away from the islands."

Sara's Mai Tai arrived and nobody said anything for a while. Eleanor kept her eyes down, playing with her paper umbrella.

Sara said, "I'm sorry if this taints your memory of your sister. Jon needed to know that his father wasn't to blame and Steve seems to have known all along that his father was an adulterer." She had a few sips of her Mai Tai and her voice took on authority. "And I needed to rid my soul of all this bottled-up resentment."

Eleanor ran her eyes around the table. "Did Xander kill him?"

"No," said Dinah. "Xander didn't kill him. It was probably an accident, but the person who called Leilani to inform her that Louis was dead may have given her an exaggerated report of Louis' misbehavior while he was in California. He was another of Leilani's admirers."

"Who?"

"Avery Wilhite called me with the news," said Sara. "I asked him if he'd spoken with Leilani. He said that he had."

FORTY

Holding fast to the passenger door of Eleanor's speeding '59 Cadillac Coupe de Ville, Dinah felt as if she had lost control of her plan. Events were spinning out of control and she was riding the tiger's back, hanging on as best she could without a seat belt. The Caddy had not been retrofitted with any new-fangled safety equipment and Eleanor seemed to have little regard for traffic lights and stop signs. The bench seat had been pushed back to its limit to accommodate her girth and, with arms at full stretch, she kept a two-handed grip on the wheel and motored down the center of the Belt Road as if she owned it. In Eleanor's mind, she did own it.

Dinah said, "It's only a theory. Avery may not have killed either Varian or Raif. And Jon's right when he says we don't have enough facts to run a good bluff. Avery will know that you're lying. We should forget about it. And anyway, I need to be with Claude Ann. Her little girl is sick." Before leaving the hotel, Dinah had called Claude Ann. Marywave's fever had worsened. She might be on the Belt Road at this very minute, rushing toward Hilo in the oncoming lane, trying to get Marywave to the hospital. "Seriously, Eleanor. Let's put this off to another day."

"Kaii. The doctors will take care of the girl and Xander will take care of his woman. Nothing you can do." She had seized the reins. The plan that Dinah had conceived and set in motion was under new command. Dinah had been demoted to aide-de-camp. Eleanor was going to attempt to blackmail Avery by claiming to have information tying him to Varian's murder. If Avery agreed to pay, it was as good as an admission.

The way Dinah envisioned the setup, Eleanor would call Avery tonight from her home with Dinah standing by to offer advice and encouragement. Eleanor would arrange a meeting with Avery in some public place tomorrow afternoon. Dinah would advise Steve of the time and location and he would go to the police and work his wiles on Vince Langford. Steve had the home-island advantage. He was a well-known attorney and an officer of the court and he was an accomplished persuader. If anyone could sell the plan to Langford, he could. Ideally, Langford or one of his subordinates would show up at the meeting with Avery to guarantee Eleanor's safety and capture the transaction on tape. Assuming everyone stuck to this script. But as the Coupe de Ville barreled down the road, Dinah began to have second thoughts.

"On reflection, we should clear this with Lieutenant Langford before you make the phone call, not after. If Avery calls your bluff and reports you to the police for attempted blackmail, you could be prosecuted, Eleanor."

She snorted. "Nobody's going to put me in jail."

"Even so, we should wait and talk it over with Jon before making the phone call. He's going to Volcano to check in on Lyssa and later tonight he'll swing by your house to pick me up. He thinks that what we're doing is dangerous and the more I think about it, the more I tend to agree with him. There are too many variables, too many ways the situation could get out of hand. Let's all put our heads together tonight and come up with a less risky plan."

"I don't care about risk." She braked hard and the lilac-colored behemoth fishtailed into the driveway past the GOD-IS-NOT-HAPPY banner. She switched off the engine and regarded herself in the rear view mirror. "All these years, I've been unjust, ho'opono'ole. I've been vindictive and stubborn, grieving over a wrong I didn't understand. Sara Sykes is cleansing her soul and making peace with the past. She is seeking ho'oponopono and I will do the same. But first I will negotiate with Avery Wilhite." She turned to Dinah and a rare, mischievous smile creased her face. "Let's chance'um, sistah."

THE ONLY INSIDE info Dinah had for this bluff was the knowledge that Varian was Avery's nephew and the fact that Varian had lived briefly in the Bayside Apartments where the police had found a few books and papers and a PC. It stood to reason that if Avery had known where Varian was staying on the island, he would have cleaned out his apartment of any potentially telltale items. The police hadn't disclosed the existence of the computer to the press or completed their examination of its contents. If, as Dinah hypothesized, Varian had made a discovery at Uwahi, he would have described his findings. The risk of losing the deal had passed, but the risk of being linked to Varian's murder must keep Avery awake nights. There was a chance that Eleanor could convince him that she had information worth paying for. And if he could be linked to Varian's murder, maybe the police could pressure him to confess to Raif's murder.

Dinah had been trailing Eleanor through her indoor jungle for an hour while the ethnobotanist watered her kupu-kupu ferns, her bromeliads, and an actual forest of areca palms that brushed against the living room ceiling. Orchids proliferated and there was an enormous fish tank in one bedroom where archerfish darted among mangrove roots. Eleanor wouldn't sit still to be rehearsed. Dinah ducked under a low-hanging philodendron vine and kept up the drill. "If he asks you how you got into Varian's PC, tell him you have a hacker friend at the U who helped you. Tell him the police would find the contents extremely interesting, but don't be specific. Keep it vague. Tell him it ties him to

Varian and leave it at that. If he thinks there's a possibility, he'll fill in the blanks from his own knowledge."

"I don't need to rehearse. I know what to say." Eleanor wasn't the least bit nervous. She dug her finger into the soil around an umbrella-shaped bonsai tree. "This one's an arboricola schefflera. Poisonous enough to kill a cat or a baby, but very pretty."

Xander had called Eleanor "the poison lady." Dinah wondered how many of these plants were poisonous. "Are there a lot of poisonous plants in Hawaii?"

"One of the deadliest is nanahonua, Angel's Trumpet. Then there's the Be-Still tree, oleander to you. People have died from barbecuing over Be-Still wood. The kukui nut tree is poisonous, but not deadly. Kava kava root is safe, but the leaves can be toxic. Then there's nightshade, foxglove, rosary peas, anthurium."

"Anthuriums are poisonous?"

"Only if eaten in large quantities." She paused to inspect the pleated leaves of an orchid and drop a few ice cubes into the pot. "Have you read about Kalaipahoa, the poison goddess?"

"No."

"She infected a copse of trees on Molokai with a poison so virulent that birds flying high above their branches fell instantly dead. The king decreed that an image of the goddess be carved from one of the poisoned trees. Hundreds of carvers perished. Eventually, the image was finished, but it was deadly to the touch and had to be wrapped in layers of kapa cloth. Kalaipahoa's priests presided over a murder rite they called praying to death. Pule-ana-ana. They chiseled off splinters of the goddess' image and sprinkled them in the food of the person they wished to kill." She made an eruptive noise which Dinah construed as a laugh. "Maybe I should invite Avery to dinner."

Jerusalem, was she serious? "We don't know for sure

that Avery is guilty of anything, Eleanor. And pule-ana-ana isn't consistent with ho'oponopono."

"Let's make the call now." She set her watering bucket in a utility sink in the kitchen and led Dinah into her office, the only room in the house not choked with plants. Her desk was surprisingly modern. She pulled out a directory. "Your eyes are better than mine. What's his home number? About now, he'll be cleaning up the supper dishes for his bossy wife."

Dinah found the number and Eleanor dialed. She sat down behind her desk and turned on the speakerphone.

Avery answered on the third ring.

"Eleanor Kalolo, Avery. We have business to discuss."

He was slow to respond. "Eleanor. To what do I owe this honor?"

"I called to congratulate you on the sale of Uwahi."

"Well, now. I must say. Didn't expect congratulations from you."

"I've been waiting for you to close so you'd be rich. No use trying to sell something to a man who can't pay. Now you can pay."

"What is it you're selling?"

"Your nephew's report on King Keawenui's bones. He was writing a book on burial customs, how the priests would assemble the skull and long bones of a king into a sitting position and set fire to them. They let them burn for ten days and then the king became a god. His successor had to build a hiding place for the sacred remains. Your nephew found Keawenui's iwi."

"Too much," mouthed Dinah. "Not so specific."

"Of no interest to me, Eleanor. Take the report to Paul Jarvis. He's the new owner."

"Rick's friend Raif told him I was fighting Xander about Uwahi and Rick came to see me. He said you'd offered him money to keep quiet for a few weeks, but he wasn't sure you could pay. And you couldn't have until now, could you?"

Eleanor, no! Dinah waved her hands. Too much.

"But I paid him, Avery. He gave me his report and I'm reading it right now. Appended to the first page is a form you signed, a form giving him permission to conduct his research on the property."

Dinah studied Eleanor's face. Was she making this up? Was she a mindreader? Had she actually spoken with Varian?

"Don't recall signing anything," said Avery, alarm creeping into his voice. "What's your game?"

"The same as Rick's, only this time the stakes are higher. This time it's not about the money, Avery. It's about your life. You couldn't pay Rick and so you had to kill him. But you've got lots of money now and you can pay me. It's what I've been waiting for."

"You're full of it. This is blackmail. I'll call the police."

"Call them. Call them and see what happens."

"You're crazy."

"My price is a hundred thousand dollars. Chickenfeed to you now. Bring the money and meet me at the end of the Mauna Loa Road at nine o'clock."

Dinah gaped in astonishment. Not tonight!

"I don't have that kind of cash lying around."

"Get it. Call your banker. Raid Kay's knitting basket. Do what you have to do. I've waited a long time for this." Eleanor cut the connection and grinned. "How'd I do, eh?"

"Is any of it, is any of what you said to him true? Did Rick Varian come to see you? Do you have his report?"

"You said to bluff Avery. I bluffed him."

Dinah was left floundering. She didn't know what to believe. The people in her life were never what they seemed. Feeling punked and more than a little fearful, she called Steve and gave him the time and location of the meeting.

"Are you kidding? Langford will go apeshit. He's not expecting the meeting until tomorrow."

"Tell him we were overtaken by events. I was, anyway. The situation has changed and things are moving fast."

"I'll tell him, but you may need that criminal attorney yet. Even before this balls-up, Langford was talking about charging you with obstruction of justice."

FORTY-ONE

THE EARTHQUAKE STRUCK at seven-forty-seven. Dinah was eating a ham sandwich. Eleanor was repotting a portulaca molokiniensis. There was an explosion like the Crack of Doom. The furniture danced and the palms swayed. Eleanor looked up and wiped the dirt off her hands and then the lights went out. From far away a siren blared. Dinah stood in the middle of the dark kitchen and listened to glass breaking all around her.

"Eleanor, where are you? Do you have a lantern or a flashlight?"

"Ai yah! Blind mullet!"

"What?"

"Da fish all buss. Kaiii! Nevahmind. I handles."

"Damn it, Eleanor. This isn't a teaching moment. Speak English. Where do you keep your flashlight?"

"In the counter drawer next to the stove."

Dinah groped her way across the floor.

"Found it!" cried Eleanor, followed by a startling burst of static and a man's voice.

"...at this time, but the epicenter was most likely under the southeast flank of Kilauea. Volcanoes National Park personnel report that Kilauea is erupting in two locations. Fountaining estimated at eighteen hundred feet can be seen from the Observatory. There are also reports of eruptions on Mauna Loa, the first since nineteen-eighty-four."

Dinah shivered. The kaula Eleanor claimed to have visited had mentioned a fountain of fire. All of the seer's visions were coming true. Dinah had been worrying about

Marywave's fever for hours. She had tried calling Claude Ann's number again and again, but her phone was turned off. Was it psychic incompetence or pure perversity that led seers to reveal their visions without providing any context or clues to the outcome? There ought to be a law.

"Eruptions of both Mauna Loa and Kilauea are underway." The civil defense siren shrieked on and on, but the voice on the radio remained inhumanly calm. "For leeward residents, strong to moderate trades are bringing with them a cloud of volcanic gas. Those with heart and respiratory ailments are advised to remain indoors or wear protective masks. Repeat, south Kona residents downwind of the Mauna Loa eruption are advised to take precautions."

Dinah bumped into the stove and found the drawer under the counter and the flashlight. She turned it on and the first thing she saw was a little gold fish float past her feet on a stream of water. She looked around for a bowl, but by the time she found one, the fish had washed under a plant stand laden with orchids.

"Hawaii State Civil Defense urges people to stay off the roads if at all possible as landslides may have caused extensive damage to roads and bridges. As they did following the quake in two thousand six, power plants will shut down automatically. Expect power outages."

If the epicenter of the quake was under Kilauea, was Hilo in danger of a tsunami or would Hawaii be sending a mega-wave on to Maui or Oahu? Dinah wished she'd paid more attention in science class.

"I saved most of them," said Eleanor, splashing into the kitchen. She carried a flashlight and a water bucket full of fish. "We should leave now for the mountain."

"What are you talking about? We're not going up Mauna Loa. It's erupting."

"Pele will protect us. She'll make us like kipukas. The fires will go around us."

"Is that another of your kaula's visions?"

"You are the one who suggested all of this. You had Steve explain it to the detectives and they have agreed to be there. You don't want to make fools of them."

"Listen to those sirens, Eleanor. The police will have their hands full. They're none too pleased with our taking the law into our own hands as it is. If they don't come, or if they can't come because the roads are blocked by land-slides, we could be in big pilikia. Avery could kill us, too. If he comes, which he probably won't."

"I'm going up the mountain. I'll drop you off at Jon's place if you're afraid."

"You can't go by yourself. It's too dangerous."

She smiled and set her bucket of fish in the sink. "Den we go awready."

THE CAR'S OVERHEAD light didn't work. Dinah tried to hold a flashlight steady on the map, but Eleanor had shunted them off onto a four-wheel-drive track and the car was buck-ing and dipping like a rodeo bull. With each dip came the sound of scraping metal. A fifty-year-old Coupe de Ville made outstanding yard décor and it would definitely turn heads cruising along the Bayfront Highway on a Sunday afternoon. It had no business venturing off-road. But the paved road had been severed by a fresh lava flow just past Bird Park. With no room to turn her lilac elephant around, Eleanor had coasted backwards down the road for over a mile, sideswiping trees and knocking over a signpost before being stopped by a mound of broken stones. The kaula's prophecy again. Undaunted, Eleanor had detoured onto this unmarked track and they were moving forward again through dense forest.

"Avery will not be able to get to this meeting, Eleanor."

"He has four-wheel drive."

"The police won't be able to get there."

"Maybe they sent somebody early, before the road was cut off."

A rock detonated under the front bumper like an IED. "Your car is taking too much of a beating. This road will destroy it."

"Minors. If there are no more lava flows, we can make it to the lookout at sixty-six hundred feet. The road ends there." Kauhiuhi, Pakekake, Mokuoweoweo. Dinah's flashlight beam bobbed haphazardly over the tongue-twisting names on the map. Dotted lines denoting trails and four-wheel-drive roads criss-crossed the mountain and there were pinkish-tan markings that indicated lava flows over the years. She gave up trying to pinpoint their location. All she knew was they were lugging uphill at a killer gradient. "Does this track go all the way to the summit?"

"Only if you're a goat." Eleanor jerked the gear stick on the steering column down hard. The engine grumbled, but continued to gain ground. "This track dead-ends a mile past a small kipuka. We can rejoin the main road there."

Previously, Dinah would not have described a one-lane sliver of asphalt that looped and tilted like a roller coaster as a main road. "Does the main road go to the summit?"

"No. The summit road starts on the other side of the mountain. Even if we could get to it, which we can't, I wouldn't attempt it in this car."

Dinah was heartened to learn that Eleanor drew the line somewhere.

Cinders pinged against the hood and windshield and a confetti of gray ash eddied in the headlights. The smell of burning rubber wafted in through the de Ville's vents. The tires? And there was a powerful smell of rotten eggs. Sulfur. The stench of hell. Except for an occasional streak of fire rocketing heavenwards, the world had bleared into a dusky, black and white lithograph. Maybe Hank was right. Maybe this really was the Apocalypse prophesied in the

Book of Revelations. Dinah sent up a silent prayer. Please, please cork the volcano.

"That's the kipuka." Eleanor slowed nearly to a stop and squinted.

Dinah strained her eyes. All she saw was a thicket of trees. Eleanor made a hard left and, after a few more dips and scrapes, they were back on pavement curling up the mountain. Three streams of orange-red magma spread out from the summit like talons, as if the mountain were about to be carried off by some apocalyptic bird of prey. Avery would not come. Only a pair of madwomen would drive up this mountain tonight.

"Reach into the back seat," said Eleanor. "There's a day-pack with dust masks and windbreakers. Put your mask on now. It'll protect you from the volcanic dust and ash."

Dinah climbed up on her knees, stretched over the seat, and grabbed the pack. "He won't come and even if he does, he won't have brought money. And he'll expect that you're recording everything that he says, so he won't say anything that can be used against him. Even if he did, recording a private conversation without the other person's knowledge is illegal."

"In Hawaii, it's legal to record a conversation if one party to the conversation consents and I consent. Give me a mask."

Dinah handed her a mask. "He could give himself consent to record you and turn the tables on us. Blackmail's illegal in all fifty states and it'll be your word against his as to what's going on in the conversation."

"He's afraid. I heard it in his voice. He will break."

"He's too smart to be taken in. Anybody would be too smart. In retrospect, this was a stupid game plan, totally full of holes. Please, Eleanor, let's turn around before it's too late."

"If Avery was smart, he would have figured out how to

stall Rick Varian and Raif Reid until after the closing without having to resort to murder. No, Avery's not so akamai. He's nervous and hasty. Those are his weaknesses. They will bring about his downfall."

Dinah had run out of arguments. A fountain of fire leapt into the black sky and she cursed herself for starting the fire in Eleanor's brain. If Langford's ugly mug materialized out of this fire-riven darkness and read her her rights, she would jump for joy. "I thought you'd want to help after you learned that Xander wasn't to blame for Leilani's death. But you've gone off the reservation, Eleanor."

She jerked the car hard around a big rock, causing Dinah to fall against the door and smack her elbow. "That's not an idiom I'd have expected from the mouth of a hapa Seminole."

"And pigheaded persistence in the face of an erupting volcano isn't what I'd have expected from a woman who fancies herself to be so akamai. Why are you doing this? It isn't to keep Xander or Claude Ann or me out of jail, is it? And it isn't because you crave justice for the two dead men. Listen to me, Eleanor. If you think you can make Avery feel guilty for the words he may or may not have said to Leilani that drove her to kill herself, forget about it. Maybe all he did was tell the truth. And if he was sadistic, I'm sure he granted himself a pardon years ago."

"Pele didn't grant him a pardon. Neither have I."

The road ended. This was the point where, on normal days, hikers began their ascent to the summit. The Caddy's headlights picked out a covered picnic table, a port-o-potty, and a small parking area barely wide enough for two cars. A Subaru Outback hogged most of the space. Did it belong to some godforsaken hikers or had Avery taken the bait?

"It's his car," said Eleanor. "Get down and don't let him see you."

Dinah slid down low in the seat. They were a half-hour early. If the car was Avery's, he must have left before the quake.

Eleanor wrestled the de Ville into the space next to the Outback and killed the engine. "Give me that flashlight. I'm going to go and sit at the table. When I get out of the car, I won't close the door completely. Put on a mask and get as close to us as you can with the recorder." She fitted a mask over her face, opened the glove compartment, and pulled out a dagger.

"What's that?" asked Dinah, knowing full well what it was and meaning what the hell do you intend to do with it.

"It's a pahoa. My great grandfather carved it from the beak of a marlin."

FORTY-TWO

ONE OF THEM will kill the other, thought Dinah, and it will be my fault. She peeped out at the darkness. Not seeing Avery was scarier than seeing him. She zipped into one of the windbreakers Eleanor had packed. It was too large, but it didn't swallow her. It must have belonged to one of Eleanor's relatives or students.

"Stay down out of sight," said Eleanor. "I'll speak loudly. You'll know when to begin the recording."

Dinah waited for a few minutes and peeped out again. Eleanor was sitting at the picnic table facing the car. She skipped her light around the empty lot, but there was nothing to see.

Dinah debated whether to end this ruse right now and reveal herself. If Avery was out there watching, he would hightail it when he realized that Eleanor hadn't come alone and then maybe nobody would get hurt. The mere fact of his coming would be incriminating and Langford could follow up the investigation in a hundred better, more logical ways. On the other hand, Eleanor seemed cool and calm and in control. She wouldn't haul off and shank Avery with her marlin's beak before eliciting an admission of some kind. The two of them would talk. They would feel each other out, do some verbal sparring. There would be ample time for Dinah to act if things started to go haywire.

Nothing moved except for Eleanor's cone of bouncing light and two divergent streams of fire oozing down the mountainside like tongs. They looked far away at the moment, but Pele was as changeful as the wind. She could redirect her streams or create new ones on a whim. Dinah missed the voice on the transistor radio. What was happening on the rest of the island? Had power been restored? Were people petrified and holding hands in the dark or popping popcorn and watching the fireworks on their HDTVs? The world felt alien and incomprehensible and she wished that Jon were here to analyze the situation and tell her whether to take heart or kiss this life good-bye.

After what seemed an eternity, the door of the port-o-potty whanged open and a beam of light emerged. Dinah ducked lower.

"Some night, eh, Eleanor? Don't go, Kay said. Probably just a humbug. Not to worry, I said. Have to see what Eleanor's found to fuss about this time."

"Come and sit, Avery. We have serious matters to discuss."

Dinah slipped on a dust mask, wriggled under the steering wheel, and eased out of the driver's side door. A flying cinder stung her neck and she stifled a yip. She brushed the rain of ash out of her face. She'd never felt so exposed. Crouching low, she walked the length of the car and peeped around the tail fin. Avery stood across the table from Eleanor, one foot up and resting on the bench. Dinah turned on Eleanor's recorder. Was she close enough? Avery had his back to her. If she could creep across the road and hide behind a tree, the reception would be better.

"Did you bring the money?"

"I told you I couldn't get cash tonight. The banks had already closed when you called. Could write you a check if you need money. Better that way. Would give me a record of the transaction."

"Something to prove I blackmailed you, you mean."

"Not the word I'd use. Negative connotation. What's this about, Eleanor? You short of money to pay your legal fees? You going to sue Jarvis?" He coughed until he began to wheeze. He sounded asthmatic. If he was, this ash must be hell on his airways. Maybe that's why he'd stayed so long in the port-o-potty. "Let's go sit in my car and talk."

"Cover your mouth with your handkerchief, Avery. I won't keep you long."

"Get to the point." He took out a handkerchief, tied it over his nose and mouth, and sat down. "Show me what you have. I'll decide if it's worth buying."

"I'm not like those foolish boys who blackmailed you and ended up dead. I left my box of papers with my attorney. If anything happens to me, he'll turn it over to the police."

"Customary to give the victim a whiff of what you've got, Eleanor. Show him it's not just a hoax."

"The papers prove that you had reason to kill Patrick Varian."

"Papers not enough. Motive, hearsay, suspicion. Not enough." His body convulsed with hacking. When the spasm was over, he stood up again. "You've got nothing. I'm leaving."

"Your tires are flat."

"What?"

Eleanor slapped the marlin's beak flat on the table, but kept her hand on the haft. "Sit. Hear what I've come to say to you."

Avery sat. "All right. Let's hear it."

"Your nephew double-crossed you. He was holding an auction. Playing you against me. If you killed him, I can understand."

Dinah didn't know if Eleanor was deceiving Avery about having contact with Varian or if she was deceiving her? She didn't know if she had slashed Avery's tires with her pahoa or whether she intended to slash his throat. What she did know was that one of the streams of fire seemed to be gathering speed down the mountain and veering toward the other stream as if it wanted to form an isosceles triangle. She willed herself not to whimper.

"Tried to help the pipsqueak. Said he needed to do research for a book, advance his career. Asked me if he could go prospecting on the Uwahi site. Have at it, I said. I knew there was nothing there. Had the damn archaeologist's report. Paid through the nose for it. Damned if Rick didn't find bones his first day out. Fine, I said. Write about it in your book, but hold your horses for a few weeks before telling anyone. I'll make it worth your while. At first, he agreed. But then he came back to me wanting money and I flew off the handle. Hit him. Didn't mean to kill him, but no help for it. Moved the body so no connection with Uwahi."

Jerusalem. Avery wasn't holding anything back. He seemed not to care that Eleanor might be recording him. Did that mean…?

"Varian was greedy," said Eleanor. "And so was Raiford Reid. He was a kolohe, a deceiver and a scoundrel, deserving only of scorn. Maybe you had no choice but to kill him."

"None at all. Rick had already shot off his mouth to Raif. When Rick's body was identified, Raif decided to pick up where Rick left off. I felt snakebit. Blackmailers crawling out of the woodwork."

"Why did you steal the Kemper girl's gun to kill him?"

"Can't say. Overheard her warn the kid to stay away from the gun. Surprised me a girl like Claude Ann would own a gun, but thought it might come in handy."

"And so it did. You must have worried that Raif had kept damaging information on his smartphone, but why did you unload it in the Pelerin girl's purse?"

"Thought it was Claude Ann's. Figured the police would assume Xander had taken it and then hid it in her purse. No matter whose. Confused everybody. I use a BlackBerry, myself. They wipe themselves clean automatically if you enter the wrong password ten times."

Eleanor picked up the pahoa and spiked it into the table. "Tell me about Leilani."

"Lani?" His body was racked by a fit of coughing and his flashlight beam bounced all over the place. When he could speak again, his voice had roughened. "What the hell do I have to do with her?"

"You knew that she was in love with Louis Sykes. That they were having an affair."

"She didn't tell you?"

"I found out just today."

"Common knowledge to all but you and Xander. But then Lani said you weren't close."

"Not close like you, Avery. You and my sister must have been very close. You called her from California the day she died."

"Don't remember. Sad day all around. Louis was a friend to us all."

"What did you say to her?"

"Knew she'd be upset. Wanted to give her time to absorb the blow before Xander came home."

"Did you tell her you'd killed Louis for her? To pay him back for cheating on her."

"Christ almighty. Your sister was crazy and so are you." He stood up and reached a hand into his pocket.

The hair on the back of Dinah's neck stood up. She took a step forward. Eleanor gripped the haft of the pahoa and pushed herself to her feet. Avery pulled something small out of his pocket and shook it. Eleanor shone her light on it. Dinah let out a breath and stepped back. It was an inhaler. She remembered that Avery wheezed a lot when he laughed, but this amount of coughing sounded dangerous. Had Eleanor known that he had asthma?

He pulled the handkerchief away from his mouth, took a hit from the inhaler, and coughed a few more times. "You came prepared, eh, Eleanor? Your talking points, your mask." He chuckled and, without warning, backhanded her across the mouth so hard that she staggered backward into a tree. He jerked the dagger out of the table and threw it on the ground. "Get up and give me your car keys."

Eleanor heaved herself off the tree trunk and moved back to the table. She reached into her pocket and handed him the keys. "Lava's over the road. You won't make it in my car."

Dinah's thoughts went into overdrive. If Avery drove off and left them marooned on the mountain, what would they do? It was eleven miles down to the Belt Road. She could jog it, assuming she weren't incinerated by lava, but Eleanor wouldn't be able to hike that distance. Dinah scoured the dark ground around her feet. If she had a big rock or strong piece of wood she could clobber him and get the keys back before he came to.

"You should have left it lay, Eleanor. I'm a family man. Work hard, play by the rules, pay taxes, give to charity, support my wife. I don't deserve this. Those spoiled whelps tried to hold me up and now you. You push a man to the brink, give him no choice."

"Before you go, tell me about Leilani."

"I wanted her once. But Xander had the looks and the money. Understood her choice. But when she went after Louis I got mad. Common as dirt. He didn't deserve her."

"And you did?" She picked up her flashlight and aimed it in his face.

"Christ. Give me that." He took it away from her and set it on the bench in front of him.

"Did you murder Louis?"

"If buying a drunk one too many is murder. I told Lani what he was, what she'd degraded herself for. Couldn't believe she flipped out and threw herself off a cliff. What's wrong with people nowadays? They act surprised when there's a price to pay for their shenanigans." He wheezed again, but recovered and this time, he pulled out a gun. "Let's you and me take a walk up the mountain."

Dinah felt the onrush of panic. Should she lunge? Should she scream?

Eleanor showed no sign of fear. "I'm too fat to walk up that mountain and you're too short of breath. Take my car and leave me here."

"Too late. You shouldn't have tried to play vigilante."

"Another killing will be harder to hide."

"I'm not going to kill you. Pele is. Now walk."

They walked toward the trailhead, Eleanor in front, Avery behind with the gun and the light. Dinah looked up at the streams of molten lava sliding down the mountainside. The moon wore a ragged gray cloud over the lower half of its face as if it, too, needed to protect itself from the polluted air. She shut off the recorder, pulled out her cell phone, and dialed Langford. Nothing. She dialed 911. Nothing. The cell phone towers must be out of commission.

She stumbled toward the table, finding it when she bashed her shin against the bench. Eleanor's flashlight rolled onto the ground and she scrabbled about in the dirt until she found it. She aimed it at the place where Avery and Eleanor had disappeared into the trees. She picked up the pahoa. How in God's name would she bring down an armed man with a marlin's beak?

"Geronimo," she said and started up the mountain.

FORTY-THREE

DINAH WAS CAREFUL not to let her light get too far ahead of her and alert Avery that he was being followed. The first part of the trail climbed through a dark tunnel of trees. At the end of the tunnel, the bald dome of the mountain loomed like the north pole of a dead planet. She was above treeline. From this perspective, she could only see one of the lava streams. She skimmed her light across the horizon.

Eleanor and Avery were walking in full view not forty yards ahead. She doused the light and waited. What was Avery thinking? He didn't want to shoot Eleanor. He wanted to make this murder seem like an accident. Would he force her to walk close to the lava and push her in? He wouldn't get too close and risk a push from her.

Dinah focused the light on her feet. This lava wasn't as jagged as the lava on the way to Ku's temple of human sacrifice. It had congealed in a circular, braid-like pattern that looked as if it had been sculpted. This must be pahoehoe, the kind of lava Jon had described as smooth and ropy, the kind that burned him. In different circumstances, she might have paused to marvel at the strange curlicues and ridges and blobs. As it was, she concentrated on trying not to turn an ankle.

The mountain sounded like a roaring gas furnace interrupted by sporadic booms that reverberated through her body. Somewhere in the I'll-look-back-and-laugh-at-this-one-day part of her brain, she wondered how she could have failed to hear the pandemonium when she was only a few hundred feet below in the parking lot. She'd been so intent on listening to Avery and Eleanor talk through their masks that she had tuned out the volcano. If any of their conversation was audible on the recorder, it would be a miracle. From where Dinah stood at the moment, the only miracle that mattered was deliverance from this roaring chaos. Maybe unbeknownst to her, Jon or Steve or Langford flew helicopters in their spare time. Maybe she would soon hear the song of rotor blades overhead and somebody would drop a harness belt and winch her up and away from this unholy mountain.

The wind had picked up, but there wasn't as much airborne ash. She threw her light ahead and picked out a pillar of flat stones stacked like scraggly pancakes. The trail curved around it and a second cairn marked the way about twenty feet beyond. Would Avery keep to the trail? If he spotted her coming after him, he might decide that shooting Eleanor was a quicker expedient than staking her out in Pele's path. But light was necessary or she'd lose them. She strafed the surrounding area with her light. Avery and Eleanor were nowhere in sight. How far ahead could they be? Eleanor was hoofing it across this ripply lava much faster than Dinah would have believed possible. They must be getting close to seven thousand feet by now and the altitude couldn't be helping Avery's asthma.

A wire fence stretched across the trail. The sign on the gate read, "Don't Let the Goats Out." The goats baaing on the other side of the fence pleaded otherwise. Dinah lifted the latch on the gate with Eleanor's dagger and stood aside as seven terrified animals stampeded through the opening and fled down the mountain. Dinah had to fight the urge to run after them.

Shit! She rolled her ankle in a crevice. Her hands were full, one holding the flashlight and the other gripping the dagger. She balanced stork-like on one leg and rubbed her throbbing ankle against her supporting leg. A sense of hopelessness swamped her. What was she going to do if she didn't find them? What would she do if she did? Like a dog chasing a car, the concept of success was problematic in the extreme.

If Eleanor and Avery had gone through the gate, would they have bothered to close it behind them? She shone her light around and saw a scrap of red cloth. Eleanor must have torn her muumuu on the wire. Dinah almost laughed. Eleanor was scattering clues like Hansel and Gretel. She expected Dinah to follow her.

Dinah's ankle felt mushy, like a rotten mango, and she didn't think she could make it much farther. Maybe it was that she didn't want to make it much farther. She passed the third cairn and the fourth. The higher she climbed, the farther apart the cairns had been placed and the air seemed to grow colder cairn by cairn. In spite of a stream of two thousand degree lava cascading in the distance, she was chilled to the bone. Hypothermia. That's how it would end for her. Not in fire, but in ice.

Her sprained ankle wobbled and almost went over again. She couldn't do anything to help Eleanor in this condition. She could turn around right now. If all Avery meant to do was leave Eleanor up here without a light and hope she would stumble into a lava flow, he had underestimated the woman. Eleanor was too tough and she was tight with Pele. Pele would cause the lava to go around her. She'd be all right. Dinah should head back toward the Belt Road, flag down help, and send people back to rescue Eleanor.

Voices. She killed her light and froze. From which direction had they come?

A scree of loose pebbles trickled out from under her foot. It couldn't have been heard above all the other noise, could it? Eleanor's voice carried above the din, but Dinah couldn't make out what she was saying. She strained her ears. The roar of the volcano was too loud.

What the hell. Sneaking up on Avery and overpowering him wasn't going to happen. She may as well announce herself. Avery would either run or he'd shoot and, if he didn't know how many people were after him...

She turned on the flashlight and shouted at the top of her voice. "Eleanor! We're over here. Where are you? Jon, you go around that way. I'll go this way."

Again, Eleanor's voice rose, but the words were indistinct. They probably couldn't hear Dinah either. She walked in what she could only guess was the right direction. A sudden sharp explosion ripped the air. Gunshot or methane gas? Overhead, there was a mad screeching. She aimed her beam up and to the right. Avery stood alone on a flat rock, waving his arms wildly about his head to ward off a pair of large, low-flying birds. They must have been startled by the explosion. Was Eleanor dead?

Dinah hid the pahoa behind her back and shouted. "Avery, hello. Where's Eleanor?"

"You hear all that foolishness between me and Eleanor down below?" He appeared to be wearing a mask over his face now instead of his handkerchief. Eleanor's mask.

"What foolishness? Jon and Steve and I just got here. Eleanor said she was driving up here and we came to make sure she didn't run into trouble. Is she with you?"

The birds swooped and dived around his head like fighter planes. Had Avery shot at them? He bellowed Jon's name. The birds flew up and Avery bent double in a prolonged coughing spasm. He sounded ready to croak. Dinah edged nearer. She was within three feet of him. The pooch had caught the car and she had no idea what to do next.

Avery straightened up, put his inhaler in his mouth, and sucked in a rasping breath.

"Jon's not here," he said. "You must have ridden up with Eleanor in her Caddy." He sounded hoarse, but perfectly amiable. The way he'd sounded before he backhanded Eleanor into the tree.

This is it, she thought. He's going to whip out his gun and shoot me. Her fingers tightened around the dagger, but even at this close range, the odds that she could hit him were astronomical.

Eleanor's voice rumbled from somewhere behind him. She was alive. Dinah took a step forward and almost dropped the flashlight as the birds swooped in between her and Avery, their wings silent as phantoms. They looked like owls. One of them hovered over Avery's head while the other dive-bombed him. It was like something out of an Alfred Hitchcock movie. Avery flapped his arms and wheezed.

"You need a doctah," rumbled Eleanor. "You bettah go wiki-wiki. You no got long, Avery Wilhite."

Dinah had a sudden brain wave that Eleanor had poisoned him, put a twig of the Be-Still tree in his inhaler or impregnated the dust mask she'd given him with deadly nightshade. Avery clutched at his chest, took another one-handed swipe at the owls and, to Dinah's utter amazement, rushed past her and headed down the mountain. The owls pursued him, circling and swooping and screeching as if he were making off with their chicks.

"Eleanor, he's gone. Where are you?"

"Can't tell you. Can't move."

Dinah followed the sound of her voice and found her lying on her side on a large boulder. "Can you walk? We have to get down before the lava blocks our way."

"No can. Broke arm. Broke foot."

"Maybe I can find something to make a splint or a crutch or a litter."

"You can't drag me. We'll have to stay the night. The pueos will protect us."

"The birds?"

"They're the spirits of my 'aumakua. The spirits inhabit the bodies of owls because owls are skilled in battle."

"It isn't that I don't believe in the skills of your 'aumakua, Eleanor, but a slumber party with Pele and the pueos doesn't appeal to me. Show me your hurt foot."

She stuck out her foot.

"Can you move it?"

She waggled it from side to side.

"It's only a sprain," pronounced Dinah, willing it to be so. "I've got one, too. If your ancestor Pele doesn't hem us in with fire, we have to try to get down. Even if Avery's tires are flat, we can stay warm inside his car until somebody comes to help us."

Eleanor didn't argue. She cradled her hurt arm and sat up slowly. She braced her good arm on Dinah's shoulder, planted her feet firmly on the ground, and heaved herself to a standing position. She grimaced from pain, but indicated that she was ready to try. With Avery's departure, she seemed to have ceded command.

"Keep your arm on my shoulder and put your feet where I put mine," said Dinah. "I'll lead us back down the trail."

And with the lame leading the lame by the feeble light of a plastic Rayovac flashlight, they shuffled down the mountain. The ash had stopped blowing and, apart from the sulfur smell, breathing had become easier. Dinah pulled off her mask. It wasn't likely to stop the deadly, microscopic particulates anyway. One of the lava streams was still visible off to their left, but the roaring had quieted. Pele's rampage was over and the pueos had dissolved away in the darkness along with Avery, leaving Dinah with a feeling of anticlimax. He would probably drive himself to the hospital, get his asthma symptoms under control, and abscond with his share of the Uwahi profits before Dinah and Eleanor could present Langford with their questionable recording. Such was life. People didn't always get their just deserts.

Eleanor stepped on the back of Dinah's heels, but it was just one pain among many. Her eyes and throat burned, her ankle throbbed, her shoulders ached, her hands and feet felt numb from the cold, she had a blister under her right big toe, and she couldn't stop thinking about the kaula's foreboding about the child with a fever.

They passed through the gate where the goats had gone through and Dinah took extra care to sidestep a deep crevice. She threw her light down the trail to find the next cairn. In the lambent beam of the Rayovac, she found Avery instead. His body lay prostrate across a mound of broken stones. He looked white and still and inexorably dead.

FORTY-FOUR

LEGEND HAS IT that there is a beach on the southeast coast of Hawaii near Ninole where the stones are either male or female and they propagate by contact with each other. It was believed that when a male stone and a female stone were wrapped up together in kapa cloth for a period of time, they produced a baby pebble. The early Hawaiians would select a nice looking stone from the beach, dress it up, and take it around with them for a while to games and sporting events, sort of like dating. If the stone pleased them and brought them luck, they would consecrate it as a household god. If things didn't work out, they ditched it or ground it down to pound taro root. This was the beach where Claude Ann chose to hold her wedding and today the air was sweet with plumerias and ho'oponopono.

Claude Ann's dress was divine and no safety pins were needed. Her wrist was healed and out of the cast and she looked transcendently happy. So did Marywave. After the wedding she would be going home to Georgia. The doctors had found no physical cause of her fever and nausea and, after running a battery of tests, they determined that her symptoms were psychosomatic, a reaction to worry and stress and acute homesickness. When the decision came down to a question of Marywave's health versus keeping her in Hawaii, Claude Ann had caved. She agreed that Marywave could live with Hank and attend school in Georgia provided that she spend her holidays and summers in Hawaii.

"I'll miss her, but maybe it's for the best." Claude Ann gazed wistfully at Marywave.

"Hank'll be the heavy now. He'll be the one raggin' on her to do her homework and clean up her room. He'll be the one who rations the TV and the textin' and the potato chips. I'll be the one who takes her paraglidin' and lets her wear lipstick." She scowled and plunked a sugar cube into her champagne. "Mama's gonna keep a real sharp eye on Hank. If he doesn't do right by my girl, I'll have his guts for garters."

Dinah had to smile. Ho'oponopono had its limits. In the case of Claude Ann and Hank, it was more of a truce than a reconciliation and conditions attached. "I suppose Phoebe will help keep Hank in line. She has told you about her plans to pick up his option now that he's a free agent, hasn't she?"

"Sheesh. Can you believe it? One of my best friends hot to move in with my ex? It's too icky. Like incest or something. I told her to choose up sides like everybody else has to do when there's a divorce. It's me or it's Hank."

For the time being, Phoebe had chosen Claude Ann. She'd caught Claude Ann's bouquet for the second time. She sat at the reception table and studied it with a plaintive expression, as if mentally counting the petals and playing daisy, daisy, who shall it be.

Da Riddum Bruddahs, a motley, four-piece band from Hilo, finished butchering "Our Love Is Here to Stay" and Claude Ann excused herself to go talk with them. Dinah slid her feet out of her tangerine pumps, stretched her toes under the table, and contemplated the faces of the celebrants. With the cessation of hostilities between Xander and Eleanor, Claude Ann had invited her parents to the wedding. Her father had brought a bottle of his own private stock to the party and, well lubricated on Tennessee sour mash, he seemed to be enjoying himself immensely. He was bending Sara Sykes' ear with a story about piloting his fishing boat through a pod of alligators in the Okefenokee.

Claude Ann's mother scraped the icing off a slice of the wedding cake as if it were putrid mold and eyeballed Xander as he strolled past strewing compliments and charm. She leaned across the table to Dinah and muttered, "If you ask me, he's all sizzle and no steak. I give the marriage two years. Three at the most."

Dinah held her peace. She had been wrong about Xander from the start and she hoped Claude Ann's mother was wrong, too.

Eleanor had admitted being wrong about Xander. She had confessed her hala and asked his forgiveness for all the years of prejudice and resentment and Xander had asked her forgiveness for profaning the land that had meant so much to her and her father. The burden of anger was lifted and they had kala 'ana. Everything was pono. Eleanor sat between Jon and Lyssa like a valued family member. Like the matriarch ready to take charge.

Eleanor still wouldn't tell Dinah whether she had, in fact, met with Patrick Varian and bargained with him over a "box of papers" and a set of bones. She preferred to keep that huna. And Dinah still didn't know if what had happened on Mauna Loa with the pueos was natural or supernatural, whether Avery had disturbed a nest or Eleanor had summoned the guardian spirits of her ancestors. Dinah had, however, done some research on the bird. It was a native species of the short-eared owl. Its habitat ranged from lowland pastures to mountain forests up to eight thousand feet. It did like to nest on the ground, but it was mostly a daytime hunter and nearly always silent. Dinah filed the experience away in the "Stranger Things" compartment of her brain.

Steve had brought Jessica the Mormon to the wedding as his date. Dinah tried not to interpret this as a message to go pound taro root. Maybe Steve's makamaka relation-

ship with Jon put her out of bounds. It was probably just
as well. She didn't want to hurt Jon's feelings either, although she wished he weren't quite so earnest and vulnerable and brimming over with oxytocin. She had given him
fair warning. A relationship that might lead to the possibility of Claude Ann as her mother-in-law could never be
consummated.

Jon hadn't taken her decision to invite Vince Langford as
her date at all well. But the spirit of ho'oponopono was upon
her and she felt moved to include Vince in the party. Also,
she still had a few unanswered questions to put to him.

Her invitation had so surprised and delighted Vince that
he'd fallen all over himself apologizing for giving her the
third degree and for his failure to make it up the Mauna
Loa Road on the night of the quake. She was actually starting to like the guy, especially since he had turned forensics
loose on Avery's car and they'd found traces of Varian's
blood and Raif's, too. It now seemed likely that Avery had
murdered Raif somewhere else and moved the body to Kalapana to dump it.

Dinah took a bottle of Cristal out of the ice bucket nearest at hand. Raif had almost ordered a bottle of Cristal that
first night at the Olopana. She wondered if Xander had
chosen it as a remembrance. "More champagne, Vince?"

"Sure. I'm off duty."

She poured him another fluteful. "Did you go to
Avery's funeral?"

"I went. And you don't have to get me pickled to talk
about the case."

She laughed. He was as cynical as she was. "Was his
daughter Tess there?"

"No. It seems she's hied off to Macau. Her agency
doesn't know when to expect her back in the office. No
reason for her to leave the country on my account. I had a
few questions about her boyfriend, nothing we can't fig-

ure out for ourselves. Far as I'm concerned, the case is wrapped up in a bow."

"But Tess and Raif were blackmailing Xander. Can't you extradite her for that?"

"Xander's the only witness against her. Unless he files a claim, it'll remain a private matter. Nothing we can hold her on."

The afternoon sun streamed through the open-air beach house and the glistening blue waters of the Pacific seemed to stretch into infinity. Da Riddum Bruddahs had picked up the tempo and Xander twirled Claude Ann around the dance floor. He wouldn't file a claim against Tess. There was nothing she could do to him now and prosecuting her would only prolong the bad feelings that all of the Garsts would rather forget.

Dinah said, "I remember the way Raif looked when he drove away from the airport that day in Hilo. He fired a finger pistol at me and when he saw Avery, he did the same. I wonder now if it was a signal and they had already agreed to meet somewhere."

"Probably. We've searched Wilhite's office and his house and didn't find any traces of Raif's blood, but we'll keep looking. Never have it said that Hawaii Five-O isn't thorough."

"Speaking of thorough, I've been wondering how Avery made Raif's phone ring inside my purse. If he erased all the data, would it still ring?"

"One of the techies in forensics says the subscriber identity memory card wasn't erased. Whether that was by design or because of some bug in the software, he can't say." Vince essayed a sincere expression. "You know, I never seriously thought that you were the one who offed Raif."

"Of course not. You merely offered me refuge in one of your lovely Hawaiian prisons if I confessed." She laughed and so did he.

Dinah was glad to see that even Lyssa was smiling. She seemed to have spent all of her anger and grief and Dinah didn't think she would throw her life away as recklessly as her mother had done. Not with Eleanor watching over her. It was all well and good if the spirits of your dead ancestors came flying when you were in trouble, but Dinah had to believe that a live guardian spirit was better than a dead one.

The blue waters of the Pacific Ocean glistened into infinity and Dinah drank in the beauty. A month ago, she had arrived in Hawaii a newcomer, a malihini without a clue, and now she felt like an oldtimer, practically a native. Wherever she went from here, she knew she would return, if not to stay, at least periodically.

The band announced a break and Xander stopped by Dinah's chair and set a small box on the table in front of her. "When Claude Ann told me you'd lost the earrings she gave you, I had another pair made. A souvenir to remind you of all the trouble you've gone through with us and for us."

"Oh, my… You shouldn't have."

He patted her on the shoulder and hurried off after Claude Ann. Dinah opened the box and held up the shiny strands of Pele's tears. Across the table, Jon erupted in laughter.

Eleanor got up and walked around to Dinah's side. "Come. We talk story."

Dinah left her shoes under the table and followed Eleanor to a quiet corner. "Don't keep me in suspense, Eleanor. Are there really bones on Uwahi?"

"Maybe, maybe not. If they're there, maybe it's mo bettah they stay buried. Like you Seminoles bury the hatchet when you make peace, eh? I'll bury my bones. I won't try to stop Jarvis. What happens, happens."

"All the same," said Dinah, "I hope they don't build that casino."

Eleanor lifted her plumeria lei to her nose, took a deep

breath, and let it fall. "I've been thinking about you. You need a life goal."

"You must have been talking to Phoebe."

"There's a position available in my department for a re-searcher. It's yours if you want it. You stay and I'll take the curse off those earrings."

"That would be a relief."

"Anyway, you'd like ethnobotany."

"I appreciate the offer, Eleanor, but I don't think so. My degree is in cultural anthropology. I've been thinking I should go back to Emory and finish my thesis."

"Ethnobotany, that's culture plus botany. My kaula, she had a dream about you. She saw a train, a green-eyed dog, an iceberg, and a box of seeds. I think you're going to need to know something about botany."

* * * * *

REQUEST YOUR FREE BOOKS!

2 FREE NOVELS
PLUS 2 FREE GIFTS!

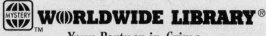

WORLDWIDE LIBRARY®
Your Partner in Crime

YES! Please send me 2 FREE novels from the Worldwide Library® series and my 2 FREE gifts (gifts are worth about $10). After receiving them, if I don't wish to receive any more books, I can return the shipping statement marked "cancel." If I don't cancel, I will receive 4 brand-new novels every month and be billed just $5.49 per book in the U.S. or $6.24 per book in Canada. That's a savings of at least 31% off the cover price. It's quite a bargain! Shipping and handling is just 50¢ per book in the U.S. and 75¢ per book in Canada.* I understand that accepting the 2 free books and gifts places me under no obligation to buy anything. I can always return a shipment and cancel at any time. Even if I never buy another book, the two free books and gifts are mine to keep forever.

414/424 WDN F4WY

Name _____ (PLEASE PRINT)

Address _____ Apt. #

City _____ State/Prov. _____ Zip/Postal Code

Signature (if under 18, a parent or guardian must sign)

Mail to the Harlequin® Reader Service:
IN U.S.A.: P.O. Box 1867, Buffalo, NY 14240-1867
IN CANADA: P.O. Box 609, Fort Erie, Ontario L2A 5X3

Want to try two free books from another line?
Call 1-800-873-8635 or visit www.ReaderService.com.

* Terms and prices subject to change without notice. Prices do not include applicable taxes. Sales tax applicable in N.Y. Canadian residents will be charged applicable taxes. Offer not valid in Quebec. This offer is limited to one order per household. Not valid for current subscribers to the Worldwide Library series. All orders subject to credit approval. Credit or debit balances in a customer's account(s) may be offset by any other outstanding balance owed by or to the customer. Please allow 4 to 6 weeks for delivery. Offer available while quantities last.

Your Privacy—The Harlequin® Reader Service is committed to protecting your privacy. Our Privacy Policy is available online at www.ReaderService.com or upon request from the Harlequin Reader Service.

We make a portion of our mailing list available to reputable third parties that offer products we believe may interest you. If you prefer that we not exchange your name with third parties, or if you wish to clarify or modify your communication preferences, please visit us at www.ReaderService.com/consumerschoice or write to us at Harlequin Reader Service Preference Service, P.O. Box 9062, Buffalo, NY 14269. Include your complete name and address.

WWL13R